IN
FOR
THE
KILL

ED JAMES

THOMAS & MERCER

Text copyright © 2018 by Ed James
All rights reserved.

Published by Thomas & Mercer, Seattle

www.apub.com

Amazon, the Amazon logo, and Thomas & Mercer are trademarks of Amazon.com, Inc., or its affiliates.

ISBN-13: 9781503947962
ISBN-10: 1503947963

Cover design by @blacksheep-uk.com

Printed in the United States of America

IN
FOR
THE
KILL

ALSO BY ED JAMES

For Helen Cadbury, a great writer and a great friend,
and Pooky, the gentlest cat I'll ever know.
Both taken from us far too soon.
Fuck cancer.

Day 1
Monday, 14th November 2016

Chapter One

DI Simon Fenchurch pulled up at the side of the road, the November rain battering his windscreen. He killed the engine, the dead wipers leaving a blood-spatter pattern on the glass. Then a wall of water cleared it away. He glanced over at the passenger seat. 'You okay?'

Abi Fenchurch sat there, cradling her belly like the baby was already in her arms and she never wanted to let it go. Her right hand shot down and jabbed the seat belt release, sending the clasp whizzing up. 'Let's get this over with.'

'Get it over with?' Fenchurch caught her hand before it went back to the bump. The baby protruded in a way their first child hadn't. The little sod was trying to batter his way out already. His son. Definitely not to be called Simon. 'She needs space to come to terms with it.'

Abi's glare sliced straight to the back of his skull. 'It's been five months, Simon. Isn't that enough time?'

'They said it could take years.'

'Years.' She smoothed her top down, stretched like the skin underneath. '*Years.*'

'I've seen ten-year-old kids who've had lifetimes of abuse. Chloe . . . Well, she didn't have that. We were lucky in that sense, but . . .'

'I don't feel lucky.'

'If it's going to take years, then the sooner we get going, the sooner she'll be back with us.'

Abi's sigh spoke a million words.

Everything they'd talked about since someone kidnapped their daughter. Eleven and a half years. On and off. Mostly off. All that time since their daughter had been taken from them. The pain of separation, but never divorce. Not knowing what had happened. Until they found her, living under their noses in South London. Kept alive by someone who had betrayed their trust. Some savages had scooped out part of her brain, bringing her up as their own.

A smile flickered across Abi's lips as she leaned over and pecked him on the cheek, her citrusy perfume cloaking him. He let go of her hand and she belted up her coat.

Fenchurch watched the busy road in his side mirror, waiting for a gap. There. He opened his door and stepped out. A puddle splashed up his trouser leg and soaked his shoe. Felt like his sock was still in the washing machine. He shook his foot off and raced round the front of the car to winch Abi out.

She tried to stand up, bracing her back with both hands. 'Christ, this isn't fun.' She snapped out her brolly and started waddling off.

Fenchurch zapped the car and followed, the University of Southwark sprawled around them. Some of its ancient buildings predated the Fire of London. Others didn't. The giant tower spiralled up into the sky, a grey box of sixties concrete darkened by the downpour. Jaines Tower, or something, the sort of name that looked French but sounded English when you read it out. A mile or so east the Shard pierced the rainclouds.

Fenchurch jogged ahead and held the door for Abi, his suit jacket already soaked through to his skin. 'I hate this bloody city.'

Abi huffed past him, all elbows and knees. A long way from jogging. 'We really should move.'

This again . . .

Fenchurch followed, clutching her hand, his shoes squeaking on the lino. 'It's not easy to get into Kent or Essex forces.'

Abi grinned at him. 'Even for a hero cop?'

'With my record, love, I'd be lucky to be on traffic.' Fenchurch scanned around the concourse. The Psychology Department was straight ahead. 'We might not be able to move, anyway, if I can't shift my old flat. London's turned to shit when we need gold.'

'Bloody Brexit.' Abi was already out of breath. 'Simon, if this is going to take years then let's take our time, sell your flat first, before we think about what to do with ours. We need to focus on making sure Chloe's okay.'

Fenchurch nodded slowly. 'Now that's a plan.' He led her down the corridor, the whole place stinking of bitter coffee and whiteboard pens. The signs for Psychology pointed to the right.

Abi's grip tightened.

Chloe stood at the far end of the hallway, her thumbs tapping on her mobile. She had her mother's figure, tall and muscular like a swimmer, and her father's blue eyes and blond hair, though hers hadn't gone to silver and still had traces of red dye at the tips. Chloe pocketed her phone and glowered at Fenchurch. Her father, the man who'd spent years of his life searching for her, who'd finally found her.

She broke off eye contact and pushed open the door.

———

Fenchurch had the worst seat in the room, sitting directly opposite the counsellor, Paddy Mackintosh, a gnome in green and beige corduroy. Looked like he belonged back on the Emerald Isle but spoke as if he was doing continuity on Radio Four. Kept pushing his glasses up his nose.

Behind his desk, the downpour sprayed the window, lashing it with each new gust. Students lurked outside, sucking on vape sticks and roll-ups as they cowered under the rain cover. A pair of police officers milled around in the distance, their acid-yellow vests bursting through the dull grey day.

Paddy leaned forward, clasping his knees, his tongue digging into his cheek, stretching the skin like Abi's belly. 'I think we're making progress here. Good progress.' He nudged his specs until they dimpled his skin. 'Jennifer, you say you're—'

'Her name is Chloe.' Abi was sitting next to Fenchurch, squeezing the life out of his hand. 'Chloe Geraldine Fenchurch.'

'My name is Jennifer.' Chloe kept looking at the floor. The West Country burr was softening, replaced by hard London. 'This fiction you've created about me somehow being your daughter . . .' Her gaze locked on to Fenchurch and Abi in turn, breaking off quickly. 'You need to stop it.'

'We're not going to.' Abi's nails dug into Fenchurch's skin. 'Never.'

'Haven't you done enough damage?' Chloe brushed her hair up at the side of her head, her fingers hovering in the spot where . . . where they'd . . . operated on her. Tearing out chunks of her brain, tearing out memories, leaving a blank page on which to build a lie. Fenchurch could barely breathe. 'My parents are locked up because of you. I get to see them once a week. For half an hour.'

'They're not your parents.' Fenchurch's throat felt like it'd been sandblasted. 'The tests were conclusive. You're *our* daughter, not theirs.'

'They raised me. You took them from me!'

'Guys, can we simmer—'

'Chloe, they're crim—'

'My. Name. Isn't. CHLOE!'

Fenchurch let go of Abi's hand and rocked forward on his chair, the wood creaking beneath him. 'You need to accept the truth. The sooner you do, the sooner we can all move on.'

Chloe pressed a finger through her hair, deep into her scar. 'I want nothing to do with you.'

'Guys!' Paddy made a T-shape with his hands. 'Guys, I need you all to take a time out, okay? We seem to be getting to this point a lot earlier in each session.'

'Twenty years ago, you were in your mother's belly.' Fenchurch stared at Abi's tummy again, focusing on the new life growing in there, then back at Chloe. 'You were born two months premature.' He caught himself before a tear formed. 'I didn't sleep a wink while you were in that incubator. I kept pestering the doctors, seeing if there was anything I could do. *Anything*. I'd never been so worried in my life.' His throat itched like he'd swallowed steel wool. 'Until you were stolen from us.'

Abi smiled at Chloe. 'Look at you now. Just look—' She broke off. Then whispered, 'Just look at you.'

'My mother's name is Cheryl. She's in prison.'

'Abi's your mother, not that animal.' Sandpaper rubbed Fenchurch's voice box. 'Abi was a student when she fell pregnant. She dropped out of university to have you.'

Tension knotted Chloe's forehead. She sat there for a few seconds, her mouth hanging open, her finger pressing her temple. 'Because of this weird obsession you've got with me, my mother is in prison. Are you a pervert or something?'

Fenchurch gasped, his voice catching in his throat. 'You—' His fists clenched. 'What did you say?'

'Forget it.' Chloe rubbed at her nose and shifted her focus to the counsellor. 'We've been doing this for, what, four months now?'

Paddy nodded. 'Do you feel uncomfortable?'

'Bit of an understatement.' Chloe ran her bottom lip against her teeth. 'I don't *have* to do this, do I?'

'Now wait a—'

Paddy's raised finger cut Fenchurch off. 'These sessions are voluntary, that's correct. I would stress that—'

Chloe got to her feet, her chair scraping back across the laminate flooring. She zipped up her jacket and hauled a laptop bag over her shoulder. 'I'm not coming to any more of these.' She stormed out of the room and slammed the door behind her. The thud echoed around the room.

Fenchurch glared at Paddy. 'She can't do this, can she?'

'This therapy is voluntary. I have to say, I—'

Fenchurch marched over to the door and flew out into the corridor. 'Come here!'

Chloe was halfway along the hall. She turned to face him, frowning, then set off again, arms folded like her mother in one of their worst arguments.

Fenchurch jogged after her and grabbed hold of her bag. 'You need to come back!'

'I don't *need* to do anything, you arsehole.' Chloe gave him all the eye contact she could muster, her father's rage burning in her eyes. 'You can stick that counselling up your arse!'

He tugged at her bag. 'Get back in there.'

She slapped him. His cheek rasped, feeling like the sort of sunburn that turns your skin to crackling. She pushed his chest and he slammed into the wall and slid down, landing on his backside.

Chloe stood over him, jabbing a finger in his face. 'LEAVE. ME. ALONE!'

All he could do was watch her charge off down the corridor, fists clenched, angled forward.

No doubting who her parents were.

Someone gripped his shoulder. 'Come on, love.' Abi, her purr bringing him back from DEFCON 1.

Paddy was standing in the doorway, arms folded. He reached up and pressed his glasses to his forehead. 'Well, now.'

Fenchurch brushed Abi off and hauled himself up.

'I know you're having solo sessions with her.' Abi smiled at Paddy. 'Please, please, please, try and make sure she doesn't give up on us.'

Paddy's glasses had already slid halfway down his nose. 'After what I saw today, I'd say the counselling you two have been on for the last few months hasn't quite cut the mustard.'

'I'm sorry.' Abi's head hung low. 'I shouldn't have called her Chloe. It's too soon.'

'She needs to come to terms with this in her own time. Okay? We've got more time next Monday. Let's focus on you two, okay?'

Fenchurch sat in his office, fingers thundering on the keyboard, trying to batter the report into submission. Or something vaguely readable. The glow from the screen made his eyes sting. His stomach rumbled. Still too early for a burrito, even if it would beat the queues. Maybe not too early, then.

He looked around the office, almost comfortable for one, but for two people, forget it. Mulholland's desk was overflowing with paperwork. Her handbag sat on top of the biggest pile, next to a book.

Fenchurch walked over and picked up the paperback. *The Right Facts* by Thomas K. Zachary. A man posed on the front. Young face, silver hair, sharp suit, sitting next to the Stars and Stripes.

Fenchurch remembered — that guy from the election coverage that Abi had been so angry about. A far-right blogger from the States who'd got a gig at Southwark University and a column for the *London Post*.

Fenchurch flicked through the pages. The text focused on the sort of shit that you would've seen in Germany in the thirties. Anti-everything — gay, trans, black, women. Especially gay, trans, black women. And members of the Jewish faith. And Muslims. And . . .

And Mulholland was reading this shit.

The door opened and Mulholland sashayed in, tucking her scarf around her scrawny neck. Turkey-skin flesh. No sign of her familiar or her broomstick. 'Oh, Simon, I thought you'd still be out?' Her public-school accent sliced through him.

'Finished early, Dawn.' Fenchurch dropped the book and returned to his seat. He tried to focus on the monitor while he typed.

Mulholland sat in the chair in front of his desk, perched forward, forehead creased. 'Are you okay, Simon?'

'I'm fine.' More typing, putting anything down on the page.

'You had a session with Chloe, didn't you?'

Fenchurch barely grunted. Had a look at what he was writing. Only so many words you can use to describe a stabbing.

'Alan asked me to cover until lunchtime.'

He reached down for a sip of tea. Cold. Tasted like second-hand sick. 'Finished early, so I'm trying to get on with work. If you don't mind?'

She smirked at him. 'Sure you don't want to thank me for covering your shift while you were out?'

Fenchurch sat back and folded his arms. 'What, have you been called out to a murder scene?'

'No. But—'

'Then you've not really covered for me, have you?' Fenchurch nodded at his monitor. 'Cos this report's still sitting here, barely written.'

'Simon.' Mulholland got to her feet, hands on hips. 'You know you can talk to me about your daughter. I worked the original case, if you remember.'

Oh, I remember.

The memory jolted at the back of his head. Her secret, the piece of incompetence only he knew about. Not that anybody would believe him. But it still stung.

'Going through this all over again must be horrendous.'

Fenchurch rested his fingers on the keyboard. 'I need to get this off to Docherty, so if you don't mind?'

'Very well.' She flounced over to her desk and sat, pouting at her Airwave Pronto. She put it to her ear and started talking. Loud, looking right at Fenchurch. 'Tom, thanks for the update. If you can drill down to a finer level of granularity before we push it upstairs, okay?'

Fenchurch sat forward, his screen blocking her out. He read the last paragraph. Absolute gibberish. He deleted it.

'Tom, if you're asking me to escalate, then I need a deep dive on the issue. I can't just run this up the flagpole and see who salutes, can I?'

The door cracked open and DCI Alan Docherty slouched in, wincing. Skinny as a rake. In fact, skinnier than ever, his dark suit hanging off him like the Grim Reaper's cloak. He nodded at Fenchurch, then sat with a groan. Yawned into his fist. 'Thought you weren't back until after you'd destroyed a burrito, Si?'

'Finished early.'

'Oh?'

'Dropped Abi at home.' Fenchurch opened his notebook ahead of the inevitable deluge of information. 'What's up?'

'You want to tell me how it went?'

Fenchurch looked away. 'Not really.'

'That well, eh?' Docherty swallowed. Took a few goes to get it down, whatever it was. 'You pair have certainly been through the mill. I hate to see you like this, Si.'

'I hate to feel like this, boss.' Fenchurch tried to smile but it wasn't happening. 'That report will be in your inbox by five tonight.'

'Good, good.' Docherty pursed his lips, then groaned. 'Anyway. Loftus just handed me my arse.'

'Moaning about me again?'

Docherty took his time to reply, nodding. 'Never a good thing when half of *my* update with the boss is spent on him repeating warnings about *your* behaviour.'

Fenchurch leaned back in his chair. Mulholland was taking greater interest in their chat than her phone call. 'Give me strength.'

'Si, I've covered your arse enough times now. Loftus is on to you. If you step out of line again, it's disciplinary action.' Docherty repeated his weird swallowing action. 'Am I clear?'

'Loud and clear.' Fenchurch cracked his knuckles. 'Now, can I get back to this report?'

'Afraid not.' Docherty coughed. Then again, harder. 'South London MIT have passed us a case. They're still working three murders and an abduction, and we're twiddling our thumbs, writing reports and escalating any slight hiccup with forensics.' He glanced at Mulholland. 'Body of a young female. University of Southwark's kind of on the border of our patches.'

Fenchurch's blood froze. 'Southwark?' Burning talons wrapped around the icicles in his veins.

Chloe's university . . .

Chapter Two

D S Kay Reed drove the pool Volvo over Blackfriars Bridge, the thick rain splashing off the grey void of the Thames and battering the new railway station standing on the river. Her left hand kept leaving the steering wheel to touch her hair, short back and sides, a long quiff swept up at the front. Didn't suit her one bit.

Her driving rattled Fenchurch's fillings. Drums thudded in his ears as he tried to keep focused on any updates to his Pronto, the posh version of the Airwave radio the Met were still forcing on them but nobody else, yet. No ID on the victim. The worry that it could be Chloe clawed at his neck. He swatted the spider climbing up. Except it wasn't there. 'You mind slowing down, Kay?'

'You're such an old man . . .' Reed stopped behind a wall of traffic, two lanes huddling at the lights, hidden in the shadow of yet another pair of towers, yuppie flats at the top, student accommodation at the bottom. She pulled into the oncoming lanes, flashing her lights, and trundled along the road snarled up with taxis and buses, Travis cars and Ubers. She hauled the wheel to the right and cut between a demolition site and some rare Victorian class in this part of the city. 'You okay, guv?'

Fenchurch didn't have a response. He sucked a pill down with a glug of stale water from the bottle in the door pocket.

'You want to talk about it, guv? Mulholland at it again?'

'Never stops. The bloody cheek of her, Kay. She asked if I wanted to talk to her about Chloe. She's the last person on earth. Especially after what she did.'

'You've never told Docherty, have you?'

'Just you. For now.' Fenchurch motioned at the wide pavement. 'Park there. We'll walk the rest.'

Reed pulled up and plonked the On Police Business sign on the dashboard. She got out first. Fenchurch had to jog to catch up with her.

The University of Southwark's halls of residence stood over the road, a modern five-storey block of glass and metal, the grey matching the sky. A gang of students hung around outside, shivering in the rain. Laughing and joking like there weren't police officers guarding the entrance. Like there wasn't a dead girl inside.

'Guv, you need to take a breather.' Reed grabbed his arm, blocking his way. 'You're going to have a heart attack.'

'I'm fit as an ox, Kay.'

'Not what I mean, guv. It's not just about Mulholland, is it?'

'Because my daughter's studying here?' Fenchurch blew air out, emptying his lungs. 'It's not a conflict of interest if she's not involved.'

She touched his arm. 'No, but you think the body might be Chloe.'

All Fenchurch could see was how the building had been back in the summer, just after the end of term. Glowing in the heat, not soaked through by the November rain. Fenchurch leading a team inside, leading them to Chloe's room.

Nothing like he'd imagined finding her would be like. Nothing like where, either. He'd expected suffering somehow. PTSD. Emotional and physical scars. Locked in a basement.

But she had been *fine*. Too fine. Cared for. Put through university. One single scar, the result of surgery to make her forget.

All based on lies, based on kidnapping, child abuse, cover-ups. The torment he and Abi and their parents and his colleagues all went through. The strain that tore his marriage apart, turned his hair from blond to white, took his mother to an early grave.

'Calm down, guv.' Reed's grip tightened on his arm, hauling him back to the here and now. 'I don't want people speaking about the state of you.'

Fenchurch sucked in deep gulps of air. Listened to the traffic, the voices, the patter of raindrops on the pavement. Smelt cigarette smoke, bus fumes, ozone from the rain. 'Thought I was over this, but it's getting worse.'

'That's better. Come on.' Reed led him along the street, where plainclothes officers thinned the lake of uniforms outside the entrance.

'Kay!' DS Jon Nelson was lurking around, chatting to that young detective constable who Fenchurch could never remember the name of. A long trench coat covered his beige suit. Rain beaded like sweat on the dark skin of his forehead. He dipped his head towards them. 'Guv.'

Fenchurch nodded back, taking in the faces of the team. Nobody from his squad. 'You got an ID?'

'Not yet, guv.' Nelson held up a SOCO suit. 'Need this if we're going inside.'

———

Nelson signed the Crime Scene Manager's form on the clipboard, the SOCO suit tight around his frame, thickened out by muscle and flab. The three-piece suit underneath didn't help.

The inner locus included a chunk of corridor, stretching out from a wedged-open door with 37 etched on a brass plate. Fenchurch couldn't remember if that was Chloe's room number.

He tried to focus on their surroundings, notice the details. Doors and walls and carpet. Budget-hotel chic, but not cheap. London prices, as if students didn't have enough to pay for these days.

A suited figure emerged from the room, tapping his fingers on his tablet's screen. Mick Clooney, the head Crime Scene Investigator. His mask puffed out. 'You got here quick.'

'Mick, you got an ID yet?' Drums still battered Fenchurch's ears.

Clooney held up his tablet. The body of a young female student lay on the bed, fully clothed but dead. Blonde hair covered her face, looking like she'd swallowed it. 'Hannah Jane Nunn.'

Fenchurch let out a breath of relief. This was never about Chloe. Too easy to fall back into that old habit, wrapped up in worry and fear.

'This her room?' Fenchurch got another nod from Clooney. The relief caught in his throat. If someone could get inside a room and murder the occupant, it could happen to Chloe. She lived nearby. His gut tightened around emptiness. Would've lurched if he'd eaten anything since seven.

Reed spoke to him through her eyes, the only part of her visible. Noticing his relief.

Fenchurch took the tablet from Clooney and scanned the image, trying to focus his nerves on something positive. 'How'd she die, Mick?'

'Pratt's doing his thing just now, but it's a fairly obvious strangulation. Quite a bit of beating, too, if you ask me.'

Fenchurch pinched the screen and zoomed in on her head. Red marks circled her throat, some deep indentations at the front. 'Can you get prints off that?'

'Tried. Failed.' Clooney took his tablet back. 'I've got to Foxtrot Oscar, Si. Managing another two crime scenes. Call me if you need anything, but you've got a good team here.'

'Not so fast.' Fenchurch blocked him. 'You owe me at least an hour of your time, Mick. Come on.'

'Simon, I can't—' Clooney tucked his tablet under his arm and dipped his head. 'Fine. Half an hour.'

'Cheers, Mick.' Fenchurch let him enter the room and waited till he was out of earshot. Nelson was crouched by the doorway. 'Jon, can you get a home address? And find anyone who she dealt with on a daily, weekly, annual basis. I want time with whoever's in charge here. Chancellor, Rector, whatever they're called. Someone got into her room — did she know them? All that jazz.'

'Guv.' Nelson sloped off down the corridor, tearing at his mask and goggles.

Reed was frowning at Fenchurch. 'You okay, guv?'

He wiped at his mask, smearing the sweat into the fabric. 'What, because it's not my daughter lying there?' He didn't give her a chance to respond. 'We're going to find this woman's killer. Don't you worry about that.' He barged past the two CSIs dusting the door surround.

Her room was filled with CSIs. Nothing much of note on the walls. One of those Charlie the Seahorse posters where he's smoking a joint. Not much of a view, just a back lane. Bars on the window, though hard to tell if it was for stopping people getting in or the other way round.

A wardrobe filled the back wall, a CSI cataloguing and dusting the contents. The rest of the room had standard office furniture, a mid-brown wood desk with a blue chair. Books stacked up on top, piled on the floor, classic novels mixed with literary theory and political stuff. So Hannah was an English Literature student, most likely.

A single bed with—

Fenchurch blinked at something hard in his eye.

Hannah lay on the bed. From here she didn't look like she was sleeping. The bruises on her face and the marks on her throat looked worse in the flesh than on the tablet screen. Took real strength to distort skin like that.

The pathologist knelt over the body. Dr William Pratt, humming a *rum-pum-pum* from some opera or something, poking and prodding the corpse. He glanced over at them. 'Look who the cat's dragged in.'

'William. You getting anything I can use?'

Pratt added a *tiddly-om-pom*. 'I can confirm that she died during the night.' *Om-pom-pom-pom-tiddly-om-pom*. 'I'm thinking between three and seven. I do need to confirm the room's heating schedule to determine an exact time. You know, body-heat loss and so forth. Then my calculations will be a lot more accurate.'

'Any evidence on the body?'

'Not my forte, Inspector.' Pratt went back to Hannah and the *om-pom-pom*.

'Room's clean, so far.' Mick Clooney was kneeling on the floor. 'A ton of fingerprints and fibres that'll no doubt all trace back to the deceased.'

'So nothing to go on?'

Clooney stood up with a groan. 'You said it.'

Fenchurch checked the desktop. 'What about her phone?'

'Good news is we've got it.' Clooney held up a mobile in an evidence bag. 'Bad news is it's an iPhone 7 and it's locked. No danger we're getting into it any time soon.'

Fenchurch took it off him. Kids and their expensive phones. Six hundred quid for the cheapest. Not much less on a contract. Gifts from Mummy and Daddy, no doubt. 'So that's it, then?'

'Well.' Clooney gestured over at the wardrobe. 'Tammy's checking her possessions. Aside from some leggings and tops and jeans, her wardrobe contains nothing but gym clothes and lingerie. Expensive stuff, too. Lacy, skimpy, corsets, you name it, it's there.'

'I'm pricing it up as I go, before you ask.' Tammy was stacking up a pile of bags at the foot of the bed, a tangle of lace and black fabric. 'Over three grand just on lingerie, according to the Victoria's Secret website. The gym gear's decent stuff, too. Under Armour and Nike and so on.'

Fenchurch picked up the top bag from the pile. Nothing much to go on until they had people to quiz. Another glance at Clooney. 'Do you know who found her?'

Chapter Three

Fenchurch stayed near the back of the kitchen, listening. The sort of communal student area that spawned arguments about stolen milk. Stank of burnt toast and acidic instant coffee. Nobody had cleaned up all weekend, either.

Reed perched on a stool. Just the one pat of her quiff so far. 'I understand you found her body?'

'This morning. Half nine on the dot.' Troy Danton stood between them, hands in pockets. Kid was fizzing with energy. Must be about seven stone soaking wet. Which he was, his hair gel slicking his forehead. Stank of the stuff, like a cheap barber's. He sounded Peckham — down that way, you can pin an accent to a street. 'I'm a cleaner here. Me and three other geezers. Split the building between us. Get half a corridor done every day. Do a proper job and all.' He kept his focus on Reed. 'Hers was first.'

'Convenient.' Reed gave him a steely glare. 'First room on your rounds just so happens to be the one with a dead body in it.'

Danton's gaze shot between them, spending more time clinging to Fenchurch now. 'I found her. That's all.'

Fenchurch wandered over to Danton, getting almost too close. The chemicals wafted off him, a lame attempt at masking the fug of cigarette smoke. 'Listen, son. Someone got in her room during the night and murdered her. Bit of a mystery how they got in. Now, you've got a good cover story.'

Danton stepped away from Fenchurch, arms up, almost knocking Reed off her stool. 'I just found her!'

'I want to hear your story, okay?' Fenchurch raised his hands in a placatory motion. 'That's all. Take us through it slowly. Remember, if you lie to us . . .' He drew a line across his throat.

'I found Hannah. That's all.'

Fenchurch waved at Reed. 'My colleague didn't mention her name.'

Danton shrugged. 'So?'

'How well did you know her, son?'

'Nice girl. Got a routine, yeah? Start at Room 37 on a Monday. 47 on a Tuesday. You get the drift. She's in 37. I started there. No crime in that.'

'Not saying there is.' Fenchurch rested against the counter and stuffed his hands deep in his pockets, trying to mirror Danton. 'How often do you speak to her?'

'Few times. She's doing English, I think. Supposed to be the laziest cu— students.' Danton blushed, rubbing his ear. 'Afternoon lectures. Not many of them, and all. So she was always in when I was cleaning. Sometimes she wouldn't let me in, so I'd go next door, do hers later. When she doesn't reply, I let myself in.'

Reed glanced at Fenchurch, flashing a warning glare. 'You ever notice anything weird about her possessions?'

'Not my business, darling.' Danton took four goes to rub his nose. His fingers sliding off somehow. Too much grease or hair gel or sweat. 'This morning, she didn't answer. I opened up and . . . that's when I found her.'

'What time did you start?'

'Seven.'

Reed looked up from her notebook. 'When did you find her?'

'About half nine.'

Fenchurch got in Danton's sight line. 'So what were you doing for that two and a half hours?'

'What?' Danton scowled at Reed. 'What does he mean?'

'You said you started at seven. Then you only got round to cleaning Hannah's room at nine thirty.'

Danton sniffed, brushing his fingernails up and down his cheek. 'Mixing detergents and that.'

'That takes two and a half hours?'

'About half an hour.'

'So the other two hours were spent on "that"?'

Danton shut his eyes. Kid was panicking, trapped between two coppers asking serious questions, putting him in the middle of something.

Reed was blocking his exit. 'What took the other two hours, Mr Danton?'

Danton stood up tall, frowning. Clearly never heard his surname that often, just TROY or YOU. He rubbed his nose on the first attempt this time. 'Had a few errands, you know. For my gaffer.'

'And this gaffer would confirm this story, yeah?'

Danton exhaled. 'I didn't kill her. Swear.'

'So where were you, then?'

'Here. Working. Helping a mate.'

'Can we speak to this mate, Mr Danton?'

'It's the truth.'

Reed wrapped her arms tight around her torso, scowling at him. 'And what about before your shift started?'

'Sleeping.'

'And after sleeping?'

'Walked in. Took me an hour.'

'Anyone walk with you?'

'No.'

Fenchurch started pacing the room again, getting in the way of the kitchen's other exit. Last thing they needed was this oik making a run for it. 'Mr Danton, you've not got an alibi for the time Hannah was murdered.'

'Swear I didn't kill her!'

'I'd love to believe you, son, but you need to tell us where you were.'

'Can't.'

'What do you mean, you "can't"? Is it because you were killing her?'

'Didn't kill her!'

'So what the hell were you doing?'

Danton stared at the floor. 'Can't tell you.'

'Try us.'

Danton thrust his arms out wide, sniffing, his mouth hanging open, tongue flopping out. 'I was selling drugs . . .'

Fenchurch couldn't make any sense of it.

'Happy now?' Danton stuck out his arms, wrists together like he was being cuffed. 'Lock me up. But I didn't kill nobody.'

'Okay, so who were you selling drugs to?'

'Students.'

'Got names for them?'

'Honest John. Bab. El Freako. The Beast.' Danton scratched his neck. 'Give everyone a name, I do. Helps me remember them.' He nodded at Reed. 'Mrs Frosty.' Then Fenchurch. 'Alan Pardew.'

Fenchurch almost laughed. 'The football manager?'

'Your hair. White all over.' Danton's gaze drifted above Fenchurch. 'Before you ask, nobody else here is involved. Well, a mate covers for me. This was the early crowd. Wake and bake, you know? Some of them ask me to drop off their gear in their rooms while they're out. When I'm cleaning. Cannabis. E. Speed.' He scowled. 'Not smack!'

Kid dipped into his own stash, that's for sure. And not just the cannabis. The denial of heroin, though . . . Kid was clearly on it, probably injected straight into the vein. Why deny selling it?

Fenchurch ran it through. All making sense. 'So, before your shift?'

'Visited my supplier.' A grin ran over Danton's quivering lips. 'Plod. Dimmest geezer you ever met. Smokes so much skunk, I think time passes slower for him. So I was at his. Stocking up, as it were.' He rubbed his neck. 'Might be hard for him to give me an alibi, though.'

Fenchurch gave a tight nod. 'All right, son. Assuming this story checks out, you're in the clear.'

'Thanks, mate.' Danton's shoulders slumped. 'How much do you want?'

'Excuse me?'

'For clearing me.' Danton got out his wallet. 'How much?'

Fenchurch gripped the kid's shoulders. 'You're in the clear over her murder, you berk. I'm taking you to the cleaners over your drug dealing. And for attempting to bribe a police officer.'

⌣

Fenchurch stood in the doorway, close enough to taste the dirty London smog as the rain hissed off the quad's flagstones.

Reed was over by a squad car, the rain flattening her hair as Troy Danton was lowered in by two uniforms. Soon as the door slammed, she jogged back over and slicked a hand through her hair. 'Stupid git'll go away for a few months.'

Fenchurch stepped aside to let her in. 'I don't think he killed her, but let's see what we can get out of him.'

'Got a couple of monsters at Leman Street, guv. They'll tear him apart.'

Out in the quad, Nelson was powering across the flagstones towards them, a frown on his forehead. He nodded behind him. 'Sir, this is Rupert Uttley. The Chancellor.'

Uttley's face was as red as the ginger patches in his mostly white beard. He was huddled under a golf brolly, wearing a suit almost as sharp as Nelson's, the wool fighting a losing battle against his gut, thickened by wining and dining, no doubt. He held out a meaty paw, shaking Fenchurch's hand like he was wielding a cane. 'Horrendous business. Not the first time we've had a death, of course, but the first murder in at least twenty years. My tenure has been relatively uncontroversial.'

'I'm sure it has.' Fenchurch reached into his pocket for his Pronto. 'Thanks for seeing us, sir. Can you confirm that security arrangements are in hand?'

Uttley's face pinched tight. Looked like he'd had botox. 'Security?'

'A student has been murdered in their room, sir. I think it goes without saying that you need to step up security.'

'Of course. How many officers can you provide?'

'This isn't a police matter, sir. You need to hire some external security.'

'Of course, of course.'

Fenchurch didn't believe it'd happen soon enough. 'In order that we find Miss Nunn's killer, my team require full access to the university, including your staff and students. Is that going to be a problem?'

'Of course not.' Uttley shook his head. His jowls took a while to stop wobbling. 'Whatever you need. Press conference, TV interviews, anything.'

'How about a home address for Hannah?'

'Well, I'll have one of my team dig it out.'

'As soon as you can, sir. In cases like this, time is of the essence.'

'Well, whatever you need. Anything at all. It goes without saying.' Uttley adjusted his jacket, thumbs digging into his braces. 'Who do you think did it?'

'We're at a very early stage, sir. Anything now would be supposition.'

'Yes, yes, of course.' Uttley flashed a smile at the three of them. 'I'll let you get on with it. My office remains open to you.'

'Thanks, sir.' Fenchurch watched him go. 'Keep on him, Jon. Blokes like that can be as practical as an underwater hairdryer.'

Nelson chuckled. 'I'll help him tie his shoelaces, guv.'

'How about the last person to see her?'

Nelson pointed down the long corridor filled with plainclothes and uniforms taking statements from students in various states of dress. A trustafarian played with his ginger dreads opposite a girl in trackies, her hair tied in a towel. 'The last we've got so far is Saturday lunchtime.'

'Keep digging.'

'Early doors, guv. We'll get something.' Nelson flipped open his handset. 'Oh. I spoke to the security guard who was on last night. He didn't hear anything. His station is at the other end of the building, so that's to be expected. Says his bosses told him not to leave it. The guy's just sitting watching Netflix all night.'

'That's my future, Jon.' Fenchurch scanned the corridor again. He doubted they'd get anything out of that lot, but you never knew. 'A girl's murdered in the middle of the night and nobody heard anything. We anywhere with CCTV?'

'One second, guv.' Nelson charged off, barging past the students.

Fenchurch followed, leading Reed through the parting tide in Nelson's wake.

The corridor opened out to an atrium, rows and rows of tables, probably usually filled with students working or chatting. Today it was almost empty.

DC Lisa Bridge was at a table on the far side, twirling her blonde hair through her fingers, scowling at a laptop.

Nelson leaned in close to her, almost caressing her shoulder, and whispered in her ear.

Reed shared Fenchurch's glower. 'They seem cosy.'

Nelson and Bridge walked over, Bridge smiling at Reed, then Fenchurch. 'Sir, I've acquired the CCTV from the corridor outside Hannah's room.' She held out her laptop, screen first.

Fenchurch snatched it off her. A shadowy figure stood outside Hannah's room. Blurry, like it was recovered from an old VHS someone found in a skip. Couldn't make anything out — it was like watching through mist.

They wore a black hooded top. Shades and a heavy duster jacket on, so it was hard to make out their build, even without the crappy video quality. The time stamp was ten to four.

'This all you've got of him?'

'That's the best I've found so far.'

Fenchurch squinted hard then passed the computer back. 'Show me the worst.'

'Okay.' Bridge rested the laptop on the desk and hit the spacebar. It started playing, the shadowy figure opening Hannah's door and entering. She hit the keys again and it cut to the corridor, empty and quiet. Then a blur left the room, sneaking away.

Reed tapped the screen. 4.21. 'This is half an hour later, sir.'

'That's our killer?'

'Not sure.' She did more typing. 'But he returned forty-five mins later.' — 5.06 — 'Then he left fifteen minutes after that.'

Fenchurch stared at the spectre who seemed to have murdered Hannah. 'So a ghost did it. The end. That's what you're telling me?'

'Not quite, sir.' Bridge wound the video back.

Fenchurch lurched forward. 'Is that all you've got?'

'Don't kill the messenger, sir.' Bridge smiled at him. 'The problem is, whoever's in charge of this place has bought the world's worst CCTV system. Don't even need to sneak past the cameras, they're not going to pick anyone up.'

Fenchurch pushed the laptop away. 'Jon, find this guy.'

'I'll see, guv.' Nelson squeezed in for a closer inspection. 'We'll cross-reference to the other cams, see what we can dig up.'

Bridge took the laptop back and switched to another window. 'There's also this, sir.'

Fenchurch's gut lurched. On the screen, Hannah Nunn stood in her doorway, very much alive. The clock showed just after midnight. She was shouting at a tall, athletic man, really going to town on him. Her face twisted with rage, a finger jabbing at him. His rower's shoulders slumped, head hanging low.

Nelson grabbed the laptop and flicked to the other window. 'Hard to tell if that geezer matches this shadow figure.'

Bridge reached over and hit play. Mr Muscles stormed off as Hannah shouted after him, then she was alone in the corridor. She slumped back against her door, crying. Bridge stopped it playing. 'I'll find him, sir.'

Her Airwave radio crackled on the desk. 'Backup needed at Room 37!'

Chapter Four

Fenchurch turned the corner and sprinted off towards Hannah's room. A huddle of uniforms clustered round Room 37 at the far end, even more than when Millwall came to West Ham. Someone shouted, 'LET ME IN THERE!'

Fenchurch barged his way through the crowd of cops.

Two burly uniforms wrestled a big man between them, a tangle of arms and shouting. They forced him to the ground, face down, and slapped a pair of cuffs on him.

His face was torn by rage. 'This is bullshit!'

Fenchurch clocked the guy from the CCTV, the man arguing with Hannah in the corridor, reducing her to tears. 'Give us some space!'

The crowd started to disperse around them, the uniforms muttering to each other as they walked off. The Crime Scene Manager was on his knees, rubbing his bloody nose. Not one of Fenchurch's team, some South London muppet. 'Kid pushed me over.'

Mr Muscles was trying to shake free, but the uniforms had him, the bulkier one digging a knee into his spine. 'You need to let me see her!' The kid looked about twenty and was over-developed. Glamour muscles, too. Couldn't even shake off two fat uniforms who hadn't graced the rugby pitch in a decade. Baby-smooth skin, though, and Hollywood looks. Lucky bastard.

Fenchurch nodded for them to let him up. Slowly. 'Can I have your name, son?'

'Sam.' He stretched out his T-shirt, but there wasn't any give in it. It hugged his torso like a lover, showing off his physique. Bloody ponce. 'Sam Edwards. Are you going to let me see her?'

Fenchurch tilted his head towards the kitchen area, currently guarded by a bored-looking uniform. 'Come on, sir, let's have a chat.'

'I need to see Hannah!'

'Are you acquainted with the deceased?'

Sam seemed to deflate at that word. Like on the CCTV, his shoulders slumped. 'She's really dead?'

'I'm afraid so.' Fenchurch clocked some of Pratt's Pathology team cowering inside the room, ready to take the body to Lewisham for the post-mortem. 'Come with me, sir.' He set off towards the kitchen, letting Sam follow, his cuffs jangling.

'In here.' Fenchurch uncuffed him.

Sam took a free stool, resting his head on the counter. Stayed that way for a few seconds.

Reed entered, her perpetual frown on her face. She clocked Sam then took a seat. 'Mr Edwards, my name is DS Kay Reed. This is DI Simon Fenchurch.'

Sam sat up and dug the heels of his palms into his eye sockets. 'What happened to her?'

'That's what we want to find out, sir.' Fenchurch stayed by the door, guarding it. Reed could handle him, knew where to hit and how to take someone down. Not that Sam looked ready to run for it.

Reed propped herself up against the counter. 'How well do you know Ms Nunn?'

'Hannah.' Sam nibbled at his bottom lip, the top one twisting into a snarl. 'I'm her boyfriend. Been together a couple of years.'

'Mr Edwards, as far as we can tell, you might be the last person to see her alive.'

27

Sam's gaze shot up to Reed, locking on tight. 'What?'

'I've seen the CCTV footage.' Reed splayed her hands wide. 'All of it. You were outside her room. She was shouting at you. You ran off.'

'That was the last I saw of her, I swear.'

'What was the argument about?'

'You think I killed her?'

'Did you?'

'Of course not. That's the last time I saw her.'

Fenchurch let out a sigh, mainly for effect. 'You didn't return later on, did you? Around ten to four?'

Sam glanced over at him. 'No.' He clenched his fists, pressing his thumbs down so hard the flesh turned white. 'After that argument, I . . . Hannah had a way of getting to me. She made me feel about two inches tall. So I went back to my room and worked out. Pull-ups from the bathroom door frame. Press-ups. Tried to take my mind off it.'

Reed tilted her head to the side. 'What did you argue about?'

'None of your business.'

'Mr Edwards, I don't think you realise the seriousness of this situation.' Reed gave him her scary-policewoman stare. 'Hannah's dead. You were the last person to see her and you had a big argument with her. That makes you a suspect in my book.'

'I can't . . .'

'Try me.'

Sam shoved his hands into the pockets of his tracksuit bottoms. 'We were talking about our plans for after university.' He swallowed. That there wouldn't be anything to plan for was sinking in. 'This is our final year. I'm staying in London. Got a job lined up. I love it here. I'm settled.'

'But Hannah wasn't?'

'She had two offers for MA courses. One at Birmingham. One at Warwick, which might as well be Birmingham.' Sam grimaced. 'That means a long-distance relationship.'

'I can understand how difficult that is, sir, but an MA is a year.'

'A year's a long time.' Sam shrugged. Then his lip quivered, his eyes welling up.

Reed gave him a few seconds. 'How did the argument end?'

'You said you saw me storm off.'

'I saw, yeah. I didn't hear, though.'

Sam nodded slowly, thinking how much to tell. His shrug suggested he'd decided on the whole truth. 'She wanted me to get a job in Birmingham. Even if she went to Warwick, we'd be able to live together.'

'What did you think of that?'

'My degree is in Psychology.' Sam scowled. 'But I want to get into AI. I've got the offer of an internship at a place in Hackney.' He nibbled his bottom lip again. 'Not much demand for it in Birmingham.' He scratched the stubble on his head. 'That's what made me so angry. She wasn't leaving me with a choice. They loved her here. She could've stayed on at Southwark to do her MA. This is a top-twenty uni.'

'And this morning?'

The life seemed to drain from Sam. 'I had a nine o'clock. Lasted two hours. My phone started buzzing towards the end. I had to ask the lecturer a couple of things about my dissertation, so I didn't check my messages until I got out.' He pinched his cheeks, slicked with tears. 'They said Hannah was dead.'

Reed seemed bored now, which was a good sign. Sam Edwards wasn't a suspect, more a witness. Or a very good actor.

Trust, but verify.

Where did that come from? Fenchurch couldn't remember, but it worked for him. Let the kid grieve, but dig into the story. Then, if it didn't stack up, haul him into an interview room.

'We found a lot of lingerie in her wardrobe.' Reed held out her Airwave Pronto. The screen showed a lingerie model. 'Expensive stuff, the kind a student shouldn't really have.'

Sam rubbed the back of his neck. 'Our sex life is private.'

'Not if it's what got her killed.'

'What do you mean by that?'

'I could mean anything by it, Mr Edwards.' Reed stood up tall. 'Thanks for your time. I'm going to leave you with a colleague for now. I'd really appreciate if you could give them a list of Hannah's friends, even the ones she met in Freshers' Week but lost touch with. As many people as you can.'

———

Camera flash shimmered out of Hannah's room. The Crime Scene Manager patted his nose. Inside, CSIs were on their hands and knees, cataloguing and bagging.

Fenchurch waited for Reed. 'What do you make of him?'

'Hard to read, guv.' She was trying to restore her quiff but it was hanging limp. 'Could be grieving, could be acting.'

Fenchurch leaned against the wall. 'Go over his statement, okay? Everything on it. I want his movements as detailed as we can get them.'

'Guv.'

A figure approached them, tugging at his mask. Tablet computer under his arm. Clooney stepped out into the corridor and snatched the clipboard off the Crime Scene Manager. 'Simon, you've had your thirty minutes. I'm leaving.' He shoved his gloves in a biohazard bag and tore at his suit.

Fenchurch glared at the Crime Scene Manager. 'Did that interlude affect anything?'

He got a meek shrug. 'The kid didn't get in the room . . .'

'And we'd already done the doors.' Clooney tugged at his jacket, snapping the zip off the left side, and stuffed it into the respective bag. His arms seemed to have another couple of tattoos that Fenchurch hadn't seen before. 'Still nothing to help you, though. Well . . .'

Fenchurch pounced. 'Well?'

'It's probably nothing.' Clooney kicked off his crime scene trousers and put them in the bag. 'Have a butcher's at this.' He held out his tablet.

Fenchurch took it and fiddled with the display. A white box stencilled with 'MacBook Pro' near the top, and below that a sleek silver laptop pictured side on. 'It's very elegant, but what does that give me?' He passed the tablet back.

'You've got a box, Si, but no computer.' Clooney tapped the screen. 'Tammy found it in the wardrobe, stuffed behind all those posh knickers and bras. She's catalogued the SKU.'

Reed nodded. 'Stock-Keeping Unit. So?'

'This is the most expensive MacBook Pro. Two thousand seven hundred. And that's before Brexit screwed the pound. And there's no sign of it anywhere.'

Fenchurch scowled. Acid burnt in his gut. He knew the lengths certain people in this city would go to get hold of Apple products. 'You're saying someone's sneaked into her room in the middle of the night to steal her laptop?'

'I'm saying nothing, Si. You're the detective.'

The bed was empty now. Hannah had died wearing the same clothes as during the argument. Hardly the sort of thing you wore to sleep in.

'I'll run a full logistical analysis of the laptop, Si. Got the serial number, so we can check with Apple and their supply chain. Even if it doesn't turn up at some second-hand shop in the East End, we'll find out where she bought it.'

'More worried about the "where the hell it is now".'

Clooney stuffed his tablet in its purple sleeve and flashed a smile. 'I'll let you know how I get on.'

'Cheers, Mick.' Fenchurch watched him go. 'What are you thinking, Kay?'

'Someone killing her to nick a laptop? Doesn't feel right, guv.' She slicked her quiff over again. It wouldn't stay still. 'Could Troy Danton have taken it when he found the body?'

'If it was there this morning. Danton could've sold it in the time it takes to roll a spliff. But it doesn't feel right. He reported her body when he found her. Called 999. He didn't have time to flog it.'

'Could've passed it to his gaffer or the mate he's covering for.'

Fenchurch snorted. 'Yeah, he's—'

'Guv!' Nelson was charging towards them, a sheet of paper flapping in his grip. 'Got a home address for Hannah. Want me to head there?'

Fenchurch took the sheet. A Suffolk village with a Bury St Edmunds postcode. Two hours' drive each way. He didn't expect it to yield anything, but it was bad form for someone other than the Senior Investigating Officer or the Deputy to break the news. Give the parents the reassurance they were after, even if it all turned to shit in the end.

He pocketed the page. 'Cheers, Jon. I'll do it.'

'Want me there?'

'Not this time. Need you to stop this place turning into a mess in a monkey shop.' Fenchurch nodded at Reed. 'Kay, you're with me.'

Chapter Five

Hannah Nunn's home village was typical Suffolk. A few houses, loosely distributed across a large area, leafy roads leading out from the central pub and post office. Never too close to your neighbours, but never too far. Beautiful stone cottages with ornate walls. Older ones with thatched roofs. Sixties bungalows with trampolines in the front gardens.

Hell of a difference to London and less than two hours' drive. Idyllic, rural, bucolic, everything. Even in November, even when it was pissing down.

Fenchurch leaned back in the passenger seat and stretched out his aching legs. 'Take it Abi's told you about wanting to leave London?'

'Many, many times.' Reed navigated the twists and bends about 10 mph too fast. Her quiff had been dried out and re-sculpted. 'Can't see you living in the middle of Middle England, though. *Daily Mail* through the door every morning. Probably get shot for reading the *Guardian* round here.'

'You think?'

'Got a cousin in Lowestoft. Eat their own there.'

'That's a dump, though.' Fenchurch waved at a pair of cottages, a wall and a hundred metres or so between them. 'This is beautiful. Even in November.'

Reed took a right and pulled up behind a squad car, a souped-up Fiesta in blue and acid yellow. 'The worst crime Suffolk would see is cattle rustling.'

'It's arable round here, Kay.'

'So someone sets fire to a hay bale or two.'

Fenchurch laughed. Couldn't help himself. 'Almost like you don't want me to leave.'

'Be my guest. Happily take your job.'

'Bet you would.' Fenchurch let his seat belt go. 'Have to fight Jon Nelson for it.'

'Don't have to tell me about the glass ceiling, guv.' Reed opened the door and held it there. 'A black man always wins over a woman.'

'How do you explain the new Commissioner? Or DI Mulholland, for that matter?'

'Can't speak for the Commissioner, but I don't have Mulholland's cauldron.'

Fenchurch got out, trying to hide his laughter as the rain spattered his hair.

Hannah's parents lived in a house that looked older than civilisation. Beautiful. Peer closer, though, and you could see the flaking paint around the windows. The missing flagstones in the drive. Settlement cracks on the gable end.

And it hit him. They were here to tell someone their daughter was dead. No matter how many times, it always felt raw, just like the first.

It took him years to stop fearing every knock on the door, every phone call, in case it was someone telling him about Chloe. Telling him she was dead.

The door rattled open and two male uniforms strolled out, hats under the arms, the sort of frowns that you made when trying to appear professional.

Fenchurch strode up to the gate and waited for them to step down the path. Broken panes of glass in the windows. 'Afternoon, gents.' He held out his warrant card, not even bothering with an introduction. 'Can I ask why you're here?'

The first one was about ten years younger than the other, not long out of school. Stubble dotted his chin, thick sideburns framing his face. 'To give the death message, sir?'

Fenchurch groaned. Couldn't help himself. 'You were told to wait.' He thumbed at Reed. 'We've just driven up from London.'

'Sorry, sir, Sarge's orders.'

'Get out of my bloody sight.' Fenchurch barged between them and splashed up the path towards the house. He rapped on the door and waited.

Reed joined him. 'Shitshow, guv.'

'Don't get me started, Kay.' Fenchurch tried the door again. Harder, more insistent.

A pink blob appeared through the glass, twisted and distorted. The chain rattled and the door opened. A tall woman in her late fifties, her red face lined. 'Sorry, we're not taking visitors.'

She got a flash of warrant card. 'Mrs Nunn? DI Simon Fenchurch.' He let her inspect his ID, her face crumpling up. 'We're here about Hannah.'

She swallowed hard. 'We've just been told.'

'I know. They should've waited. We're Met detectives, Mrs Nunn. We're investigating her murder.'

Tears streaked down Mrs Nunn's face. She sank to her knees, rocking hard as she cried. 'My poor, poor baby.'

⁓

'My wife's not handling this very well.' Gerald Nunn walked over from the kitchen door, stooping like he'd grown since he'd bought the house. Or the building had shrunk. He sank into an armchair beside a roaring fire, blue flames kicking up from the red coals. He rubbed a hairy fist around the thick silvery beard covering his face.

Fenchurch sat on the left side of a sofa, Reed at the other end. The floorboards were battered and bent. Felt like the sofa could fall into a hole at any point. 'We can come back, sir.'

'It's fine, fine. Fine.' He gripped the arms of the chair as if he was on a rollercoaster. 'I'm sorry this place isn't up to much. Every spare penny went to Hannah. We wanted her to get the best education. The best.'

'That's very noble, sir.'

'Is it?' Nunn frowned at Fenchurch, rubbing his thick beard. Couldn't take his hands off it. 'Isn't it what any parent would do?'

'You'd be surprised.'

'I'm sure you've seen *things* that'd make your hair stand on end.' Nunn's fingers dug into the armchair, twitching like they needed to get back to the beard. 'Yes, things.' His gaze settled on Fenchurch. 'Have you got anywhere in finding who . . . did this?'

'It's still early, sir.'

'Then what do you want to know?'

'How would you describe your daughter?'

'Impetuous. At times. At others, she'd think things through almost too much. Almost too much.' He battered his fists onto his thighs. 'She had a very loving upbringing, very loving. Didn't want for anything. Anything at all.'

'Like computers?'

Gerald's brow twitched a few times, then settled into a deep frown. 'Of course, of course. We scrimped together and bought her one for Christmas. A good one, according to my brother. Very good one.' He frowned at them. 'We got it from the . . .' He clicked his fingers a few times. 'From the, uh, from PC World. Had to go into Bury. Near the Sainsbury's. My brother said it was a good one, anyway. Of course, he said that about that mower he sold me.'

Fenchurch got out his Pronto and dug through the forensics until he found the photo of the laptop box. 'Was it this one?'

'An Apple? Heavens, no. I'm not made of money. It was Hewlett Packard. Used to have one for my accounts back in the day. Very good machine, it was. Four hundred pounds, this one cost. Came with a student licence for that Microsoft Office thingy.'

Fenchurch searched through the case files while Nunn muttered about his daughter's computer, and found the inventory. No mention of an HP, not even a stray charger or a box.

So now they had two missing laptops.

Reed smiled at Nunn, warm and reassuring. 'Did Hannah like clothes?'

Nunn stared at her for a few seconds. 'That was Hannah's thing, yes. Her thing. Clothes. Always the best clothes. Her mother took her to London every so often. She'd get the best. The very best. Jeans. Tops. You know how it is. But the best stuff for her. Next and River Island. Maybe Debenhams. But the very best for her. Our daughter.'

Not posh lingerie, then.

Fenchurch found a note in the inventory — the lingerie was estimated at over four grand. Almost half of her annual fees. He glanced at Reed, then leaned forward. 'We found some expensive . . . lingerie in her wardrobe.'

'Lingerie?' Nunn screwed up his eyes. 'Are you sure?'

'Positive. Do you—'

'I don't know anything about that, sir. Nothing. Like I say, she was into clothes. Nice clothes.'

Another dead end.

'Did she ever mention any friends from university?'

'All the time. Not to me, of course. Never to me. But Hannah talked to her mother about them.'

Fenchurch checked the kitchen door again. Mrs Nunn was sitting by the window, clutching a photo of Hannah. Not in any state to help answer their questions.

'Did she ever talk about a boyfriend?'

'Sam. Was it? Sounded like a nice man. Nice, yes. Never had the pleasure, I'm afraid.'

'Did you ever worry about your daughter's safety in London?'

'No.' His fingers needled the armchair. 'Listen to me, at school . . . at school, there was a boy in the village who had a thing for Hannah. I threatened to knock his bloody block off, but . . . You know how some men are, don't you?'

———   ———

'I mean, it might be the grief, guv, but . . .' Reed knocked on the front door of a sixties bungalow on the other side of the village from the Nunns'. The house seemed like it had been grown in a field, plonked between a load of horse chestnut trees, the ground pockmarked with rotting conkers. 'Given up a lot for their daughter's education.'

Fenchurch raised an eyebrow. 'Tell me you're not the same.'

Reed knocked again. 'Fat chance either of mine will get an A-Level, let alone a degree.'

'Makes you think, though.' Fenchurch tried to swallow down the lump in his throat. 'I've no idea how Chloe's paying her way through her degree. Nine grand a year, isn't it?'

'And the answer's debt, guv. Student loans bigger than my first mortgage.' Reed knocked again. 'Doesn't—'

The door opened a crack and an eye peered out, shrouded by wispy sideburns. 'What?'

'Police, sir.' Reed showed her warrant card. 'Looking for a Graham Pickersgill.'

'That's me.' Still didn't open the door.

Reed scowled at him. 'Sir, we have reason to believe you were causing distress to a schoolgirl. Is that—'

'That's my son.' The door opened a bit further. Guy was a rough forties or a spritely sixties. 'Graham Pickersgill the fourth. I'm the third.'

'Can we have a word with him?'

'Chance'd be a fine thing, love. Not seen hide nor hair of the bugger in almost two years. I've no idea where the thieving little shit is now. Good day.' And he slammed the door.

Chapter Six

Fenchurch pulled up on the pavement across from the halls of residence, where Reed had parked hours earlier. Still cordoned off. Uttley had stepped up the security, though. Bulky men and women in acid-yellow jackets lined the street. Possibly too many, but that was preferable to the alternative. Suspiciously normal, like all the excitement and drama of a dead body had been contained. Typical London, always pushing forward.

'You okay, guv?' Reed was still focusing on her notebook, scribbling and scrawling God knows what. 'I mean it. You've been a grumpy sod all afternoon.'

'Just as well you've only had to spend five hours in my company.' Fenchurch unclipped his seat belt and sat back. The pool car annoyed him. The clicking from the passenger's side. The lump in the chair. The armrest was too high. Even the bloody weather. Everything.

Another glance at Reed, typing on her Pronto. 'You getting anywhere with this Pickersgill geezer?'

She held up her Airwave. 'Did a PNC. You not listening?'

Fenchurch gripped the door handle, watching for a gap in the thrum of traffic. 'Wasn't listening.'

'You never are. Nothing on him, anyway.'

Fenchurch twisted round, frowning. 'So this geezer was stalking her at school and he just disappears? That's not good.'

Reed snapped her notebook shut. 'If only we'd discussed this during the drive back, guv.' She got out and slammed the door.

Fenchurch waited for a row of three Ubers to pass before he got out. He locked the car and sprinted down the street to catch up with Reed. 'What's up?'

'Five hours for nothing, guv.' She waved over the road at Nelson, talking on his phone. 'You could've taken Jon instead. You could've sent him for all we learned.'

'But I trust you, Kay.' Fenchurch hammered the button at the crossing. 'Your insights are good.'

'Guv . . . if Docherty's busting your balls about behaving properly, think about how you use your resources, yeah?' Reed set off over the road. 'If you took me to show the sort of shit a Deputy SIO has to put up with, then I get it.'

Fenchurch leaned close to Reed. 'Getting *anything* out of grieving parents is the hardest trick to pull off. We got a lead thanks to your persistence. This Pickersgill might be nothing; then again, he could be that figure in the corridor outside her room. You've done something instead of just looking important, okay?'

Reed seemed to think it through. Could see her go through all the stages. The denial of a frown, the anger of a scowl. Then depression as her forehead tightened, her jaw clenching. She sighed. Acceptance. 'Guv, sorry. I'm acting like a child.'

'I know, Kay. Same as it ever was.'

'Come on, then.' She set off.

Nelson finished his call and took a suck on his vape stick, exhaling a fine mist. 'Kay. Guv.' He pocketed the device, but just stood there, waiting. 'You get anything up in Suffolk?'

'What do you think?' Reed sent a glare at Fenchurch. Not at acceptance yet, then.

Nelson had another puff of vape. 'Anyway, we've pretty much finished here.'

'Already?'

'Students, guv. They've all been in their rooms or someone else's. Or hanging about. We've spoken to everyone in Hannah's corridor, plus the two adjacent ones. Both security guards on last night.' Nelson waved at the guard standing by the doorway, acting like he was an American patrol cop in some film. 'Nobody saw anything.'

'And this man in the corridor on the CCTV?'

'Still nothing, guv. The guards don't have anyone coming in or out around that time, which makes me think it's a student.'

'Or they're lying.'

'Watched the CCTV myself, guv. They're on the level. All of the exits were covered.'

Fenchurch tried to think it through. Too many holes. 'So this bloke, whoever he is, was already in the building by lights out?'

'They dim them at ten.'

'So between ten and three fifty, we've got nothing?'

'That's right. Other than Hannah and Sam's argument.'

'And nobody knows how they got in her room, I suppose?'

'Wasn't locked.'

Fenchurch slapped his forehead. 'You're bloody kidding me.'

'Tammy confirmed it. She could tell by how the mechanisms were . . . arranged.'

'Even though that cleaner went in?'

'He's got a different key. She can tell these things.' Nelson held out his handset. 'Check this.'

The screen showed a street in greyscale, bleached hard by the streetlights. Zoomed out to show ten or twelve buildings. Shoreditch, round the corner from the Brewdog bar on Bethnal Green Road. A few people milling about, hipsters and suits, girls in dresses and dungarees.

Nelson breathed stale coffee all over Fenchurch. 'Here.' He hit a play button on the screen and the scene came to life.

A young woman walked in from the right of the frame, arms crossed, gaze on the pavement in front of her. The gang of hipsters drinking outside an old pub gave her some chat. She started mouthing back at them. Got a round of applause from the hipsters. Then she turned and continued her angry walk, temporarily blocked by a bus.

Fenchurch hit pause and squinted at it. 'Is this Hannah?'

'Yep.' Nelson zoomed in on the figure, turning it blocky. The footage skipped forward a few nanoseconds and sharpened up. 'This is her, guv.'

Hair out in ringlets, a long dress almost covering her feet, tight around her legs. Difficult to miss how defined her thighs and buttocks were. Muscular, like she'd worked hard at it. Not the sort of athleticism you got from rowing or swimming, or the chunkiness of hockey or rugby. Something else, something he couldn't pin down.

Fenchurch didn't want to say anything in case it made him look like a dirty old pervert, but it didn't hang right.

'Watch this, guv.' Nelson zoomed out and hit play again.

Hannah continued her walk, now three buildings away from the hipsters. Four, five, then another pub, quieter. She walked across a side street and someone stepped in behind her, matching her pace. She continued over to the left-hand side of the frame, then disappeared, her tail following.

'What the hell is this, Jon?'

'Keep watching.'

The man staggered back into the shot, his arms windmilling. He hit a wall and slumped down, his arse touching his ankles.

Hannah appeared in the shot and stood over him, shouting. He got up, arms outstretched, pleading with her. Then she cracked him one, her right fist denting his cheek. Hannah tried sticking the boot in, but she was pulled back by the hipsters, a flurry of beards, skinny jeans and waistcoats.

Nelson hit pause again and circled a finger round them. 'Spoke to this lot about half an hour ago. Sod's law, guv, but they're off-duty cops out on the lash. Cyber Crime Unit, based over in Scotland Yard. Can you believe it?'

'Believe anything, Jon, given enough evidence.' Fenchurch glanced at Reed, still transfixed by the screen. 'So these guys stopped her beating up this bloke?'

'She got two good hits in before they got her off him. Broke his nose, blood everywhere. She was a strong girl. Whoever killed her must've surprised her because I doubt they could've overpowered her.'

Reed tapped the screen. 'Got a name for this guy?'

'Not yet.' Nelson drew a circle around the hipsters. 'They thought they were being clever, putting the frighteners on her, showing their warrant cards.'

'You're kidding me.' Fenchurch groaned. 'And they didn't think to arrest her for assault?'

'No, guv. And it gets worse. While they were doing that, our chum ran off.' Nelson hit play again. Hannah's victim retreated up the side street. 'It's all laptops and spreadsheets with those guys, guv. Wouldn't have the first clue about community policing. Not real cops, are they?'

Fenchurch found it hard to argue. 'If they'd arrested her, we'd have a much better lead on who this plonker in the video is. I'll mention this to Docherty.'

Nelson looked like he was about to say something but he just gave a slight shrug.

'Still, this is interesting.' Fenchurch cracked his knuckles. 'How did you find it, anyway?'

'That boyfriend of hers came through. Gave us a list of Hannah's friends. One of them told us about this.' Nelson took the Airwave back from Reed. 'Hannah broke her hand. Still waiting to speak to a couple of them who were out drinking with her that night.'

'Why the delay?'

'They're in the gym, guv.'

Reed charged through the hangar-sized gym, rammed with cardio equipment, virtually all of it taken. The cross-trainers and cycles hissed and whirred. A man in tight shorts held himself up on a treadmill blurring past underneath, then dropped for a mad sprint. Then up again. Crazy.

In the corner, a tall guy was swinging a kettlebell, his grey T-shirt soaked through with sweat, the slogan just about visible. MAYBE IT'S BECAUSE I'M BAVARIAN. Could smell him from here.

Reed was scanning round the gym. 'Focus on the machines, guv.'

Fenchurch tried to match the faces Nelson had given them. 'What's that supposed to mean?'

'I saw how you were looking at that video of Hannah, guv.'

'I wasn't perving, okay?' Fenchurch let out a sigh. 'Come on, Kay, you of all people should know that.' He rubbed at his neck. Burning red, a trickle of sweat. Must be all the exercise pushing the humidity through the roof. 'Go with me on this. On that video, her skirt thing was really tight, yeah? To show off her legs and . . . her bum. It was all overdeveloped, like she was going for bulk and size.'

'Guv, quit while you're behind, yeah?'

'Kay, come on. I'm serious. She put a lot of effort into it.' Fenchurch clocked two girls in the corner, hunched over stair-climber machines, clinging on for dear life. Sweat soaked their long hair, leaving traces of blonde in the murky brown. Steel thighs and diamond buttocks pounded the machines. 'Like those two.'

'You dirty pervert.' Reed squinted at them. 'Hang on, that's who we're looking for.' She set off.

The two girls wore matching white T-shirts, soaked through with sweat, VICKS and LIBBY stencilled on the back in dark blue. SOUTHWARK TO BRIGHTON ULTRA MARATHON 2016

Reed tried to catch their attention. Both had earbuds in, white tails trailing up to smartphones cradled on the machines. She waved a hand in front of them.

The girl on the right took an earbud out and scowled. 'What?'

'Police. Need to speak to Victoria Summerton and Olivia Magrane.'

'I'm Vicks, she's Libby.' The sort of Essex accent Reed was losing by the week. Out on the estuary, Grays or somewhere feral like that. 'What do you want?'

She was still pounding away. The machines were on long multi-hour programs: 2.56:34 remaining. Set to level 15, too. Made Fenchurch's eyes water just thinking about it. Could grind your hips to dust doing it for that long.

Reed flashed her warrant card. 'Need to speak to you about Hannah Nunn.'

The machines clicked as they both stopped. Victoria got off first. 'All right if we get showered first?'

Reed smirked in Fenchurch's direction then gave them both a tight nod. 'Don't be too long, yeah? Otherwise, I'll send him in after you.'

⌣

Fenchurch took the coffees from the barista and set them on a tray. The café was closer to a Caffè Nero than the sort of greasy spoons you'd find in most gyms he'd frequented at that age. A glass window looked out on the free weights area, two idiots daring each other to deadlift increasingly more stupid weights.

Reed stood next to him, watching the door. 'What do you reckon, guv, divide and conquer?'

Victoria and Olivia walked in, bags slung over their shoulders, wet hair dripping on the floor.

Fenchurch picked up the tray, careful not to spill any. He smiled at Victoria and nodded to a free table in the corner. She followed him and slumped in the chair. Frowned at the cups. 'Which is mine?'

Fenchurch pushed one across the table. 'Hazelnut skinny latte.'

'Thanks.' She tore off the lid and peeked inside, like he was lying to her. She took a deep sniff of it and sat back, legs crossed. 'So, what do you want to know?'

Fenchurch cradled his coffee, letting it cool. The heat spread through his fingers. 'I gather you were good friends?'

'Met her at Freshers' Week at a cheese and wine thing in halls. Not that either of us had any cheese.' She took a sip of coffee. 'Too fattening.' She gave Fenchurch a flash of long eyelashes. 'We drank too much vodka together that year.'

'You talk like you're not friends any more.'

'Hannah started seeing Sam.' Her gaze swept around the room. Then it settled on Fenchurch with a smile and another flash of the lashes. She dipped a finger into the foam, then licked it off slowly, eyes trained on him. 'You work out, don't you?'

Oh Christ. The last thing I bloody need . . .

Bloody girl's flirting with me. Same age as Chloe, give or take.

'Three times a week.' Fenchurch took a sip of coffee, his mouth burning like his neck. 'I saw the program you were doing on the machines.'

'Got to keep in shape.' Victoria patted her stomach, flat through her lilac T-shirt. 'I listen to lectures and audiobooks while I'm doing it. Beats sitting in the library.'

'Did Hannah ever talk about a Graham Pickersgill?'

She blew air up her face, sweat pricking the skin round her eyebrows. 'Not to me.'

'Sure? Because we heard about Hannah assaulting someone in Shoreditch in June.' Fenchurch took another biting glug of coffee. 'I gather you were with her that night?'

'Me and Libby were, yeah. Clubbing. Thursday nights can be wild up that way. It's not exactly cheap but we have ways of getting drinks.' Victoria shifted forward on her seat. 'We were flirting with these bankers, real City boys. Two of them, yeah? They kept on buying us bottles of rosé and shots. I didn't notice that Hannah had gone until an hour later. She got fed up. She was seeing Sam, so she wasn't trying it with these guys. Taking candy from a baby. But I never commit.' Another flash of lashes. 'Waiting for the right man. Someone with experience.'

'So you didn't leave with Hannah that night?'

'No.' She cradled her cup, the realisation that he wasn't going to flirt with her starting to sink in. 'Heard she beat up some guy who followed her or something.'

'Did she say who?'

Victoria took another drink, slowly licking her lips. 'Can't remember. It was some random, wasn't it?'

'She didn't mention the name Graham Pickersgill?'

'Sorry. Never heard of him.' Victoria fanned out her hair, leaving it frizzing around her ears. 'She told us the cops let her off with it because the bloke ran away.'

'We noticed a few things we can't explain in her room.' Fenchurch spun his paper cup round. 'A missing laptop, for starters. You ever see her with a MacBook Pro?'

Victoria sunk the rest of her coffee in one go then stuffed the lid back on, pulling it tight until it snapped. 'I do a lot of the same lectures as Hannah. Never saw a MacBook, just a small laptop. HP or something.'

'That's missing, too. When did you last see it?'

'Not for a while, actually.' She peered into Fenchurch's coffee cup for a few seconds, her forehead creased. 'It had a pink Charlie the Seahorse sticker on it.'

Fenchurch noted it down. Might narrow their search a little. 'The other thing we found was a few grand's worth of lingerie.'

'Didn't know she had any.' No coquettish smiles. No lashes. No flirting. 'What she wore when her and Sam were at it, she kept secret.' Victoria rolled her eyes. 'It's a bit of a puzzle, isn't it? Missing laptops, lots of expensive lingerie. Glad I'm not a cop.'

Cheeky. Fenchurch held her gaze for a few seconds, then took a long drink of coffee. 'She ever have any disagreements with anyone?'

'Hannah was good people.' Victoria bit her bottom lip. 'You heard what happened with Zachary, yeah?'

Chapter Seven

The lift pinged but the doors didn't open. Fenchurch hammered the button, but they stayed shut.

Bloody, bloody hell.

He held it down again, still nothing. 'Are we bloody stuck?'

Reed pressed the button for the twentieth floor. There was a thud, then the doors ground open, as though someone was taking a diamond-tooth chainsaw to them. 'Stairs next time, yeah?'

'Yeah.' Fenchurch stepped out into the atrium. Three corridors led off, the one opposite them marked CHANCELLOR'S OFFICE. 'Take it you've heard of this Thomas Zachary?'

'Abi was moaning about him last time I saw her. This place has gone to the dogs since we were here.' Reed grimaced as she led down the corridor. 'How could they vote a scumbag in as Rector?'

'The way Victoria talked about it, it was a choice between him, that bloke off *Strictly Come Dancing* and some ex-footballer she can't remember. Zachary won.'

'In my day, the Chancellor would've cancelled it. They're screwing these kids over, guv.' Reed's mouth was almost snarling. 'Nine grand a year and voted for a Nazi as Rector. People respond to tough talk and hate, don't they?'

A receptionist straight out of a black-and-white film sat outside the office. Twinset and pearls, hair that would take a good hour of curling every evening. She took one look at Fenchurch and got to her feet. 'Can I help?'

'DI Fenchurch. I called the Chancellor, he said to come straight up?'

'Mr Uttley's waiting for you.' She held open the door and let them pass.

Rupert Uttley was on his feet before Fenchurch could even get in. His office was near the top of the Jaines Tower, one giant window trained across the South Bank skyline, filling up with newer towers. The Shard was centre stage, almost like Uttley had planned his office around the view. 'Inspector, good evening. This is Gordon McLaren, Hannah's Director of Studies.'

A big man sat in front of the desk, legs crossed. Short hair, jeans and a hooped shirt, almost skintight. Open-toed sandals with painted nails, matching the purple on his fingers. Tasteful make-up, his face creasing as he smiled, stood and offered a hand. A silver band wrapped round his wrist. And a wedding ring. 'Also her lecturer in English Literature, for my sins.' Glasgow accent, though with less of a threat of knife crime than most. 'And yeah, you've probably noticed that I'm non-binary.' Looked like he had that discussion twenty times a day and had decided to get in first.

Reed remained standing. 'Okay.'

'Pleasure to meet you, sir.' Fenchurch shook McLaren's hand and took the seat next to him. 'As I suspect Mr Uttley's mentioned, we're investigating the murder of Hannah Nunn.'

Uttley took a sip from a china teacup, bone white and unadorned. Didn't seem in a hurry to offer any to Fenchurch or Reed. 'We've just been discussing this horrendous, horrendous matter.'

McLaren's lips formed a full stop. 'Hideous.' He drank from his own cup. 'I had a catch-up with her scheduled for tomorrow. Such a shame.'

'Were you close?'

'Ish. Hannah was great. Really smart. Could destroy a book in a day. And I'm not talking skimming, she'd pick up on all the subtext and thematic constructs. She was gifted. Such a shame.'

'Inspector.' Uttley set his teacup down and rested his palms on his desk. Giant oak thing that probably dated back to the university's founding in the mists of time. 'What does this pertain to?'

'Thomas Zachary.'

'Ah.' Uttley circled his lips with his tongue a few times. 'Our Rector.'

'Why was Hannah Nunn organising protests against him?'

'The Rector is a ceremonial position voted on by the student body.' Uttley exchanged a look with McLaren, but it wasn't sympathetic. 'As part of their tenure, the Rector is allowed to give an optional series of talks. Usually, this isn't taken up or the topic relates directly to the life of a student. Rent prices, tuition fees, life after college. Mr Zachary was very keen to share his worldview with our students, especially after such a resounding victory in the contest.'

An open transgender man at the same institution as someone a couple of stops from Fascist Central. That had to open wounds.

Fenchurch brought McLaren in with a glance. 'And you're happy with this?'

McLaren grimaced, deferring to Uttley without a word.

'Experiencing multiple worldviews will only serve to enrich the education of our students.' Uttley groaned like he'd done this a million times before. 'Mr McLaren here isn't on Mr Zachary's Christmas-card list, it's fair to say.'

'Seems nice enough.' McLaren spoke through a twisted grin. 'Charming as hell and all that, but Christ, some of the shite he writes . . .'

'This is evidence of the broad school of thought we have at Southwark.' Uttley's eyelids fluttered as he spoke. 'This isn't some Facebook echo chamber or a lefty commune. I want my students to experience all schools of thought and challenge their own beliefs. It'll help them contribute to wider society.'

'Mr Uttley, my officers have questioned your students and staff all afternoon and this protest only came up this evening. You could've mentioned it when I saw you this morning. You wouldn't be trying to cover anything up, would you?'

A flat smile spread over Uttley's lips. 'You may wish to divert attention to your own officers' inadequacies.' He held Fenchurch's gaze for a few seconds. 'There is absolutely no way that Mr Zachary is involved in Hannah's death, Inspector. Hannah was indeed leading the protests, but they're the sort you see everywhere. Students expressing themselves. Harmless fun.'

Fenchurch clocked Reed shaking her head.

'When I look back on my time here, Inspector, I'm proud of establishing a university that lets all voices speak.' Uttley touched the tips of his fingers together, as if he was praying. 'Our last Rector was Yvette Farley of the *London Post*, who is at the opposite end of the political spectrum from Mr Zachary. And having both Thomas Zachary and Gordon McLaren at the same institution. Two very difference voices, that can only serve the greater good.'

'Sure?' Reed's nostrils flared. 'Sure it's not just stoking flames? You saw what happened to Jo Cox. You've got to be very careful when you let certain voices speak.'

'Are you accusing me—'

McLaren silenced the Chancellor with a wave. 'Rupert, if I may?' He smiled at Fenchurch. 'Listen, all of that nonsense . . . Hannah put it behind her, got on with her studies.'

'What nonsense?'

'She organised a mass drop-out because of Zachary.'

Chapter Eight

McLaren shuffled along the corridor, his shoes slapping against his feet like he hadn't tied his laces properly, chatting to Reed.

Fenchurch followed behind, trying to process it. Zachary, paragon of the alt right, annoying Hannah so much that she arranged protests against his very presence there. Another suspect, possibly. Probably. Had to make sure they didn't jump to any conclusions with the guy, try to throw him out of the window because of his beliefs before he'd even had a chance to defend himself. Innocent until proven guilty.

'Don't get me wrong.' McLaren opened a fire door to an empty corridor, letting out the faint smell of Pot Noodle. He blocked their way. 'Zachary seems nice enough, aye? Funny. Charming, even. But you have to read some of his bile, man.'

'Not a fan?'

'Hard to be a fan of a man who wants you drowned at birth.' McLaren held up a finger. 'His words, before you start. Not even a drop in the ocean of the bile he's spreading at the university, mind. Very clever man, though. Always careful to toe the line when it comes to hate crimes.' He blew air up his face then pointed to a door down the corridor. 'That's his office there. I try not to get too close to him.'

'Thanks.' Reed smiled and let McLaren go, waiting until he was out of earshot. 'Can't imagine he had a fun childhood in Glasgow.'

'Does anyone?' Fenchurch marched down the corridor and rapped on the door. 'Mulholland was reading Zachary's book.'

'That's an escalation from the *Mail*, isn't it?'

'Not sure. Worried I'm prejudging him, Kay.'

'Isn't that what his type are all about, guv? Prejudice?'

The door slid open and a guard lumbered out, more muscle than bone. Black suit, shades, earpiece. 'Can I help you guys?' Seemed to be capable of speech. Sounded like he was from Wolverhampton via Chicago.

Fenchurch flipped out his warrant card and held it between them, like dangling bait above fish. 'Need to speak to Thomas Zachary.'

'You've found him.' The man inside the room was frowning at them. Silver hair, mid-forties at a guess. Dark-brown suit, crisp white shirt and a bright-purple tie a few shades lighter than his black eye, despite the make-up covering it. A soft American accent, high-pitched but deep and resonating at the same time, like a musical instrument.

Reed grinned at Fenchurch; shiner aside, she clearly thought Zachary was a dead ringer for Fenchurch, didn't she? Then she caught herself and showed her own warrant card. 'DS Kay Reed. DI Simon Fenchurch. Need to ask a few questions, sir.'

'Brad, can you give us a few minutes?' Zachary waved his security off and held out a paw for Fenchurch to shake. Yellowing bruises circled his wrist. 'Please, come in.'

The security guard twitched, then he let them through.

Zachary's gaze followed him out. 'He's solid. Ex-marine, as they all are. Loyal and almost cheap. I had to hire Brad after someone in the street gave me this.' He gently patted his shiner. 'Some people think free speech extends to violence.'

'Our laws are more about what you can't say than what you can, sir.'

Zachary appraised him for a few seconds then stood aside. 'Come in.'

The office was on the small side, but immaculate. Oak panelling, thick curtains. A projector filled the far wall, showing a photo of Donald Trump shaking hands with Zachary, both of them grinning, the word INSTRUMENTAL overlaid across. The background was filled with MAKE AMERICA GREAT AGAIN placards, fewer of TRUMP / PENCE.

'Sorry about this. Just putting the final touches to my lecture tomorrow night.' Zachary sat behind his desk and hit a few keys on his laptop. 'Word to the wise: if you're giving a public speech, don't memorise a long screed. Have a series of images you can talk to. People engage better and you get less nervous.'

Fenchurch waved at Donald Trump's gurning face on the wall. 'You know him?'

'We're close friends.' Zachary beamed. 'I was, uh, kinda instrumental in his victory.' He rubbed at the dark rings under his eyes. 'Slept maybe twelve hours in the last two weeks.' He slammed the laptop's lid. 'Still, the world marches on and I'll get my reward in heaven.' The way he smiled, you could see he believed it.

'We need a word about a student.'

Zachary drummed his fingers on the laptop lid, nodding. 'Hannah Nunn?' He rubbed at his eyes again. 'I heard what happened. Tragedy.'

'You knew her?'

'Not really.'

'She'd organised protests against you, right?'

'You think The Donald knows all the ants planning marches?' Zachary grinned wide. 'He might know the people paying them to march.'

'But you were aware of the protests?'

'Listen, all I heard was that some girl was trying to shut me up and prevent my free speech.' Zachary drummed his fingernails on the laptop lid again. 'In five years, all these protestors will be married housewives or in plum City jobs.'

Fenchurch held his stare for a few seconds. 'Hannah won't.'

Zachary raised his hands. 'God, I'm sorry. I don't mean that.' He swallowed, still grinning, but you could see the cogs whirring behind his eyes. 'Liberalism is transitory. They'll stop caring about whether freaks use the wrong bathrooms when those same freaks start raping their children.'

'That's quite close to hate speech.'

'I'm not discussing their religion or sexual orientation, sir. I'm not causing them distress, I'm trying to stop those perverts raping children.' Zachary's gaze switched to the door. 'We have one here, dude called Gordon McLaren. Got a lot of time for him. I love that dry sense of humour Scottish guys have. So ironic.' His expression darkened, his nostrils flaring. 'But he's not normal.'

'Should be drowned at birth, yeah? That's what you said, wasn't it?'

'You're misquoting me. I said that in less enlightened times, he would've been. I don't want these people to die, I just wish they'd stop holding out the begging bowl and expecting to be treated as better than straight white men.'

Zachary's sort had a defence or justification for everything. *Don't get involved.* 'I gather Hannah Nunn threatened to drop out because of you.'

'Listen.' Zachary tried a smile a couple of times, then replaced it with a scowl. 'It's her free choice to protest and get her voice heard. But I was voted in by the student body here. If some little girl hates me, whatever. It's democracy, first past the post wins. Everyone else is a loser. I'm here to share my experience with the students and spend some time working on my next book.'

'She threatened to leave the university because of you. Giving up her career and future on a point of principle.'

'And it was an empty threat.' Zachary rubbed at his eyes again. 'Hannah sent Rupert Uttley an email with a list of three hundred or so students who would drop out if I didn't leave. I met her, very briefly, right before I flew back to the States in early October. I wanted to make sure she wasn't being rash. Hannah said she was dropping out. She wasn't a fan of my work, didn't want my voice heard.' He scratched at his chin. 'In the end, the Chancellor made a few calls to some concerned parents. The next day, ten of them pulled out. Then twenty. Pretty soon the whole thing crumbled. What they're doing is censorship, my friend. They're denying me a platform. Denying my *rights*.'

'And that was the only time you spoke to her?'

'Right before I left for Don's final push.'

'You didn't visit her room last night?'

'Of course not. I've nothing to hide here. Listen, when I met her, she brought a friend along. Why don't you speak to her?'

———

Fenchurch stomped down the corridor so hard he thought he might dislodge a floorboard. Or his knee. Some students ran out of his way, eyes wide like sheep at the side of the road. He swung round the corner and opened the kitchen door. A few DCs were using it as an interview room.

Victoria Summerton was sitting opposite a male DC, wearing the same clothes as in the gym café. Her hair had settled into some tight curls, tamed by a ponytail. 'Are we done?'

Fenchurch caught the male DC's gaze. Poor guy had fallen in love with her. 'We need a word with Ms Summerton, so . . .'

'I need to go.' Victoria got to her feet. 'I'm meeting a friend.'

'Your friend can wait.' Fenchurch shot her a dark glare. 'Just a couple of minutes, that's all.'

Victoria folded toned arms across her chest. 'I *really* need to go.'

'You told us about Thomas Zachary.' Fenchurch smiled at her. 'But you didn't tell us Hannah had threatened to quit over him.'

Victoria settled back down. The DC wasn't going anywhere. She muttered to herself, then let out a sigh. 'We tried to get rid of him. We failed. He's still here. We lost.'

Fenchurch couldn't argue. 'Mr Zachary told us he met Hannah to persuade her to not quit. You were there too, weren't you?'

Victoria rubbed her face, smudging her make-up. 'We met in the union for a coffee. He wanted to talk about the protest, about us all quitting. It'd all fallen apart by then but Hannah was still threatening to quit.'

'Did her parents know?'

'I don't think so.' Victoria undid her scrunchie and dropped it on the table. 'Zachary wanted to see if he could come to an agreement, keep her at the university.'

'Did anything happen during this meeting?'

'I was with them the whole time, nothing bad happened.' Victoria stretched out the scrunchie. 'He listened to us. Hannah was practically screaming at him at one point. Everyone was staring at us.' She tossed the scrunchie back on the table. 'But the thing was, he was actually concerned about her future. He sat there and just took it from her. He was very patient. Then he won her round by listening to her. Most of them here just try and shut you up. But Zachary wanted to hear what she had to say. In the end, she promised that she wouldn't drop out.'

'So why the new protests?'

She nibbled her lip, in a completely different way than earlier, worry biting this time. 'When he left for the States, Hannah got really pissed off with him. Saw who he was with in the States. Made her feel like he'd played her so he could look good with the Chancellor. That he didn't care about her feelings. So she arranged those protests for when he came back.' Her hands formed fists. 'Christ, if you read about him, he thinks he single-handedly got Trump elected. Sickening.'

'How far did these protests get?'

'Hannah had one arranged for this week. Might be Wednesday. Can't remember.'

'Any press or anything like that?'

'Not that I know of. Sorry. There's like a Facebook group, but it's private.' Victoria checked her watch. 'I've really got to go. Sorry.'

Fenchurch studied her for a few seconds, trying to figure out if she was hiding anything. In the end, he just shrugged. 'Fine.'

'Thanks.' Victoria snatched her scrunchie and her sweating gym bag, then stormed off.

Fenchurch waited for the door to shut. 'Think there's any more in it, Kay?'

'Could be something, could be nothing.' Reed was fiddling with her own hair. 'But I don't think we should let Zachary out of our sight . . .'

Fenchurch got out his phone and googled 'Thomas Zachary London'. The first six hits were *London Post* articles, all with the same byline. 'Here we go.' He found the number and hit dial, walking off. 'Liam, I need a word.'

Even on a cold November night, suits lurked outside the Barrowboy and Banker, gulping pints of real ale and sipping Peroni. Sucking on cigarettes, red faces glowing as the buses and taxis trundled past.

Fenchurch walked in and hit a wall of sweaty warmth. Central heating cranked up too high. The place was busy, filled with a good chunk of the South Bank's post-work crowd. An oak-panelled bar downstairs, curved but not quite a horseshoe.

Liam Sharpe sat under a marble staircase leading up to a mezzanine, his fingers cradling an IPA glass half-full of fizzing amber liquid. Flicking through his own newspaper, probably looking for his own byline. Kid had come a long way in the short time since Fenchurch first met him, his girlfriend the victim of knife crime, a slaying that Fenchurch witnessed. But his feature on Chloe had forced the insects out from under their rock. He looked up and grinned. 'Simon!' He clamped a hand round Fenchurch's and patted his back. He'd shrunk in the wash since the last time Fenchurch saw him. His hipster beard was trimmed down to designer stubble, his thinning locks military-short. Thick glasses, like giant goldfish bowls. 'Can I get you a beer?'

'I'm good for now, Liam.' Fenchurch took the seat opposite and wished he'd gone for a nice ale. The bar had Bristolian and Suffolk pumps, along with the ever-present Doom Bar, the Cornish ale stocked everywhere in London. He leaned forward and immediately soaked his elbow in stale beer. 'So, Thomas Zachary.'

'There this much foreplay with Mrs Fenchurch?' Liam sat back, beaming, and folded his arms. He took a sip of beer, his eyes glinting in the light. 'How's Chloe?'

Fenchurch wanted to drown himself in Liam's pint. His mouth was as dry as the sands around Dungeness. 'She's still not speaking to us.'

'Sorry to hear that.'

'I appreciate everything you did for us.'

Another sip and a doffed imaginary cap. 'All part of the service.'

'It helped flush those scumbags out into the open.'

Liam sank half of the remaining beer in one go. 'I heard Zachary got assaulted last night, battered good and proper.'

'Why wasn't that in the paper?'

'No police report, either.' Liam rasped his fingers over his stubble. 'He's a nasty bastard, but it didn't stop the *Post* giving him a monthly column. Bloody clickbait for the far right. I mean, I'm not sure what's worse, the content of it or the fact it's called "A New York Man in England". I mean, who names anything after a Sting song? I mean, *Sting*.'

'Liam, the first two and a half Police records are good.'

'I know.' Liam adjusted his glasses. 'But this is *solo* stuff.'

Fenchurch leaned back in the chair, almost toppling over. 'So, have you got any juice on him?'

'I've met him a few times. He came to some editorial meetings, didn't need to be there, but he was. Some of the . . . positions he was taking were . . .' Liam sighed. 'I hope that he's the killer you're looking for and that you lock him up.'

'I didn't mention anything about killers.'

'Fenchurch . . .' Liam finished the beer and grinned. 'You never speak to me unless it's about killing.'

'I'm interested in him.'

Liam frowned. 'This isn't because Chloe's at Southwark, is it?'

'It isn't. It's about a case.'

'The girl's murder this morning?'

'Surprised they've not got you on that story.'

'I've got bigger fish to fry, I'm afraid.' Liam shrugged. 'Well, different fish.'

'So, tell me about him.'

'Nasty bastard. When I heard he had a column, the first thing I did after getting Yvette's PA to delete my resignation from her inbox was to investigate the guy. Know your enemy. Fight fire with fire.'

'Did you find anything?'

'Have you seen his website?'

'RightFacts.' Fenchurch nodded slowly. 'Abi's uncle shared a load of it on Facebook when Donald Trump got elected. She wasn't happy. I've seen his book. You really think this guy's a Nazi?'

'The sort of people who read RightFacts, all they want is to wind the clock back to the thirties and be in Germany. Ironically, that book got prosecuted for hate speech in Germany. I'm writing a profile on him, but they don't want to publish it while he works for the paper.'

'You found anything interesting?'

'His criminal record in the States is.' Liam fiddled with his smartphone, the backlight making his face glow. 'He was at Rutgers University in New Jersey in the nineties. I found a police report online.' He held the screen round to show a news story, a young Zachary grinning at the camera, wasted like a movie star in career meltdown. 'He beat the shit out of a gay man. Hospitalised him, knocked out six teeth, broke both arms. Got community service. Picking up rubbish at the side of the road.'

'You're serious?'

'This is America, my friend. So long as you're not black, female or gay, everything is open to you.' Liam gritted his teeth. 'Worse still. In 2002, his blog outed a chat show host as transgender. Ended his career. Guy killed himself.' He flashed up his mobile. 'And he's spent the last two years campaigning against transgender rights in America. You've heard of the bathroom ban?'

'Stopping transgender women using a female toilet.'

'Total bullshit. Painting these girls as sexual predators. "Oh, think of the children." But these aren't the sort of people you need to worry about, are they? In actual fact, in the vast majority of cases, they're the *target* of abuse and violence. By Zachary's people. He's a nice suit and perfect teeth. The real animals are the knuckle-dragging mouth-breathers who read his bile. Assuming they can actually read. More likely watch his YouTube channel.'

'Okay, Liam, that's—' Fenchurch's mobile throbbed in his pocket. Nelson. He stuck it to his ear. 'What's up, Jon?'

'Guv, we've got a lead on Graham Pickersgill.'

Chapter Nine

Fenchurch drove along the narrow street, a miserable corner of Southwark lined with a lot fewer trees than it had fifteen years ago. Nelson was lurking on the other side of the traffic lights, puffing on his vape stick. Fenchurch pulled in opposite the shop and sidled over.

'Guv.' Nelson nodded as he took one last toot. The fog misted out of his nostrils, a slow cloud building. He gestured around the street. Pizza restaurants, letting agents and boutique hotels. 'I remember when this was all needle dens.'

'Yeah, about five minutes ago.' Fenchurch peered down the side street, one of those ancient London avenues that had lost whatever it was winding round, now all new flat developments with more glass than brick. And roof gardens. 'So, where is he, Jon?'

'This way.' Nelson set off towards a pale-blue railway bridge, just tall enough for the queue of buses to squeeze under. Go Fix Yourself beneath a tick mark, an almost complete rip-off of the Nike logo, screamed out of a hoarding.

The place had that new-computer smell, probably canned and sprayed every morning. Second-hand laptops rested in display cases, covered in stickers. Two high-powered gaming rigs stood either side of the door, glowing and throbbing, the 3D shooter looking more real than reality.

The man behind the counter patted his turban, as though he could smell Old Bill. 'Can I help you, officers?'

Nelson showed his warrant card. 'You the owner?'

'Myself and my brother, yes. How can I help?'

'Looking for a Graham Pickersgill.'

'I'm afraid that Mr Pickersgill isn't here.' The owner rested on the counter, the glass misting around his fingers. 'Asked for a few days off. Told me he's moving flat on Saturday. Needed a few days to sort things out.'

'You believe him?' Nelson waited for a response, snorting mist out of his nostrils. Just got a shrug. 'Got an address?'

'Just a second, sir.' The owner reached down and picked up a ring binder, stuffed full of paperwork, pages hanging out. He flicked through it, the pace betraying his hidden anger at the cops visiting his shop. 'Sorry, no. I've got his old one.'

Nelson put a business card on the counter. 'The second he comes through that door, give me a call, yeah?'

'Sure thing.' The owner slid the card across the desk and stuffed it into his ring binder. No chance that was getting looked at again.

Fenchurch led out onto the street. 'Well, Jon, thanks for getting me out here for nothing.'

'Guv, I know how you—'

'Don't worry, Jon, we're just running a murder case. We've got all the time in the world.'

'Guv, I can't—'

'It's fine. I'm messing with you.'

'Right.' Nelson's vape stick was already in his mouth. He took a suck then started rattling it. 'Bloody cartridge is empty.' He patted himself down and found one in his coat pocket.

The owner was already on the phone. Fenchurch hadn't heard it ring, so it was outgoing. Better not be warning his mate Pickersgill . . .

Something caught his eye. A pink HP laptop sitting in the window. With a Charlie the Seahorse sticker on the lid.

Fenchurch was through the door before he even thought about it. 'You!' He jabbed his finger at the owner, then at the window. 'I want that laptop, now!'

'I'll have to call you back.' The owner frowned at Fenchurch. 'I'm sorry, sir?'

'That HP, the one in the window.'

'It is mine, sir.'

'I need it for evidence.'

'But I only bought it yesterday. For a lot of money.'

'This is a murder case. Get it now!'

The owner flipped up his counter and sidled over, huffing. He got out a jailer's key set and unlocked the window display. 'This one here, sir?' He treated Fenchurch like any other customer, full of contempt.

Fenchurch snapped on a pair of evidence gloves. 'The one with the sticker on it.'

The owner took it from its mount and rested it on the counter.

Fenchurch grabbed the laptop and spun it round in his gloved fingers, searching for anything pinning it to Hannah. 'We'll need to take this into evidence, sir.'

'I'll need a receipt.'

'Jon?'

Nelson groaned as he got out his notebook and started scribbling. He held a page up for the owner.

'You'll get nothing off it.' The owner took the receipt from Nelson. 'I zeroed it this morning and rebuilt it with Windows 10.'

Fenchurch glared at him. 'At least you didn't take the stickers off.'

The owner shrugged. 'Why bother? It'll leave a mark. Some people think these things are funny. Sometimes that's why they buy the machine.'

Fenchurch reached into his jacket pocket for an evidence bag. Looked big enough to fit. 'Who sold it to you?'

'Just one second.' The owner huffed as he lifted up a bulky ledger, then flopped it open at a page. His finger traced across a line. 'His name is Troy Danton.'

'They what?' Fenchurch drove along the South London roads, following Nelson's pool car, engine roaring. 'They let that little shit go?'

'Sorry, guv, but yes.' Reed sighed down the line. 'Not enough to hold him.'

'But Danton confessed to dealing!'

'They're going to formally interview him tomorrow. Sent him home for the night.'

'So much for taking a tough line on drug crimes.' Fenchurch braked hard and let a Fiesta trundle round the junction. 'Can you get his address?'

'Guv.'

Fenchurch scanned around as he set off, tearing through Camberwell, the sort of place where new streets were going up every week, new developments dominating areas still struggling with their history. 'You got it yet?'

'Neville Court, guv. Twenty-nine.'

'Peckham, right?'

'Yup.'

'Cheers, Kay.' Fenchurch killed the call. He battered the horn and indicated left.

Nelson ignored him, staying on the main road.

'Bloody hell.' Fenchurch dialled Jon's number but it kept ringing. 'Have to do everything myself.' He took the first left, then the next right and pulled up in a tight space surrounded by low-rise brick buildings on all sides. Enough to give you claustrophobia. He got out and assessed the area. Never knew when you needed to be prepared.

Garages filled the ground floor on both sides, propping up three storeys of flats on the right, just one on the left. The lane kept on going, no signs of any turnings up ahead.

Fenchurch found a set of buzzers in a door. Number twenty-nine. He grabbed his phone and noticed a text from Reed. Flat four. He jabbed the buzzer for three and waited.

'Hello?'

'Police. Need access.'

'Sure thing.' The door buzzed and Fenchurch pushed it open. He set off up the stairs, two flats on the first floor, another two above. Stank of cats and mould and piss and skunk. At the top, the door on the left was open a crack. Fenchurch showed his warrant card and it clicked shut. He thudded the door to flat four with the heel of his hand. Caught a blur of movement in the eyeglass. 'Mr Danton, it's DI Fenchurch. Need a word.'

The door slid open. Danton stood in a fug of dope smoke, his navy tracksuit zipped up to his chin. A bright light shone straight at Fenchurch, almost blinding. 'What's up?'

Fenchurch could make out a couple of faces in the gloom behind Danton. Doubtful they were staying there legally. 'You didn't happen to sell a laptop to a shop on Tower Bridge Road, did you?'

Danton shrugged. 'Might've done.'

'Well, well.' Fenchurch thumbed behind him. 'Need you to come with me.'

Danton's shoulders collapsed, together with his resolve. He pulled the door shut behind him and trudged alongside Fenchurch. 'You know I didn't kill her.'

'Do I?' Fenchurch stopped at the top of the stairs. Some of Danton's fizzing energy from the morning interview had returned, climbing over the cannabis wall. 'Come on, son.' He gripped Danton's arm. 'Maybe you can work out your story by the time we get there.'

Danton lashed out with his foot and cracked Fenchurch's left knee. Bastard thing spasmed. Fenchurch windmilled backwards, bouncing off the wall, then tumbled forward, landing on the carpet tiles. His fingers bore the brunt of the fall, his weight pushing them flat, his chest thumping off the floor. Felt like the tendons in his wrists had snapped.

Danton's foot dug into his back. Twice. Again. Then he was off, his footsteps rattling round the stairwell.

Fenchurch pushed himself up onto all fours and sucked in a deep breath.

Stupid, stupid bastard.

Schoolboy error. No matter how little they weigh, it's always the scrawny ones you've got to watch out for.

His left knee tingled, could barely move it. He grabbed the banister and pulled himself up to standing. Searing pain burnt up from the knee, like it'd been stuck on a hotplate. He put some weight on it and started down the stairs, each step burning with fresh blasts of pain.

Can't let that little bastard escape.

Another step, more pain.

Shouting that he didn't kill her.

Why's her laptop in the shop, you little bastard?

Fenchurch had to take a break at the bottom. Tried stretching out his knee, but it wouldn't move past halfway. He hobbled over to the door, keeping his left leg straight, and jerked it open.

Danton lay on the ground outside, face down, wriggling and lashing out with his feet, scratching with his fingers. Nelson had a knee in his back, pushing his face into the cobbles. '—in evidence. Do you understand?'

Fenchurch collapsed against the door. 'Jon . . .'

Danton twisted round. 'I understand.'

'Come on.' Nelson pulled Danton up to his feet. 'Don't run off again, guv.' He scowled at Fenchurch. 'You okay?'

Fenchurch hopped over towards them, each step feeling like his leg had fallen off. 'Little shit got my knee. Sent me flying. Lucky it wasn't on the bloody steps.'

'Wish I'd seen that.' Nelson grinned wide, his teeth glinting in the light. 'I've cautioned him.'

'Good to know.' Fenchurch grabbed Danton by the scruff of his tracksuit. 'Why did you nick her laptop, you little shit?'

'I never!' Danton was bracing himself for a punch in the face.

Fenchurch tried to pick him up but his knee wasn't having it. So he growled at Danton instead. 'The truth. Now.'

'I didn't kill her.'

'So why the hell did you sell her laptop to a shop!'

'She . . . Hannah . . . She . . . swapped it . . . I sold her some dope and MDMA.'

Fenchurch clocked Nelson's frown. 'You serious?'

'Yeah, ten Q of resin and thirty ecstasy pills. Good stuff, too.'

'Did you steal the drugs from her room?'

Danton's head lowered. 'I panicked when I found the body. Didn't want to get caught. So I nicked it back. Most of it. She'd smoked most of the dope. Taken a couple of Es.'

'I'm going to need that as evidence.'

'Ain't got it no more.'

'Like you didn't have the laptop, either?' Fenchurch wanted to smash the lying little shit's skull off the pavement, crack it into a million fragments. 'You sold it to Graham Pickersgill, didn't you?'

'Who?'

Fenchurch frowned. 'The guy at the shop? Go Fix Yourself?'

'It was this Sikh bloke, I swear. Big fella, cheeky bastard was smoking in the shop.'

Fenchurch stepped towards Nelson. 'Jon, get him down the station. He's not leaving until we get the truth.'

———⌣———

As if driving back wasn't hard enough, the stairs are killing me.

Fenchurch had to stop on the first floor of Leman Street station. His left kneecap felt like it was hanging off. Max-dose ibuprofen and paracetamol could only do so much. He rubbed it, popping a little back into place with each stroke, gritting his teeth and swallowing hard.

Then a sharp pulse of pain made him gasp. Never had that before, no matter how many times he'd had the shit kicked out of him or vice versa. Usually just dusted himself off, got some fresh trousers and he was good as new.

Need to see a doctor.

Fenchurch hobbled over to the door and pressed against it. The corridor did that horror-film thing where the lens turned itself inside out to make it look twice as long as it actually was.

Need to get halfway. That's all.

He set off, bracing himself against the wall, taking it a step at a time.

Stupid bastard. Should've gone to hospital.

He was making slow progress. So bloody slow. He put his right foot down first. Then placed the left. Seemed to be okay. His right, then his le—

'Aaaah!' Another dart of pain in his knee, stabbing his thigh, hip, back.

Fenchurch leaned against the wall, waves of pain up the whole left side of his body. He pressed his thumbs into the kneecap until something popped. Another throb, then it dulled down to less than half. He touched a finger to it. Nothing. So he pressed down, followed by a wash of quick panting. Something didn't quite click, but it felt better. He set off, taking it slow, hobbling along, but at least twice as fast as before. He opened the Obs Suite door.

On screen, Nelson and Bridge were interviewing Troy Danton, getting his confessions about the drugs and the laptop on tape and in the case file, where it couldn't escape.

'There you bloody are.' Docherty was sitting in the room's sole chair, leaning back, feet on the desk.

'Boss.' Fenchurch hobbled over to the table by the back wall and rested on it. Docherty was blocking out a thin strip of the screen. But Nelson and Bridge didn't need any management support.

Docherty pushed himself up to standing and immediately doubled over, coughing like he'd got something stuck in his throat. He rubbed at his mouth and stood up tall. 'I told you to stop that nonsense, Simon. Bloody hero cop going after the suspect on his own.' He waved at the screen, teeth bared. 'Christ, you're lucky that boy's a skinny wee clown, otherwise we'd be looking down the barrel of another police brutality case.'

'He assaulted me.' Fenchurch straightened out his leg. The ache was a dull twang now. 'Buggered my knee.'

'Least you deserve. This reminds me of when I worked with your bloody father. He was the same. Pair of clowns.' Another battery of coughs racked through his body.

Fenchurch didn't know whether to go over and thump his back. 'You okay, boss?'

'I'm fine.' Docherty picked up a bottle of water and slugged it in one long drink. 'Last thing I need, Si. Last bloody thing. I *told* you Loftus is on my neck about this exact thing, so why the hell did you go in on this kid like Graeme Souness in the first minute of an Old Firm game?'

Fenchurch folded his arms. 'I thought Nelson was behind me, boss.'

'Bullshit. You *knew* he wasn't. I spoke to him when he came back. He was heading to' — his cough sounded like it had scraped flesh off his lungs — 'to the uni. You went off on yet another Rambo crusade on your tod.'

The truth was the only option here. 'Boss, I wanted to speak to him, get ahead of—'

'Hero cop.' Docherty shook his head, panting like a dog stuck in the back of a car. 'Si, the pressure we're under on this case. We took it from South London, okay? Loftus said I could've passed it to West or Central, but no, we've stood up and, boy oh boy, are we being counted here. And all the shite that goes with it.'

'Boss, I'm sorry, I—'

'Sorry?' Docherty glared at him. Looked like his eyes were going to pop out of the sockets. 'As my Deputy SIO, I need you to be on top of your anger issues. Once and for all. You really want me to hand this case to DI Mulholland?'

'She's the last person.'

'You keep saying this but I don't get what it is she's ever done to make you so angry at her.'

Fenchurch stared hard at him for a few seconds. *Bugger it, time to give him the truth.* 'When we found Chloe, I did some digging into that whole operation. There was this bloke, one of the scumbags who . . . kidnapped kids. His name rang a bell and I couldn't work out where from. He was a taxi driver, part of that whole pass-the-parcel thing they had going. He didn't take them off the street himself, but he had these kids in the back of his cab. Anyway, I worked out where I remembered the name from. Eleven years ago, Mulholland was a DC, working the case. Remember?'

Docherty stifled a cough. 'Jesus Christ, Si. You can't blame her.'

'She had a bloody lead, boss. This guy knew who took Chloe. And she let him go without him giving up anything.'

'Bullshit.'

'I'm not making this up, boss. I mean, yes, I'm being petty. She made a mess on the case involving my daughter. But her screw-up cost us finding Chloe for eleven years.'

'It's been going on for years, though.'

'I just don't like her, guv. She's a smug git.'

'Well. This has to stop.' Docherty folded his arms, grimacing like he was going to tear the flesh off Fenchurch's legs. 'You've got to' — another cough — 'stop buggering about with' —COUGH — 'chases and fights and—'

Docherty collapsed, sending the chair spinning round, and toppled to the floor.

Chapter Ten

B oss?' Fenchurch lurched across the Obs Suite and grabbed the chair by the arms. Stopped it spinning.

Docherty lay slumped beneath it, tongue hanging out, eyes shut.

Fenchurch stuck an ear to Docherty's chest and held it there. Thought he could hear a faint heartbeat. Maybe it was his own.

Shit.

Shit, shit, shit.

Fenchurch reached into his pocket and dialled Control on his mobile. Answered immediately. 'This is DI Fenchurch.' Pressed a finger against Docherty's neck. Still a pulse. 'Someone's collapsed in Leman Street police station.'

'I'm afraid there's an incident in central London and—'

'Then I'm taking him to the Royal London. Have a doctor meet me at the entrance!'

'Of course. I'll stay on the line.'

'Thanks.' Fenchurch pocketed his phone, then reached down to grab Docherty's body. A fifty-year-old sack of bones, as light as Chloe had been when she disappeared. He put him over his shoulder and staggered towards the door, every step sending jabs of pain through his knee, right up his body.

No choice but to be a hero cop.

———

Fenchurch pulled past a hissing bus and tore on down Whitechapel Road, the row of shops with their Arabic squiggles, then old East London with its betting shops and hipster bars. The Royal London hospital's old facade hid behind a row of shops.

Need to take that turning.

Fenchurch waited for a break in the traffic, a steady throng of taxis heading into the centre. Behind, the Gherkin glowed in the sky, flanked by new towers.

Docherty lay on the back seat, his chest barely moving. Fenchurch reached round and shook him. Got a slight grunt in return.

Fenchurch spotted a gap and hit the accelerator, pulling across a pair of motorbikes into the side street.

A dead end, no sign of the bloody hospital. Siren stabbed his ears. A small road led through a tunnel in a sixties building. A red sign. EMERGENCY DEPARTMENT.

Fenchurch picked up his phone from the passenger seat. 'Nearly there. Two seconds.'

'Of course.'

The Royal London hospital's new section rose out of the ground next to him, the blue and green windows glowing in the night sky. A row of cars blocked the entrance. Fenchurch got out into the biting cold. 'I'm here now.'

'Hang on.'

Fenchurch tore open the back door and grabbed Docherty. His pulse was still there, getting fainter with each beat. 'Come on, boss, you don't get out of this that easily.' He dragged out Docherty's legs and pulled him up to standing. Tried to put him on his shoulder, but his left knee locked. He stumbled into the car, his shoulder smacking off the glass. Almost dropped Docherty.

'It's okay, sir, we've got him.' Two burly paramedics winched Docherty down from Fenchurch's shoulder and rested him on a gurney. 'We'll take him inside, sir. You need to sign in at reception.'

'Okay. Okay.' Fenchurch leaned back against the car, rubbing at his shoulder. Sheer bloody agony. All he could do was watch them trundle Docherty inside.

'Hello?'

Fenchurch put the phone to his ear. 'They've got him. Thanks for your help.'

'I'm sorry we couldn't get an ambulance out, sir.'

'Not your fault. Thanks.' Fenchurch killed the call, his fingers clenched around the phone case. Nothing to do but stand around and wait. Nothing to influence, nothing to challenge. He scanned through his contacts and found the one he never wanted to see popping up. After a long breath he hit dial.

'Detective Superintendent Julian Loftus. To whom am I speaking?'

'Sir, it's DI Fenchurch. I've had to take Docherty to hospital.'

'I see.' Loftus's footsteps cannoned round a stairwell somewhere. 'Have you spoken to Margaret?'

'Next on my list, sir.'

'Don't bother. I'll phone her.'

———

Fenchurch slurped machine tea and leaned against the windowsill. Cleaning chemicals assaulted his nostrils. Even the tea tasted of it. A long white corridor, doors regularly spaced, windows looking out across East London's evening, households stuck in their cycle of addiction.

Coronation Street, EastEnders, that baking nonsense. Football, Netflix binges, Facebook, Snapchat. God knows what else.

Another sip of tea and he tried Abi's phone. Straight to voicemail. A text popped up. *Bloody hell.*

Fenchurch tried to avoid thinking about Docherty. Collapsing in the Obs Suite. Lying on the back seat of the car, limp and lifeless. Weighing less than a small child. All the stress and strain of managing a cop who gets results the wrong way. Someone who pushes and prods and needles and bends the rules way past breaking.

Another stab of pain in the knee.

Troy Danton.

Little bastard. Little, little bastard. Six stones of arsehole, barely weighing as much as Fenchurch's legs. Pure instinct, blind luck.

Always bet on the scrawny bastard.

'Inspector.'

Fenchurch looked over as he took another slurp of tea.

Detective Superintendent Julian Loftus approached, wearing full uniform. His bald head gleamed under the light, polished with Pledge or something. A good five years younger than Fenchurch, though the gap looked greater. The sort of athletic physique that wouldn't get caught out by a scrawny bastard in a crappy flat. Then again, he wouldn't deign to try to interview a suspect. Hand out, ready for a shake. 'Simon, I can't even begin to . . .'

Fenchurch clasped his hand and shook. 'It's horrible, sir.'

Loftus joined Fenchurch, resting against the windowsill. 'I can't even . . .' He let out a gasp. 'Did you—'

'No, sir, I didn't punch him.' Fenchurch finished his tea and put the cup on the sill. 'He was talking to me, discussing this case. Then he seemed to have a fit.'

'Managing you has finally taken its toll.' Loftus was grinning, but his eyes told Fenchurch to watch his step. 'This Hannah Nunn case at Southwark University, isn't it?'

'Correct.' Fenchurch wished he hadn't finished his tea. Nothing to play with. No decoys, just twitching fingers. 'We're getting there, sir.'

'Not quickly enough for Alan, I'll wager.' Loftus dusted off his left shoulder, seemed bothered by something still there. 'You know, Southwark is my alma mater. For my undergraduate degree. St Andrews for my postgraduate, up in Scotland. Couldn't get much different.' His expression darkened. 'Alan's originally from near St Andrews, as well.'

'Thought he was Edinburgh, sir?'

'Fife. Crail. Lovely place. Visited a few times while I was up there.' Loftus rubbed at his forehead. 'How do you begin to . . .'

By finishing your sentences?

Fenchurch nodded slowly. 'I can't even, sir. Can't even.' As if on cue, his gut started bubbling, burning at his oesophagus. 'Had he mentioned anything to you about being ill?'

'You know Alan, Inspector. Always about the job. Stats this, evidence that, office politics, protecting you. Married to the Job, I thought, only I happened to discover he was actually married when my wife met his at a function near where we live.'

'You're Grays, too?'

'Heavens, no. Hornchurch. A lot less of the estuary up there.' Loftus checked his watch, frowning. 'Wonder where she's got to? Said she'd meet me here. Anyway, I had a call from the DI in charge of Cyber Crime saying that this case is linked to one of theirs.'

'Hardly, sir. They should've arrested someone but were too busy getting drunk. That lot are just playing at being cops.'

'I see. You do know that I ran that unit for five years?'

A door opened not far from them and a doctor appeared, drawn and haggard. His body looked melted, like someone had left him in a conservatory on a hot summer's day. 'Ah, Inspector Fenchurch?' He was looking at Loftus.

'Detective Superintendent Julian Loftus.' He marched over and gave the doctor a thorough handshake. 'Alan works for me.'

'Ah, I see.' The doctor focused on Fenchurch. 'Thanks for bringing him in, sir. You've, ah, probably saved his life.'

'Probably?'

'Ah, well, we're trying to figure out the full extent of his ailment.'

'Was it a stroke? Heart attack?'

'We've ruled out any, ah, cardiovascular event. Stroke, myocardial infarction, angina pectoris, you name it, ah, which leaves us with a mystery.'

Fenchurch frowned at Loftus then at the doctor. 'So you don't know?'

'We're running tests just now. He's, ah, very heavily dehydrated, of course. Now, officers, I must get back to the patient. Is Mrs Docherty here?'

Loftus shook his head. 'I'll tell you the second . . .'

'Ah, tell the nurse, please.' And with that, the doctor swooshed off in a trail of white coat.

Loftus let out a deep breath. 'Well, that's helpful . . .' He frowned down the corridor, at the rattle of heels clicking towards them. 'There's Margaret now. Might be time for you to get off home?'

———

Fenchurch hobbled into the Incident Room in Leman Street, his knee feeling like it'd dropped off at the hospital. That or he should've got someone to look at it. Trying to pop it in himself wasn't the smartest move.

The room was almost empty. Nelson was over by the whiteboard, the pen squeaking as he scribbled an update. He noticed Fenchurch and his wonky knee. 'Listen, guv, I need a—'

'Did you get anything else out of Danton?'

A frown twitched on Nelson's face. 'Just what he told us outside his flat.'

'You believe him?'

'Feels legit, guv. Lisa's returned to that laptop shop to confirm the story. Students pawning their possessions for drugs. The world doesn't change.'

'No . . .' Fenchurch collapsed into a chair and put his left foot up. Took out some of the sting from his knee. 'You honestly think he's just her friendly neighbourhood drug dealer? Hasn't got anything to do with her death?'

'No idea, guv.' Nelson sat next to him and took in his handiwork on the board. 'Listen, I spoke to some old mates in the drugs squad Danton's going to be spending the rest of the week with them. He's promised to pass on some information on his suppliers.'

'Reckon he will?'

'Doubt it, but if anything else points to him in this case, guv, we know where he is.' Nelson grinned at Fenchurch. 'And you won't have to knacker your knee chasing him again.'

Fenchurch laughed it off, but couldn't look at Nelson. 'It'll be fine by tomorrow.'

'You sure?'

'No idea. It's sore. Should've gone to A&E at the hospital.'

'What hospital?' Reed was standing behind them, eyebrows arched. 'Is Abi okay?'

'She's fine, Kay.' Fenchurch checked his mobile again. Nothing from her. 'You got anything that'll make me happy?'

'Winning the lottery wouldn't make you happy, guv.' Reed hauled over a chair and perched on it. 'Had a trip out to Lewisham. No further progress with the forensics, though Mick said his team are pulling an all-nighter to get over the backlog.'

'Like no sleep will make them any less error-prone.' Fenchurch rubbed at his knee. Getting better, but slowly. 'Anyway. I . . .' He swallowed down the lump in his throat, tried to brush away the tingling in his nostrils. 'I had to take DCI Docherty to hospital. He collapsed in the Obs Suite while Jon was interviewing our little drug-dealing cleaner.'

Reed's shoulders slouched. 'You okay, guv?'

'It's Docherty and his wife I'm thinking about.' Fenchurch pinched his nose. 'I don't have any update for you, but it's not looking good. He was out of it. Thought he'd died.'

'Poor guy.' Reed let out a deep sigh. Then she hefted up her bag. 'Well, I'm going to see my kids before they forget they've even got a mother, okay?'

'See you, Kay.'

'Night.' Nelson waited until the door clicked to turn to face Fenchurch. 'Think he'll pull through?'

Fenchurch shrugged. 'In the lap of the gods now, Jon.'

'Right.' Nelson put the pen down under the whiteboard. 'Guv, earlier, I said I wanted a word?'

'And?'

'You sold your flat yet?'

'The jewel in the crown of the Isle of Dogs property market is still available, yes. Why?'

'Kate's kicked me out.'

⌣

Fenchurch pulled up outside his old flat and killed the engine. Typical turn of the Millennium — white roughcast walls dyed yellow by sodium lighting and burst pipes, balconies with seating covered in forgotten washing. All under the flightpath for City Airport, but spitting distance of Canary Wharf. The FOR SALE sign caught the breeze, flapping back and forth like one of those things you saw outside garages in America.

Fenchurch got out and leaned against his car, waiting.

Nelson's Audi pulled up in the space next to Fenchurch. Ten years old but purring, like he was still a management consultant and not a

DS in the Met. He hauled himself out of the tight gap between the cars and nodded up at Fenchurch's flat. 'We shared a few bottles on your balcony over the years, didn't we, guv?'

'Not very happy times, Jon.' Fenchurch blocked his exit. 'You going to tell me why she kicked you out?'

'Guv . . .' Nelson barged past him, aided by Fenchurch's knee locking, and set off towards the building. 'How much is it on for?'

'Put it this way, Jon: if you can afford it, I'm reporting you to Professional Standards as you've clearly been taking a bung.' Fenchurch left a space for Nelson to open up. He didn't. 'Spill. What did you do?'

Nelson stuffed his hands in his pockets. 'How did you afford it back in the day?'

'Bought it off plan. Saved forty per cent when I only had about fifty.' Fenchurch scratched his neck, feeling his eyes welling up. 'Mum died the year before and Dad was holding my inheritance. So when Abi told me to leave, I got the rest off him and it all worked out. More than doubled since.' He looked around the car park at the flash cars and hipster scooters. 'I was lucky. Cops can't afford to live in London any more, Jon. It's sickening.'

'Don't have to tell me.' Nelson beamed wide. 'Got any wine in?'

Fenchurch folded his arms. 'What did you do?'

'Nothing.'

'Kate kicked you out for nothing?'

'Guv . . .'

'Jon, we're off duty. You can call me Simon. Or wanker, whatever. Not guv.'

'She's overreacting.'

'Jon, I know a thing or two about being a selfish arsehole and getting kicked out by your better half. Have you been a selfish arsehole?'

'I was in the shower and my phone was in the living room.' Nelson was clawing at his neck now, close to drawing blood. 'Got a load of texts from a colleague and she took it out of context.'

'Who?'

'Gu— Simon, there's nothing in it. She just read too much into an innocent chat.'

'You swear?'

Nelson barked out a sigh. 'Come on, what is this?'

Fenchurch's mobile blared out. Abi. He answered it. 'What's up, love?'

'Where the hell are you?'

Fenchurch tossed his spare keys over, then pointed a finger at him and mouthed, 'No more lying.' He opened his car door and got in. 'I'll be about ten minutes, love. Where have you been?'

'My bloody parents are in town.'

Chapter Eleven

Fenchurch trudged up the stairs, his knee a dull throb now. His key hovered over the lock but he couldn't put it in. Bedlam inside, the kind he hadn't heard since . . . since Chloe was a child.

She'd be in her room in halls, a few corridors over from Hannah. Someone had got into Hannah's room. What if they could get into Chloe's? In and out. What if Troy Danton was her cleaner? What if it was one of his mates?

A snake slithered up his leg and coiled itself round his guts, squeezing and squeezing. All that pain, just to find her and lose her again.

He slotted the key in and twisted. The noise swelled up to engulf him. Abi and her mother at loggerheads. Shouting about Basildon and Chelmsford and Sevenoaks and Rochester.

Same as it ever was.

He pushed the door shut and hung up his jacket. Abi's dad piped up about the M25, his deep voice booming out. Fenchurch tossed his keys into the bowl and hobbled through to the kitchen, sticking a smile on. 'Jim, Evelyn, we weren't expecting you.'

Jim Ormonde was standing in the window, cradling some red wine in one of those giant glasses Abi bought as a joke. 'Simon.' He took another sip, then reached over to top up his glass, his red face almost the same colour as the reserve Rioja he was quaffing. Hairy arms crept out of his navy T-shirt, *Ace of Bass* scrawled on the front, a cartoon Jaco Pastorius playing his fretless. Jesus, another Weather Report fan. Still, him and Dad might cancel each other out.

Abi was trapped on the far side of the kitchen table, behind her mother and a pile of house brochures. Obviously, the whole internet had stopped working since he'd last checked.

A stack of plates, smeared red with pasta sauce.

'Simon, have you eaten?'

'Not yet.' Fenchurch stifled a yawn as he checked his watch. 'Could still get a burrito.'

Abi's mother took her time scraping her chair round. The blonde hair framing her face was about thirty years too young, looked trapped in the mid-nineties. She'd pushed her sunglasses up her head, as though it wasn't November in London. 'You're *still* eating burritos, Simon?' She hardened the Ts like she was a DJ.

'Yes, Evelyn. Most days. The old acid reflux is under control.' Fenchurch reached into the cupboard for a normal-sized glass and poured the last dribble of wine from the nice stuff Docherty gave him for his birthday. A lump thickened his throat. 'So, what brings you to sunny London?'

'Well, we've been going through all these brochures.' Evelyn fanned herself with a thick pamphlet for a new development near Tunbridge Wells in Kent. She waved around the room. 'With the amount you'll make out of this place and your old flat, you really should invest in something in a nicer part of the country.'

'What about Cornwall?'

Jim smiled at his son-in-law. 'That'd be too close for comfort, Simon.'

'You still sailing?'

'Every day, if I can get out.'

Fenchurch drained his glass. Didn't want to start another one, given he'd cleaned out the last of the drinking wine at the weekend and hadn't been to Aldi since. Not the time to dip into the good stuff with Jim around. 'What brings you up here?'

'Abigail told me about the counselling session you had with our granddaughter.' Evelyn moved round to the other side of the table and sat next to her daughter. 'We drove straight here.'

Abi's expression showed she regretted the phone call as much as her father did, no doubt missing an afternoon out on the sea, away from his wife.

'It wasn't *that* bad.' *Sod it.* Fenchurch reached for the Châteauneuf-du-Pape and tore at the foil. 'She needs time.'

'That's what I said.' Abi looked like she'd been saying it all day and all evening.

'No! We were just saying how important it is that we intervene.' Evelyn reached over the table for her glass, almost spilling out of her low-cut top. 'We should all go round and force her to speak to us. She's our granddaughter and we need to remind her of that!'

'Hear, hear.' Jim raised his glass between thumb and forefinger and took another sip.

'I don't think it's wise.' Fenchurch stuck the corkscrew in deep, twisting and turning, pretending it was Troy Danton's neck. He popped out the cork and hobbled over to the bin.

'You okay, love?' Abi was frowning at his leg.

'Hurt my knee.' Fenchurch tossed the cork in the bin. 'I don't think it's—'

The toilet flushed in the hall and footsteps clattered through, some-one tunelessly whistling a Weather Report riff. 'I'd leave it a minute if I were you.' Fenchurch's old man wandered into the room, drying his hands on his trousers, and reached into the fridge for one of his son's beers. 'Jim, did I tell you me and Bert saw Weather Report in—' He frowned. 'Simon?'

'Well spotted, Dad. And they say a detective never loses his instincts.'

'I'm not on the force any more, son.' Dad grabbed the corkscrew and pried off the cap. 'Anyway, cheers.' He sucked at the beer and gasped. 'Lovely stuff, son. Lovely.'

'I was saying I don't—'

'Simon, what do you think you should name your boy?' Dad started peeling the label off the beer.

Fenchurch frowned at Abi. Her grimace told him this had been chewed over for at least an hour. 'We've not really settled on a name yet.'

'I think it should be James.' Jim was nearing the end of his glass, checking out Fenchurch's fresh bottle. 'Been in our family for years. I'm the fifth.' His eyes misted over. 'Shame we didn't have a son.'

'Jesus, Jim.' Fenchurch saw his shock reflected in Abi's eyes as disgust and anger. 'You ever thought about being sensitive?'

Jim took another sip of wine. 'I didn't mean it like that. We love Abi. It's just, well. Tradition is important.'

'Tradition is an arsehole.' Dad had torn off most of the label, picking at the edge with a nail. 'I've seen so much stupid bollocks in my career all done because of tradition.'

Fenchurch smiled at him. 'And what do you think it should be?'

'Don't care, so long as it's not James.' Dad took another swig of beer. 'So, anyway, are you actually going to do this intervention wotsit?'

Fenchurch waited for Abi to say something. She didn't, not to her parents. Same as it ever was. 'I think if anyone's going to speak to Chloe, it's got to be us. We're her parents.'

'Simon, you need to let us in.' Evelyn couldn't bring herself to look at him, staying focused on her daughter. 'We *can* help.'

'I don't want anyone hatching plans and conniving, okay?' Fenchurch dumped the corkscrew back in the drawer and took a small glass from the bottle. 'You need to leave it to me and Abi.'

'But this is important!'

'Mum.' Abi swallowed hard, caressing her swollen belly. 'Simon's right. We should be the ones who do it.'

'But we've driven up from Newquay!'

'And I'm happy to see you, it's just . . .'

'Evelyn, Jim.' Fenchurch shot his gaze between them. 'If either of you so much as visits Southwark without speaking to me or Abi first, there'll be trouble.'

Jim barked out a laugh. 'Are you threatening us?'

'I'm just saying.' Fenchurch settled his gaze on his father. 'Dad's kept his distance. I expect you to do the same.'

'Simon, this isn't—'

'Jim, I know you've got a vested interest, but we need you to back off, okay?' Fenchurch put his glass down. 'Back in a sec.' He set off out of the room and went into the toilet.

Little yellow droplets covered the seat, down the side and on the floor.

Jesus, Dad . . .

Fenchurch tore off some toilet paper and started wiping up. *This is what having a young boy will be like . . .*

'Night!' Dad's voice. The flat door slammed.

Shit, I didn't tell him about Docherty.

Fenchurch flushed the toilet and chased after him as fast as his gammy knee would allow. Had to take the stairs one at a time, right foot then left on the same step, shuffling down. Out onto the street and the cold air. A taxi droned off round the corner.

Shit, just missed him.

Fenchurch's gut rumbled. Still time for a burrito. He patted down his pockets. Phone and wallet stretching the fabric, as ever. He set off for Upper Street.

Fenchurch unlocked the door, his knee throbbing from the walk, the Chilango's bag swinging at his side. Could almost taste it. He found Abi in the kitchen on her own. Jim had finished the bottle of Châteauneuf-du-Pape in the twenty minutes he'd been away. 'Have they gone?'

'In the spare room.' She sipped some chamomile, one hand on her belly. 'Dad shifted those typewriters into the corner.'

The pile of broken machines she'd taken to fixing, trying to make some sense of what the hell was happening in her life . . .

'Told you to send them back.' Fenchurch sat opposite her and unwrapped his burrito. 'Watch what you tell them in future.'

'I've learned my lesson yet again.' Another sip, then a smile. 'How was your day?'

'You know when someone says "bad to worse"? I'd kill for that.' Fenchurch took a bite of burrito and chewed and chewed and chewed until it was mush. 'Caught a case at Southwark Uni.'

Abi's frown dragged him back to his reaction that morning. 'Chloe?'

'Trust me, if it was her, I'd have told you a lot earlier than now.' Fenchurch took another bite. 'Got into a scrap with a little shitbag and I've really hurt my knee.'

'Thought it was nothing?'

'It's something, all right.' Fenchurch picked up his wine glass and sipped some down. Least, he thought it was his. 'Not enough to get compensation, and besides it was my own stupid fault.' He checked his phone. Still nothing from Loftus. 'Then Alan Docherty collapsed on me. He was having a right old go at me, then he fell back into his chair. Out cold. Drove him to the Royal London.'

'Jesus Christ. You didn't punch him, did you?'

'No!' Fenchurch finished chewing. 'No. It's serious, though. Not his heart, but . . . it didn't look good.'

'Poor guy.' She took another sip of tea. 'You okay?'

'Not really. The guy's my mentor. Looked after me since I got my stripes, got me this gig, kept me in when I've been a naughty boy. I hope the big Scottish wanker pulls through.'

'That's more like it.' Abi rested her tea on the table. 'That stuff Dad was saying. Calling our son James. Over my dead body.'

'Don't joke about that.' Fenchurch's gut clenched. 'I can't bring up a son on my own. Wouldn't know where to start. At least with a daughter, I've done the first eight years.'

She reached over and grabbed his hand. 'I'm not going anywhere, okay?'

'It's fine, it's just . . .' Fenchurch dropped his burrito onto the table. 'This case . . . The girl's the same age as Chloe. Someone snuck into her room in the middle of the night and killed her. We've got guards on but . . . that could happen to Chloe and . . . and . . .' He wiped at his cheek. 'And there's nothing we could do to save her.'

'She's a grown woman, Simon.' She pointed at the window to the street where Chloe had been taken from. 'She's not the little girl we lost out there. That's not who she is any more. She's an adult now. And someone messed with her brain to stop her remembering us. And . . .'

Fenchurch could only nod.

'Sometimes I wonder if this is the world we want our child to grow up in.'

Fenchurch grimaced. 'It's more like "do we want to bring a child into this world"?'

Abi patted her belly. 'Bit too late for that.'

'I don't mean anything by it.' Fenchurch reached over to stroke her bump. 'But the shit I see, the . . . I can't do everything to protect young James.'

Abi's lips curled up. '*Not* James.'

Day 2
Tuesday, 15th November 2016

Chapter Twelve

*D*addy!' *Chloe shouted at him, baby-blue eyes, blonde pigtails, England shirt with* ROONEY *almost readable over her shoulder. 'Daddy, you can't save me! You need to save yourself!'*

'I'm going to find you, Chloe.' Fenchurch looked around the street, in the shifting shadows of their flat. Monsters lurked on the corner, cars with giant teeth sat there, engines roaring like lions. A police car full of vampires pulled up, all claws and teeth and snarls. 'I'm going to—'

And the biggest vampire policeman snatched her up and ran off. He threw her in the back of the car and bellowed with laughter. 'Even though I'm dead, you can't kill me! You can't save her!'

A witch with her cauldron helped him take Chloe, her scarf trailing until it was infinitely long.

Fenchurch jolted awake, panting. Sweat soaked his pillow, his chest. His knee locked, trapped in a vice. He reached over and flicked on the light. No Abi. Up already. He settled back into his soggy pillow and tried to get his breathing under control.

Going to have a heart attack at this rate.

Become Docherty, a sack of bones lying across his back seat. Going from berating an idiot officer to . . . what? The doctor said it wasn't a heart attack. What else could it be?

And the dreams were never ending. They kept reappearing, tearing and biting and clawing. The giant vampire cop who told the truth, after all the mortal sins he'd committed. Who led them on the path to finding Chloe as he died in a pool of his own blood.

For what that was worth.

It was worth everything. Fenchurch would've given his life for her to be free. Just wished she'd speak to him now that she was.

Mouth dry, bladder full. Fenchurch got up and rubbed at his knee. Might, just might, not fall off anytime soon. Still hurt like a bastard. He padded through to the hall. The bathroom door was locked. Whistling reverberated inside, that infernal Weather Report tune.

Fenchurch knocked on the door.

'Sorry, I'm in the bath!' Jim's voice, deep like he was hung over. No surprise given how much expensive wine he'd destroyed last night.

Fenchurch huffed out a sigh. He trudged through to the kitchen and found Abi staring out of the window, same as most days. He tried walking over but his knee locked.

She swung round, frowning at him. 'Simon. Are you okay?'

'I'm bursting for a piss and your bloody father's in the bath.'

'I'm just as annoyed, by the way. They just turned up.'

Fenchurch groaned. 'Like vampires.'

Abi frowned at him. 'You had that nightmare again, didn't you?'

Fenchurch felt for the back of his knee and started rubbing at the tendons and muscles. 'How did you know?'

'Lying next to someone muttering about their daughter and vampire policemen isn't exactly restful.' She sat down at the table. The dishes from last night were still out. 'You're not supposed to wake someone up from a nightmare, according to Mum.'

'What, in case I get trapped in there? Those big vampire cops are all dead, but I keep thinking they'll come back to life and take her again. I've been living this nightmare for the last eleven years, love.'

'It's not that bad now, is it?'

A big clunk in his knee. Then a wave of pain rattled up his thigh, got stuck around his belly. 'I can't control her. Couldn't save her then, can't save her now. This case at her university, there was sod all anyone could do to stop whoever killed Hannah getting into her room. What's the point in anything?'

'It wouldn't be much different if we'd had her all this time, you know? You'll never stop worrying about her and that's natural. Chloe's twenty next year, she'll graduate the following year. It's only been five months since we found her. We need to give her time.'

Fenchurch tried to focus on what she was saying. She was correct, but . . . it didn't feel right. None of it did. 'I'll get into work early, get a gym session in before my shift.'

'I'm sorry, but . . .' Abi patted her belly. 'Listen. The most important thing is that we need to take care of young Ian in here.'

'Ian? No way.'

Her straight face cracked. 'Jim it is, then.'

⌣

Fenchurch stopped outside the Incident Room, his forehead still damp. Like he'd just had a shower. Oh, he had. Didn't stop him sweating, mind. Someone had the heating on full blast. Probably Mulholland.

The Incident Room was swarming with cops. His officers, none of them vampires. Probably. Only one witch, but he couldn't spot her. Nelson and Reed were at the front, deep in a chat. *Hopefully a lead that'll blow the case open. Probably Nelson's pending divorce.*

Fenchurch grabbed the door handle.

'Inspector?' Loftus was marching down the corridor, arms swinging like he was on the parade ground. 'A word?'

Fenchurch stepped away from the Incident Room. 'Is Alan okay?'

Loftus grimaced. Shit, the news was going to be bad.

Mulholland was behind him, cast in his slipstream, small enough that she was blotted out. She shared Fenchurch's frown. She didn't know either.

Loftus took a sip from a coffee beaker. Must be bitter, because his grimace deepened, sucking his forehead in. 'It's not good, I'm afraid.' Another sip. 'I stayed at the hospital until after midnight. Margaret's not taking it well and . . . I'll be brief. I'm rambling.' His lips twitched. 'Alan has cancer.'

Fenchurch's gut sank to the floor, taking his buggered knee with it. *Cancer? Shit . . .*

And it couldn't be good. Collapsing and staying unconscious as Fenchurch sped through East London.

Loftus tried a smile on for size. Probably be going back on the rack. 'No prognosis at present, but it's not looking rosy, given . . . well . . .'

Mulholland tightened her scarf. 'It's definitely cancer?'

'They've found a series of, uh, lumps on his, uh . . . You get the picture.'

Fenchurch's hand shot to his groin. His balls were almost in his stomach. 'Does the doctor think it's late-stage?'

'I'm no expert, but I've got my eye out for a black tie. He said it's spread to the liver and the lungs, hence all that coughing.'

'Sounds like stage three or four.' For once, emotion in Mulholland's face. Tears. Clenched jaw.

Loftus gripped both of their shoulders at the same time, tight. 'You guys okay to work today?'

Fenchurch gave a slight nod. 'Keep me updated.'

'The very second I hear anything.'

———

Nelson shrugged, then looked around the assembled officers like he was doing stand-up. 'Unless you've got a flux capacitor and enough road to get up to eighty-eight.' He soaked up the laughs for a few more seconds. 'What I'm saying is we need more time, okay?'

'Use it wisely.' Fenchurch picked up his tea mug and took a deep gulp. He couldn't taste anything. Lumps growing on his balls, evil cells swimming around his body. His gaze settled on Clooney. 'Mick, have you got any good news?'

Clooney hid behind his tablet. Seemed bigger than yesterday. 'Okay, so Hannah's room is clean as far as we're concerned. Same with the corridor.'

'Wait.' Fenchurch frowned. 'There's no DNA in either place?'

'There's too much. We've got about ten thousand pieces we could process. None of which will likely give you any evidence pointing to the killer.'

'You're saying it's someone she knew?'

'I'm saying nothing.'

Fenchurch waited until Clooney looked round his tablet. 'Mick, I want an action plan by the end of the post-mortem. No later.'

'There's no budget.'

'I'll worry about that. You give me a plan, I'll get the budget, okay?'

'Fine.' Clooney snorted as he stabbed something into his tablet. 'Fine, fine, fine.'

Nelson didn't look away fast enough. Fenchurch caught him, spotted something he wasn't telling him. 'What is it, Jon?'

'I got an email from the drugs squad.' Nelson cleared his throat. 'They've charged Troy Danton and he's appearing in court later this morning. No chance he'll be getting bail.'

'Have they got anything that might help us pin her murder on him?'

'Don't know, guv. Well, other than he couldn't offer a plea.'

'Typical. Keep on it. I want his statement closed down, okay?'

'Guv.' Nelson's voice had dropped an octave, like he'd stopped vaping and had gone back to the hard stuff. 'And, in other news, we're still searching for Pickersgill.'

'I want him found. Today.'

Reed was glaring at Fenchurch. Bridge looked as though she wanted to run off.

'Guv.' Nelson wrote something on his Pronto.

'Thanks.' Fenchurch swallowed his tea, scalding the lump in his throat. 'I suspect some of you will have heard. DCI Docherty was taken to hospital last night. I don't know precisely what's wrong with him yet, but I will keep you all updated as things progress. Everyone okay?'

Bridge raised her hand. 'How serious is it, sir?'

'I honestly don't know.' Fenchurch's mouth was dry, his voice thin and shrill. 'But, it's not looking good.' Sounded better. 'I'll visit him at some point today and update you tomorrow.'

Looking round the room, it was clear most hadn't heard about Docherty. *Hope it doesn't affect morale too much.*

Fenchurch tried a smile. 'We've got a case to solve here. I know everyone will still give this one hundred per cent. We've got a young woman lying in the morgue, dead long before her time. We will find who killed her.' More of a threat than encouragement. 'Let's get down to it.'

The crowd dispersed with a puff of chatter.

Fenchurch finished his tea and stood up tall, trying to take control of his emotions. He set off towards the exit, doing up his top button.

Reed blocked his path. 'Guv.'

'Kay, I'm going to the PM.'

'You okay?'

'I'm fine.'

'You don't look it.' She kept her voice low. 'What's up?'

'There's nothing wrong, Kay, other than Abi's bloody parents setting up camp in my bathroom this morning. Almost got a ticket driving in, I needed to—'

'It's not that, is it?' She held his gaze for a few seconds. 'Come on, talk to Dr Kay . . .'

He leaned in and whispered, 'Docherty's got cancer, okay? It's bad.'

'Shit. Do you want to—'

'I'm fine, Kay.'

'Guv. Simon. You can talk to me.'

'I know.' Fenchurch smiled. 'And I appreciate it.'

Reed stared at him. Looked like she didn't believe any of it.

Fenchurch couldn't look at the body. Just over twenty-four hours earlier, Hannah Nunn had been alive. Living, breathing, shouting at her boyfriend. Thinking of going to Birmingham or Warwick or . . .

Thinking.

Doing.

Being.

The wall opposite was painted white, stained with coffee and faint specks of blood.

Should really head to the Royal London, see Docherty myself. Get a handle on what he's going through. If he's awake. Give him support.

'Simon, am I boring you?' Pratt looked up from the incision on Hannah's belly. 'Mm?'

'It's fine, William. Just finding this one a little close to home.'

'Ah, yes.' Pratt restarted his probing. 'And, of course, we've all heard about what happened to DCI Docherty.'

'The jungle drums are still up to speed.'

'Of course.' Pratt squinted at his scales, then made a quiet note into his microphone. Then back to focusing on Fenchurch. 'I heard cancer.'

'That's what Loftus told me. Doesn't sound good.'

'Good lord. I've a lot of time for Alan. He knows his onions, as they say.'

The door juddered open and Clooney staggered through, clutching his tablet. 'That's your plan pulled together, Si. Please don't tell me Docherty's got three hundred grand squirrelled down the back of the sofa for this.'

Fenchurch kept staring at the wall.

'What's up?'

Pratt's forehead started twitching. 'Michael, you have heard, haven't you?'

'What?'

'About the aforementioned DCI?'

'Ah.' Clooney leaned back against the counter and set his tablet down. 'I didn't think. Sorry.'

Fenchurch caught himself grinding his teeth together. 'Accepted.'

'So who's going to replace Docherty?' Mischief twinkled in Clooney's eyes. 'Fenchurch or Mulholland, eh?'

'*Mick.*'

'DCI Simon Fenchurch doesn't have a ring to it?'

'I'm getting on with the case. Like you should be.'

'You know *she* won't.'

'Mick, grow up.' Fenchurch glared at him for a few seconds. Then he shifted his focus to Pratt. 'William, do you want to summarise where you've got to for the boy wonder's benefit?'

Clooney held up his tablet. 'It's okay, I've been watching it on here while I was doing your urgent report.'

'Fine.' Fenchurch glanced at Pratt. 'Okay, summarise where we are for my benefit, then.'

'Dear lord . . .' Pratt stood up tall and snapped off his mask. 'Well, I can confirm that young Hannah was very definitely strangled to death. Manually, judging by the contusions on her throat. Once I've opened her lungs, I'll perform some additional tests and confirm. I'll do that in the next five minutes or so.'

Clooney frowned at his tablet. 'So have you worked out if the sex was post-mortem or what?'

Fenchurch scowled at Pratt. 'What sex?'

'My good sir, you really haven't been paying attention.'

Fenchurch huffed out a sigh. 'I've been listening; you just didn't say.'

'Oh. Well.' Pratt caressed Hannah's cold abdomen. 'It would appear that someone raped Ms Nunn. After she died.'

Chapter Thirteen

Fenchurch couldn't wrap his head around it. Turning a murder into a murder-rape . . . Made his blood boil. 'She was definitely raped?'

'If the girl's dead, she can't consent.' Clooney shrugged, then sniffed in Pratt's direction. 'Correct?'

'That would logically follow, yes.'

Fenchurch gripped the edge of the table he was leaning against. The pair of pricks just stood there, grinning and humming, like they weren't standing over a dead girl who'd been raped after death. He stood up tall, fists clenched, and stared at them, Clooney then Pratt. 'You're sure it was post-mortem?'

'At least ninety per cent.' Pratt's tongue wiggled around in his mouth, a pink splodge in his thick beard. Added an *om-pom-pom*. 'But how sure is "Good Ol' Pratty" that the intercourse was post-mortem?' He stuck his tongue out so far he was risking it if the wind changed. 'Very. Some perimortem bruising could have delayed presentation, of course, but it's definitely over ninety per cent certain that this is post. There are traces of latex and spermicide. Whoever it was had the presence of mind to rape a corpse wearing a condom. Now, that is *cold*.'

'Didn't want to get her pregnant.' Clooney was staring at the tablet, but smirked like he was pleased with himself. Like his brain was made of the same silicon as the tablet. Like Fenchurch wasn't going to make him swallow the bloody thing straight down in one go. Clooney looked up like he could Fenchurch's mind. 'But whoever's raped her has replaced her clothes. Trouble is, I've got sweet Fanny Adams from her body on which to run a DNA test.'

'William, that can't be right?'

'Afraid so. Whoever forced himself on young Hannah was careful to cover his tracks.' Pratt shook his head violently. 'This is a sickening, sickening act. This doesn't appear to be a crime of passion. You don't tend to strangle someone when you're wearing a condom.'

Clooney wrapped his fingers around his own neck. 'Unless you're into edge play and don't want to take the pill.'

Fenchurch thumped his fists against the table and rounded on Clooney, someone to focus his anger on. 'Edge play?'

'S&M. Strangling. That guy from INXS. That Tory MP.'

'Any evidence of that, William?'

'Well.' Pratt frowned, the flesh on his forehead buckling. 'Not really. If she was a seasoned practitioner of bondage, or even if she'd done it a few times, you'd expect . . . rough skin and chafing and bruising and whatnot. Marks somewhere, wrists or ankles. But there's nothing that I can see. And I'm the best there is.'

'Okay . . .' Fenchurch dared to look at Hannah again. Her dead eyes focused on the ceiling. Sent another shiver down his spine, meeting a jolt of pain from his knee halfway. The same age as Chloe. This could happen to her. After all they'd been through, to find her and lose her in something like this. Hannah was someone else's daughter, someone who felt the same way about her as he did about Chloe, the same as Abi did. 'Mick, can you process your forensics based on proximity to the body?'

'Even that's more than you've got, Si.' Clooney tilted his head, a sly grin crawling over his face. 'You want to stick your mortgage on the three thirty at Chepstow?'

'I don't care, Mick. We're going to find her killer. Start processing the DNA and I'll get your money.'

Clooney typed into his tablet. 'You're the boss.'

'I am.' Fenchurch kept his gaze on him, in case he sneaked off. 'What else have you got on her?'

'Nothing.' Didn't even look up.

'Nothing? You've been at this twenty-four hours, Mick.'

'Not my fault, Si.' Clooney locked his machine and tucked it under his left arm. 'Oh, before you start chasing me, I passed the laptop logistics to DC Bridge.'

'That's your job, Mick.'

'Well, she offered. She's forensics trained, said she could complete it.'

'Good. At least she does something when I ask her.'

The mobile Incident Room filled four spaces in the car park behind Jaines Tower. Fenchurch hauled open the door and stuck his head in. Got a wall of stale farts for his trouble.

Two male officers in there, hammering keyboards, burping, laughing and joking about Arsenal. The nearest looked over and did a double take. Shot to his feet, almost saluting. 'Sir.'

'Either of you two seen DC Bridge?'

'Gone for coffee.' A nod over towards the university. 'There's a Starbucks in the main courtyard.'

The Starbucks lurked in the corner nearest the lecture theatre, the queue winding towards the door. For all the moaning about student loans and tuition fees, they could afford a few quid for a latte to drag them through the day. Inside, students stared at laptops, giant headphones clamped to their skulls. The nearest girl was a dead ringer for Chloe, just the wrong hair colour.

Fenchurch scanned around for Bridge, but couldn't see her in there. She was dressing down like a mature student, contrasting with Fenchurch's business suit. Fine if you're investigating a City bank rather than a university. Not that Loftus gave them any choice. Wanker.

The door clattered open and Sam Edwards wandered out, clutching a coffee. He clocked Fenchurch and made to head off in the opposite direction.

Fenchurch grabbed hold of him. 'Sam, I need a word.'

'I'm late for a lecture.' Couldn't look at Fenchurch.

Fenchurch checked his watch. 'They start at ten twenty-five, do they?'

Sam's shoulders slumped. 'What?'

Fenchurch led him to the far end of the concourse and pulled over two metal chairs. 'Have a seat.'

Sam was too big to fit in his. He opened the lid of his coffee and sprinkled on sweetener, just like Fenchurch's old man for the two weeks after his doctor told him to watch his sugar. 'You getting anywhere with Hannah's murder?'

'We might be.' Fenchurch stretched out his knee, took the dull pain down a couple of notches. 'This isn't easy to ask, but . . . did you have sex with Hannah on Sunday night?'

Sam almost dropped his coffee. 'Excuse me?'

'Did you not hear me?'

'No, I did, it's just . . . it's a bit—' His frown became a scowl. 'Wait a sec. Have you found something?'

'Did you and Hannah have sex?'

Sam slumped back in his chair. 'I didn't.'

'Did she?'

'I . . . helped her out.' Sam took a gulp of coffee and wiped foam off his nose. He got a card out of his wallet and slid it across the table. 'I'm a sperm donor. It helps pay through uni. I abstain for a couple of days before, so I . . . *We* didn't. I went down on her, if you must know.'

The card looked official, genuine.

'Do you mind me asking when the last time was?'

'Of course I don't.' A bittersweet smile fluttered on his lips. 'Friday night. We were out at a club. She stayed at my flat. Had a nice time.'

That tallied with the missing drugs. A pair of MDMA pills, taken with her lover at a club on Friday. Something finally making sense amongst all the bullshit. Still, she'd swapped a half-decent laptop for some drugs. Fenchurch wondered what Sam brought to the table.

Sam looked up, tears filling his eyes. 'Why are you asking?'

'I can't tell you.'

'Shut up, of course you can.'

'I'm afraid not.'

'After all that? Won't even give me the common decency.' Sam jerked to his feet and stormed off. 'Prick.'

Fenchurch could've chased him, dodgy knee or not, but he'd got enough out of the kid. He looked around the café. No sign of DC Bridge. He pulled himself up and set off.

In the mobile Incident Room, the two amigos were sipping coffees, locked in a discussion on whether Chelsea would stay top of the league all season.

Bridge sat on the other side, fingers locked around her cup. She glanced over at Fenchurch. 'Sir.'

'Lisa.' Fenchurch sat next to her and clicked his tongue a few times. 'Mick Clooney said you'd taken over the logistical analysis of the laptops?'

'DS Reed asked me to, sir. Highest priority.'

'And yet you were off getting coffee?'

'I'd just finished it, sir. I phoned DS Reed while I was in the queue, but she bounced it. Interview, according to her text.' Bridge opened up her own laptop and tapped the keyboard. 'I might have something, though.'

'On the HP?'

'No, Clooney's still got that.'

'Do me a favour and chase him, please?'

'Sir.' Bridge swivelled her screen round to show a scanned document. 'I've spoken to Apple. That MacBook was part of a batch sold to a preferred supplier who sold it to a limited company registered in Mile End.'

Fenchurch squinted at the paperwork. 'What the hell is Manor House?'

'I imagine it's a knocking shop, sir.'

Chapter Fourteen

Fenchurch pulled up the pool car outside a squat office in the arse end of Mile End. Low-rise post-war houses surrounded it, half of them with builders working, the constant drone of TalkSport accompanying the thumps and bangs. The area was slowly gentrifying, DLR trains trundling in both directions, into central London and out to the eastern badlands. 'What do you make of Lisa Bridge, Kay?'

Reed looked over at him. 'She's okay. Solid, but nothing flash.' She frowned. 'You do remember that Jon's managing her now, don't you?'

'Of course I do.' Fenchurch felt himself blush. *Have to dig out that email again.*

'Why are you asking, guv?'

'Keeping tabs on my team, that's all.' Fenchurch killed the engine and let his seat belt flop down. He got out and started off towards the office. 'This is solid work. Usually takes Clooney an age of man to finish logistics analysis. She's been pretty quick.'

'Still hasn't found the computer, though, has she?'

'True. But this place . . .' Fenchurch couldn't see any office workers on smoke breaks, which raised the threat level a bit higher. 'She thought it was a knocking shop. Manor House sure sounds like one.'

'Classy sort of place, if you know what I mean.' Reed pointed over at the office, gnawing at her top lip. 'It's not on anyone's radar, is it?'

'Nobody we need to speak to before we're allowed to visit, anyway.' Reed pressed a button, then patted her quiff.

The security door buzzed and a small screen flashed on. A tall man stood in an office, grinning at them. 'What can I do you for?'

Fenchurch recognised the face from intelligence briefings. The sharp snarling mouth, a row of rings above eyes full of glee and menace. Dimitri Younis. The new ganglord running East London. 'Wouldn't mind a word with you, sir.'

'Well, I'm pretty busy.' Younis didn't just wear the clothes of a preppy Chelsea twat, he spoke like one too. 'How about you come back later, yeah?'

'The word I need concerns one of your laptops, sir. A MacBook Pro. Decent spec on it, too.'

'This is what the great Simon Fenchurch is reduced to, is it?'

So the new broom recognised the local cops. Interesting.

Fenchurch shared a brief look with Reed. 'It belonged to a Hannah Nunn.'

Younis clicked his tongue for a few seconds. 'Okay, I'll bite. In you come.'

The door clunked open, like a bolt into wood.

Fenchurch led Reed inside. Looked like a waiting room at a posh hairdressers' on a Saturday afternoon, loads of girls sitting around in skimpy clothes. A few English accents, but more than a few Eastern Europeans. Two local girls stood near the back, tanned with hair in long ponytails, comparing their bums in the full-length mirrors, settling into deep squats, hands clasped tight.

'Strippers, guv.' Reed's gaze prowled the room. 'Remember that case at Christmas?'

'Never forget it. Young girls taking their kit off for fat wankers in back rooms. You think Hannah's been stripping?'

'Let's find out.'

A muscle-bound man joined the squatters, getting down so low that his arse touched his basketball shoes.

Younis stood leaning against the door frame admiring them, licking his lips. 'If you'll follow me?' He led them along a corridor, then held open a glass door marked CEO. He winked at Reed as she waltzed in. 'Call me Dimitri.' He held out an arm, his snakeskin suit frayed round the edges where it'd been cut to fit him.

'I know where you got this.' Fenchurch ran a hand down the sleeve of Younis's jacket. The material was a lot smoother than he expected. 'The slimy prick whose illegal businesses you're now running, I suspect.'

'Illegal businesses? Get real.' Younis waved into the room. 'Get your arse down on my couch and we're talking, otherwise you can piss off, the pair of you.' The Chelsea accent was straight out of Mile End now. 'Well, you can stay, Ms Reed.'

'Mrs, and I'll knock you into—'

'Kay.' Fenchurch took a seat by the desk. He patted the one next to it and waited for Reed to sit. Then he trained his glare on Younis. 'Can you explain why one of your laptops was in Hannah's room when she was murdered?'

Younis stopped by his desk. 'She's dead?'

'Haven't you heard?'

'No.' Younis collapsed into his office chair and spun around. 'Shit.'

'You run Manor House, correct?' Fenchurch passed him the scanned delivery note. 'That's your signature, isn't it?'

'I don't know what you're talking about.'

'This place is either a brothel or you've got a lap-dancing club somewhere down the back here.' Fenchurch thumbed back out at the corridor. 'Either way, I doubt much of it is legal.'

'Should kill the pair of you, then, shouldn't I? Dump your bodies in the Thames, yeah?'

'Cut the shit. Why did she have your laptop?'

'Must've bought it after I'd sold it on.'

Fenchurch nudged the delivery note a little further over the desk. 'This computer was almost three grand. Bought in August. You really sold it that quickly?'

'Happens.'

'But you recognised her name when we came in.' Fenchurch let him suffer for a few seconds, caught out in the lie. 'I'm thinking there's some connection between you and Hannah. Something more than you giving her a laptop to help with her studies.'

Younis crunched back in his office chair and nodded slowly, assessing the odds. 'Fine.' He picked up the paper and folded it, slitting it down the middle and tearing it in half. 'I'm running a business here. Manor House. Classy. All legal. Punter consent is needed.'

'Consent for what?'

'What do you think?' Younis held up the two half-pages. 'Are you stupid or something? So they can access my girls and boys.'

'Guv.' Reed nudged his arm. 'He's running a cam site.'

Younis winked at her. 'She's smart, this one.' He looked her up and down. 'Could definitely get a few punters paying for your time, love. Lot of interest in MILFs right now. And you are a mother, I can tell. Got that *House of Cards* thing going on, too. Very popular.'

'Okay, son.' Reed smiled at him. 'When you're man enough, you give me a ring, yeah?'

'I'm serious.' Younis blew her a kiss, then switched his gaze to Fenchurch. 'So your smart cookie here's bang on the money. I run a website, a very legitimate business between consenting adults. All the girls and boys give theirs before I let them through the door. You probably saw a few on the way in, yeah?' He reached down and plonked a huge folder on the desk. Hundreds, maybe thousands in there. He started flicking through. 'And all they do is take their clothes off and dance. Think of Stringfellows or the Chippendales but from the comfort of your own sordid one-bedroom flat. They just take their kit off.

Harmless fun. Nothing illegal. No real porn, certainly nothing you could even suggest as extreme.'

Reed barked out a laugh. 'And what would be extreme to you?'

Younis settled back in his chair. He picked up a little cube from his desk and clicked it. Really loud, really annoying. 'Anything violent. Child, corpse, animal, that kind of thing.' He tossed the cube in the air and caught it. 'There's no penetration here. Just girls slipping out of their lingerie. Boys getting their old fellas out, waving them about a bit.'

'Boys?'

'Got twenty-five of the buggers at the last count.' Younis stuck his finger to his chin. 'Quite fancy the look of that lummox in reception. They're all over-age and they don't even get a hard-on while the customers rub one out.'

'You said lingerie.' Fenchurch flashed up his eyebrows. 'Are we talking expensive stuff?'

'The best. Unless the punters want dirty little scrubbers. Why?'

'We found at least three grand's worth of lingerie in Hannah's room.'

'Nothing to do with me, mate.' Younis held up his hands. 'Standard practice is to wear a corset or a frilly bra. If she wants to waste her money on all that shit, fair play to her.'

Fenchurch tapped on the folder. 'Can I see Hannah Nunn's form?'

'Piss off.'

'You gave her that laptop so she could strip for you, didn't you?'

'I said, piss off.' Younis stuffed the folder back where it came from. 'Now, I need to get on with my work.'

'The laptop isn't here, is it?'

'No, and it's time for you to clear off. Now. You ain't got a warrant so get out. This is bordering on threatening behaviour.'

Reed stopped outside the mobile Incident Room and grabbed the door handle. 'What do you mean, cut down on the flirting?'

'He was all over you, Kay.'

'If he'd kept it up, I would've snapped his cock off, guv. Dirty little pervert.'

Fenchurch took a step back, far enough that she couldn't smack him. 'He was playing you.'

'Oh yeah? The number of times I've seen you thrusting yourself at a young witness? Think Abi wants to hear about that?'

Fenchurch blushed, even though it was utter bullshit. 'Hardly.'

'You don't think I'd cut it as a camgirl, do you?'

'Kay, you're fine, okay?' Fenchurch opened the door. 'Drop it, please.'

One last glare then she entered the van.

Bloody Younis. Flattery will get you everywhere. Need to take that little shit down a peg or two.

He followed her inside. Bridge's pals had cleared out, taking their farts and football chat with them. Left a pile of empty coffee cups by their laptops.

Bridge was pointing at her screen. Reed squatted next to her, scowling. Then she looked up, still frowning. 'Guv, you want to see this.'

Bridge smiled at him. 'I've been looking into this Manor House, sir. It's a camgirl site.'

'Yeah, we know. If DS Reed plays her—' Her glare shut Fenchurch up. 'What have you got?'

'Well, I can explain the lingerie and the high-end laptop.' She sat back and hit the space bar on the keyboard.

The screen filled with a video. That Lana Del Rey song played, the one Abi loved. A face was up close to the camera, all blurry. Then she stepped back and started dancing. Hannah Nunn in her college room, wearing a tight red corset, swaying her hips in time to the thumping beat.

Bridge paused it. 'She goes by Natasha Sparks, but it's definitely Hannah Nunn. Was. Probably paying her way through university by working as a camgirl.'

'Thanks for doing that, Lisa.' Fenchurch smiled at her. 'Sorry that you had to watch all that shit.'

'It's not the worst thing I've seen, sir.' Bridge ran a hand through her hair. 'Had a case a few years ago where our whole team had to look through a pervert's laptop. The weirdest was people having sex with an octopus.'

Reed grimaced. 'That's a thing?'

'If you're so inclined.' Bridge stuck her tongue in her cheek. 'But this has been a lot more interesting. The psychology of the punters . . . I've seen so many videos where the girls just talk about their days, buying shoes and bras and tins of beans. They're at least as popular as when they're shaking their moneymakers.'

Reed barked out a laugh. 'The guys fall in love with them, don't they?'

'These sad, lonely men. They think they're their girlfriends or something.' Bridge tapped her laptop's keys. 'Anyway, I've looked into this Dimitri Younis character. Been running East London for four months. There's a squad in Scotland Yard digging into his background. All of his other businesses are based out of the Caymans or the British Virgin Isles. We were lucky that he was sloppy with Manor House.'

'Sloppy just about covers it.' Fenchurch stood up tall.

Something pinged on Bridge's laptop. She frowned when she looked at it. 'Just a sec.' She hit a few keys then set another video playing. Similar to the last one, the camera focusing on Hannah's blurry face. But the title read 'Natasha Sparks and Keira Lovelace'.

Music began playing and Hannah started dancing. The posters were different and . . . and the room was left-handed instead of right, the doors on the wrong side.

Another girl appeared in the shot, dancing too. Really slutty stuff. Victoria Summerton.

Chapter Fifteen

A hairdryer droned inside Victoria's room. A couple stood down the corridor, arguing silently. Probably breaking up.

Fenchurch knocked on the door and waited. 'Can't believe what these girls do to pay their way through uni, Kay.'

Reed looked away, her neck red. 'I did it.'

'What, stripping? You?'

Her fury burnt into Fenchurch. 'Jesus, Simon, two kids down, and you can't believe I used to strip?'

'So Younis was on to something.' Fenchurch stifled a laugh. 'Kay, you can't let him get to you.'

'I'm not letting anyone get to me. Other than you, you twat.' Her glare hardened as she thumped on the door, much louder than Fenchurch had. 'Bar in Shoreditch, club in Mayfair, which was a lot better, trust me.'

'You didn't mention this when we had that case at Christmas.'

'You were in your own world back then, guv.' Reed thumped the door again. 'I wish I hadn't done it. Ended up with a shit degree and a drink problem. Then working in the police for a boss who's a complete arsehole.' She flashed a smile as she stuck her ear to the door. 'She's definitely in, by the way. I can hear music. Lana Del Rey, if I'm not mistaken. Same song that Hannah was dancing to in the video.'

Fenchurch booted the door. 'Police!' He battered the door so hard it hurt. 'Ms Summerton?'

The arguing couple sloped off, nervously checking behind them.

Victoria opened the door, wearing a robe pulled around her. A fresh coat of spray tan covered her face. Her orange palms confirmed it. 'Yeah?'

'Been working, have you?' Reed was smiling.

'What?' Victoria's gaze switched between them. 'What the hell are you talking about?'

'We know how you pay your fees.'

'Shit.' Victoria focused on the floor. 'It's not illegal.' She pulled her gown even tighter. 'It's stripping, but I make much more money and I don't have to work in shitty bars with dirty old men running their fingers all over me.'

'I know.' Reed's smiled widened.

Victoria swung the door fully open, pushing a draft across their faces. 'I'm not the only one round here who does it.'

'Hannah did, right?'

Victoria gave a slight nod. 'If you want me to talk, you'll have to arrest me.'

'That's not going to happen, Victoria.' Reed blocked Fenchurch's view of her face. 'You work for Younis, don't you?'

'Sorry. I can't tell you anything about it.'

'We found a video of you and Hannah.'

'Just us?'

Fenchurch caught Reed's look and threw it back at Victoria. 'There are others?'

'I can't tell you!'

Fenchurch got in her face, his nose inches from hers. 'Listen, you tell us who got you into this and we'll be on our way.'

Victoria slumped against her door frame, her head dipping. 'Sam.'

Sam Edwards lived in a flat on Page's Walk, almost on the corner with Willow Walk. Bermondsey, half an hour's walk from the university. Old factory buildings lined one side of the road, the brick flats on the far side sandblasted new, pricing them out of student tenancy. Sam's address was a ground-floor flat in the rougher half.

Fenchurch walked up the drive and clattered his fist off the door. He crouched down and peered in through the letterbox, gloved fingers carefully prying it open. A wide hall, three doors. One had a sign up: DON'T BANG IF I'M BANGING, next to a poster of Yosemite Sam.

Something crashed inside. Glass, maybe. The bedroom door splintered open, bouncing across the hall. 'YOU COMPLETE BASTARD! COME HERE!'

Didn't sound like Sam Edwards.

'COME HERE!'

'AAAAH! THAT HURT!' Sam Edwards tumbled through the doorway, blood slicking his arm.

Fenchurch thudded the door. 'Sam?'

'YOU ARE A FU—' Another smash, deeper. A dull thud. 'YOU SHIT!' A tall man stuck the boot into a prone Sam.

Fenchurch gave the door some shoulder. The wood creaked and bent. Another push and he was in.

Sam lay on the floor. A man stood over him, kicking his stomach. 'YOU SLAG!' Black tracksuit bottoms and a green T-shirt, a beer gut twisting the slogan. Another boot. 'YOU'RE WORSE THAN HER! YOU SLAG!' His boot slapped off Sam's hands.

'Police!' Fenchurch launched himself across the hall and tackled Sam's assailant, hauling him off. They landed on the carpet, the attacker crunching into Fenchurch's left knee. He screamed out, pain roaring up his thigh and hip. Then he got a faceful of fist and a different flavour of pain. 'Get off me!'

A boot cracked Fenchurch's side. 'YOU'RE AS BAD AS HIM!'

Fenchurch lashed out with his right boot, the sole bouncing off the attacker's chin. The attacker pulled back his fist, ready to strike again.

Reed lashed out with her baton and cracked the man's wrist. He spun round, looking ready to punch her.

Fenchurch grabbed his wrist from behind and locked his arm, pushing him face first to the ground. 'Stay!' He wriggled, so Fenchurch tightened the lock. 'Stay still!'

Sam was prone on the floor, tucked up in a ball, groaning. Clutching his arm, his hand caked in blood.

Fenchurch waited a few seconds, then loosened his hold. The attacker tried to elbow him, so he tightened his grip again. 'Kay, for God's sake, call in backup!'

Chapter Sixteen

That prick bit me!' Sam let the paramedics help him to his feet. 'Bit me! Guy's an animal!'

They led him limping out of the door, dark blood caking his arm. 'We'll take him to the Royal London, sir.'

'Thanks.'

Still no bloody uniform. Medics had now been and gone and his lot couldn't be bothered showing up.

Useless.

But the Royal London . . .

Docherty's there, lying in a bed. God knows what's happening to him. Maybe if I don't go, he'll . . .

Of course he won't, you stupid bastard. Stop thinking about fairy tales.

Fenchurch tried to straighten his knee, but struggled. Beyond pain now. He stretched it off by walking into Sam's room.

Bare walls, a MacBook on an IKEA desk, unlocked, covered in stickers. SAM IS THE MAN! and CUCK OFF!

The attacker sat on the bed, head between his knees. Handcuffs rattling as he rocked back and forth. Moaning. Muttering. Mid-forties. A wallet lay at his feet.

Fenchurch reached down and picked it up, started flicking through. Driving licence said Ian Galbraith. A passport-sized photo of the man on the bed and a blonde-haired woman gurning. On the back someone had printed 'Ian & Jo, 04.09.16'.

Fenchurch tried to make eye contact with Reed. She wasn't having it.

Galbraith let out the mother of all sighs. 'Should never have . . .'

Fenchurch waited but he'd clammed up. 'Never have what?'

'You can piss off.' Galbraith lay on the bed. Looked like he hated himself as much as Sam. 'I'm saying nothing until my lawyer turns up.'

'Is your wife sleeping with Sam?'

Nothing. Not even a glance. Then: 'Bitch.'

'Did you catch them at it?'

Galbraith shook his head.

Something sparkled at his feet. A sheer black box. A smartphone, facing down, light haloing on the carpet.

Fenchurch slipped a glove on and knelt in front of Galbraith, his knee grinding like a chainsaw. He picked up the phone. Hadn't locked itself. Playing a video, full of blurring. Shouting, screaming, then it focused on Sam Edwards.

Fenchurch held it up. 'Sir, I need your consent to search this phone.'

'Do what you like.'

'Take that as a yes.' Fenchurch stood up tall and wound the video back to the start, turning up the volume.

The screen filled with a hotel corridor, shaking as the holder walked. 'This is what we both want, not just her.' Galbraith held up the camera, selfie-style. He raised a bag up, clinking with glass bottles. 'Hope they're getting acquainted.' He swiped his key card, the phone focusing on the floor.

The camera swivelled round. A woman was on her knees, in front of Sam, her head bobbing back and forth, her hands working in front of her. Sam was yawning, then nodded at Galbraith.

'JO, WHAT ARE YOU DOING?'

The video focused on Joanne, peering round Sam's buttocks, grinning. 'I couldn't help myself.'

'You were supposed to wait for me . . .' His voice was close to a whisper.

Fenchurch paused it before it got to the shouting. 'Care to explain this, sir?'

Galbraith took a glance at it and let out a deep, deep sigh. 'You don't want to know.'

'Trust me, I do.'

Shame twisted Galbraith's face, all puffy and red.

Fenchurch sat next to him, getting the weight off his knee. 'What is this? Some kind of threesome?' He waited, but Galbraith wasn't speaking. 'You walked in on them starting without you, so you beat the shit out of him. That about the size of it?'

Galbraith clicked his tongue a few times. 'Sod it, I'm in enough shit as it is.' An intense grin crawled onto his face. 'It's not what you think.'

'Try me.'

'That Edwards fella is working as a cuck.'

'A what?'

'A cuck. Cuckold.' Galbraith's lips twitched. 'The kid rents himself out to couples to . . . satisfy certain fantasies.' He rubbed his hands together. 'Jo's my second wife, fifteen years younger than me. Lovely girl, but . . . Jo's . . . disappointed with . . . something about me.'

'And she's not disappointed with Sam?'

'Sam's got a . . . He's well hung.' Galbraith rubbed at his neck. 'I mean, I've never had any complaints before but . . . Jo, man. Anyway, I . . . hired him for her birthday. I was going to record the whole thing so we could watch it together and . . . I told them to wait for me . . .'

'You wanted to watch them?'

'That's not a crime.' Galbraith frowned. 'Is it?'

'Need to look that one up. Go on.'

'Sam turned up and I thought I'd let them have a chat, get acquainted. Went to the Tesco next to the hotel, got in some beer and wine. But she couldn't get enough of him, could she? I tell you, mate, I don't get women. At all.'

And I don't get perverts who want their wives to sleep with other men.

'Anyway, they didn't stop. She just kept on sucking his cock. Didn't stop. I sat and watched. They . . . they made love. Didn't take too long, either. Jo enjoyed it. I think.'

'When was this?'

'Saturday. Lunchtime. We've got season tickets at Selhurst Park. Watched Liverpool battering us later.'

Watching Crystal Palace after your wife had sex with a stranger . . .

That didn't quite tally with Sam's poor sperm donor story.

'Mr Galbraith, I'm still struggling to understand why you decided to kick the living shit out of him three days later?'

'Because . . .' Galbraith slumped back on the bed. 'I play Sunday League for our local down in Sutton. The Old Post Office. I got there, but it was pissing it down. Waterlogged pitch so the game got cancelled. Instead of going for a few jars with the lads, I came home to spend time with Jo. Only, I get there and her car's leaving the drive, going the other way. Hello. So I followed her. She came here.' He stabbed a finger at Fenchurch. 'I waited outside. Heard her getting *smashed* by that prick. Can you believe it?'

Fenchurch leaned forward. 'Did you confront her on Sunday?'

Galbraith grabbed his knees. 'Could hear her screaming from the bloody street. I came back here yesterday after work, but that punk was out. His flatmate said something about someone dying. So I took a long lunch today and came back.' He shrugged. 'Lucked out, I suppose.'

'And what happened?'

'Confronted him. She paid him three hundred quid for that. More than I paid for the hotel thing!'

'So you kicked the shit out of him?'

'Wouldn't you?'

Before Fenchurch could pretend to answer, a pair of burly uniforms filed into the flat. He got up and waved at Galbraith. 'Take him to Leman Street.'

———

The Royal London didn't have that hospital smell. The air tasted of airport duty-free, all aquatic aftershaves and smoky whiskies. Fenchurch stopped at the junction between ACCIDENT & EMERGENCY and URGENT CARE.

Sam Edwards or Alan Docherty.

Should really go and see Docherty.

After Edwards.

He took the left and spotted the uniform presence outside a sheeted-off area. A big lump of muscle stepped forward as he approached. Early twenties, but seasoned enough. He clocked Fenchurch's limp. 'I'm sorry, sir, Accident and Emergency is—'

'DI Fenchurch.' He showed his warrant card. 'Sam Edwards, yeah?'

'Sir.' His badge read Kirkpatrick. Scottish or Irish name, but his accent was Billericay. 'Sorry, I'm so sorry, I—'

'Don't sweat it, son. I make much bigger blunders than that every week. Is Sam in here?'

Kirkpatrick stepped aside. 'Yes, sir, he's being seen to, sir.'

'Cut it with the sirs, okay?' Fenchurch smiled and tore back the curtain.

Sam Edwards sat on the bed, hunched over and topless. He winced as a nurse dragged a needle through a deep gash on his arm, threading stitches, knitting the flesh back together.

Fenchurch's gut clenched. Ian Galbraith had done that. Maybe tackling him hadn't been such a good move, after all . . .

The nurse gave him a hard glare. 'Sir, this is a—'

'I'm police.' Another flash of his warrant card. 'Need a word with Mr Edwards here.'

'Two seconds, then.' He ploughed on with the stitching, getting a couple of sharp gasps from Sam.

Fenchurch took a seat next to the bed and tried to get Sam's attention. Nothing. He waited.

Should've gone to see Docherty. Daft sod.

'And that's us.' The nurse passed Sam a green hospital top, matching his bottoms. 'We need to X-ray your leg, so I'll be back in about half an hour, okay? But that wound on your arm will heal up nicely in a few days. Be right as rain.'

'Thanks.' Sam stayed focused on the floor while he left. Then his gaze shot up to Fenchurch. 'He bit me. Can you believe it? Actually bit me. Then kicked my leg . . .'

'Think you maybe deserve it?'

Sam looked up at Fenchurch for a few seconds. 'I'm not saying anything.'

'I'm not surprised.' Fenchurch got up and started walking around. The buggered knee wasn't helping him act the tough guy. 'Trouble is, Mr Galbraith has been saying something. And not only saying . . .' He reached into his pocket for his Pronto and played the video, holding it in front of Sam's face.

Sam couldn't watch. 'I'm not going to deny it.'

'That's good.' Fenchurch pocketed the phone again. 'Mr Galbraith says you had sex with Joanne Galbraith on Sunday. That right?'

Sam shrugged.

'Cos you told me you had to "save yourself" for your sperm donation.'

'Listen, mate, Hannah was cool with it.'

'She was happy that you were having sex with other men's wives?'

Another shrug. 'Need to earn a crust.'

'Sam, it's prostitution.'

'It's not a crime. I know the law. Nobody else was involved in me selling myself. You can't touch me.'

Fenchurch stared hard at him. The kid had done his homework. 'The second I find that Younis was involved, son, I will charge you.' He'd lost Sam. Time for a different tack. 'You know, when I saved you from worse than getting bitten like this, we wanted to speak to you. Someone told us you were involved in Younis's business. I thought you were pimping out the girls. But it's not like that, is it?'

Sam bunched up his fists. 'Who told you?'

'What, that you got Hannah into stripping on her computer?'

'Victoria, yeah?'

'Can't say. You should appreciate that with your knowledge of the criminal justice system.' Fenchurch leaned in close to Sam's face, trying to force him to look at him. 'Let's cut the crap. Did Younis know Hannah?'

Sam flinched. 'She auditioned for him.' He prodded the cut the nurse had sewn up. 'Filled out a form, same as the rest of us. Had some questions on the background checks, but that's Younis messing with us.'

'She ever do anything to annoy Younis?'

'Made a lot of money for him.'

'What about you?'

Sam nibbled at his thumbnail. He kept twitching. 'What about me?'

'You do shows, don't you?'

'I do, but I don't make enough.' Sam's baby-blue eyes twinkled. Fenchurch could see why all the girls went for him. 'Mate. My parents are poor. Very poor.' He huffed out air, like he'd confessed to the world's biggest crime. 'I'm the first in my family to ever go to university. When you were young, that might've been quite common. Now, everyone goes. But I had a shit upbringing. Really shit. Dad's not worked since the nineties and I was born in 1997.'

'Getting into Southwark's a big achievement.'

'I know.' Pride fought with shame on Sam's face. 'But it's nine grand a year. And that's just fees. It doesn't cover how much it costs to stay in London. Food, coffee. Might even want to go out once in a while.'

'And this is how you pay your way?'

'Not that I've got a choice.' Sam rubbed his hands together slowly. 'It started with cam shows. The audience was mostly fellas to begin with, but then a few women joined. I get a hell of a lot of couples watching me. Then these messages came through on the website, asking to meet up.'

'Was Younis aware of them?'

Sam nodded slowly. 'There's a messaging system on Manor House. I think it's so he knows who's turning tricks.'

'Does he take a cut?'

'You don't get it, do you? You lot are interested in what he does, so he screens the users to keep an eye on which girls and boys are meeting people on the side.'

'People like you?'

'He doesn't mind about the boys. It's the girls you lot have a problem with.'

'You're close?'

Sam started inspecting his nails. 'I'm one of his favourites.'

'How favourite?'

'He watches my shows. That's it.'

'Was Hannah turning tricks?'

'She didn't. Wouldn't. There's money to be made, but she made a killing out of the shows.' He twitched again. 'She was fine with my sidelines, so long as I was careful.'

'Getting the shit kicked out of you is careful, is it?'

Sam raised his shoulders. 'It's dangerous.' He touched the bandage over his cut. 'As I'm finding out now.'

'Did you meet Hannah through this?'

'No.'

'And Younis?'

'Just after I came to London, I was . . . He . . . saw me dance a couple of times at this club in Soho. One of the last ones. Very hands-on.'

'He's gay?'

Sam barked out a laugh. 'Omnisexual is how he sees it.'

'I need to get this on the record.'

'Yeah, fat chance.'

———

Fenchurch hauled himself up the stairs at Leman Street, his knee locking every couple of steps. Too proud to take the lift.

Sam Edwards. Bloody hell. Usually, Fenchurch would rely on instinct, batter into Younis, accuse him of everything under the sun. Get nowhere, except into a fight.

But this time . . . This needed strategy. Deep thought. Time. And Hannah wasn't getting any less dead.

Younis was an unknown quantity. Rising up to take over the East End. Not exactly a Kray, but still formidable. Still a lucrative place if you knew what you were doing. Trouble with the younger generation, though, is they'd just rip the snakeskin suit off your back.

Fenchurch opened his office door and limped through.

Mulholland was behind her desk, smiling at him. 'Afternoon.'

'Is it?' Fenchurch glanced at his watch. How did it get to one o'clock? He slumped behind his desk and unlocked his computer. Whirring and grinding as it opened his emails.

'I visited Alan this morning.'

Shit.

Shit, shit, shit.

Forgot to bloody go.

'How was he?'

'Awake.' Mulholland got up and paced across the office, resting to the side of his monitor. 'I heard you were at the hospital. How was he?'

'Dawn, I'm running a murder case.' Fenchurch stared at her long and hard. 'Do you mind getting out of my hair?'

She left their office with a huff, her scarf dragging behind her.

Save me from this bullshit . . .

Fenchurch logged into the PNC and searched for Dimitri Younis. Just took him to the same intelligence file he'd seen a few weeks back. They had so little on him, it was like the guy didn't exist.

Who'd know about him? Howard Savage, maybe?

He flicked into his inbox and scanned down the list of emails, hundreds of unread, unactioned messages.

Reed's holiday requests, Nelson asking for a 'chat'. Five from Docherty yesterday. Enough to pump up the lump in his throat. And one from 'A friend'. No doubt the sort of penis-enlargement drugs that the spam filter was supposed to kill.

But the subject was 'Your daughter'. Another nutter who'd read the articles in the *Post*. Against his better judgment, he opened it.

> See her in action.
> — Your friend

And a link to a video site.

Sweat trickled down Fenchurch's back.

Don't click on it. It's just some sick bastard messing with you.

The pixels on the screen resolved to tiny dots.

Thinking it through, planning what the hell to do with it.

Can't watch it.

Can't not watch it.

See her in action. What the hell did that even mean?

He clicked.

A video opened and started playing, the sound muted. Chloe sat on a couch, short skirt, bare legs crossed. Tight black top, hair scraped back from her face. Well-lit room, very much like Younis's office in Manor House.

Fenchurch's mouth was dry, his fists clenched.

She said something, but the sound was off. Fenchurch unmuted it.

A male voice droned out, 'Are you going to dance for me?' London, but indistinct.

Chloe gave a nervous nod to whoever was behind the camera. Then music, tinny and thin. Robert Palmer, 'Addicted to Love'. She got up and started strutting around, swaying her hips and shoulders.

Fenchurch couldn't watch. Couldn't tear his eyes off it.

She nibbled her bottom lip as she played with her top, lifting it up to show bare flesh.

Fenchurch tried turning it off without looking at it again.

On the screen, Chloe stormed off out of the room. 'I can't do this.'

Chapter Seventeen

Fenchurch stood in the corridor, clutching his phone. His finger hovered over Abi's number. He tried to press it but . . . couldn't.

How do you tell your wife that her estranged daughter is . . .

Is . . .

He hauled open the Incident Room door and scanned around, stuffing his phone in his pocket. DC Bridge was in the corner, working on a laptop, headphones in. He wandered over, smiling at the two DCs he passed, trying to act calm and rational. 'Lisa, did you get that email?'

She pulled out her earbuds. The audition video was on her screen. Up to three views now. Shit. Someone else had it. 'Who is this girl?'

Fenchurch pulled up the chair next to her, sweat trickling down his back. He looked her in the eye. 'I think it's connected to the Hannah Nunn case.' As big a smile as he could manage. 'Can you trace who sent it?'

'That's really Mick Clooney's department, sir.'

'But you can do it?'

'Well. I can try.' She hit a few keys and typed into a little black window, tiny white text. A bar stretched across the screen. 'Balls, that IP address is masked.'

'Dead end, then?'

'Dead end.' She tapped at the video screen. 'But . . . Nah, it's nothing.'

'No, go on.'

She pointed at the monitor again, circling the sofa and the pot plant. Her face twisted up. 'She's familiar, though.' Her hand shot to her mouth. 'Is this another victim?'

'God, no.' Fenchurch got to his feet. 'Thanks for this, Lisa. I'd appreciate it if you kept this to yourself for now.'

'No problem. Do you want me to dig into it?'

'No, I know who to speak to about it.' Fenchurch jabbed a finger at the laptop. 'But see if you can get that site to take it down for me.'

⌣

Fenchurch locked his car and sucked in a deep breath.

Why the hell is that prick sending videos of Chloe . . .

Stripping.

Jesus. Is she being forced to strip to pay her way through university? Taking her kit off so some obese pervert can masturbate.

But she pulled out, didn't she? That's what it looked like.

He pocketed his keys and sucked in another deep gulp of air. Time to—

'Can't get enough of this place, can you?' Younis was standing by a blue BMW X5, the SUV sparkling with glitter. The male squatter from earlier was waiting next to him, about to do something he'd regret. 'It's much easier if you do it on your computer. Now, boy or girl?'

Fenchurch took his time walking over, trying to keep a smile on his face, trying to stop his knee from locking. 'Here to ask you about a girl, as it happens.' He grinned at the beefcake. 'Though I hear your tastes are a little more male?'

Younis patted his friend on the arm. 'You get in the car, Leon, okay?' He waited until the door slammed. 'Who I ride isn't your concern,

Fenchurch. And, anyway, I'd shag anything. Anyone. Your DS earlier.' He leered at him, adding a wink to make it that little bit seedier. Then Fenchurch got the up and down. 'Even you.'

Fenchurch flushed. 'Did you send the video?'

'There's a video of you?' Younis folded his arms, nodding, giving Fenchurch another detailed inspection. 'Solo, is it? Male-on-male? You going down on Mrs Fenchurch?'

Fenchurch's mouth was dry. 'Chloe.' It was all he could manage to say. *Stop this prick getting at you.*

Younis reached out and touched Fenchurch's arm. 'My, you are a big one.'

'The girl in the video, her name is Chloe.'

'Don't know her.' Younis thumbed into the car. 'Sure you don't want to have some fun with me and Leon?'

'What about Jennifer Simon?' Fenchurch hated saying it, felt his gut recoil.

'Sorry, mate.' Younis squeezed Fenchurch's arm. 'Offer still stands. We can have a lot of fun.'

'I'll get myself all lubed up, shall I?'

'Fenchurch, Fenchurch, Fenchurch.' Younis exhaled slowly. 'If only you were interested.'

'Just in who sent me the video.'

'Well, I don't know anything about it.'

'That mean you didn't send it?'

'You got evidence that I'm involved, eh?' Younis held his gaze until Fenchurch looked away. 'Thought as much.' He sniffed. 'Now, I've no idea who or what you're talking about.'

Fenchurch pulled out his Airwave Pronto. The video was ready to play. Chloe in that office, looking alone and ashamed for what she was about to do. 'Do you recognise her?'

Younis nodded slowly, staring hard at the screen. 'What did you say her name was?'

'Stop messing with me.'

'Chloe, wasn't it? Or Jennifer.' Younis smirked. 'I remember her. Very sexy, but shy. That makes it even sexier. She came in, filled out all the paperwork, then we filmed her. But she changed her mind halfway through the audition, didn't she?' He ran his tongue over his lips. 'A lot of girls can't cope with knowing that they're dancing for thousands of seedy degenerates. Finding a man who can is even harder. Like hen's teeth.' He laughed. 'Weird thing is, some hens do have teeth. A genetic throwback. Vestigial, they call it. Like a snake with a leg.'

Fenchurch nudged Younis back against his car. 'Why did you send it?'

'I'm getting all hot and bothered here, Inspector.' Younis licked his lips again, his eyelids quivering. 'But I'm afraid that I've no idea what you're talking about. I haven't sent anything to anyone. Call me a tinfoil-hat nutter all you want, but I don't trust computers. Someone's always watching.' His gaze shot down to Fenchurch's crotch. 'Though I'd love to watch you.'

'Did you send that video?'

'We've discussed that, sweetie. No.' Younis winked and patted the car window behind him. 'And if you want any more, then how about you come back to mine with Leon here. My pillow talk can be quite open.'

Fenchurch thought about threatening him. *Don't want the prick to think he's won.* 'I'll be seeing you.' He walked off towards his car.

'Cooee!' Younis was pouting at Fenchurch, a business card between two fingers. 'Take this. You never know when you might need to phone me.' He shot a wink. 'Or want to.'

A plastic bag soared past Fenchurch, blowing across the university quad, now thronging with bodies. Students coming out of lectures, others going back in.

'Inspector.' Gordon McLaren nodded at Fenchurch. A touch too much eye shadow today. His lilac cravat matched his pink blouse and dark-brown skirt. 'Have you got anywhere with finding Hannah's killer?'

Fenchurch grimaced. 'Not yet.'

'I see.' McLaren passed him a flyer. 'Well. I'm hosting a candlelit vigil tonight for Hannah. She was well loved here and . . . it just seems the proper thing to do.'

Fenchurch held up the flyer then pocketed it. 'I'll see what I can do.'

Besides, someone might turn up that shouldn't . . .

'Hope to see you.' And McLaren shot off, passing out flyers to students.

The flyer burnt in Fenchurch's pocket. He really should go. Show solidarity with the students, show them the Met cared. Put a human face to it.

A newspaper trundled past, caught up with the plastic bag. This morning's *Metro*, splashed with a photo of Hannah cadged from her Facebook profile. Tomorrow it'd be something else. Another dead girl in a city that didn't give a shit about anyone or anything. Could be Chloe lying in Lewisham. Just a twist of the knife away.

This is someone's daughter. Someone's girlfriend. Someone's student. Someone's friend. But Hannah had also been someone's enemy. Too many to list, even now.

The plastic bag swished, staying out of his reach.

And there she was, standing by the Starbucks, fiddling with a mobile phone. A dimple denting her cheek, her forehead creased with concentration. Or worry.

Chloe.

She bent down to snatch up the plastic bag, then stuffed it in a bin. *Like in the dreams . . .* She clocked Fenchurch and walked off.

Fenchurch caught up with her by the alleyway, dodgy knee or not, and blocked her path. 'Did you send it?'

'What?' She tried to barge past but he wouldn't let her. 'Get out of my way!'

'Chloe, someone sent me a video of you auditioning for a . . .' He swallowed hard. 'For a stripper website.'

She folded her arms, giving him a scowl Abi would be proud of. 'You expect me to dignify that, do you?'

'Well, it's in my inbox. Whoever sent it is trying to get a reaction, seeing if they can use it as leverage.'

She let out a sigh. 'Well, since you and your mates decided to lock up my parents and freeze their assets, I have to pay for my degree somehow.'

'Stripping's not the answer.'

'I know that. Christ. If you'd watched it, you'd have seen that I couldn't go through with it.'

'I can help.' His mouth was dry. She was winning and he'd no chance to get her back. Losing her all over again. 'I'm selling my flat. I can give you the money. The profit. Help you pay your fees.'

'I'm working in Tesco. I'm fine.'

The tiniest weight lifted off Fenchurch's shoulders. She was handling it herself. 'Someone got hold of your audition. Who suggested you do it?'

'You did watch it, didn't you? You . . . pervert.' She shook her head, her mouth twisting up with rage, her neck burning red. 'All that bullshit about me being your daughter. If incest porn is what gets you hard, you really need to speak to someone. Jesus.'

'Let us help, Chloe.'

'I wouldn't throw water on you if you were on fire.'

'There's nothing wrong with wanting to help your daughter.'

'You're not my father!' Her scream tore his eardrums. Turned a few heads outside the café. She pushed his chest and he bumped into the wall. Her footsteps rattled around the alleyway as she ran off.

Fenchurch steadied himself and started to follow. His knee felt like it was going to pop out. He ran out to a crossroads, one way leading to Jaines Tower, another to the halls of residence, the third a mystery. No sign of her.

'Inspector?' Thomas Zachary was frowning at him, mobile to his ear. 'Are you okay?'

Chloe was nowhere to be seen.

'What's up?' Zachary held his phone away from his ear. 'Seen a ghost?'

'I'm fine.' Fenchurch took the third path, to avoid Zachary as much as anything else.

What an idiot, tearing after her. Did that so many times when she was a little girl. She was an adult now. And throwing money at her to buy affection?

But she was getting close to the case. And someone knew about her, knew about him and their history. And they were trying to use it against him.

Fenchurch turned a corner, limping badly now, and spotted his car parked on the main road.

Halfway over, Chloe was standing with a couple of friends, talking, nervously looking his way. A woman who probably should still be at school, and a man even older than Fenchurch.

He hobbled towards them, ignoring the glares from her friends. 'Chloe, I really need a word.'

The man intercepted him, dropping his rucksack as he walked. A mature student, probably one of those City traders who burnt out in their thirties, cashed out and did something else with what little time their ravaged bodies had left. He got in Fenchurch's face, standing like someone who could handle himself. 'She doesn't want to speak to you, mate.'

'Who the hell do you think you are?'

'Listen to me.' The mature student had the same silver hair as Fenchurch, the same gnarled skin, aged by the bullshit of a career that took more than it gave back. He thumbed behind him. 'That poor girl's been through hell since the summer. She doesn't need you sending her back.'

Fenchurch glanced over at her. Terrified, huddling behind her young-looking friend. 'She's my daughter.'

'If you really believe that, then you need to let her come out the other side, okay?' He opened his palms. 'Chasing after her isn't helping you and it certainly isn't helping Jen. Give her space. Okay?'

Fenchurch glanced at Chloe. Close to tears. He nodded at her friend and walked off. 'Tell her I'm sorry.'

Chapter Eighteen

Fenchurch took the back stairs up to his office, a naughty schoolboy trying to avoid being caught messing around.

Docherty was right. Loftus was right. He was an idiot. A complete idiot. Trying to protect his daughter but only succeeding in pushing her away.

Voices inside his office. No doubt Mulholland and Loftus, carving out the new empire before Docherty had even left the building.

Shit. Docherty. Really need to get out and see him. Stop avoiding it. Stop avoiding everything.

He opened the door and walked in like he owned the place. Reed and Bridge were sitting at his desk. 'Sorry, I'll come back later.'

'No, guv. You don't get off that easily.' Reed was already halfway towards the door. 'You didn't think to tell me about the email?'

Fenchurch shot Bridge a hard stare. But really, she was right. He was wrong. 'Sorry, Kay. I . . .'

Reed spoke in an undertone, 'Guv, you've got to stop this secret-squirrel shit, okay?' She clapped his arm. 'Okay?'

He gave her a nod then crouched. 'Lisa, have you got anything else?'

'Not on that email, sir.' Bridge glanced at Reed. Didn't want to jump the gun. 'Sarge?'

Reed smiled at Bridge. 'Lisa's been through the HP laptop you got from the shop.'

Bridge held the bagged machine in the air. 'Even though the guy had zeroed it, sir, I've managed to undo it with some tricks from a mate in MI6. Got a full clone of the hard disk as Hannah had it.'

'Bloody hell. I'd hoped but didn't expect we'd get anything out of it.'

'You don't know the half of it.' She put the laptop back down. 'Anyway, I'm in. And I've got access to Hannah's Gmail account.' She reached over the desk for a pile of papers. 'I found an email on Hannah's laptop from an Oliver Keane.' She passed a page to Fenchurch. 'He asked to meet up with her for sex.'

Fenchurch scanned the email. The guy was a fan of Hannah's camgirl shows and wanted to take it to the next level: Bridge tapped at her own laptop. 'I'm running a server search for anything else from him.'

'Any idea who this Oliver Keane guy is?'

'None.' Reed was staring at her Airwave handset. 'Got far too many hits on the PNC to narrow it down. Twelve of that name in the South-East alone. He could be anywhere. America, maybe.'

Fenchurch ran through the second page. Hannah's replies were flirty and playful, but kept a professional distance. Keane's were sinister and direct. 'Is there any more of this?'

'Not yet, guv.' Reed dropped her Airwave on the desk, giving up on her side of the hunt. 'But those emails were sent last week, which means he was stalking her before she died.'

'Stalking's a bit harsh.' Fenchurch waved the printouts around. 'I don't approve of what he's doing, but he's not exactly stalking her, is he?'

Bridge's computer pinged and she glanced at it. 'Jesus.'

'What?' Fenchurch hovered over her, trying to peer at her screen, but it was far too small for his old man's eyesight.

'More emails from him.' Bridge ran her finger down the screen. 'A load were deleted on Sunday night. Whoever this guy is, he's been messaging Hannah constantly. He was obsessed.' Her forehead twitched as she read. 'Shit. He said he paid thousands to watch her strip on his computer. Meeting up was the least she could do. That was sent on Sunday.'

Fenchurch swallowed. All adding up to a credible suspect. Another one. 'Is this the Natasha Sparks account?'

'Shit.' Bridge groaned. 'No. These are in her personal account, sir.'

Fenchurch's gut fell through the floor. 'So this guy found out her real name?'

'Oh here we go.' Bridge pointed at the screen. 'He's sent her his address.'

⁓

Mansell Street was a quick hobble over from Leman Street, half-City, half-East End. A fresh wave of traffic hurtled up from the Tower of London, mainly vans and lorries.

Fenchurch led Reed up the street, trying to match Keane's address to a building. A council estate occupied the middle of the street, four stories of red brick, precarious balconies and satellite dishes of all sizes. The sort of council housing that trapped people. Except, the grime stopped halfway up. The end block was shrouded in scaffolding, the sandblasting droning out. The end flats had been cleaned and refurbished, the window frames painted the latest shade of grey that all the posh pubs wanted. Looked expensive inside, too, all spotlights and Farrow & Ball.

'Got anywhere with the PNC yet, Kay?'

'Sorry, guv.' Reed was checking her handset. 'This is the only address I can find for Oliver Keane. Just moved in, by the looks of it. Says he owns the whole building.'

'So, nothing. Great.' Fenchurch tried to spot the joins. Couldn't find any. Keane had turned eight flats of misery into a bachelor pad for a single male pervert. Not that Fenchurch was prejudging him based on his internet activity . . .

'Bet it cost a bloody packet.' Fenchurch crossed over and walked up the path. Workmen filled the front yard next door, standing around a cement mixer like tramps at a brazier. Keane had a nascent garden, dark earth dotted with baby bushes and shrubs, probably the wrong time of year for it to start growing. Fenchurch was the last person to give gardening advice. Could drown a cactus.

He knocked on the glass door. A well fitted-out kitchen inside, black units with a granite worktop.

The door slid open and a man peered out, frowning. Dark hair streaked grey, thick red beard. He wore one of those Japanese dressing gowns. A kimono? Or was that something else? Music blared out, early XTC by the sounds of it. 'Towers of London', ironically enough. The stench of dead fish wafted out, like he was smoking kippers or fermenting his own nam pla. 'Can I help?'

'Oliver Keane?' Fenchurch had to cover his mouth to avoid the stink.

Keane stepped back into the house. 'Alexa, stop.' XTC died. 'How can I help?'

'Police, sir. We need to—'

Keane held up his mobile phone. 'I am recording this. I am maintaining my silence.'

Jesus, what did Younis say about tinfoil hats?

'I know my rights.' Keane's gaze darted between Fenchurch and Reed. 'If you want to speak to me, you will have to arrest me.'

'This is about Hannah Nunn, sir.'

'Who?'

'Natasha Sparks.'

'I am refusing entry!'

Fenchurch got in his face. Trying to goad him. 'You managed to get her real name, didn't you?'

'I am refusing entry and maintaining my silence.' Keane grabbed the door handle. 'I am refusing entry and maintaining my silence!'

'We've seen the emails you sent her.'

Keane tugged at the door. 'I am refusing entry and calling my solicitor!'

'This is your last chance, sir.' Fenchurch grabbed the sliding door and tried to stop it. 'Come with me now and I'll look favourably on it.'

Another push and the door lurched forward. Fenchurch let it shut.

———

Fenchurch opened his office door. Luckily, Mulholland wasn't in. He sat behind his desk and let out a sigh of relief. 'Okay, what's our plan here?'

'Not a lot we can do, is there?' Reed sat opposite him, hands on her knees. 'You think he's our guy?'

Fenchurch found the pile of emails on his desk. 'This is pretty convincing to me. Enough to make him a person of interest, as they say.'

'He's the, what, fourth suspect, guv?' Reed started counting on her thumb and fingers. 'Troy Danton, Graham Pickersgill, Sam Edwards, now Oliver Keane. We're not clearing them.'

'Add Thomas Zachary to that list, too.' Fenchurch tossed the emails onto the desk. 'We can probably cross Danton off.'

'Don't disagree.' Reed was frowning. 'But much as I despise him, I don't buy Zachary as a suspect. Speaking of which, you've missed off Younis.'

'He's another one, isn't he?' Fenchurch blew out a deep breath. 'Think we should focus on Keane. We're not getting in there, Kay. That guy isn't going to be intimidated by us dirty pigeons, is he? He knows how to play it. Wouldn't be surprised if that house of his is under video surveillance. Any wrong moves and we're stuffed. If he can afford that, he can afford a lawsuit against the Met. And I've had more than my share of them.'

A knock on the door. Nelson, sucking on his vape stick. 'You wanted me, guv?'

'Jon, thanks.' Fenchurch shrugged off his jacket. 'I need you to have a very long word with Sam Edwards.'

'You mean, man-mark him. Got surveillance approval?'

'I mean keep on him, Jon. Ask him very detailed questions, so detailed that he doesn't slip out of the hospital without us knowing, okay?'

'Fine.' Seemed anything but.

Reed's phone blasted out. 'Back in a sec, guv.' She got up and left. 'Michelle . . .'

Nelson waited until she was out of the door. 'Seriously, guv, I'm a Detective Sergeant.'

'I ask you because I trust you, Jon. Edwards is deep in this. He introduced those girls to e-stripping or whatever it is. He's sharing himself with couples, getting his todger out on his laptop. God knows what else he's doing. And I really, really don't believe anything he tells us.'

Nelson took a puff on his vape stick. 'I'm not happy about it, but fine.'

'Such a team player, Jon.'

Nelson took another puff, letting the vapour rest in his chest before a slow exhale through his nostrils. 'Fine.'

Footsteps stomped out in the corridor. Not Reed, but Bridge thundering towards him, cradling her laptop like a newborn. She flashed a smile at Nelson as she sat next to Fenchurch. 'Sir, I've been digging into more of the messages. What I was saying earlier about these men thinking those girls are their girlfriends?'

'I'll never forget.'

'Well, I found some messages from this Keane person . . . It might be me, but I'm worried, sir.' Bridge rested the computer on Fenchurch's desk, far enough away that the text was a blurry blob on a white background. 'He started telling her about how he's going to change the world, cleanse it for their people.'

Fenchurch clenched his fist. 'Their people?'

'White people.' Bridge glanced nervously at Nelson. 'One big act, he says she'll love him for it.'

'Any idea what it is?'

'I might know.' Reed was peering into the room. 'Just had a call from Special Branch, guv. My PNC search alerted them. Keane is flagged as a terror suspect. They want us over there now.'

Chapter Nineteen

M ore of a hotel than a police headquarters, Kay.' Fenchurch climbed up the steps to the front entrance, his knee clicking like his mother was knitting. Scotland Yard loomed above them, eight storeys of stone grandeur. Cost a pretty penny to move from the old place, but some bean counters thought it was worth it. New Scotland Yard was becoming posh flats and the Met were back near where they started. He pushed through the revolving door and showed his ID to the security guards. 'Thought Michelle Grove was CO11, Kay?'

'Was.' Reed held out her own ID. 'Moved from Public Order to Counter Terror last month. SO15.'

'And it's DI Grove now, Sergeant.' Grove was walking towards them, her heels clacking off the flagstones. Plain grey trouser suit and pink blouse, her dark hair trimmed short. Black-framed glasses with neon-lime flashes on the legs. She grabbed Kay and wrapped her in a hug. 'How're you doing?'

'Still a Sergeant.' Reed's smile glared at Fenchurch. 'Anyway, we need to talk about this Keane geezer.'

'This way.' Grove led them towards some glass-sided meeting rooms, pitch-black inside. She popped her head through the door and waved them in.

By the time Fenchurch got there, the lights had flashed on and Grove was sitting at the head of the table. He sat at the opposite end.

Reed took a seat halfway up. 'So, Counter Terror Command, eh?'

'Yeah, it's chaos at times, but it's a promotion. Precious few of them about these days.'

'Tell me about it.' Reed pulled her Pronto out of her jacket pocket. 'So, we've got this murder case. Oliver Keane.'

'And I have to say, it intrigued me when the alert came through.'

'So he's a terror suspect?'

Grove nodded slowly. 'What's your interest?'

'Our victim was a student, worked as a camgirl. She received a lot of messages from Keane. Sexual, businesslike, if you follow me. But there's also some stuff that'd make your hair stand up on end, but for a different reason.'

Grove waved at Reed's quiff. 'As opposed to a can of hairspray each morning?'

'It's only half and it's organic.' Reed smoothed down the page in her notebook. 'So, what can you tell us about him?'

'Precious little, I'm afraid.'

Reed held out her hands. 'Michelle, we've driven over from Leman Street at rush hour. You could've said "no, piss off" over the phone.'

'It's not that . . .' Grove's glower faded. 'I would if I could. He's a terror suspect. That's pretty much all I can tell you.'

'Come on, Michelle . . .'

'Seriously, Kay. Terror trumps murder every time. Now, how about you tell me what you've got, then we'll see where we stand. Okay?'

Fenchurch drummed his fingers on the table. 'I haven't played "you show me yours, I'll show you mine" since primary school. But, anyway, you first.'

'I'll tell you what I can share.' Grove settled on her seat and unbuttoned her jacket, letting it hang loose. 'Okay, so Keane grew up in London, went to Cambridge, then to the States for his PhD. Think he went to Stanford. But anyway, he got a gig in Silicon Valley working for Google. Then a few years running a start-up. Fast forward to now and he's returned to London, having sold up.'

Reed was following it. 'He didn't do an IPO?'

'Sold the start-up.' Grove shook her head. 'Can't remember who to, but it was a decent amount. Saved all the hassle and he didn't have to stay on over there.'

'What's an IPO?'

'Initial Public Offering.' Reed smiled at Fenchurch. 'The owners sell a big chunk of the company to the stock market. It's how they're all billionaires.'

'How much did Keane make?'

'He's not in the three-comma club.' Grove winked at him. 'I mean, he's not a billionaire. But I think it's a hundred million or so. Never needs to work again unless he's very stupid. He's semi-retired now, doing a second degree. Mature student at Southwark, studying Sociology and Social Anthropology. Something that interests him rather than will get him a good job.'

'So why are Special Branch investigating him?'

'I told you, Fenchurch, this can't be quid pro quo.'

'I could've got that from Wikipedia.'

'And it would've saved you a trip across London at rush hour.'

'Come on, none of that's remotely suspicious. You lot don't keep tabs on someone because they're a mature student.'

Reed's hand flashed up, telling Fenchurch to back off. 'Michelle, was Keane planning something?'

'What?'

'Some of the emails he sent the victim, they were terror-related. Said he was going to change the world for white people.'

'Bloody hell.'

Reed got to her feet. 'Guv, time to head back to Leman Street.'

'Wait.' Grove sat forward, bracing against the table edge like there was an earthquake. 'The reason he's on our radar is because he posted a manifesto on his website a few months back. It's fairly eye-watering, to say the least. So right-wing it's practically left again. He was talking about absolute white rule in this country. Deportations, work camps. Then he wanted to reclaim the Empire and populate it with white British people.'

Fenchurch's gut tightened. Acid started spitting. 'How is this guy not in prison?'

'Because . . .' Grove settled back in her chair, gripping the arms. She craned her neck to look out into the corridor. 'I didn't tell you this, but we think he's connected to the English Defence League and its splinter groups. Also, our American cousins think he has ties to some militias from his time over there. Silicon Valley is in northern California. Ish. East and you're into Nevada. North and you're in Oregon. Bandit country. White supremacists, biker gangs, meth labs. Everything.'

'What have you done about him?'

'We've been monitoring him.'

'Surveillance?'

'Of a sort.'

'What about the early hours of Monday morning. Between three and seven.'

'I know for a fact that we didn't have anyone on him then.' Grove held up a finger. 'Now, you show me yours.'

Fenchurch reached into his jacket pocket and got out an email. Slid it over the table to Reed, who passed it along. 'What do you make of this?'

'If this is true, I better change my knickers.' Grove flipped it over and kept on reading. 'We know he's planning something, but we think he could just be all mouth and no trousers.' She put the printout on the desk. 'That's why we haven't moved on him yet.'

Reed scowled. 'Even after the Paris and Nice attacks?'

'This is a different kettle of fish to Islamic terror.' Grove traced her finger along the folds in the paper. 'Highly organised, hierarchical. Not just a load of nutters exploiting angry kids, or some angry kid self-radicalising and blowing himself up. Someone like Oliver Keane isn't going to kill himself for seventy virgins, is he?' She tapped the printout. 'But, anyway, I can't have you going in there and jeopardising our operation.'

'Wouldn't let us in, anyway.'

Grove pinched her nose. 'Kay, tell me you're joking?'

'Wish I was. Quite some place he's got.'

'Those flats on Mansell Street got me this gig. Previous DI dropped a bollock during a raid there in March. Now he's managing traffic on the Westway.' Grove's forehead knitted tighter. 'One of Keane's manifesto points is "forced gentrification of ethnic areas". He bought that whole estate off Tower Hamlets Council to prove what he can do.'

'Michelle.' Reed gave her a broad smile. 'We need to speak to him.'

Grove got up and stood in the doorway. Actually blocked them from leaving. 'You're not going in there.'

Fenchurch walked over, standing face-to-face with Grove. 'This isn't related to hate crimes or American militias. He's a murder suspect, cyber-stalking our victim, pressing her to meet up and have sex. Nothing to do with terror.' He left her a gap, but she didn't fill it. 'So, we're going to speak to him.'

'You've got nothing.'

Fenchurch reached into his pocket and got out a screenshot of the shadowy figure entering Hannah's room. 'This was captured just before the murder.' He held it out, waiting for her to take it. 'You'll agree that it fits Keane's description, yeah? And you can't account for his whereabouts at the time, meaning you're blocking access to a suspect.'

'Look, guys, I know where you're coming from. Believe me.' Grove returned the sheet. 'But this is a monitoring job. That's an order from the Commissioner. If you disagree, you need to escalate.' She checked the emails again. 'And if you want to speak to him, you really need better evidence than this.'

Fenchurch was all out of ideas.

Reed piped up. 'Michelle, does the smell of dead fish mean anything to you?'

'What?' Grove stepped back towards her chair. 'Oh, shit. HMTD.'

'HM-what?'

'Hexamethylene Triperoxide Diamine.' Grove ran a hand through her hair, sending it sticking skywards. 'It's a home-made explosive. Can stink of fish.'

'His house was reeking of it.'

Grove slumped down in her chair. 'Kay, you're making this shit up, aren't you?'

'Michelle, I've known you for years. We went through Hendon together. I wouldn't lie about this.'

'Your guv'nor would, though.' Grove squeezed her knuckles into her eye sockets. 'You can't speak to him. I'm sorry.'

'Come on, if Keane killed Hannah, that gives you leverage to find out what he knows. Plea deals. You name it.'

'Kay, that's a big if. And you know how much of a shitshow the Crown Prosecution Service are in thanks to what happened in June.'

Fenchurch grimaced. 'Don't need to mention that to me.'

Grove hauled herself to her feet. 'I'm not promising anything, but let me run this up the flagpole. Okay?'

———

'She's bloody piece of work.' Fenchurch sat in the window of the Pret a Manger on Mansell Street, drinking coffee from a paper cup. The sort of posh tar that Nelson would drink. Nah, Pret wasn't hip enough for him. 'So you went to Hendon with her?'

'For my sins.' Reed was halfway through a pack of mango fingers. Hadn't even squeezed out the lime. 'She had her son between my two.'

'Son? Thought she was gay.'

'She is.' Reed smiled at him as she chewed. 'One of her colleagues provided the, uh, sperm for her and Ashley.'

'Sam Edwards told me he's a donor.'

Reed put the lid back on her fruit. 'Is there no way that boy won't abuse his body for money?'

'Clearly not.' Fenchurch scanned down the street. 'Unless it's a front for his cuckold services.'

The builders were still at it at this hour, turning old hell flats into yuppie townhouses. Made the place seem different when some white supremacist was using it to prove his mad-bastard theories.

Fenchurch pointed at the crew. 'Must be paying them a pretty penny to still be working.'

'Notice how half are black? Bet the others are Polish, too.' Reed took a sip of tea. 'Couldn't make this shit up, could you?'

His phone blared out. Nelson. 'Guv, I'm still at the hospital.'

'Glad to hear it, Jon.'

'I've taken Sam's statement, not sure what else I can do.'

'Are they letting him go?'

'Still not had his X-ray.'

'Keep on him, Jon. I don't trust him.'

'Guv, I'm not happy about this. I think we're wasting our time with him.'

'Has he said something that gives you that opinion?'

'No, it's . . .' Nelson's sigh hissed down the line. 'Guv, he's a kid. If he killed her, there'd be some signs of him doing it. We've got nothing.'

'He was in a screaming match with her outside her room. A few hours later, she's dead. And he can't account for his movements at the time of death, can he?'

'Says he was asleep. We've checked his housemates, but nobody can confirm or deny it.'

'Keep him there, then we'll talk about it later, okay?'

'Guv, I'm a Detective Sergeant. You really want me to babysit a suspect?'

'I ask you because I trust you, Jon.' Fenchurch killed the call with a sigh. He sipped his coffee, getting too cold to drink now. 'Has he got a point? Should a DS be doing that?'

'I wouldn't be happy.' Reed stuffed her mango tub in the bin. 'And I'm not chasing the career ladder like he is.'

Fenchurch took another drink of coffee. Couldn't get the memory of Nelson's last appraisal out of his head. Him going on and on about getting a promotion. 'He's gone all quiet on that front.'

'That's cos Mulholland's coaching him.'

'What?'

'I've seen them in the canteen, guv.'

'Jesus Christ.'

'Everyone's getting promoted but us.' Reed laughed. 'Am I too close to you?'

'What, you think I've got a shit vortex around me or something?'

'You're at the plughole, guv. And you've not got Docherty to protect you any more.'

'You trying to cheer me up?' Fenchurch sat back and finished his coffee. Definitely too cold to drink. 'I can't stop thinking about Docherty. The guy protected me through the hardest part of my life, now he's . . . And I can't even bring myself to visit him in hospital, Kay. What's wrong with me?'

'It's natural, guv. You'll see him when you're ready—'

'Very cosy.' Grove stood in the doorway, dressed in body armour. An armed officer next to her, similarly attired, drawing as many glances from the rest of the punters in there as he was giving to Reed. Worse than Younis, earlier.

'Okay, so my bosses have reviewed the evidence and, assuming you're on the level about this fish smell, they've approved a raid. We bring him to your station, interview him about the murder, then if there's something there, we'll see where we take it from there.'

'Thanks, Michelle.'

Grove gave a tight nod, as though wearing the armour turned her into a soldier. 'Look lively.'

Fenchurch dumped his cup in the bin and followed Grove and Reed out onto Mansell Street.

A squad huddled outside the Sainsbury's, rifles hanging from their shoulders, gripping the handles, waiting for some direction. Grove headed over and chatted to them. Then it was go.

Two armed officers sprinted up the path towards Keane's house and pushed themselves flat against the wall. A third joined, lugging an Enforcer battering ram.

Fenchurch stayed back with Reed, waiting.

His Airwave rasped. 'This is Serial Bravo. Rear exit secured.'

The officer by the door spoke into his sleeve. 'Serial Alpha. Kitchen entrance secured.'

Grove nodded at them. 'Let's go!'

By the time Fenchurch and Reed were at the door, the two officers had the glass door off the rails and were stomping into Keane's flat. 'Kitchen, clear.'

Grove joined them, then set off into a hallway. Fenchurch followed, gripping his baton tight. Hard to feel it was adequate when they were all wandering round with guns.

The hallway was a glass-roofed atrium, probably would've been a garden between two blocks before the renovation. A staircase climbed up to the higher floors.

A pair of officers bustled past them, taking a door on the right. Grove took one ahead of them.

'Lounge clear.'

'Bathroom clear.'

Grove pointed up the staircase. 'Thwaite, you go first.'

'Ma'am.' The officer from the Pret took his time idling up. Grove followed, repeating the manoeuvre. Fenchurch's baton was sweaty in his grip. Grove and Thwaite went over to the first of three doors.

'Bedroom, clear.'

They came back out and Grove pointed at a second door. Thwaite opened it slowly, then raised a finger in warning. 'Contact.' He waited until Grove was in position, then stepped inside.

Fenchurch followed Grove, Reed close behind him.

Keane sat by a window framing the City skyline, working at a laptop, bobbing his head in time to a beat blasting out of huge speakers. He wore a plain black polo neck and bleached jeans. He jerked round, eyes wide, then raised his hands. 'I am not speaking to you. I am maintaining my silence.' His phone lay on the desk, flashing.

Thwaite swivelled round the room until he was behind Keane. Grove got in next to him. Another two armed officers piled in, squeezing Fenchurch and Reed to the sides.

'I request legal advice! I am maintaining my silence!'

Grove frowned at Fenchurch through her mask, then raised her pistol to point at Keane's head. 'On your knees!'

'I request legal advice!' Keane shot to his feet, looking round the room. Spent a few seconds checking out Thwaite.

Someone muttered, 'Shut up, gimp.'

That's the last thing we bloody need. His phone picking up that sort of shit.

Fenchurch nudged past an armed officer and stepped over to Keane. He locked eyes with Thwaite, trying to figure out if he was the culprit. Then he focused on Keane. 'We know about the HMTD.'

'What?' Keane stepped forward, his forehead twitching. 'HMTD?'

'You're making a bomb in here.' Fenchurch glanced at Grove. 'We smelled it earlier.'

'You've got nothing on me.' Keane twisted so he was side on to them. Then he lurched back to the desk.

A gunshot blasted round the room, white noise whistling in Fenchurch's ear.

Keane tumbled over. Landed hard. A knife toppled to the floor, digging into the wooden boards.

Fenchurch raced over to Keane. Gargling, face down, a red pool spreading out across the floorboards, dripping between the cracks. Fenchurch flipped him over. A bullet wound dug into his chest, right in the heart.

Dead.

Grove grabbed Thwaite and pushed him against the wall. Fenchurch couldn't make out a word she said.

Chapter Twenty

Oliver Keane lay on the floor, his pale jeans mostly red now. Fenchurch was leaning against the wall. A police shooting. On Fenchurch's watch. Grove's watch, really, but . . . Shit.

'You okay, guv?' Reed was by the door, her phone pressed against her chest.

'Need a hearing test, but otherwise I'm fine. You?'

'I've got to get back to the Incident Room.'

'I'll take it from here.'

'Guv.' She left him to his thoughts.

A gang of CSIs arrived and started doing their thing. A house this big could take weeks to process. On top of the work that was already overdue on Hannah's room.

Disaster.

Keane had lunged for the knife, though. If Thwaite hadn't shot him, maybe Fenchurch would be the one going to Lewisham in a body bag.

But that was the end of the line with Keane. Whatever he meant by the messages to Hannah had died with him. Any plots or plans were gone. Any links to extremist groups.

Unless his computers could give up any of his secrets. At least ten machines in the room, all humming. Laptops and desktops. Decent kit, too.

The one Keane had been working on was still unlocked. Fenchurch slid a glass paperweight onto the spacebar to stop it locking.

Grove's breath hissed out slowly. 'Well.'

'I'm sorry, Michelle. This is on me.'

'My operation, Simon. My mistake.' Grove raised her eyebrows. 'Why did he have to shoot?'

'Might've saved your life or mine, Michelle. We were closest.'

She took one glimpse at the blood pool and gave her own entry to the world's biggest sigh contest. 'Did you hear someone say "gimp"?'

'Was it Thwaite?'

'Could've been. So much happening and I was focusing on Keane.'

'The IPCC will be in before we can blink.'

'Don't doubt it.' Grove's mobile chimed. She checked it and upgraded her sigh-contest entry. 'Okay, that's the boss. Back in a sec.' She got up and wandered off, phone to her head.

Fenchurch caught a glare off a CSI. Clooney, if he had to bet on it. 'You getting anything, Mick?'

'Sweet Fanny Adams, Si, but then we've only been at this five minutes.'

'We thought he was making a bomb.'

Clooney surveyed the room, frowning at his team. 'Are you winding me up?'

'I was here earlier, smelled dead fish. Grove thought it was something.'

Clooney shot off across the room. 'Everyone out!'

'I need to speak to Superintendent Loftus.' Fenchurch clutched the phone. His hands were still shaking. Either too much caffeine or . . .

Or someone getting shot inches from him.

'I'm sorry, Inspector, but Julian is in a session with DI Mulholland.' Loftus's assistant's voice could've been some AI home assistant thing, so cold and unemotional. 'I'll get him to—'

'I need you to get him out. It's urgent.'

'It's always *urgent*, Inspector.'

'Tell him there's been a police shooting.'

The assistant growled down the phone line, finally showing some emotion. 'I shall pass on the message.'

'Thanks.' Fenchurch hung up and took another look around Keane's front garden.

Still no sounds of bombs going off, just Clooney stepping in a deep puddle. 'Crap!' He glowered at Fenchurch. 'False alarm.'

'No bomb?'

'Oh no, we found some HMTD, but it's in a gel container.' Clooney showed Fenchurch his tablet, an image of a fish tank, some small orbs floating in yellow liquid. 'It's not going off this side of a sizeable earthquake.' He snorted. 'Nasty stuff, though. Some al-Qaeda types tried using it in New York and New Jersey back in September. This could've been a disaster if it'd got into the wrong hands.'

'Keane is the wrong hands.' Fenchurch frowned at Clooney as he pointed over the road. 'One of those New World Order, white-supremacist types.'

'Oh, Christ.' Clooney exhaled slowly. 'That kind of changes things a bit. Why does this shit always happen to you, Si?'

Fenchurch took a sip of tea. 'Wish I knew, Mick.'

Clooney charged off, shaking his head. Poor bastard.

'Simon.' Grove was lurking beside him, pocketing her phone. 'My boss just told me that the IPCC are here already. The second there's a police shooting . . .'

'Who are they sending? Abercrombie?'

Grove focused on him again. 'You know her?'

'Not intimately.' Fenchurch looked around conspiratorially then gave her a flash of his eyebrows. 'I really need to interview Thwaite.'

'Why?'

'Trouble has a habit of following me around. I want to satisfy myself that it's just a police shooting. Nothing more. This doesn't quite sit right with me. We wanted Keane for a murder. You lot wanted him for all sorts of terror malarkey. I can accept it if this shooting was just an accident, but I want to *know* it's just an accident.'

Grove stared off into the middle distance, in the vague direction of Leman Street. 'We can't just blunder in there and grab hold of him. More than our careers are worth.'

'Well, how about you and me have a little chat with Abercrombie, see if we can get some time with Thwaite before all the stupidity starts?'

Grove ran a hand through her hair. 'There's no persuading you otherwise, is there?'

They found Zenna Abercrombie in a meeting space near the interview rooms, huddled with a six-strong team. Amazing how fast the IPCC can mobilise. She was hammering a laptop, only pausing when Grove knocked the door jamb. 'One second.' Every inch the Greek princess living on her daddy's yacht, just with the voice of a Wapping docker. She shut the lid and looked up, then let out a groan. Very professional. 'Fenchurch. Had to be you, didn't it?'

'That's no way to greet me, Zenna.'

She passed off her laptop to a colleague. 'Sarah, can you complete sections four to eleven, please?' Her underling took it without any more than a nod. Zenna focused on Fenchurch, her dark eyes narrowing at him. 'Now, you do understand that the Independent Police Complaints

Commission is independent, right? We're here to make sure you're accountable for your actions.'

'And here was me wondering if we could scratch each other's backs.' Fenchurch rested against the door frame. 'Richard Thwaite killed a murder suspect.' He thumbed at Grove. 'Michelle here wanted that suspect in connection to a domestic terror case. Possibly international links.'

'And?'

'And we've got evidence against the victim here. He might be a murderer. Might be working with people who want to do some very nasty things to a lot of people. I want to find out if the reason he's dead is anything to do with my investigation into a young student's murder. Michelle wants to stop people blowing each other up. This might be related.'

'And operational policing butts up against my agenda yet again.' Zenna let out a well-worn sigh and puckered her lips. 'Just so we're clear, this is my investigation. I'm only interested in finding out the truth here. Who did what. Who is culpable for what.'

'And we can help. Let us in the room with Thwaite. Let me satisfy my curiosity.'

'You're not letting this one go without a fight, are you?'

'You know me. I can escalate if I need to.'

'Right.' Zenna picked up a bulging document holder and hugged it tight. 'I'm going to start interviewing him while he's still fresh and traumatised, see what he spills. If I can guarantee full co-operation from both of you, then we can clear your queries first. Okay?'

'Fine with me.' Fenchurch gave his best grin. Seemed to dent her armour a little.

'And me.' Grove nibbled at her lip. 'Only thing is, he was off with stress for six months, beginning of last year.'

'That's all I need . . .' Zenna barged between them, heading to the interview room.

PC Richard Thwaite sat playing with his St Christopher. Bastard thing kept catching the light as he twisted it round. *Someone should take it off him. If he opens a vein . . .*

'Richard, you shot him, didn't you?' Grove was drumming her fingers on the table. Kept glancing at Zenna next to her, as if she was seeking approval. 'You shot my operational target. We were supposed to bring him in.'

More fiddling.

Fenchurch was leaning against the door, arms folded. 'Why did you do it, Richard?'

A sharp tug, not quite enough to yank the chain apart. Thwaite didn't look at him, didn't look at either Grove or Zenna. Just stared at the desk, twisting the cross.

'Why did you murder him, Richard?'

'It was an itchy trigger finger. I swear. I was saving you.' Thwaite dug one of the corners of the cross into his thumbnail. 'Keane reached for the knife. You were closest. Then DI Grove.'

'So you shot him?'

'I reacted. Aimed for centre mass.'

'Centre mass isn't his heart, Richard.'

Thwaite let go of the St Christopher. 'He moved. Fast. Like a greyhound out of the traps.'

'I don't believe you.' Grove leaned forward on the table, elbows thunking against the wood. Thwaite picked up the St Christopher. 'He looked at you for a good few seconds. Did you know him?'

'Course I didn't.' Thwaite pushed himself from the table. 'Course I didn't. You must think I know half of London, or something.'

'No, just Oliver Keane.'

'You're full of shit.' Thwaite ran his tongue over his lips. 'How could I know him?'

'Happens more often than you'd think.' Fenchurch folded his arms. 'Someone muttered "gimp" in there. It was you, wasn't it?'

163

Thwaite clutched his St Christopher like it would ward off the devil. Or at least Fenchurch. 'He went for a knife.' He rocked back and forth, twisting to the side. 'Went for a knife.' Then he retched, spraying vomit on the floor and up the wall. He wiped his lips, swallowing with some pain.

Fenchurch got up and snatched the St Christopher off Thwaite's neck, snapping the links in the chain. Then he got in Thwaite's face, getting a lungful of vinegary sick. 'Why did you shoot him?'

Twitching fingers searched for the St Christopher. 'I want a lawyer. Now.'

⌣

'That's about the bloody *limit*.' Loftus thumped a fist on Docherty's desk. Made the Rangers mug jump in the air. Landed perfectly, but spilled coffee over the varnished wood. 'Another death on your conscience, eh? It should go without saying that I will *not* be covering for you.'

'I'm not asking you to, sir.' Fenchurch wanted to look away, but didn't. Kept up the eye contact, wanting Loftus to look away. 'This was a joint operation with SO15. They ran it, given their skillset and the likely terror angle. DS Reed and I were only there in a support capacity. The shooter, Richard Thwaite, is one of their officers.'

'Trying to wriggle out of it, eh?' Loftus sneered at him. 'You've beaten the snot out of suspects like it's still the seventies. You've had an officer lose an arm in an ill-advised chase. Five months ago, a suspect died in custody. Then there's all that stuff with your father and . . .' He squeezed his thumb and forefinger tight together. 'Inspector, you're *this* close to triggering an internal investigation.'

'Why don't you? Could it be because *none* of those were my fault?'

'Always back to blame with you. You're made of Teflon. Nothing sticks to you, does it?'

'I've been a DI for over ten years, sir. I'd say that stuff does stick to me, otherwise I'd be in your chair by now.'

Loftus bellowed out a laugh. 'Dear God, I haven't heard anything that funny in a long time.'

'I'm serious, sir.' Fenchurch grabbed the arms of the chair tight, in case he lurched across and smacked Loftus in the chops. 'You can distrust me all you want, but I'm clean.'

'Really.' Loftus picked up the Rangers mug, his nostrils twitching as he gulped. He set it down with a thump. 'So, where does this death leave us?'

'We've lost a suspect, sir. That's not good in anyone's book.'

'No. No, it's not. And how likely was he?'

Fenchurch shrugged. 'Probably a Champions League spot.'

'Do you have anything that might set into concrete?'

'All our evidence is vague and indicative at best. We needed to get Keane on the record.'

'And what did SO12 have on him?'

'SO15, sir.'

'I don't like a smart-arse.' Loftus took another sip from Docherty's Rangers mug. 'What did they have on you?' He growled. 'I mean on him. Keane.'

'Terror suspect on watch, sir. Links to the far right, both here and in the States. We suspected he was making a bomb. Mick Clooney found one, safe enough, but a bomb.'

'When you say "we", did this suspicion come from you?'

'It did, sir. DS Reed and I visited his property this afternoon and smelled dead fish.'

'Dead fish?'

'Sir. Like he was smoking kippers or something. Really strong. We raised it with DI Grove and she told us that it's indicative of a certain type of home-made explosive. HMTD. Can't rememb—'

'I *know* what it stands for.' Loftus stared deep into the mug, licking his lips slowly, then back at Fenchurch. 'If I find out that you fabricated this evidence, the hot coals I haul you over will be the least of your worries.'

'Sir.'

'I need you to report this to DI Mulholland. Immediately.'

Fenchurch froze. So this was how it was going to play out, was it? Reporting to Mulholland. Bugger that. 'Sir, there's something you should know about DI Mulholland.'

'I'm all ears.'

Someone knocked at the door. Mulholland stood there, grinning like she'd got a new cauldron. Speak of the devil, and she will appear. 'Sir, we've got something you might want to see.' DC Bridge was next to her, clutching a silver laptop in an evidence bag.

'Come on in, Dawn. Make yourself at home. DI Fenchurch was just about to enlighten me as to something critical.' Loftus held out a hand to Bridge. 'Don't think we've had the pleasure?'

'DC Bridge, sir.' She shook it. 'Lisa.'

'Good, good. Well, Fenchurch, out with it.'

Fenchurch locked eyes with Mulholland. He could tell she knew what he was about to say. He cleared his throat and shifted his gaze to Bridge. 'Lisa, what have you got?'

'Forensics are in Keane's house just now.' Bridge put the bagged laptop on the table, the white Apple logo cut out of the silver metal. 'They've found two MacBook Pros.'

'*Two?*' Fenchurch frowned at her. 'Are either—'

'One of them matches Hannah's serial number. The other's from the same batch.'

'Can you get into either?'

'IT are cloning Hannah's just now, sir.' Bridge produced her own laptop from somewhere and showed a clone window, a copy of the computer accessible on hers for evidentiary reasons. 'I've been looking at the other one. Thing is, we don't know who owned it. The account says "Administrator".'

'It's probably Mr Keane's own.' Mulholland was practically purring. 'But the fact we've found Hannah's missing laptop in his house, well. I'd say that this means we've got a prime suspect for her murder.'

'Indeed.' Loftus nodded slowly, a smile flashing over his lips. 'But one who's unfortunately dead.'

'Better a dead murderer than a live one.' Mulholland shut her eyes, as though she regretted it before she said it.

Loftus ignored it and got to his feet. 'Okay, please get this logged, Louise.' Bridge stood there, nodding. Didn't correct him. 'Dawn, you and I shall have a word with the CPS.'

Fenchurch frowned. 'What about me, sir? It's my—'

'It's late, Inspector. Time you got home.'

Chapter Twenty-One

Fenchurch squeaked down the hospital corridor, unsure whether his shoes or his knee needed oiling more. No sign of Nelson outside Sam's room, just the same pimply uniform as earlier. 'Have you seen DS Nelson?'

'Eh, no, sir. Not for an hour, sir.'

'Bloody hell.' Fenchurch entered the room.

Sam was lying on the bed, staring at the ceiling. He glanced over, then went back to counting cobwebs.

Fenchurch pulled up a seat and perched on it. 'How you doing?'

'What do you care?'

'I do worry about people, you know.' Fenchurch settled back into the chair and folded his arms. 'I stopped that bloke killing you, for example. All part of the job.'

'I can handle myself.'

'Yeah? That why he put you in here?'

Sam didn't reply.

'What's the prognosis?'

'No bones broken. Slight tear to a ligament in my ankle. The bite will heal. Just leave a small scar.'

'Why are you still here, then? You're frightened of Galbraith, aren't you?'

'Wouldn't you be?'

'I wouldn't be giving his wife a portion.' Fenchurch spotted the smirk on Sam's face. 'Then again, I've not got the equipment for that line of work.'

'Neither have I.' Sam looked down at his crotch. 'Believe me, mine's normal-sized.' He scratched at his neck. 'According to his wife, Galbraith's isn't.' He put his thumb and forefinger together. Reminded Fenchurch of how close Loftus thought he was to getting the boot. 'As small as Hitler's, if you believe the stories.'

'You should register as a charity, or something.'

Sam chuckled, then sat up in his bed. 'Why are you here?'

'Does the name Oliver Keane ring any bells?'

'A couple.'

'Any idea why he'd have Hannah's laptop?'

'What?'

'We just raided his house. He was working on it at the time.'

'Jesus.'

'When did you last see that machine?'

Sam frowned, like he could see back into the past. 'I mean, I don't make a habit of keeping an inventory of her stuff, but I think we watched some Netflix on Sunday night. Before the . . . you know. Argument.'

'Remember what?'

'Think it was *It's Always Sunny in Philadelphia*. Our third time through it.' Sam adjusted his position in his bed. 'Do you think this Keane guy killed her?'

'We've put him at the top of the suspects board. Moves you down a bit.'

Sam's mouth hung open. 'You *honestly* think I killed her?'

'You had a big argument with her.'

'Piss off, you prick.'

'You could help me.'

'What? How?'

'Hannah's laptop password would be a start.'

'Does Mrs Fenchurch know yours?'

'Of course. She had to set it up for me.'

'Well, Hannah didn't share it with me. She wasn't an idiot.'

'Any ideas what it could be?'

'Passwords are supposed to be secret. If I could guess, it wouldn't be secret, would it?'

'We found another MacBook with hers. Any idea whose it was?'

'How should I know?' Sam pulled himself up to sitting. The bed sheet dropped to the floor. His ankle was strapped, the pyjama bottoms rolled up. 'I'm getting out of here.'

'Sam. Whose laptop is it?'

'I have no idea.' Sam reached down for a shoe and tugged out the laces. 'Now, if you want anything more out of me, I'll need a lawyer.'

Kid wasn't messing about. 'This because you know Oliver Keane?'

'I don't know him, but . . . Hannah talked about him. Guy was stalking her.'

'You didn't think to sort him out?'

'I tried the whole chivalrous thing but she wouldn't let me.'

'You didn't go behind her back?'

'No.' Sam was working at the other foot now, wincing. 'Look, I want a lawyer.'

'Son, your girlfriend's lying on a slab out in Lewisham and I would've thought you'd want her killer brought to justice.'

Sam stared at him for a few seconds then looked away. 'Listen, my old man was fitted up by the police. Lost his job because of it. It's not personal, but . . . I just don't trust cops.'

'You can trust me.'

'Can I?' Sam's shoulders deflated. 'I'm sorry. I'm finding this hard.'

'It's not easy, son. What did Hannah say about Keane?'

'Nothing. Guy was sleazing over her online. Watching her Facebook and Twitter pages. Sending messages.'

'She never went to the police?'

'Wasn't that serious, far as I could tell. I can ask her mates, see if any of them heard anything?'

'Do that. And give me a ring, okay?' Fenchurch left him in the room.

PC Pimples stood up to attention. 'Sir.'

'Give him a lift home, okay?'

'Sir.' Pimples put his hat on, pulling the strap below his chin. 'Oh, Control said DS Nelson is off duty.'

'Is he, now?'

'You're Fenchurch, aren't you?'

'Why?'

'DS Nelson said some old man was here to speak to that lad.'

'You got a name?'

Pimples checked through some paperwork. 'Yeah, it's Ian— Oh. Fenchurch.'

Jesus Christ, Dad.

Fenchurch tried to cover his sigh with a smile. 'Get DS Nelson to call me, please.' He walked off, putting his phone to his ear. Nelson's number rang and rang. He tried Reed instead.

'Guv?'

'Kay, seen Jon recently?'

'Not for a while, why?'

'No reason. Have a good evening.'

'Guv, Lisa said they're treating Keane as the chief suspect?'

'That's right. She still there?'

'Nah, she knocked off about twenty minutes ago. She's been stuck with Mulholland and Loftus.'

'Bet she has. See you tomorrow.' Fenchurch killed the call.

No choice but to go and see Docherty.

Fenchurch stood outside the ward. Felt like he'd been there for half an hour, trapped in indecision. He checked his watch. He had been.

Come on, you twat. Get in there. Just. Go.

Fenchurch pushed the door open and walked in. Six beds. The first three could've been body bags the state their occupants were in. Nearest, a young lad sat with his family, pipes and wires coming out of the poor bastard.

Docherty was nearest the window. Eyes open, at least. Headphones on, reading a book, coughing like a miner.

Can't be too bad.

Fenchurch sidled up to the bed and rested against the chair, leaning forward. 'There you are, boss.'

'Simon?' Docherty's frown creased his forehead. 'About bloody time.'

'I got you this.' Fenchurch passed him a bottle of Lucozade.

Docherty shot him a wink. 'This isn't going to be much use against terminal cancer.'

Fenchurch's gut clenched. He collapsed into the chair. 'There's no hope?'

'It's just sugar and water. Unless you've stuck some single malt in it?'

Fenchurch felt like he'd fallen through the bottom of the chair and kept on falling, down and down. 'They told you it's terminal?'

'Heathrow Terminal Five, but worse.' Docherty twisted the lid on the bottle. Still had enough strength to do that, at least. 'Get yourself a cup.'

Fenchurch picked up two, his hands shaking almost as much as Docherty's as he poured. He handed one over and took a drink from the other, nowhere near quenching his thirst. 'I'm sorry I've not been in.'

Docherty took a sip and grimaced. 'Jesus, that's vile.' Then started coughing again. His lungs sounded ready to burst out through his mouth. 'Heard you got a result in that girl's death, though.'

'How did you hear?'

'Loftus.' Docherty rubbed his fingers over his lips. 'Sounds promising, though.'

'We'll see how it goes.' Another sip of the orange gunk.

'South London call him Lord Julian.' Docherty grinned. 'How you getting on with him?'

'House on fire, boss.' Fenchurch's fingers tightened around the cup. 'But I'm stuck inside and he's not letting me out.'

'Ah, good old Julian.' Docherty snarled. Then started crying. Tears streaming down his cheeks. 'I'm such an idiot.'

'What's up?'

Docherty held his gaze for a few seconds. 'Si, I found a lump on a ball about a year ago. Wanted to go to the doctor's but . . . something always came up. Work. Kids. Something. Anything. So I didn't get round to going to the doctor's.' He pinched his nose. 'Stage four. Stage fucking four.'

Fenchurch's own balls had tightened, stuck up to his guts. He couldn't speak. He tried but just croaked. Another splash of Lucozade and a sip. 'Boss . . . I wish there was something I could do. Something I could say.'

'Nobody can do anything for me. Six weeks, they said. Six. Weeks.' Docherty rubbed his tears across his cheeks. 'Enough about me. Si, you need to clean up your act. All the covering up I've done for you, all that anger, battering people like Kamal and those vermin that stole your daughter. Loftus won't stand for it. Your next boss won't stand for it, whoever that is.'

'I've already had my nuts toasted.' Fenchurch regretted the words as soon as he'd said them. 'Sorry.'

'It's fine, Si. Christ, I'm the idiot here. Not you.' Docherty finished his cup. 'So, this suspect?'

'That case is the last thing you should be worrying about, boss.'

'Shut up. I need something to take my mind off this.'

'I shouldn't—'

'Doc!' Fenchurch's dad strolled over, grinning, tomato soup coating his moustache.

Docherty laughed. 'How you doing, you old bastard?'

'A lot better than you, by the sounds of things.'

'Si, get your old boy a glass, eh? Finest ten-week-old Lucozade. Very peaty, though, Ian.'

'Smashing.' Dad did the honours himself, downing a glass in one go. 'Either of you ever have this stuff with vodka? Lovely.' He poured another and held it up in a toast. 'Simon, I hear you've caught that girl's killer?'

Docherty scowled at him. 'Why didn't you tell me?'

'Because I'm not convinced yet.' Fenchurch leaned over to his dad. 'You've clearly still got irons in the fire.'

'Jon Nelson told me.'

'Dad, you're not a cop any more. You can't be snooping around suspects and witnesses.'

'I'm discreet.'

'Hardly. Either way, you need to keep your distance.'

'My lips are sealed, son.'

Fenchurch thundered up the staircase towards his old flat, the carpet getting a bit rough round the edges. He thumped on the door and waited. *Bloody Nelson. Never give your friends anything.*

The door opened to the security chain and Nelson peered out. 'Guv?'

'Open up, Jon.'

'Can we do this tomorrow?'

Fenchurch laughed. 'You really think I'd come out to the Isle of bloody Dogs on my way home to Islington just so we can do this tomorrow?'

'Guv, I'm in the middle of something and—'

'What have you been telling my old man?'

'Just a second.' The door clicked shut.

Cheeky bastard. Not even paying rent. Never do anyone a bloody favour ever again.

The door opened wide and Nelson stood to the side, wearing a silk dressing gown. 'In you come.'

'That's a smashing blouse, Jon.'

'Piss off.' Nelson shut the door and led him through to the kitchen. Looked like Oliver Keane's bomb had gone off in here. Foil curry containers on the counter, red and orange sauce dripping on the fake granite. Empty bottle of red. Plates everywhere. And all in one day. 'Sorry about the mess.'

'Glad you acknowledge it. I'm supposed to be having viewings, Jon.'

'It'll be clean, I swear.' Nelson rested on the stool at the breakfast bar and forked out a lump of meat from the nearest container. 'You had much interest?'

'Jon, I'm not here about that.' Fenchurch scanned around the room for any other damage. Seemed fine, but you never knew. 'I visited Docherty.'

'How is he?'

'They're talking weeks.' A stab in the gut, like someone had stuck a knife in. 'Weeks . . .'

'You can talk to me, guv.'

'Jon, you left Sam Edwards on his own. After I explicitly told you to stay with him.'

'My shift ended.'

'You didn't call me.'

'Really? "Please, sir, can I go home now? Please, sir, can I go to the toilet?" Eh?'

'Don't be stupid, Jon. I expect you to tell me what the state of play is before you piss off for the night. Act like an adult. But if you want to be treated like a child . . . ?'

Nelson broke off eye contact to focus on cold curry. 'Sorry. You're right. I should've phoned.'

'You should've. And you definitely shouldn't have let my old man anywhere near him.'

Nelson dropped the fork into the red mush.

'Jon, he spoke to Sam Edwards. Why did you let him in?'

Nelson started stacking up the curry boxes in the sink. 'I . . .'

'He's not an officer any more. Not since . . . that shit in June. He might not have killed Blunden, but he let himself get into the state where they could frame him.'

'Then you need to keep him under control, guv.'

'If you let him speak to suspects, then what's the bloody point in me warning him?' Fenchurch let the question rattle around the room.

Nelson turned on the tap and water blasted the curry trays.

'Why was he asking?'

'He's got it in his head that this is connected to Chloe's disappearance and—'

'Oh, Jesus.' Fenchurch had to prop himself up on the breakfast bar. 'Seriously?'

'Seriously.'

'How did he find out about this?'

'Not me, guv.' Nelson was blushing. 'He's got contacts. Hundreds. Could be any one of them.'

Fenchurch clicked his tongue a few times. 'I suspect Sam'll be home by now. Leave dealing with my old man to me, okay?'

'Guv.' Nelson was scrubbing at the top tray, really working it. How much curry did one man need? He had to shout over the white noise. 'Only problem is, DI Mulholland told me to get evidence against Oliver Keane?'

'That's right.'

'We're going after a dead man?'

Fenchurch sat on the stool, the energy seeping out of him. 'It all fits. He had her laptop. Guy was making a bomb. He wanted to impress Hannah. Threw thousands at her for that computer stripping shit.'

'And the guy was worth millions, wasn't he?'

'At least a hundred.'

Nelson stopped with the dishes. 'I'm struggling to see why he'd kill her.'

'That's what Loftus wants Mulholland and me to focus on now. Close it all off.'

'Guv, if she's wrong, the real killer's still out there. Could strike again.'

Fenchurch couldn't help but look out of the French doors to the cold outside. Couldn't help but think of Chloe, lying asleep in her room in halls when the killer breaks in during the night and—

Click.

'Did you hear that?' Fenchurch knew every sound in his flat off by heart. Every door. The electricity meter. Every click of laminate. The fridge hum. That was the front door opening. Someone was in the flat. Someone trying to kill Fenchurch. Or someone who knew Nelson was in here on his own.

Fenchurch edged through the kitchen, taking it slow.

Nelson was behind him. 'Guv, I didn't hear anything.'

Out into the hall and Fenchurch caught the flat door shutting. He grabbed it before it hit the lock, pulled it, then flew out into the corridor.

Lisa Bridge spun round. 'Shit!'

Chapter Twenty-Two

Nelson pushed the door shut and put an arm around Bridge. Neither of them could even look at Fenchurch. 'Guv, I—'

'Jon, hold that thought.' Fenchurch caught Bridge's attention. 'Lisa, I'll see you at the briefing. Eight sharp, okay?'

'Sir.' She pecked Nelson on the cheek and left them to it.

'Guv, I don't know what to say.'

'You could start with the truth.' Fenchurch got in Nelson's face, even though he was a few inches taller. 'Then you can move on to apologising for lying to me, Jon. This is why Kate kicked you out, isn't it?'

'Sorry.' Nelson collapsed against the door and sighed, ready to confide in someone. 'Wasn't just text messages. We'd been seeing each other for a few months. One Friday, Kate was supposed to be at her sister's for the whole weekend. I bumped into Lisa in the pub after work. Went for dinner and . . . Well, one thing led to another and, instead of going to her place, we went to mine.' His head hung low. 'And Kate caught us.'

'I hate people lying to me.' Fenchurch bared his teeth, some animal instinct taking over. 'You're not a management consultant any more. Lying's about ninety per cent of the game with that lot. You're a cop,

Jon. You've got to give evidence in court. People have to know you're telling the truth.' He stabbed a finger into his own sternum. '*I* need to.'

'This is the *only* time I've not been straight with you. Ever.'

'You expect me to believe that?'

'Have you any reason not to?'

'Jon, you decided to screw a direct report in your own bed.' Fenchurch prodded Nelson's chest through the silk. 'Not only are you an idiot, but it's seriously unprofessional.'

'Guv, I'm sorry, but . . . we've got something.' Nelson's head hung low again. 'I'll switch her back to Kay tomorrow.'

'And what about your wife, Jon? Ten years down the tubes for a tumble with her?'

'It's *my* life, guv.' Steel glinted in Nelson's eyes. Could see he believed he was in love with Bridge. 'Besides, Kate and I don't have any kids.'

'You want kids with Lisa?'

Nelson shrugged.

'Oh, Jesus H. Christ.' Fenchurch rubbed his palms into his eye sockets. 'Make sure she gets on with her work. I need her to focus on getting evidence off those laptops, okay?'

'Guv.'

'And no more leaking shit to my old man.'

Nelson scratched his head. 'Old Bert who worked with your dad at the Archive?' He rubbed at his nose and thumbed at the door. 'He's Lisa's uncle.'

'Why doesn't anybody tell me anything about my own bloody case?'

'She had to go over there, asking for some stuff on Keane, as per your orders. Then, well. Bert and your old man, they pressed and pressed, then started taking over.'

'You don't let them in, Jon, okay? Those pair . . . Never let them anywhere near a case. Right?'

'Message received, guv.'

What a shambles. Where to go from here?

Fenchurch's phone chimed out a reminder. 'Hannah candlelit vigil.' He grabbed Nelson's arm. 'Jon, get dressed. You're coming with me.'

———⌣———

'Guv, seriously, what's the point in this?' Nelson walked alongside Fenchurch toward Jaines Tower.

Singing came from the quad, hard to make it out. They turned the corner and the music was clearer. Someone singing 'There Is a Light That Never Goes Out' by The Smiths.

Gordon McLaren stood on a makeshift stage, wearing lime dungarees and a pink top, strumming an acoustic guitar, veins in his neck straining, his voice raw with emotion as the crowd sang along. They continued chanting the refrain as he passed the guitar to a male student.

'This is an Ed Sheeran song that Hannah loved.'

Fenchurch looked for faces he recognised. Victoria Summerton was with a group of girls singing along. Uttley and some of his support staff were over at the entrance to Jaines Tower, arms folded, solemn and officious.

As the chords jangled out, McLaren walked away, wrapping his arm round a woman. Tall and slender, wearing jeans and a shirt, her wedding ring matching McLaren's. Two kids swarmed around their parents' legs. McLaren hefted his daughter up into his arms and pinched her cheek. His son hugged him tight.

Fenchurch set off towards him, but his phone blared out 'Thank You' by Led Zeppelin. Abi's personal ringtone. His heart skipped a beat. *Is the baby okay?* 'You okay, love?'

'Yeah, why wouldn't I be?'

Fenchurch shooed Nelson away. 'What's up?'

'Wondering where you are, Simon. Jesus, is that *Ed Sheeran*?'

'It's not him. I'm at Hannah Nunn's vigil.' Fenchurch locked eyes with Nelson. 'No accounting for taste.'

'Okay. My parents are insisting on taking us out for dinner. We're meeting your father in Shoreditch.'

'I'll be twenty minutes. Text me the address.' Fenchurch killed the call. 'Jon, can you stay and see if anyone turns up that we don't think should have.'

'Guv, come on—'

'Jon, no messing about, okay? You owe me.'

'Guv.'

Fenchurch parked on the street, already feeling dread. Not at seeing his father or Abi's parents. Well, not completely.

The address in Abi's text, the restaurant . . . It was where the Alicorn used to be. A lap-dancing bar Fenchurch shut down at Christmas. Typical London, blink and half the city changes. The place used to be black, even the windows, but they'd opened out all the painted-shut windows. And named it Noir.

Abi was in the window, smiling politely at her parents opposite her. Fenchurch walked through the front door and nodded at the maître d' as he wandered over to the table.

Dad sat at the end, resting on his elbows. 'Simon!' He got up and wrapped his son in a hug. At least three sheets to the wind.

Fenchurch sat next to Abi and pecked her on the cheek. 'Nice of you to give me advance warning.'

'Abi's already ordered for you.' Dad took a gulp of beer. 'We couldn't wait.'

Jim and Evelyn stared into their full wine glasses, clear of finger-prints. Like they were at a wake, not a slap-up dinner. Jim managed a slight nod.

'Have a taste of that, son.' Dad passed his glass. 'Lovely stuff.'

Fenchurch had a sniff. Smelled like a can of Lilt. 'Cheers, Dad.' He took a sip. Tasted like Lilt. 'What's that?'

'Made by some microbrewery in Hackney. Called "Lilt", I think.' Dad shrugged and took another glug. 'Bert's been on about this place to me. They serve black pizza.'

Fenchurch leaned in close. 'Dad, I've told you about the racism.'

'Simon, for crying out loud.' Dad held out his arms. 'The dough's cut with charcoal.' Then patted his stomach. 'Helps the digestion.'

Abi clasped Fenchurch's hand. 'I've ordered you a steak fajita one.'

'Thanks. I'm starving.' Fenchurch reached over for the red and splashed some into his glass. The bottle said it was from Shrewsbury. He had a sip. Surprisingly nice. He leaned in to whisper to Abi. 'What's up with your parents?'

'It's a nightmare.' Then Abi smiled at her mum. 'Tell Simon what you got up to today.'

'Abigail . . .' Evelyn glared at her daughter like she was ten years old again.

'Come on, Mum. You came all the way up from Cornwall, so why don't you tell Simon what you got up to?'

'Abigail, that's unbecoming.' Jim reached for his wine and took a gentle sip. 'Well, if you must know, Simon, this afternoon, we paid a visit to Chloe.' Another sip, longer this time. 'She refused to see us.' He gritted his teeth and rested his arm round his wife's shoulders. 'She used to call us Mumpy and Grumpy, do you remember?'

'Of course I do.' Something stung his eyes. 'What happened?'

'She wouldn't see us.' Jim sipped some wine. 'Then we tried to have a session with your counsellor. Asked him if he'd be able to help but he flat-out refused.'

'*Nothing* is helping.' Evelyn shrugged off her husband's arm. 'Nothing. It's as if she's still lost.'

'She's not lost. She's still in denial.' He focused on Evelyn, but she stared up at the ceiling. 'What she needs is time to get used to the new situation.'

'She's had *months*.'

'Evelyn, this isn't a standard thing. She wasn't handcuffed to a radiator in a damp basement and fed on live crickets while she was pining for us.' Fenchurch drank an inch of wine. 'They took care of her.' His fist tightened around the glass. 'And they operated on her, erased her memories. Stole her mind after they stole her body.'

Fenchurch finished his glass. 'Evelyn, I know you're only trying to help, but please, please, please, can you stop butting in? We're working with a professional on this. We're trying, but we've got to accept that Chloe might *never* remember who any of us are.'

Fenchurch's dad finished his pint and spun the glass on the table. 'While nobody's interested in my opinion, I think you need to stop meddling.'

'Meddling?' Jim looked like he might fly out of his chair and thump Dad. '*Meddling?*'

Dad clicked his fingers, trying to attract a waiter's attention. 'You and Evelyn, you're meddling in this Chloe business. It should be for Simon and Abi to resolve. She's their daughter and they found her. I tried, for so long I tried, but they're the ones who actually rescued her.'

'We're not *meddling*, Ian.'

'Sorry I used a five-pence word instead of five grand.' Dad beckoned the waiter towards him. 'But you need to let the process take shape. That's all I'm saying.'

'Meddling . . .' Jim sank the rest of his glass. 'And we wouldn't catch you meddling in anything?'

'I've kept my distance.' Dad leaned to whisper to the waiter.

Fenchurch let him order another beer. 'What about when it comes to police business, Dad?'

Dad winked at him. 'Touché, son. Touché.'

Another waiter appeared, somehow juggling four pizzas, all of them with black bases. 'Okay, who ordered The Second Hole?'

———

'Well, that was fun.' Fenchurch pulled onto City Road, following the long line of traffic heading north. 'We really must have your parents to stay more often.'

'Be thankful they've checked into a hotel.' Abi's phone lit up her face in the darkness. 'Your dad went a bit overboard on them.'

'Don't disagree. He had a point, though. This isn't for them to solve.'

'It was worth seeing if it'd work, wasn't it?'

'Maybe.' Fenchurch stopped at the lights, the engine catching every so often. 'I had some . . . bad news today.'

'Docherty?'

Fenchurch grimaced. 'That as well.' He swallowed down some tears. 'He's got weeks to live.'

'Jesus.' She reached over and stroked his cheek. 'You okay?'

'It's not really sunk in yet. He's being strong about it. So strong. And I'm . . . I'm a bloody mess. All the support he's given me over the years. You know what he's been like. He helped me when we lost Chloe and we . . . Well. He was there for me.'

'Poor guy.' Abi pecked him on the cheek. 'What was the other bad news?'

'Shit, yeah.' Fenchurch set off again, but he had to blink away fresh tears as he drove. 'Someone sent me a link to a video file.' He bit his lip, tore off a chunk of flesh. 'It was Chloe, doing . . . an audition for a website. Stripping.'

Abi's mouth hung open. 'Are you serious?'

'She ran out before . . . before anything happened, but yeah. I can't believe she's been reduced to that, to make ends meet.'

'You know Kay did that at uni, don't you?'

'She told me.' Fenchurch's nostrils flared. 'We're failing Chloe.' He turned onto Upper Street. 'I'd give anything to have stopped this shit all those years ago. To not let her play on the bloody street. Even though we've found her, have we really made this any better?'

'Of course we have. She's got the truth. We've got some closure.'

'Maybe.' Fenchurch pulled up outside their flat and killed the engine. Didn't sound healthy as it died. 'This case I'm working . . . I'm already worried out of my skull about her, about someone getting into her room. But the victim, Hannah, she did shows on the site Chloe auditioned for. It's possible she was murdered by one of the men who watched her.'

'This bloody world, Simon. I swear.' Abi let her seat belt go and massaged her belly. 'Who's to say she's not on another site somewhere?'

A chill ran up his spine. 'She told me she's working at Tesco to pay her way.'

'You spoke to her?'

'I saw her at the university. It just came out.'

'Simon, do you think that sort of shit is helping?'

'Come on. Someone sends me a video of her . . .' Fenchurch's throat tightened up. 'Of her . . . And I'm not supposed to chase it down?'

'Was finding her a mistake?'

'Never say that, love.' Fenchurch grabbed her hand and squeezed. 'Never. Okay?'

She nodded. 'Okay.'

Day 3
Wednesday, 16th November 2016

Chapter Twenty-Three

*D*addy, you ate my last sweetie!' Chloe threw the bag on the ground and mashed her foot into his shoe. 'Buy me more!'

'You ate the whole packet.' Fenchurch bent down to pick it up. 'And you don't throw things away, okay?'

'You do it.'

Fenchurch leaned back on the bench and tried to soak in the sun. 'If you pick it up, you might get some more.'

Rather be working than dealing with this strop.

No. Don't say that. Never say that. Never even think it. In three weeks, someone will take her from you. You'd do anything to have this again. To have her with you as she grows up.

Chloe got up from her seat and started skipping around, muttering to herself. Took a few seconds for Fenchurch to tune in. 'My daddy is a bad, bad man. My daddy catches bad, bad men. My daddy is the best daddy. My daddy steals my sweets.' She skipped off to the side, round the bench. 'My daddy is a bad, bad man.'

Remember this. Focus on it. Stay with it. This keeps you going. Stops all the bad shit staying in your head.

Then fingers coiled round his neck, ran down to his shirt. 'My daddy is very, very bad.' An adult voice, purring in his ear.

Fenchurch stood up, spinning around.

Chloe stood there, as an adult, wearing the tight top and short skirt from her audition, swaying her hips. Lifting up her top, running her fingers across her stomach. 'My daddy is a very, very bad man.'

'Stop it.'

'Do you want me to check your balls for you? I can get rid of your cancer when you burn to black coal.' Chloe vaulted onto the bench and started strutting around, her heels sparking off the painted metal. 'I've got bad daddy issues and you're my daddy.' She jumped onto him, trying to stick her tongue—

'Stop it!' Fenchurch lurched up. 'Stop!'

Fenchurch sat up, drenched in sweat. He was in the bedroom. Of their flat. It was November 2016. Chloe was alive and . . .

Jesus.

'What's up?' Abi was lying on her side, stroking her belly. Staring straight at him.

'Nothing.' Fenchurch lay down. His pillow was soaked through. 'Go back to sleep, love.'

'I can't. James has been kicking all night.'

Fenchurch managed a chuckle. 'We're *not* calling him James.'

'Was it another dream about Chloe?'

'One of those memory ones.' Fenchurch hauled off his T-shirt and dabbed at his forehead. 'She was doing a strip, like on that video. I shouldn't have watched it.'

'You *watched* it?'

'I didn't know what it was. Jesus Christ. What's wrong with me?'

'The trauma of losing your daughter, then finding her, only for her to disown you?'

Fenchurch pushed himself up out of bed. 'You want any tea?'

'I've stopped drinking it. Making me feel terrible.'

'Since when?'

'Eh, about four weeks?'

'Bloody hell.' Fenchurch padded through to the bathroom and switched the shower on. Got a good look of a seedy old man in the mirror, his hair lank and greasy like a true sex case. What a bloody idiot.

He stripped off and had a good feel of his balls. Was that a lump? That bit on the top. Was it?

'What the hell are you up to?' Abi stood in the doorway, staring at his nether regions.

Fenchurch blushed. 'Checking myself for, you know.' He let go. 'Docherty told me he had a lump for about a year. Now it's going to kill him.'

'I can help.' She brushed her belly up against him, fingers scanning all over his balls, reaching for his cock.

Fenchurch pulled back. 'Abi, sorry.'

'What?' She probed his balls to the point of pain, her nails digging into his scrotum. 'The midwife said it's good for him.'

'The dream . . . It's . . . Can we do this tonight?'

'Fine.' Clearly wasn't.

———

'Our focus today is collating evidence against Oliver Keane, who remains our prime suspect.' Fenchurch stared around the Incident Room, concentrating on Nelson. Gritting his teeth, giving a slight shake of the head. 'DS Nelson has a list of actions, please consult with him.'

A list of actions DI Mulholland left overnight in his bloody inbox. Emailed. A note left on his desk.

Nelson's phone rang and he checked the display. Seemed to miss Fenchurch's glare too. He held up a finger as he left the Incident Room, already talking by the time he was at the door.

Loftus pushed through behind him, dressed in full uniform. He mouthed, 'Carry on.'

Fenchurch pointed at a photo on the whiteboard, the first in the long rogues' gallery they were collecting. 'Sam Edwards is still a person of interest, mainly for continually lying to us. As it stands, we have no specific motive for Hannah's death, but I want his statement to be torn apart and see what's left. If he's innocent, fine.' He tapped at the next photo along. 'I also want us to keep tabs on Thomas Zachary. Hannah was organising protests against his presence at the university and I want to eliminate any possible involvement from him.' Then the last photo. 'And finally, we still haven't located Graham Pickersgill. He was stalking Hannah back in her home town before they went to university, then her old laptop turned up in the repair shop he works in. We need to get him on the record and eliminate him.' He smiled at Loftus. 'Sir, anything to add?'

'Thanks, Simon.' Loftus marched over to the front of the room and leaned back against a desk. 'Can I just echo what DI Fenchurch has said? Oliver Keane is our lead suspect in this case. It appears that he had acquired a laptop from Hannah's bedroom on the night of her murder. Not long after, well, I'll not bore you.' He flashed a grin at Fenchurch. 'Now, it pains me that Mr Keane unfortunately died during the raid on his home yesterday. I shall be working with the IPCC. Zenna Abercrombie is the lead investigator and those of you who were present should extend as much of your time as required.' He gave Fenchurch a nod.

'Okay, that's all for today. Thanks for your efforts so far.' As the room exploded with noise, Fenchurch picked up his tea mug and drank. 'You dealt with Abercrombie before, sir?'

'Couple of times now.' Loftus pursed his lips. Clearly the experience hadn't been a good one. 'The most recent you know all about, of course, but DI Winter in South London got himself into a spot of bother a couple of years back.'

'I know Rod.'

'Yes, well, you're peas in a pod, aren't you?'

Fenchurch let it go, but not without a glare. 'When is she starting interviews?'

'Their initial focus is on the Terms of Reference. Things were a tad rushed last time around and we've agreed to nail that down beforehand. Then they'll interview the Firearms Trained Officers first. I expect you'll be the tail end of next week. But that depends on whether SO15 are deemed higher priority. It was their operation, after all.' He folded his arms. 'So, that will give you enough of a chance to concoct a story with DS Reed.'

'Sir, we've nothing to hide here. It was one of Grove's officers who shot Keane.'

'Then it's all gravy, Simon.' Loftus doffed his imaginary cap and sauntered off out of the Incident Room.

Fenchurch finished his tea. Cheeky bastard. Poor old Docherty having to cope with that clown all the time. Shitting on his head every day, preventing the proper coppers doing their jobs.

Nelson waltzed back in, grinning wide, and patted Fenchurch on the arm, like they were mates again. 'Guv, can I get you a coffee?'

'Not now, Jon.'

'Fine.' Nelson put his hands behind his head. 'I'm still not happy about going to that vigil last night.'

'Did you get anything?'

'Was I expected to?'

'I'll take that as a no.'

'It's a no.'

'Okay, Jon, I'll let you get on with the actions.'

'Listen, guv.' Nelson held up his mobile. 'That was the front desk downstairs. He's got Sam Edwards in. Someone's stolen his laptop.'

Fenchurch groaned. 'Tell me it's not a MacBook Pro . . .'

'Wish I could.'

Chapter Twenty-Four

Fenchurch paced down the corridor towards the interview room. 'Jon, if someone's nicking these MacBooks, tell me it doesn't look like Younis is covering something?'

'Looks that way.' Nelson rounded the corner first and stopped, frowning. 'Kay?'

Reed was outside the Obs Suite. She glanced at Nelson. 'Guv, Sam Edwards told us—'

'—his laptop's missing. I know.' Fenchurch felt a sigh beat its way out of his lungs. 'We're going to speak to him. Why are you here?'

Reed pointed at the door. 'Mulholland and Loftus are in there.'

'Thought they were focusing on Keane?'

'They got wind of this, guv. She asked me to lead the interview.'

Fenchurch stared at the door, trying to decide what to do. Burst in on the interview or play the political game. Sam Edwards or Julian Loftus. He opened the door and entered.

Loftus sat in front of the giant monitor. Mulholland loomed over him, like she was eating his soul. She glanced over at Fenchurch and frowned. Then stared back at the screen. Fenchurch's presence wasn't worthy of anything more.

On the screen, Sam Edwards sat across from one of Mulholland's DCs, a young male officer. He frowned at Reed as she sat opposite. 'Have you found it?'

Reed glanced at the camera. 'We've only just discovered that it was missing. When did you notice it was gone?'

Sam scratched at his neck. 'I only noticed when I got home from the hospital. I was going to report it, but it was late. So I'm here now.'

Reed sat back and folded her arms. 'The truth about Oliver Keane would be a start.'

'Oliver Keane?' Sam stared at Reed for a few seconds, then shrugged. 'He was making a nuisance of himself with Hannah. I had to sort him out, yeah?'

Reed leaned across the table. 'You told us Hannah wouldn't let you.'

'I didn't let it stop me.' Sam ran a hand over his scalp. 'Okay. I visited him and threatened him. Asking her for sex wasn't appropriate. Told him to stop it.'

Bridge opened her laptop and frowned at something. 'But *she* didn't stop it, correct?'

'She kept emailing him.' Sam ran a hand across his shaved head. 'She . . . she had to. Made a lot of cash out of him. It's a tough gig, you know? You've got to tread the line between keeping them keen and pissing them off. His spend was at least half of her income.'

'And he wanted more, didn't he?'

'A lot more. So he threatened her, told her he'd stop paying her.'

'What about when you spoke to him?'

'Guy's a dweeb.' Sam rocked his chair to the side. 'Too busy shitting himself to be smart.'

'Did he ever threaten Hannah?'

Sam stopped messing about with his chair and settled back on all four legs. 'You think Keane killed Hannah, don't you?'

'I can't comment on that, sir.' Reed held his gaze. 'Did he, to your knowledge, ever threaten Hannah?'

Sam focused on the desk. Seemed to think through a decision. 'Sunday night. We had that argument. The . . . the last time I ever saw her. It was about him. Oliver Keane. Hannah was getting worried about him killing her.'

Fenchurch stood up tall. *Come on, Kay . . .*

Reed was frowning at her laptop. 'You didn't think to mention it earlier?'

'There's nothing to mention. She was overreacting. From what I saw, he was getting weird in those messages he was sending her.'

'By messages, you mean emails, right?'

'No. Manor House has a private message server. We sometimes use it with clients. Keane talked to Hannah on it. Like, a lot. I think he knew how secure it was.'

'How did that make you feel? Her messaging this man for sex? Did it make you angry?'

'They never met. It was all part of the game. The thrill of the chase.'

'Then your argument was partly about Keane. You looked very angry in the CCTV footage. So did Hannah.'

Sam sighed. 'I wanted to kill him.'

Reed's forehead couldn't stay straight. 'Oliver Keane died yesterday.'

Sam gripped the table edge. 'Shit, I didn't mean it. I didn't know.'

'You're not a suspect for his death.' Reed waited until his shoulders slouched. 'Mr Keane sent Hannah emails, though.'

'Guy wasn't the type to stick to one method of communication.'

'He sent them to her real name.'

Sam jolted upright. 'What?'

'Mr Keane had found out that Hannah wasn't born as Natasha Sparks. Got her real email address somehow.'

'Shit.'

'Would she have given him it?'

'Must've done. Don't see how he'd get it otherwise.'

'Mr Edwards, we're currently struggling to access these Manor House messages between Hannah and Mr Keane. Can you help?'

'Wish I could.'

Mulholland muted the display. 'When we get those messages, that'll be it. Definitive evidence against Keane, at last.'

No reaction from Loftus, just stony silence, the threads on his forehead twisting. 'We need those messages, Dawn. Until then, this still isn't stacking up.' He scowled at Mulholland. 'We need to drill down here.'

'I intend to, sir.' Mulholland rubbed her hands together. 'We've got Hannah's laptop and IT are tearing it apart for me. And I'll pull together a warrant to access these messages on this Manor House site.'

'Dawn, weren't you listening?' Fenchurch couldn't even look at her. 'It doesn't matter if you get access to the platform — if it's encrypted, all you'll get is gibberish.'

Mulholland gave him a withering look then smiled at Loftus. 'Do you know of any judges who can approve it immediately, sir?'

'I know a few. Okay, you've got my full support, Dawn.' Loftus stood up and buttoned up his uniform jacket. 'This is a good start. Excellent work, Dawn.'

Fenchurch got out of there before Mulholland could speak. Not that she'd bloody listen.

———

Bridge and Nelson were sitting at the back of the Incident Room, locked in a deep conversation. They broke off when they saw Fenchurch. Nelson got to his feet first. 'Coffee, guv?'

Fenchurch couldn't even be bothered to be angry with him any more. 'Americano with milk, please.' He stuffed a tenner in Nelson's hand. 'Get one for Lisa as well.'

'Guv.' Nelson charged off out of the room.

Fenchurch sat in his space and logged into the machine.

Bridge leaned over and spoke in an undertone. 'Sir, I'm sorry about last night.'

'It's fine, Lisa. Your private business. One of you should've told me by now, though.'

'I'm sorry, sir.'

'Listen, can you do me a favour?' Fenchurch waited for her to nod. 'Sam Edwards lost his laptop. Another MacBook Pro. Can you dig into it for me?'

She made a note. 'Sir.'

Fenchurch settled into the chair next to Bridge and checked his email. He stared at the screen, letting the pixels blur.

Five messages from Loftus, all requesting progress updates. Prick could ask. An email from Reed about the Christmas night out, not that he'd be able to attend for longer than an hour at most. Mulholland had sent out three emails in the last ten minutes, all marked Urgent. Fenchurch deleted them. Nelson actioning the transfer of Bridge back to Reed had generated six emails Fenchurch needed to approve. Fenchurch logged into the HR system and clicked through the forms. They didn't make it any easier than the old paper stuff.

His machine pinged. A new message. The sender was listed as 'A friend', same as the message with the Chloe video. The subject was 'Open this now!' The preview popped up, another link to a video.

His mouth was dry. *If this is more goading, if this is Chloe . . .*

He clicked on it, out of breath. The video opened up and started playing. Sam Edwards having sex with a woman from behind, her blonde hair fanning out as she tossed it around. The sound was muted, but she was shouting something.

Fenchurch grabbed Bridge's headphones, plugged them in and unmuted it.

'Sam! Oh, fuck me, Sam!' Harsh, sibilant like she was lisping. 'Fuck me like you fuck your girlfriend! Fuck me hard! Fuck me like I'm Hannah!'

'Cheers, Martin.' Fenchurch left the burly Custody Sergeant and charged towards the rear entrance, his knee a constant sting. He hauled open the door.

Sam Edwards was waiting by the security door. 'You've missed your chance. I've got a lecture.'

'This is important, Sam.'

Sam smacked the door and got a clang.

'I can give you a lift.'

Sam's eyes narrowed. 'What do you want?'

Fenchurch held out a screen grab from the video, Sam thrusting at the mystery woman. 'Recognise this?'

Sam seemed to shrink back. 'I made it.'

'Someone sent me this. It isn't Joanne Galbraith. It's not Hannah. So who is she?'

'I don't know.'

'Sam, quit it.' Fenchurch pointed behind him. 'We can take this into an interview room, if you'd prefer.' He tapped the page. 'This woman asked you to "Fuck me like I'm Hannah".'

Sam's tongue poked out between his lips.

'Earlier, you said Hannah was cool with you sleeping with other people. Did she know about this woman?' Fenchurch caught himself before he did the air quotes. 'Did it make her angry? Is that what she was angry about on Sunday?'

'How the hell did you get hold of this?'

'You're playing that trick, are you?' Fenchurch pocketed his phone. 'You sent me it, didn't you? That and the video with— You sent it, didn't you?'

'I genuinely didn't. This is me and a . . . client. I record the sessions to show there's consent. I don't want to get done with rape.'

Jesus.

Fenchurch got up. 'Was Hannah angry with you for turning tricks?'

Sam blinked away tears. 'I have to do this. I don't make anywhere near as much from cam work as she did.'

'Remember that you're speaking to a police officer.'

'You would've charged me if you were going to.'

Fenchurch was tempted. Dirty little bastard, renting himself out. Tricks. Games, while his girlfriend rotted in the morgue. 'What's her name?'

Sam held up his hands. 'Zoe. I don't know her surname.'

'Was that the first time?'

'No. She was a regular. Every week. Sometimes twice. But it'd been a while since the last one. Then she asked me again.'

'I need to speak to her, Sam. Give me her address.'

He sighed. 'I can't tell you.'

'Can't or won't?'

'We met in a hotel. Always the same one. Place on the Minories. Hotel Bennaceur.'

'Did she contact you through Manor House?'

'This was private.'

Fenchurch stepped forward, blocking Sam's exit. 'You're telling me this has nothing to do with Younis?'

'No, I mean, she got in touch through Manor House originally.' Sam tried to get past but Fenchurch had him trapped. 'But I gave her my burner number. She texted me on that.'

'Younis has home addresses for all of the punters. Verified ones. Right?'

'IP addresses, maybe. Not physical ones. You're barking up the wrong tree there.' Sam nudged him away. 'Now, unless you've found my laptop, you can piss off.'

'Sure your flatmates haven't got it? Played a joke?'

'I'm telling you, someone's nicked it.'

'Who? Why?' Fenchurch waited until Sam looked away. 'What's on there that someone would want to nick?'

'It's an expensive machine. Still get at least fifteen hundred for it, second-hand.'

Fenchurch narrowed his eyes at Sam. 'You seem to know a lot about selling them. You didn't sell it for drugs like Hannah did with that HP?'

'Shut up.'

'We know what happened. Swapped it for some dope and ecstasy with her friendly neighbourhood drug-dealing cleaner. Turned up in a shop in Southwark. Danton had a mate there. Connected to Hannah.'

Sam scowled at him. 'Graham?'

'Pickersgill. You know him?'

'Not really. Guy was at school with Hannah, bit of a creep. He freaked her out. I checked him out for her. He wasn't a threat.'

'What did she say about him?'

'She beat the shit out of him. She got worried he'd come back and . . . you know.'

'When did you check him out?'

'Sunday. Guy had just moved flat. Had to threaten his boss at that shop.'

Chapter Twenty-Five

I n five years, guv, this'll all be expensive flats.' Nelson scanned the block again. 'Can't believe that Shadwell is on the rise.'

Five storeys of painted brick, with corridors outside of the building. Washing hung off the metal barriers acting as banisters. Christ knows what they would've been like when they were built, probably a drop down to the car park. Some construction work was underway, but council repairs as opposed to the gentrification machine.

'Some areas will stay stuck like this, Jon.' Fenchurch leaned back against the car park's metal fence. 'This block will be full of Poles and Bulgarians, ten to a room, poor buggers. Some racist bastard coining it in off them. Only way anyone can live in London and still send money back home.'

'Even the worst shithole in there would be worth the best part of half a million quid.' Nelson nodded slowly as he sucked on his vape stick. Then another check of his watch. He grunted, then took another suck. 'Guv, about last night . . .'

'I think I made myself clear, Jon.' Fenchurch gave him a sideways glare. 'You get up to that sort of shit, that's your business. You deal with the day-to-day ramifications of your behaviour, fine. Just don't expect me to trust you, okay?'

'Come on, guv.'

'Jon, you're out of line.'

Nelson let out a sigh. 'Guv—' His mobile rang and he checked the display. 'That's Mulholland.'

A squad car rattled in from the main road and pulled across Twine Court, almost blocking the exit. Four lumps got out, one of them packing an Enforcer over his shoulder.

'She can wait. Bounce it.' Fenchurch set off towards them. 'You're leading here, Jon. Chance to prove yourself.'

Nelson pocketed his phone and met the squad halfway. 'Let's take this easy, gents, okay? We don't want a repeat of the incident on Mansell Street yesterday. Bring him in for questioning.'

He got a wall of nods. One of them spat a toothpick on the concrete.

'Come on.' Nelson led over to the building.

Fenchurch followed him. No outside door, no security system. The flight of stairs stank of piss and the marshmallow tang of smoked heroin.

Nelson took the first floor and headed back out into the long external corridor, the red-painted brick flaking off. November sunshine beat down, drying some Arsenal bed sheets. Nelson stopped outside a brown door — brass letterbox and knocker, almost dignified — and waited for the uniforms. Then he thudded on the door.

It slid open and a little man squinted out. 'Yes?' Sounded Polish, maybe Slovenian.

Nelson held up his warrant card. 'Graham Pickersgill in?'

'Nothing to do with me!' His arms shot up, palms splayed. 'Room at the back! Nothing to do with me!'

Nelson barged past him and Fenchurch followed. Dark-green carpet in the hall, big clumps eaten by moths. Magnolia walls, the glossy paint chipped and cracked. The door at the back was ajar. An absolute racket of electronic music blared out, the sort of dance that was more metal than house.

Fenchurch snapped out his baton and let Nelson go first.

Pickersgill stood in the middle of the room by a pile of boxes, hands stuffed inside the top one. Tall and skinny, but he was dressed like he was in a hip-hop video, layers of American sports tops thickening his torso. 'What the hell?'

'Police.' Fenchurch had his warrant card out. 'Graham Pickersgill?'

'Er, yeah?'

'I need you to get your hands out of that box for me, sir.'

'What have I done?'

'Get your hands out of the box!' Nelson raised his baton to strike.

'What's this about?'

'Hannah Nunn. You—'

'Shit, okay!' Pickersgill sank to his knees and interlinked his fingers. 'Please, you've got to lock me up for what I did. Hannah didn't deserve it. I couldn't help myself.'

Fenchurch frowned at Nelson. *What on earth?*

One of the uniforms tore at the stereo system, killing the racket.

'I've been watching her. Following her. Waiting outside her room. I'm a filthy pervert. You need to get me help!'

'You killed her?'

Pickersgill frowned at Fenchurch. 'What?'

'She's dead.'

'Shit.' Pickersgill shot to his feet and shoved the boxes over. The pile landed on Nelson's foot and he screamed. He tumbled back, grabbing hold of Fenchurch and pulling him over as well.

Pickersgill made a run for it, vaulting the pair of them in one stride.

Fenchurch lashed out with his baton and clattered Pickersgill on the back on the knee. He yelped as he fell. Then Fenchurch grabbed his arm and twisted it hard. 'You're going nowhere, sunshine.'

Fenchurch sat opposite Pickersgill in the interview room. No lawyer. Just the way he wanted it.

Pickersgill rested his head on the brand-new table's unblemished wood. Only a matter of time before someone defaced it. Buddhists would say it was already carved and graffitied and burnt and pissed on. 'She can't be dead.'

'She is.' Nelson was leaning against the wall by the door. 'Do you want me to show you the autopsy photographs? They might upset you.'

'You're not kidding, are you?' Pickersgill ran a hand down his face. First some tears swelling, then flooding down his cheeks. 'Shit, shit, shit.'

'How did you know Hannah?'

'We were at school together. Sat next to her in chemistry and maths.' Pickersgill brushed his tears away. 'I liked her. A lot. I followed her to London. We were both at Southwark. Only two from our town.' He scratched at the pristine wood with his thumbnail. 'I dropped out in first year. Doing Computer Science, but I hated it. Competing against all these nerds on the course who'd been coding since they were five. I could never catch up, not in a billion years.'

'And now you're fixing laptops in a shop in Southwark.'

Pickersgill looked up from his scratching. 'Pays my rent and that's about it.'

'Enough for some dope, though?'

'What?'

'We know.' Fenchurch smiled. 'Troy Danton, right? Met him when you were a student?'

Pickersgill looked away. 'Shit.'

'I don't want to do you for that, son, but a squad is going through your room just now.' Fenchurch grinned. 'Having all your stuff packed in boxes makes our work so much easier.'

'There's nothing in there.'

'That the truth?' Nelson kicked off from the wall and sat next to Fenchurch. 'When we arrested you, you said we should lock you up for what you did to Hannah.'

'I didn't kill her.'

'Okay. So what did you do?'

'I was in love with her at school.' Pickersgill went back to the scratching, picking out a thin line in the wood grain. 'I might've . . . become obsessed. I didn't know how to control myself. Didn't know what I was doing.'

'So she told you where to go and you killed her, yeah?'

'No!' Pickersgill thumped the desk. 'I never did anything to her!'

'Really?' Nelson got a page from his pocket and slid it across the desk. 'She didn't kick the shit out of you?'

Pickersgill stared at the photo, slack-jawed. 'I was in a bar in Shoreditch and I saw her. Tried to speak to her, tried to apologise. She said I made her life hell. That I was bullying her. Then she left. So I followed her, really wanted to make it up to her. She spotted me on the street and . . . beat me up. Think she'd trained in a martial art. I hadn't.'

'Is that why you killed her?'

'I didn't! Listen to me!'

'Tell us what you did, Graham, and it'll all feel better.'

'No!'

'It's funny how you've been off work since you killed her. Sick with guilt, yeah?'

'I moved flat on Monday. You saw the boxes. I've got so much shit to unpack. My old man kicked me out after I left uni. Had to take all my shit down here. I didn't know she was dead.' Pickersgill rubbed at his cheek. 'It's why I was outside her room on Sunday night.'

'What did you just say?'

'I was outside her room. I needed to apologise to her.'

'You're not on CCTV.'

'Please. I can run rings around that. I know where the cameras are. I was away from the one outside her room, but I could see her door.' Pickersgill frowned at them. 'My security card still works. I . . . used to visit. Hang around outside her room.'

'You were stalking her, but she wouldn't speak to you. Then you killed her, didn't you?'

'I keep telling you! No!'

'Did you see anything?'

'She wouldn't let me in.'

'Did you see anyone?'

'Sorry.'

———

Fenchurch shut the door, leaving Pickersgill inside with the Custody Officer, ready to take him downstairs for further processing. 'What do you think?'

'Guy's messed up.' Nelson got out his vape stick for a quick toot. 'Do I think he killed Hannah?' He shrugged. 'Could've.'

'If he didn't kill her, Jon, he's the last person near her room before the killer struck, but . . . I don't know. He's got a motive, he's got means, he's clearly had an opportunity.'

'Guv, let me dig into his background a bit more.' Nelson pocketed his e-cigarette. 'He's not going anywhere for a while. We can get him in court for pushing that box on my bloody foot.'

'How does it feel?'

'Not good. A solid-state amp landed on it. Vintage thing. Weighed a ton.' Nelson stretched out his foot. 'I'll get a detailed witness statement from the cops who stopped her killing him in the street. See if we can get him for any of that, too.'

'Good idea.'

———

'This is excellent work.' Loftus was outside the Incident Room, giving Mulholland a thumbs-up. He seemed to groan at the sight of Fenchurch. 'Inspector.'

'Sir, I need to—'

Loftus pointed at Bridge, now chatting to Nelson by the whiteboard. 'She's good, isn't she?'

'I think so, sir. Lot of potential. I need—'

'Nice to see that we can still produce stars.' Loftus tilted his head to both sides, cracking his neck. 'Anyway, I need a word with you, Simon.'

'Sir, this is important.'

'Very well.'

Fenchurch flashed a smile. 'We've got another suspect, sir. A strong one.'

Mulholland swung her scarf round her neck. 'We don't need any more.'

'Graham Pickersgill.'

Mulholland nodded at Loftus. 'The chap who Hannah beat up.'

'You found him?' Loftus cracked his neck again, even worse this time. 'Do you think that he wanted to kill her because of that incident?'

Sweat trickled down Fenchurch's spine. 'He's an ex-student, his card never got cancelled, so he could get into the halls at any time. Knew how to avoid the cameras. He said he was outside her room on Sunday night. Add in the history of stalking, extrapolate the escalation in his behaviour, and he's a clear suspect.'

'That spectre . . .' Loftus glanced at Mulholland. 'You think it's him?'

'DS Nelson's digging into it, sir.'

Loftus clicked his tongue a few times. 'Okay, let's deal with them both as valid suspects at this juncture.'

'Sir.' Mulholland stood, hands on hips, scarf trailing behind her. 'We need to focus on Keane. You heard the interview?'

'I did, Dawn, but I want no cowboy behaviour here, okay?' Loftus nodded at Fenchurch. 'We're treating Keane as our primary suspect and we'll work on that basis. But if Pickersgill was at the crime scene at that time, he may be another witness. Okay?' He waited for them both to nod then walked over to the door. 'Good. Now, Dawn, can you take lead on both aspects? Thanks.' And he was gone.

'Thanks for that.' Mulholland walked after Loftus, her parting gaze digging deep into Fenchurch's soul, like she could freeze his bones and scoop out the marrow.

She was probably correct, though. Keane was the most likely suspect. He had Hannah's laptop. If he hadn't killed her, then who gave it to him?

Fenchurch peered inside the Incident Room, most of them looked like Mulholland's officers. Loftus was doing the presidential thing, wandering round and waving to the little people, chatting to a few. If there'd been a baby in there, he'd have kissed it.

The door rattled open and Bridge walked out, carrying her laptop. 'Sir, didn't see you there.' She bit her lip. 'Can I ask you something?'

'Sure.'

'Okay, so I've been doing some work for DI Mulholland, but . . . Well, she's not listening to me.'

Fenchurch looked around for any of her spies or familiars. 'What isn't she listening about?'

'Jon— Sorry, DS Nelson gave me the actions this morning to dig into Oliver Keane's background. And . . . You're probably not interested.'

'Hit me with it.'

'Fine. Okay. Keane owned an app called "Inside". It's basically a big blog platform. To entice people in, they gave away some of the columns for free. One of the first was by Thomas Zachary.'

Another suspect piling on the Keane bandwagon. 'So Keane knew Zachary?'

'Potentially.' She opened a window on her computer. Keane and Zachary pictured at a press conference, sharing a stage, in front of Inside's logo. 'DI Mulholland has some of her team working on it, she said. But I don't believe her.'

'Okay. Keep digging. And if she asks, tell her it's at my request and she needs to speak to me.'

'Thanks, sir.'

Fenchurch walked off, away from the Incident Room, and called Liam's number. Answered immediately. 'You got a minute?'

'Better be literally a minute.' Liam Sharpe was somewhere noisy. Like an airport. Gatwick, if Fenchurch had to put any money on it. Shit.

'You know your profile on Thomas Zachary? Are you aware of any connection between him and someone called Oliver Keane?'

'Whatever you've heard, it's all true, mate. They worked together in the States on Inside. Hideous platform. We had a hook into it for some online content and I got involved in it. Those guys are complete pricks.'

Fenchurch didn't like the sound of it. 'So Keane definitely knew Zachary?'

'They were good friends, is what I hear. Close.' Liam sighed. 'Look, my flight's boarding. Off to Marrakesh for a week. Have fun.' Click and he was gone.

Fenchurch pocketed his phone and leaned against the wall.

Another link between Zachary and a murder victim. Is it enough? Is it anything?

Sometimes the guilty do innocent things. Is that all this is? Search for evidence against the big racist monster and you find it. Am I trying to pin shit on him because I don't like his politics?

'Simon.' Loftus beckoned Fenchurch over from the door. 'I gather you're not as sold on this Keane chap as Dawn is?'

Fenchurch tried to think it through. Playing five-dimensional chess. In space. Sod it, be honest. 'That's right, sir. Feels too neat. And someone's stealing these MacBooks. I hate easy explanations and I worry that's what Keane is.'

'Occam's razor can certainly slice through any prosecution.' Loftus did up the buttons on his uniform. 'Follow me.' He led Fenchurch further down the corridor, away from the squad of uniforms approaching the Incident Room. 'DI Mulholland told me there's now a connection between Keane and Thomas Zachary?'

'That's correct, sir. DC Bridge told—'

'I've had Dawn's team investigate any connection.' Loftus folded his arms. 'When a celebrity pops up, well, let's say I'm concerned that their fame can serve against us and any prosecution. So due diligence and all that.'

'Seems wise.'

'It is. But my issue isn't about Mr Zachary and Mr Keane. It's that he's been dating one Jennifer Simon.'

Fenchurch opened his mouth to speak.

'I know who she is, Simon. Your daughter.'

Chapter Twenty-Six

Footsteps cannoned around the university's circular stairwell. Loftus was powering ahead, out of sight round the bend. But he could bloody hear him. Fenchurch clung to the banister, pulling himself up another flight, one step by one step. Strip lights caught the rough concrete surface. Sweat soaked his shirt, dripped down his forehead. His knee was on fire by the second floor; by the twentieth, it was self-medicating.

Another corner and Loftus was by the door, doing stretches. 'You should've taken the lift, Inspector.'

'I'm fine, sir.' Fenchurch was about to vomit. Took everything to keep it down. 'Fine.'

'You look very far from fine.' Loftus held open the door but stopped Fenchurch getting through. 'I can see you limping.'

'I had a tumble down some stairs arresting a suspect, that's all.' His knee locked and sent a jolt of pain up his thigh. 'I'll be fine.'

'Ah, an ill-advised chase after a "scrote".' Loftus did that air-quotes thing, his chunky fingers dancing like rabbit ears poking up over a barley field. 'We're supposed to push scrotes down stairs, not them us.' He flashed a grin, but it was soon lost, a stone dropped in a fast-flowing river. His forehead creased. 'Simon, I'm going to be frank here. You'll know as well as I that, all along, there's been a possible conflict of interest in this case.'

'Because my daughter's a student here?'

'Correct. DCI Docherty liked to sail close to the wind on such matters and I respected his judgement. But . . . it's not beyond the realms of possibility that a savvy defence lawyer could get your testimony thrown out.'

'Sir, she's not been—'

'Let me finish.' Loftus kept his hand in the air as he spoke. 'If our intel is correct and your daughter is involved with this chap, then you're off this case. Okay?'

No point in arguing. So long as he keeps Reed, Nelson or Bridge on it. Someone I can pressure for info . . .

'Understood, sir. I wouldn't want it any other way.' Fenchurch nudged past and hobbled down the corridor, lopsided.

The same goon was stationed outside Zachary's office, wearing shades in a London November. 'Sirs, I need you to stop.'

Loftus smoothed down his uniform. 'I don't know who you think you are, but—'

'I'll stop you there, sir. Mr Zachary had a death threat this morning so we're locking this place down.'

Loftus poked his tongue around his cheek. 'And why weren't we informed?'

'Standard protocol, sir. Now I need you to back off.'

'I'm a police officer, son.' Loftus clenched his jaw. 'You're the one who's going to back off.'

'Sir, my job is to prot—'

The office door clattered open. 'Brad, what the hell?' Zachary was waving his arms, scowling at the security goon. 'Can't even think in here, man!'

Fenchurch stepped forward, as smoothly as his gammy knee allowed. 'Need a word.'

Zachary huffed out a sigh. He arched his eyebrow and nibbled at his bottom lip, thinking it through. Not that there was much to think through. Then he nodded at his security. 'Brad, go make yourself useful.'

'Sir, I—'

'These are cops, you moron.' Zachary came out into the corridor, his suit jacket flapping behind him. 'Get yourself a cup of Joe and be back in five.'

Brad's massive shoulders slumped as he glared at Fenchurch. Then he sloped off, tearing out his earpiece and letting it dangle free. Prick thought he was guarding the President, not some big-mouthed racist. Not that there'd be any difference, come January . . .

Zachary was already inside his office.

Loftus took a seat in front of the desk, waiting for Fenchurch to sit. Didn't seem to have calmed much, his skin a few shades redder than normal. He gave Zachary a professional smile, eyes narrowed and thin. 'Does the name Jennifer Simon mean anything to you?'

'Oh God, yeah.' Zachary picked at something stuck between his teeth. 'We dated for a couple of weeks.'

Loftus glanced at Fenchurch. 'But not any more?'

'Nope.' Zachary rooted around in his desk drawer and pulled out a toothpick, then went to town on his teeth. 'We had a few wild nights, I can tell you. But she broke it off with me a couple weeks back.'

Fenchurch let his held breath slip out. 'Did she say why?'

'Sorry, dude.' Zachary swallowed something, but left the toothpick dangling, like he was a Mexican gangster in a mid-nineties film. 'You'd have to ask her, I'm afraid. I'm a gentleman, I know when to listen to a "no".'

Loftus was already on his feet. 'Thanks for your time, sir.'

'Through here, gentlemen.' Uttley's secretary flashed them a false smile. 'Rupert won't be long now.'

Loftus sat at the huge oak desk, keeping his silence. He brushed some fluff off his shoulder. Didn't look particularly satisfied that he'd got rid of it all.

Fenchurch joined him, but couldn't stay sitting. His knee kept wobbling and locking. He got up and walked over to the window. Rubbed his kneecap until he got another satisfying clunk. The pain dulled a touch.

The door clattered open and the Chancellor came through, wearing a gown over his suit as though he was in the middle of a ceremony. 'Gentlemen.' A tight nod, then he found a chair.

Chloe followed him through, head bowed, clasping her elbow.

Uttley stood behind his desk and gestured at the free chair next to Loftus. 'Jennifer?'

Fenchurch hated to hear the name, felt like someone crushing glass in his eardrums.

'I'm fine standing.' But not anywhere near her old man. Chloe stayed by the door, leaning back against the oak panelling, her backpack at her feet. Couldn't even look at the half of the room Fenchurch was in for longer than a second.

'Very well.' Uttley hauled off his robe and rested it on a dressmaker's mannequin behind him. Took great care buttoning up the front. Then he collapsed into his chair like some slob in a Balham flat. 'Gentlemen, Jennifer has kindly agreed to answer any questions you may have in my presence. Okay.'

Loftus smiled at her. 'Nice to meet you, Chloe.'

'It's *Jennifer*.'

'Okay.' Loftus frowned at Fenchurch, then gave her another smile. 'You'll be aware that we're investigating a murder case, yes?'

'So I gather.'

'When your name comes up in connection with a suspect, we have to investigate very carefully.'

She frowned at Uttley. 'Shouldn't we be doing this down a police station?'

'Not yet.' Loftus leaned forward on the chair, his forehead creasing. 'Did you date one Thomas Zachary?'

'Why—' She gasped. 'You think he killed her?'

'We're investigating a series of leads. Ms Nunn was organising a protest against Mr Zachary's presence at the university. As such, we are deeming him a person of interest. Now, I need to confirm whether you were romantically involved with him?'

Uttley's face could've soured cheese. Clearly not a fan of his staff consorting with students. Or of them keeping it from him.

Chloe rubbed her temples for a few seconds. Then she hefted up her bag over her shoulder. 'I need to go.'

'I don't want to stand in your way.' Loftus smiled. 'After you've answered the question.'

'This is my personal business. You've no right.'

'It's a simple yes or no, Ms Simon.'

Chloe stared at her father, long enough to get his heart thudding in his chest. 'Fine. We dated. For a couple of weeks. But it was just sex.' She held Fenchurch's gaze, then focused on Loftus. 'But I got to know him. And I couldn't stand the guy's politics. So I ended it.'

'How did you meet?'

'Tinder.'

Fenchurch's throat thickened, hardening around the truth. 'Tinder?'

'Yeah.' She tilted her head to the side, frowning. 'I saw his profile and swiped right. Might even have swiped up, which is a super-like.'

'You know how dangerous—'

'Simon, can you give us a minute?' Loftus waved him out of the room. 'Please?'

'Sir, I—'

216

'Now, Inspector.'

'Okay.' Fenchurch took his time leaving, trying to get Chloe to look at him again. She wouldn't. He shut the door behind him, fizzing with energy.

Tinder.

She was using Tinder to . . . have sex with predatory old racists. Christ. Who else is she meeting on there?

Uttley's secretary scowled at him like he'd smeared dog shit over her carpet. 'Everything okay?'

'Just dandy.' Fenchurch walked off, dropping his mobile as he got it out of his pocket, the device cracking off the floor. He bent over to pick it up. Screen was mercifully intact. He hobbled away from the desk and phoned Abi.

'Simon? You okay?'

Fenchurch stopped around the corner, out of earshot. 'Chloe . . . She's . . . she's involved in this case.'

Abi gasped. 'How?'

'She . . .' The words didn't come out.

'Is she okay?'

'She's fine.' Fenchurch pressed his lips together. 'She's been using Tinder.'

'That dating app?'

'It's more of a pick-up app, but yeah. That. Trouble is, she's swiped right on a suspect in this case.'

'Swiped right?'

'That's what you do when you like someone. Apparently.'

'Should you be telling me about this?'

'Abi, that's our little girl.' Fenchurch wanted to punch the walls, smash through to Uttley's office and grab hold of her, shake her until she saw sense. 'We found her again, but she's lost to us. This is worse than—'

'No, Simon, it's not. Don't even . . . Don't even—'

'She's been . . . sleeping with the Rector. That hipster Nazi.'

'Zachary?'

'Him.'

'Of all the bloody people . . .' Abi paused. 'She's obviously got her mother's lousy taste in men.'

'I want to throttle him, Abi.'

'I think there's a long queue.' Abi's breath rasped against the speaker. 'Just because it's all apps nowadays, doesn't mean it's any more dangerous.'

'I don't like it.'

'This is what you committed to twenty years ago, whatever happened. You knew she'd grow up, become a woman and, as much as you hate it, she'd have sex with someone. Man, woman. Doesn't matter. Someone would take your little girl from you.'

Fenchurch leaned back, resting on the wall. Tried to shake out his leg.

She's right. God, is she right.

Why's everything so broken? Why can't it just stay fixed? Even just for an hour. A minute, even.

He let out a deep, deep breath. Still no sign of anyone leaving Uttley's office. 'How are you doing, love?'

'I'm with your old man and my parents again.' Her sigh made the speaker click in his ear. 'Mum keeps saying that we're not doing enough. They're talking about an intervention. I'm sick of this, Simon. It keeps reminding me of when Chloe was young. Nothing I did was ever good enough for your mum or mine.'

'We're doing all we can, love. It's up to Chloe now.'

The Chancellor's door opened and Loftus stomped out, fists in his pockets.

'Got to go. Love you.'

Loftus nodded at the phone. 'Mrs Fenchurch?'

Fenchurch put it away with a grunt. 'Did you get anything useful?'

'Precious little.' Loftus grabbed his shoulder like a vice on a chunk of wood, branding his fingerprints into Fenchurch's flesh. 'I can't imagine how difficult this whole thing must be for you and Mrs Fenchurch.'

'Thanks, sir. I keep worrying about her. What if she's next?'

'I've got two daughters, you know. Three and five. I worry about them every second of every day.' Another pulse of Fenchurch's shoulder. 'I can't begin to understand how you've coped with what's happened.'

'Thanks, sir.'

'Am I correct in thinking that she refuses any contact with you?'

Fenchurch leaned against the wall, his sweat leaving an imprint on the paint. 'We were getting counselling and she . . . said we were getting nowhere. She resents us for freeing her. Well, for imprisoning who she thought were her parents. She won't accept the truth.'

'You think she hates you? Really?'

'After all I did. Eleven years, searching for my little girl. Finding a young woman. Yes. She hates me.'

'I'm no expert, but . . .' Loftus waved him away. 'Forget it.'

'But what?'

Loftus poked his tongue into his cheek then nodded. 'I'd suggest that she's got . . . "daddy issues".'

Fenchurch wanted to grab his stupid stubby fingers and break them. 'What?'

'Zachary doesn't remind you of anyone?'

'You don't think she's—'

'Simon, she was separated from you and Mrs Fenchurch at an early age. Those who took her spent time and effort blotting it out, even resorting to surgery. Her current boyfriend is the same age as you, isn't he?'

The guy with her by the halls? The mature student? That's . . . that's her boyfriend?

'You're off the case, Simon. Okay?'

Fenchurch held his gaze. Tempted to fight it. But . . . Off the case. He felt a few stone lighter. The worry was on someone else's shoulders. He could put his focus into getting Chloe back into their life, not pointless worry about what-ifs. 'Fine.'

Loftus marched over to the lift and pressed the button. 'I appreciate you being so gracious, Inspector. I'm going to need you to keep your distance from this case. And from the staff working it.'

'Just find Hannah's killer.' The lift pinged and Fenchurch guarded the door with his hand. 'The most important thing is securing a conviction, sir. If it's Keane, I want to know.'

'Understood.' Fenchurch's phone blasted out. He checked the display. 'It's DS Nelson, sir.'

'Stick it on speaker, please.'

Fenchurch answered and tried to find the right setting. Took a few goes. 'Jon, you're on with DSI Loftus.'

'Guv. Sir. I've been digging into Keane's background for DI Mulholland and we've—'

Loftus hit the screen and muted Nelson, then walked off, phone to his ear. 'You're just on with me, Sergeant. Go on.'

Fenchurch dug the heels of his palms into his eye sockets. Out of the loop already. The lift rattled and the door tried to shut. He pressed the hold button.

Loftus's free arm windmilled as he spoke.

Daddy issues . . .

The weight pressed down again with new worries. *My little girl is on Tinder, dating a man my age.*

'Okay, Sergeant.' Loftus marched over and tossed Fenchurch's phone back to him. 'Let's—' He paused, frowning, clicking his tongue. 'You know what? I may have a use for you.'

'Go on?'

'DS Nelson has discovered that Oliver Keane was using his fortune to fund a law firm specialising in defending rape suspects. It all goes back to his manifesto. He's convinced there's a conspiracy against white men.'

'Give me strength . . .'

'And it gets worse.' Loftus paused. 'Sergeant Nelson connected this legal fund to a case the South London MIT are running. One Christian Greenwood is the suspect in a rape-abduction. I don't imagine the case has anything to do with Keane . . .'

'You want me to check into it?'

'Dig deep, okay? But the very second Keane's name pops up, you're off this. Am I clear?'

'Crystal, sir.'

'And keep away from your daughter. There's been a murky grey area all along, but now it's become very black and white.'

Chapter Twenty-Seven

Fenchurch pulled up in the car park outside Sutton police station and got out into a howling gale. Must be closer to Brighton than Leman Street and they'd have their work cut out for them down here. For every Beckenham that had gentrified, there was a Croydon, ten times the size, fifty times the crime rate. He trudged over to the entrance, his aching knee the least of his worries.

A pathetic figure was huddled in the doorway, sucking on a cigarette, lucky to get any of the smoke before the wind ripped it from his lungs. 'There you are, you old bastard.' DI Rod Winter, his contact, grinning away. His dirty black hair flopped forward, greasy and lank. Needed a good wash. Grey stubble dusted his jawline. He snapped off the ciggie and popped it back in a crumpled box, then stuffed it in his coat pocket. 'Thought you'd be hours getting here.'

'Couldn't escape fast enough, Rod.' Fenchurch slapped his hand into Winter's. 'How's tricks?'

'You know how it is, Si.' Winter swiped his ID through the reader. 'Win some, lose some.'

Fenchurch followed him into the station, limping like he'd been shot in the leg. 'Losing more than you win?'

'Working for the Met, eh?' Winter unlocked an office door and waved until the lights flashed on. He sat behind a big desk, rammed with paperwork. The computer was perched on the edge, not far from toppling off. 'Could do with Alexa in here.'

'Don't tell me you've got one?'

'Wife got me one at Christmas, now I've got one in every room in the house. Spent more than a grand on lightbulbs, IR blasters, you name it.' Winter put his feet on the desk and picked up a coffee mug. He sniffed it then took a swig, snarling like it was whisky. 'Anyway. Anyway, anyway, anyway. Little bird tells me you're interested in Christian Greenwood, yeah?'

'Loftus's orders.'

'Lord Julian. What a prick.' Winter flipped open his cigarette box and peeked inside. 'You're flying high if you're dealing with him.'

'Docherty's dying of cancer.'

'Bullshit.' Winter snapped the pack shut. 'I spoke to him on Monday.'

'He collapsed in front of me on Monday night. They're giving him weeks to live.'

'Shit.' Winter collapsed back in his chair. Seemed to hit him harder than most. 'Shitting hell.'

'You need a minute?'

'Nah, it's cool, Si. Just . . . Shitting hell.'

'Sorry, I thought you'd know.'

'The jungle drums don't beat down here. Out of sight, out of mind. Have to rely on smoke signals.' Winter stuffed the cigarettes in his desk drawer. 'Anyway, this case. It's a doozer, mate. One of those ones that's a toss-up between East, South and Central. You know Central, those shitheads always try and shirk out of any hard graft. And you were still up to your nuts in that stuff in the summer. Anyway. Why did Loftus send you of all people? And why now?'

'This Christian Greenwood geezer. The guy who's bankrolling his defence died in a police shooting. IPCC are all over it.'

'And I know how much you love those guys, Si.' Winter shrugged off his jacket and started rolling up his left sleeve, each twist revealing another inch of his caveman arms. 'Bloody stifling in here.' He switched to the right sleeve. 'Anyway, stop me if you've heard this one before, but Greenwood's the suspect in a brutal rape. Abduction too, hence us picking it up and not the sex crimes lot.' He leaned forward. He'd got worse, could never sit still, always fidgeting with something. 'Anyway. Christian Greenwood is a white, upper-middle-class student. He "allegedly"' — the rabbit ears were catching — 'kidnapped a young woman from outside her house in Bermondsey. Then tied her to a radiator and brutally raped her over three days. We're in court next month. Supposedly.'

'Who's his defence?'

'The law firm is Dickson, Pitt and Owenson. Lawyer is Anna Xiang.'

Fenchurch groaned. 'Dealt with her a few times.'

'Yeah, me and all.' Winter frowned at Fenchurch. 'Anyway. Heard you found your daughter?'

'Sort of.' Fenchurch rubbed at his knee. 'Loftus asked me to dig into this for him and see if there's a connection to our case. Think it'd be worth my while speaking to this Greenwood geezer?'

Winter hauled on his jacket. 'If it's for Loftus, mate, you ain't got a choice.'

⁓

Wandsworth still smelled like Wandsworth. Had a particular aroma, you could almost taste it. Probably the worst prison in London. Scratch that; *definitely* the worst. Everything about it was wrong. But especially the smell, like the evils of every single prisoner had turned into a stench and it had seeped into the bones of the building. They never cleaned it well enough. Even when this place was inevitably shut and converted into flats, you'd still smell it then.

The interview room door clanked open and Christian Greenwood slumped in, led by a guard. Every inch the upper-crust buffoon, lank blond hair, weak chin, Roman nose. But he looked broken, remand in Wandsworth enough to destroy his spirit. If he was guilty, there was no chance he'd get through a twenty stretch.

His lawyer followed him in, her leather document case strapped to her chest, matching her hair colour almost perfectly. Anna Xiang, no sign of any Chinese ancestry. Making a bad habit of representing dirty criminal bastards. 'Inspectors.'

The guard helped Greenwood into his chair then stepped back to the door, clutching his baton. Meatier than standard police issue.

Fenchurch waited until they'd settled down. 'Mr Greenwood, I need to ask you a few questions.'

Xiang got a notepad out of her document holder and dated the top page. 'Inspector, my client is maintaining his silence, so I ask you to respect that.'

'Well, that's disappointing.' Fenchurch focused on Greenwood. 'Does the name Oliver Keane ring any bells?'

Didn't seem to. Greenwood glanced over at his lawyer.

'This is a pending case, Inspector.' Xiang jabbed a finger into her notepad. 'You can't expect him to influence his defence.'

'You might be able to help us out more than your client, then. I understand that Mr Keane has given financial—'

'Okay.' Xiang gritted her teeth. She smiled at Greenwood. 'Christian, I'll take this.' She beckoned over the guard. 'Thanks for your time.' She waited until the guard led Greenwood out of the room, then snarled at Fenchurch. 'You could've visited my office instead of dragging him in here.'

'The palace paid for by Mr Keane?'

'A baseless accusation.'

Fenchurch waved at the door. 'I don't understand how you can bring yourself to defend that monster. He kidnapped someone and raped her repeatedly.'

'Allegedly.' Xiang gave him a warm smile. 'I understand this might be pushing certain buttons, Inspector, but I request that we end this here.'

'You've defended fifteen rapists. White men, upper class. I don't get it.'

'You want to know why?' Xiang slapped her document holder shut. 'Because my brother was imprisoned for false rape allegations. Five years he was inside, until new DNA evidence countered the testimony. The alleged victim had a vendetta against him. He'd spurned her at school. That's it. And that's why I do it. My work stops people lying, makes sure the law is about the truth, stops innocent people going to prison.'

'And Keane pays for it?'

'I think he's formally a partner in the firm. A silent one, of course. He doesn't have a law degree.'

'You know Keane died, don't you?'

'I . . .' Xiang's gaze shifted to Winter, then back to Fenchurch. 'I hadn't heard.'

'He was a murder suspect and, wonder of wonders, rape is involved in that case, too.' Fenchurch sat back. He had her exactly where he wanted her now. Panicking, edgy, her shields down. 'Did Mr Keane know Mr Greenwood?'

'My client is innocent, gentlemen.' Xiang got to her feet and marched over to the door. 'I'd rather you kept these baseless accusations to yourselves.' She left them to it, her footsteps clicking out in the corridor.

Winter got up and started pacing around. 'That went well.'

'Smelling smoke, Rod, and it's not your cheap cigarettes.'

Winter laughed. 'Who is this Keane fella, anyway?'

'Our main suspect in a murder.' Fenchurch frowned at Winter. 'Any chance I can speak to the victim?'

⌣

Fenchurch got out of the car onto Emba Street, a nothing road in Bermondsey, a nothing part of London. Could almost taste the Thames. Could definitely hear the waves splashing at high tide, hissing like the wind rippling through trees.

Winter opened a gate and walked up the path to a tiny flat, a row of windows about ten metres across, lurking in the bottom-left of a giant box. He knocked on the door, gentle and soft. 'You're on your best behaviour here, okay?'

'Me?' Fenchurch held out his hands like an Italian centre-half who'd just kicked a striker into the middle of next week. 'I'm here for intel, Rod. She's your witness.'

'My victim. And her name is Sharon Reynolds.' Winter knocked again. 'The girl was given the full Terry Waite treatment.'

'Terry Waite wasn't raped, was he?'

'You know what I mean.' Winter hit the door harder this time.

Fenchurch tried to peer through the window but the shutters were drawn too tight. 'Rod, aren't you—'

'You're such an old woman.' Winter got out his phone. 'Used to be an outgoing girl, but after what happened, well, she became a recluse. Stopped going out, stopped answering the door.' He fiddled with his phone and stuck it to his ear. 'Sharon, it's DI Winter. Give me a bell, yeah?'

'Still unconcerned?'

Winter walked over the gravel to a feral rose bush and rooted around. He held up a key. 'She's a bit funny about speaking to people, that's all.' He unlocked the door and opened it. 'Sharon! Where— Shit.'

Sharon Reynolds lay on the hall lino, her face pale, dead eyes bulging. Thick red marks around her throat.

Chapter Twenty-Eight

This is a bloody disaster, mate.' Winter tipped off a big pile of ash from his fifth cigarette in half an hour. 'Supposed to be in court next month.'

'Open and shut, though.' Fenchurch couldn't get out of the way of his smoke. Everywhere seemed to be downwind of it, the thin wisps coiling towards him. 'Isn't it?'

'Hardly. You saw Greenwood, mate. He's denying everything.' Winter took another deep suck. 'The case is "he said, she said". I told you, mate. He grabbed her off the street, took her to a warehouse, cuffed her to a radiator and raped her, again and again. Anyway, he was smart. Wore a condom, washed her with bleach afterwards. When we found her, her skin was burnt. Permanent pigment damage.'

'Jesus.'

'Anyway, Greenwood's doing Criminology as part of his degree. Knows a thing or two, or so he thinks—'

A tall figure strolled towards them. *Om-pum-pum.* 'Simon.' Dr Pratt nodded at Fenchurch then at Winter. 'Rodney.' Then he entered the crime scene and disappeared inside the house.

'Rodney?' Fenchurch frowned at Winter. 'Had you pegged as a Roderick.'

'Don't start, mate.' Winter sucked on his cigarette. 'I was born not long before *Only Fools and Horses*. School was hell. Only so many times you can call someone a plonker before they snap.'

'And become a cop?'

'That.' Winter finished the cigarette and stamped it out on the ground. 'Anyway, the last time Greenwood raped her, as he was cleaning her in the bath, she scratched his face and ran off. Unfortunately, she didn't remember where the warehouse was.'

'How did you find Greenwood?'

'She identified him, described him down to a tee. His flat's near the street she was found in, couple of blocks over from the warehouse. When we arrested him, his face was covered in scratch marks. Faded, but we've got the photos. Anyway, it was a simple matter of matching Greenwood's DNA to the skin under her nails from the scratch.'

Fenchurch held up his hands. 'Thought it was "he said, she said"?'

'Just being negative, mate. Saves me getting kicked in the balls later.'

'You'll never change, Rod.'

A random attack, vicious and sadistic, but still random and different to the shit Keane was up to.

'Picked her up just over there.' Winter pointed at the house across the road, an overflowing skip sitting outside, bags of cement spilling out into the rain. 'Pulled up, balaclava on, knife to the back and off.'

Fenchurch waved at the crime scene. 'Whoever killed her found out where she lived.'

Winter groaned. 'Ah, shitting hell. Here comes trouble.'

An exec-class Audi trundled along the street and pulled up by the skip. Loftus got out and stepped in a pile of cement. He gave Fenchurch a nod as he walked over, saving a glare for Winter. 'Gentlemen. This is . . . Well.'

Mulholland got out of the passenger side, talking into a phone. 'Yes, Jon, another one. Goodbye.' She ended the call and sidled over. 'Simon, Rod.'

'Dawn.' Winter exhaled out of the side of his mouth. 'Sir, this is my fault.'

'Nonsense.' Loftus clapped his shoulder. 'Just one of those things. Happens to the best of us.' He paused to run his tongue over his lips. 'I do expect you to make good on it, however.'

'Of course, sir.'

Pratt wandered out of the flat. *Om-pom-pom-pom-tiddly-om-pom.* He threw his medical bag on the ground next to them. 'Ah, there you are.' He popped a mint in his mouth and pushed it into his cheek. 'Well, that's fairly unpleasant inside. I'll get at her in Lewisham as soon as Mick Clooney lets me.'

'Appreciate it, William.' Loftus gestured at the house. 'So, what have you got?'

'She died yesterday lunchtime.' Pratt grabbed his own throat. 'Manual strangulation, of course. And I'd place the time at one o'clock, plus or minus an hour.'

Mulholland flashed her eyebrows at Loftus. 'When Keane was still alive.'

Loftus focused on Fenchurch. 'Are you in agreement, Simon?'

'I don't want to jump to a conclusion, sir.' Fenchurch shrugged. 'The only connection is that Keane was paying Greenwood's defence.'

'Well, confirming it is something, isn't it?' Loftus clapped his hands together. 'Come on, Dawn, let's venture inside, shall we?'

Fenchurch watched them go. 'She's a . . .'

'What's your problem with her?' Winter got out another cigarette and sparked his lighter. The wind kept blowing it out. 'Bastard thing!'

'Rod.' Fenchurch snatched the lighter off him. 'I was saying that someone found Sharon's address. Did Greenwood target her?'

'We think Greenwood found her online, then managed to track her down in real life, as the kids say.'

Fenchurch gave back the lighter, groaning. 'Tell me he saw her on Facebook or something.'

Winter got his lighter to stick, managed to get the cigarette going. 'Why?'

'Tell me Sharon Reynolds wasn't a camgirl.'

Winter almost choked on his smoke. 'How did you guess?'

'Jesus Christ.' Fenchurch felt like he'd been punched in the gut.

The biggest connection of all and he'd missed it. Not that he could've saved Sharon Reynolds, but . . . Searching the wrong bloody places, fixating on rape defence funds when the answer was different.

He grabbed Winter's wrist. 'Tell me everything. Now.'

'Let go of me!' Winter pushed away from Fenchurch. 'Christ, you don't get any better, do you?' He sucked on his cigarette. 'Sharon left school with one GCSE, got a job in Boots. Then a friend suggested she did a camgirl show.'

'On Manor House?'

'Shitting hell. How did you know that?'

'You're sure it was that site?'

'We visited them. Spoke to some freak who tried to get one of my officers to do a strip for him. Anyway, Sharon did this whole goth thing on there under the name Elektra De'Ath. It became really successful and she was earning a good full-time wage from it. And I mean good. Way more than a cop earns.' Winter took another long drag. 'Then she got kidnapped and raped. Girl's been a shell since.'

'Rod, mate. You should've told me this back in your office.'

'Wouldn't have saved her, Si. You saw her. She's been dead since yesterday.'

Fenchurch tried to think of a counter, but Winter was right. Nothing could've saved her. Nothing short of taking every last raping monster off the streets. Even then, another would pop up in their place.

All it did was link her to Hannah's death. Maybe. Could just be coincidence. Then again, the method of murder and the fact the perpetrators had been careful after the sex . . .

But Greenwood was in Wandsworth and he was the careful one. Wasn't he?

Still, Sharon had been very much alive when she was raped; Hannah, well.

Yep, it still sickened Fenchurch. He nodded over at the house. 'Did Greenwood act alone?'

'Possibly not.' Winter finished his sixth fag and stamped it out. 'Said there was someone else with him during at least one of the . . . incidents.'

'Keane?'

'No idea. Sorry.' Winter was fidgeting with his cigarette packet. 'Shit. I'm out.'

'You've already smoked enough for a week.'

'Never enough.'

Fenchurch glanced at Winter. 'Rod, I'm thinking this might be linked to my case.'

'No, no, no.' Winter stepped towards Fenchurch. 'Loftus is going to steal this off me, isn't he? Give it to that witch.'

'No idea.'

'Shitting hell.' Winter lurched off, jogging across the road, blocking off a figure in a crime scene suit. 'You get anything?'

'Rod, you're even worse than—' Clooney tore off his mask. 'Oh, here he is . . .'

'Mick.' Fenchurch smiled. 'You need to practise your straw-drawing. Or at least check that there are actually long ones in the cup.'

'Tell me about it.' Clooney tore off his jacket and stamped on it. The wind buffeted it, threatening to steal it. 'Bloody hell.'

Fenchurch nodded at the house. 'You get anything inside?'

'Nothing.' Clooney stuffed his tablet under his arm as he started on his trousers. 'A dead woman, Si. Need to stop making a habit of it.'

Is he lying? Probably.

Fenchurch grabbed the computer off him. The flat inventory. 'Are you doing monkey work, Mick?'

'Inventory's the most important job. Christ.' Clooney almost fell over as the wind billowed in his trousers. 'If you don't know what you've got, how can you focus people on tasks?'

'Fair enough.' Fenchurch read the list in detail. Lots of lingerie, like Hannah. Tracksuits too. Fitness equipment stuffed into her shoebox of a flat. Surely a gym membership would be better? But something was missing. He held the tablet out. 'Mick, where's her computer?'

'It's not mandatory to own one, you nipple.'

'She's a camgirl, Mick. She'd have a computer with a webcam. This lot all have MacBook Pros.' Fenchurch scanned the rest of the list. 'Hang on, there's no smartphone either.' Fenchurch passed back the tablet. 'Whoever killed her took her computer and phone.'

⌣

Fenchurch knocked on the door and a lumbering goon opened it. 'Looking for your boss.'

'He's not in.' More of a dull roar than actual speech. 'Mr Younis is doing some personal business, sir. He'll be back shortly.'

'Okay.' Fenchurch walked back to his car. Winter was on another call, sucking down yet another cigarette. He got out his mobile, found a business card and started dialling.

Younis answered, driving sounds rumbling in the background. 'Oh, Fenchurch, so you *do* want a tumble in the back of my BMW!'

Fenchurch sighed. 'I need a word.'

'Ooh, two for one. You and another big stud. Have you dumped the delectable Ms Reed? Mm, mm.' Click.

'What the hell?'

A car horn blasted out, headlights flashing. A BMW X5 pulled up, the tinted window sliding down, George Michael's 'Fast Love' pumping out at high volume. 'Hey, baby.' Younis peeked out over mirrored shades. 'Looking good. Mm, mm.'

Fenchurch leaned into the car and got a blast of menthol cigarettes. 'Need a word, sir.'

'So hop on in.' Younis reached over and opened the door.

'I'll stay here, if it's all the same.'

'Don't know what you're missing.'

'Sharon Reynolds.'

'Excuse me?'

'Might know her as Elektra De'Ath.'

'Ah.' Younis turned down the music. 'And what of her?'

'She died. Yesterday. Only just found her body.'

'Oh, sweet Jesus.' Younis stared down at the pedals, twisting his fingers around the steering wheel. 'That's a real bloody shame. She was a good earner. Been off the scene for a few months, though.'

'You hear what happened to her?'

'Fenchurch, baby, you're so hot but so cold between the ears. I tell my girls to keep themselves to themselves. Online only. Anything more is illegal.'

'I meant about her being kidnapped by a punter and tied to a radiator. Raped repeatedly until she escaped.'

Younis held up his hands. 'Nothing to do with me.'

Fenchurch pulled open the door. Wanted to grab his throat and kick the shit out of him. He rested against the car instead. 'I want access to all of her messages.'

'If Sharon was turning tricks, then it's news to me. You might not like it, but I've got to keep this all above board. Last thing I need is you pricks all over me. Well, except you, sweetie.'

'Who's been messaging her?'

'Good luck.'

'We have a warrant.'

'Very pleased for you. Still can't help.' Younis slouched back in his chair and pulled off his sunglasses. 'You really need to listen more, sweetie. We encrypt the private chats. I don't want to be party to what these girls and boys are doing behind my back. Dancing? Fine. Chatting to their customers? I don't really care. Meeting them for sex? I *can't* know about it, otherwise you guys will be straight up my arse.' He looked Fenchurch up and down. 'Though that's only a bad thing depending on who they send.'

Fenchurch was about to tear the door off, or at least give it a good go. 'Listen, you dirty scumbag, two of your girls are in the morgue, so—'

'Fenchurch, listen to me.' Younis sucked on the metal leg of his shades. 'They're not *my* girls or boys. They're all independent contractors who run their own businesses through my platform. I give them the equipment and charge them a percentage and that's the end of it.'

'You don't mind that your punters are sending them death threats?'

'Nothing surprises me, but they're big girls. And boys. I run the platform, that's it. This isn't my issue.'

Fenchurch stared him down, got the prick to look to the side. 'Tell me about Zoe.'

Younis folded his shades and put them down. 'Zoe?'

'A girl Sam Edwards was . . . seeing. Met her on your site.'

'Not my issue, Fenchurch. In case you haven't been listening, the chats are encrypted.'

'I don't really care what they've been talking about. I need to speak to her.'

'Fancy her, do you?'

'In case you've not noticed, you've got two dead strippers on your hands. You need to start playing ball.'

'Well, I'm not giving you anything.' Younis held up a finger. 'Not without a warrant.'

———————

'Bloody hell, Rod.' Fenchurch got in the passenger side of the car. Across the courtyard, Younis was hugging his security like they were teammates and they'd just won the World Cup. 'See what we're up against?'

Winter was already unwrapping a fresh box of cigarettes, clicking a dirty finger against the tear. 'Did he give you the whole spiel about zero-hour-contract strippers?'

'Doesn't even *want* to know what they're up to. Doesn't care, just takes the money from them.'

'Makes sense, though. He's interested in the money, not any of the hassle from us.' Winter put his key in the ignition and turned the heating up, keeping the engine off. 'He's getting to you, isn't he?' He twisted the key and sparked the pool car to life. 'You think he sent that video of your Sam Edwards, don't you?'

'I could do him under revenge porn laws. Just need to prove it was him. I know he's hiding something. Every time I get at him, he's all over me like a snakeskin suit.'

'He's not as good as the guy he got the suit from. He'll stumble. And when he does, we'll catch him.'

'I'm not so sure, Rod.' Fenchurch eyeballed Younis giving a body-builder type a high five. What was he hiding? Not his sexuality, that's for sure.

Fenchurch let out a sigh. 'Come on, Rod. Let's get back to the station and dig into that prick's business.'

Chapter Twenty-Nine

I don't really care, Rod.' Fenchurch held open the Leman Street stairwell door. 'So long as it's not Mulholland.'

Winter blasted stale cigarette breath across Fenchurch's face. 'It'll be Mulholland.'

'Shut up, Rod.'

'Seriously. It's not going to be you.' Winter took out a cigarette from his latest packet. 'Sure as hell won't be me. Can't think of many others. And Loftus won't want to bring someone else in. East London is hardcore, mate. Whoever gets Docherty's job will need bollocks as big as my head.'

Fenchurch played it through his politics filters, trying to sand off the rough edges. Still looked like shit, smelled like shit, tasted like shit. 'Let's get on with work and leave the politics to the arseholes.'

'Bloody Leman Street.' Winter followed him along the corridor. 'Not been back here in years.'

'It's not changed much.' Fenchurch limped over to the Incident Room door and pushed it open.

A gang of DCs were huddled by the whiteboard, one of Mulholland's DSs leading some sort of update session. Nelson was chatting to Bridge in the far corner, though she was focusing on her laptop. Fenchurch shot Nelson a warning glare as they approached.

'Rod!' Nelson stood and grabbed hold of Winter's hand. 'Mate, I've not seen you in ages!'

'Yeah, likewise. You look well, mate.'

'Never better.'

Fenchurch sat in Nelson's seat and leaned in close to Bridge. 'Lisa, do you know if Keane sent emails to any other camgirls?'

Bridge punched her desk. 'We still haven't been able to unlock Hannah's MacBook. Mulholland's got three guys in IT working on it.'

'What about the one I found in his house?'

'Jon told me to focus on Hannah's. Evidence trail and all that shit. And I'm blocked.'

'Lisa, I need you to get into that other MacBook, okay?'

'But DI Mulholland—'

'—is over there.' Bridge nodded at the door.

The room hushed as Mulholland entered, undoing her scarf as she walked, almost gliding. Her expression darkened as she spotted Fenchurch. She came over and gripped Bridge's shoulder. 'Lisa, how are we doing? Anything linking Keane to Sharon Reynolds?'

'Sharon Reynolds? Ma'am, I'm—'

'His movements during her time of death are unknown.' She pouted at Fenchurch. 'Unless you disagree with me, Simon?'

Fenchurch kept his focus on Winter. 'Dawn, if you're asking me, I think you need stronger evidence against him in general.'

'Well, I'm not, Simon. In the brief time that you've been off the Hannah Nunn case, we've somehow managed to push the evidence forward a few miles.' Mulholland squeezed Bridge's shoulders. 'Mr Keane is the shady figure entering her room.'

'What?'

Mulholland opened her own laptop and held it in front of Fenchurch's face. 'Have a look.' She flicked through the case file. 'This is the street camera from round the corner from the halls of residence.'

Fenchurch snatched it off her.

The screen showed a man walking down the street towards the camera, his face shrouded in a hoodie. 4.56. The next was 5.32, showing him walking off. Enough time for him to get inside and enter her room.

He hit pause and focused hard on the screen. 'Is that a laptop under his arm?'

'That's what I think.'

'So it's Keane?'

Bridge hit play again. The screen shifted to a zoomed-in shot, focusing on the face. Definitely Oliver Keane.

Fenchurch's blood ran cold. She was correct. All the pissing about he'd done, letting his tedious feud with her get in the way of the case.

There was a reason Docherty kept them apart. Fenchurch hated to think it was him.

She took the laptop back. 'Mick Clooney sent on the preliminary analysis from Mr Keane's house. Turns out he left some clothes in his washing machine. The hair on them matches Hannah's DNA.'

Fenchurch's skin prickled. 'Should have his prints on Hannah's laptop, though. Right?'

'Which you found in his house.' She waved her finger in his face, like she was chiding a naughty child. 'Which he took from her room.' Her smile spread across her face. 'And we've got CCTV of Mr Keane's Lexus LS600h driving from Mansell Street to this address around the time of Hannah's murder.' She tapped the screen, the sharp figure not ghostly any more. 'He did it, Simon.' Fenchurch still couldn't look at her for longer than a second. 'Why kill Sharon Reynolds, then?'

'He's obviously involved in the abduction. Him and this Christian Greenwood.'

'That's what *my* team will be working on next.' Mulholland flashed a smile at him. 'You're welcome to watch.'

Fenchurch hated himself for admitting it, but Mulholland was right.

Or was she? Something nagged at the back of his skull, growing like a tumour. He snatched her Pronto and scanned through the photos.

Got it.

'Have you got him arriving the first time?'

Mulholland frowned at him, then at Loftus. 'Excuse me?'

'This shadowy ghost figure entering Hannah's room. They left at four twenty-one, if my memory serves.' Fenchurch flicked to the other set of screen grabs. 'But you've only proved that Keane was there on the second visit at five oh six.'

Mulholland took hold of the laptop and frowned at it for a few seconds. Then she nodded slowly and marched off towards the whiteboard. 'Gather round! Okay, I need all hands focusing on validating this hypothesis.' She uncapped her pen. 'DS Nelson, your team are to validate his movements prior to the camera picking up his car on Mansell Street.'

Bridge took back her laptop, glaring at Mulholland.

Fenchurch leaned in to whisper. 'Everything okay, Lisa?'

'Sir.' Bridge let out a sigh. 'Mick Clooney said he found three MacBooks in Keane's house.'

'Three? I know about Hannah's and this mystery one. Is it Sam's?'

She sighed. 'Could be.'

'So Keane broke into Sam's flat now and nicked his laptop? What the hell was he covering up?'

'Lisa?' Mulholland was shouting over from the whiteboard, her gaze drilling into Fenchurch. 'If you've got a minute to spare?'

Bridge got up with a smile.

Fenchurch caught her eye. 'Get hold of the laptop's image and give it the once-over.'

'Sir.'

Winter was fiddling with his cigarettes. 'Anyway. You don't think she's going to be your boss?'

'If she is, I'll hand in my notice.' Fenchurch ran a hand across his face. 'I can see the writing on the wall, Rod. People like her are taking over from people like us.'

'Here, don't tar me with your brush, mate. I've got smart lightbulbs to pay for.'

'Inspector Fenchurch?' Zenna Abercrombie was by the door. 'Time for us to have a word, if you've got a minute?'

'You said it was going to be later this week?'

'And plans change. Life's shit, Fenchurch.'

'Rod, can you make sure Lisa checks that laptop?' Fenchurch got up, clocking Winter's nod, and met Zenna halfway, out of earshot of the rest of the room. 'We meet again.'

'Okay, well, I suppose that's consistent.' Zenna yawned into her fist. Even she was bored. Two hours of this shit while the case trundled on down Mulholland's road. Zenna peered up from her notepad. 'Were you aware of Richard Thwaite's depression?'

Depressed cop shoots suspect during terror raid. The papers would go ballistic. Not that many read them these days.

'Just when DI Grove mentioned it.'

'Indeed.' Zenna passed him a sheet of paper. A printout from the HR system. 'Mr Thwaite was off work for three months, returned two weeks ago.'

Fenchurch didn't even pick it up. 'From all the statements you've taken, you'll know that I wasn't the one who enlisted the Firearms Squad.'

'No, but Mr Thwaite is based in this building.' She pointed at the ceiling. 'As are the rest of the Firearms Squad for this side of the city.'

'And I don't know the janitor or the tea lady or half of the uniform squad. Does his depression have an impact on the shooting?'

'Well, it's fair to say that Mr Thwaite is struggling with his position. Being expected to kill someone, if needs be.'

'So why did he get firearms training?'

Zenna let out groan. 'Quite.'

'You think he shot the guy deliberately?' Fenchurch scowled at her. 'To get off active duty?'

'He's not said as much, but . . .'

Fenchurch scraped his chair back across the lino. 'Okay, so are we done here?'

Zenna ran a finger across a list on her notepad, then peered over her glasses. 'We are. For now.'

Fenchurch got up and walked to the door. 'Where is he? Thwaite, I mean.'

'He's at home, suspended on full pay while we investigate.'

'Thought you'd have locked him up.'

'The man is suffering from severe depression, Inspector. He doesn't represent a danger without a gun.'

'Why not have him in a hospital?'

'We're considering it.'

'Well. Keep me posted, please.' Fenchurch left the room.

Thank God that's over.

'Inspector.' Loftus was standing in the corridor, tugging at his cap. He entered the room without a further word.

Fenchurch set off, trying to get as far away as possible.

———

'Si, coffee?' Winter was by the Incident Room door, fingers twitching like he needed his eightieth cigarette of the day.

'Tea, if you're going.' Fenchurch let him past and set off. Bridge was still in the corner, her forehead denting as she worked at the machine. Mulholland still led a huddle by the whiteboard, facing away from the door. Fenchurch snuck over and sat next to Bridge. 'You getting anywhere?'

She jumped. 'Christ, sir. Didn't see you there.'

'You okay?'

'I'm fine.' Bridge's nostrils flared. 'Where were you, sir?'

'IPCC interview. Two hours of my life I won't get back. You get hold of that laptop image?'

'I've been digging into it.' She chanced a look over at the whiteboard, then tapped her laptop's screen. 'I think this one belonged to Sharon Reynolds. Well, she's definitely been using it. And I can get into her messages.' Her fingers rattled the keyboard. Her screen mirrored the MacBook, could easily pass for it. The Manor House logo appeared in the web browser and Bridge tapped the top-right corner of the screen. 'The username and password fields were pre-populated, sir.' She clicked the button below. 'This is the back-end platform, where the users send emails to the girls. And boys. This is Sharon's account. Elektra De'Ath.'

Sharon's photo on the site was a strange mix of a Cure video and a burlesque show. Below was a chain of messages from Christian Greenwood, every other line a reply from Elektra.

'Have you read these?'

'Every last one.' Lisa clicked on the first one. 'The guy was obsessed with her. She was keeping him at a distance, but still, he wouldn't let go. Kept on suggesting they meet, but she palmed him off.'

'Here you go, Lisa.' Winter brought in Bridge's coffee and Fenchurch's tea on the cardboard tray. 'She's good, this one.'

'Hands off.' Fenchurch ripped off the lid and let the steam out.

Bridge was frowning. 'Sir.' She pressed a button and other messages filled in between the rows. 'I've found something.' She tapped the screen. 'Oliver Keane sent her a message yesterday morning.' She clicked on it.

Sharon. We've warned you. Keep quiet or we will kill you.

Chapter Thirty

Fenchurch sat back and took a sip of scalding tea. Irritation scratched at his back.

Oliver Keane, the uber-suspect who was intending to kill half of London before being shot himself, now threatening a camgirl. The case was building itself.

Was he irritated because it played into Mulholland's narrative? Or because it disrupted his?

'Greenwood attacked Sharon months ago, right?' Fenchurch blew on his tea, sending ripples across the surface. 'So why's she sending messages on there now?'

'That's the thing.' Bridge flicked to another view. 'The attack was in July, but she's logged in every day since she got out of hospital. Chatting to her punters. Stayed on for over eight hours at least twice a week. Still earns more than me and she's not even dancing. Just feeding their fantasies. Telling them stories. Keeping them interested.'

Fenchurch took a long glug of tea and swilled it round his mouth. 'Okay, so Greenwood abducted her, but *Keane* threatened her. Used her real name, too.' He stared at Winter. 'Why?'

'He's in league with Greenwood.' Winter nibbled at a fingernail. 'You told me that Keane's paying for his defence. We think someone else was in on it.'

'Keane?'

'Makes sense to me. Sure the Coroner at the inquest will buy it, too.'

'Okay, I get killing her to shut her up. But stealing her machine?' A tiny avenue opened up in Fenchurch's brain, letting the troops file through. 'And why warn her?'

'Who knows?' Winter shrugged, then he frowned at the screen. 'Before the raid, you and DS Reed visited Keane's house and he didn't let you in.'

Fenchurch spilled some tea on his lap. 'Shit.'

'And, because he'd already warned her, he thought that Sharon had spoken to us about him.' Winter waved at the screen. 'So he killed her. Probably took her laptop in case we found these messages.'

Fenchurch dabbed at his trousers, frowning. 'Where does this leave us?'

'Us? This is my case, Si. And you've solved it.' Winter seemed surprised at the logic and its simplicity. 'Anyway, I'll brief Loftus and my gaffer. Please keep a distance from this, okay?'

'If that's how you want to play it, Rod.'

'It is, Si. And you'd do the same to me.' Winter put the lid back on his coffee and stood up tall. 'But this is brilliant work. Thanks, Si. Lisa.' He clapped Fenchurch's shoulder and charged off.

'Don't mention it.' Fenchurch pushed himself up to standing. 'But he's right, Lisa, this is good work.'

'Thanks, sir.' Bridge nibbled at her lip. 'You're annoyed with him, aren't you?'

'I've seen it all, Lisa.' Fenchurch logged into a machine and scanned down his inbox. 'It's important to know when to push and when to sit back, munching popcorn.'

'Which one's this?'

Fenchurch found his most recent emails. The HR system had kicked out his approval of Bridge's transfer. Bastard thing. 'Maybe.'

'I said, which one is this? Popcorn?'

'I don't know.' Fenchurch clicked on the link and re-approved the form. He finished his tea. Needed another one already. 'Do you know if Mulholland got the warrant for Manor House?'

'She emailed about it half an hour ago.' Bridge glanced around the room. 'It's where everyone's gone. It's what I'm supposed to be working on.'

'You can go back to it.'

'Sir, I appreciate the coaching.'

'Lisa, I'm the last person you need coaching from.'

'Well, it's interesting working with you and DI Winter.'

'I'll try and take that as a compliment.' Fenchurch checked her screen. Filled with messages he couldn't quite read. 'So you've got access to Manor House?'

'Got access to the system, but not the messages.'

'Explain?'

'They're encrypted. The only way to see the messages is if you're a user. Like that message Sharon got from Keane. Once a message is sent, it stays sent. I was in her account, so I could see it. But Keane couldn't delete it. Might be why he stole her laptop.'

'There's no back door?'

'Not that I've found. Younis is genuinely covering his arse, sir.' Bridge hit the trackpad. 'Out of sight, out of mind.'

Fenchurch tapped at the glass, yet another computer mirrored on her laptop. 'And what's this?'

'We think it's Keane's personal machine, sir.' She bit her lip again. 'DI Winter asked me to search for messages from Greenwood.' The screen filled with messages. 'He was talking to Oliver Keane. Seems to be in code. I *think* they've got nicknames for the girls they're watching, but I can't pin them to any faces.'

'Any likely suspects for Sharon Reynolds?'

'Maybe.'

Fenchurch swallowed hard. 'Sam Edwards?'

'DI Winter thinks so, but I don't buy it.' Bridge flashed a grin, then clicked her fingers. 'That reminds me. Mick sent over a photo of that other laptop. Found it down the back of Keane's sofa.' She showed him the forensic photos of a MacBook Pro, the silver skin covered in patches where stickers would've been, just one remaining. Cuck Off!

Fenchurch rubbed his hands together. 'Can you get in?'

'Need his passcode.'

'One sec.' Fenchurch got out his phone and dialled the number he had for Sam. He started walking away.

'Who is this?' Sounded like Sam was at a rave.

'Sam, it's DI Fench—'

'Goodbye.'

'We found your laptop.'

Sam paused. 'I need that back.'

'See, that's the thing. I need to ask you a few questions about it. Starting with the passcode.'

'I don't have to give you that.'

'We found it at Oliver Keane's.'

'Whatever. It's private. And I know you can't brute-force it.'

'You seem to know all the lingo.'

'I did a course in Information Security in first year. I don't have to give it up.'

'So you're hiding something?'

Sam sighed. 'It's private and I'd rather it was kept that way.' Click.

Cheeky bastard.

Bridge frowned at him. 'Did you get it?'

Fenchurch grimaced. 'No.'

'Typical.'

'Anything else we can do?'

'Not on that.'

'Meaning you've got something else?'

'Possibly.' Bridge opened another window. 'This is the MacBook Sharon Reynolds used. I've found an interesting message.' She clicked on the Manor House link and a message appeared:

Elektra—

Just wanted to say that I loved your little show. I really like your style.

Tom

'Sent a month ago.' Bridge highlighted a chunk of numbers. 'Sir, this is the IP address the message came from. It's from the machine in Thomas Zachary's office.'

'It's definitely him?'

'Takes a lot more to prove that, but it's up to him to prove it wasn't now.'

'Right.' Fenchurch scowled at the text again, trying to wring some meaning out of it. Trying to figure out if he definitely sent it. 'Assuming it's him, what does that message mean?'

'He wanted to have sex with her?'

Fenchurch didn't buy it. Too vague. 'Did she reply?'

'Nothing.'

'That's it?'

'That's it.' Bridge was flicking between windows, far too fast for Fenchurch to process. 'Do you think we should speak to him about it?'

Fenchurch grabbed the machine and squinted at the screen. Took his time thinking through the next move. 'Maybe. Maybe not. He watched her on video, then sent her a message. That's not a lot, is it?' He pointed at the time stamp. 'And this is six months old, too. He's not exactly stalking her. It's not like he's tried to meet or anything.'

'Do you think I should mention it to DI Mulholland?'

'Keep digging for now. It's got my spidey-sense tingling.'

And it had. Zachary kept popping up. What irritated Fenchurch more? The man's politics or the fact he had dated Chloe?

Fenchurch leaned in close. 'Lisa, I need to tread carefully here. Can you see his messages on there?'

'I can see the metadata. I mean, I can see who's messaging who. And we can't break the encryption.' Bridge patted her hair. 'But, I found a lot of messages between Sam and Zoe.'

'Can you get in?'

'I've been trying. But I won't see them until I unlock Sam's machine.' She nibbled her lip. 'The other thing is, I've found some messages between Zoe and Thomas Zachary.'

Fenchurch scowled at the screen. A constant back and forth between them, maybe thirty or forty a day. Whatever they were sending was hidden from the police.

Fenchurch tapped on Zoe's profile picture, a manga woman with blonde hair and giant eyes. 'Can you get anything on her? Phone number, email address?'

'That's the thing. I thought I had an address, sir, but it's a PO Box in Clapham. I mean, I could find out who owns it?'

Fenchurch leaned back in his seat and folded his arms. 'Do we know anything about her?'

'Just that she was paying to sleep with Sam Edwards.' Bridge shrugged. 'That's it.'

'So why is Zachary involved with her?'

'No idea.'

Fenchurch stared back across the Incident Room. 'We should speak to Zachary.'

'You're still alive, then?' Reed was leaning against her car, shivering in the cold.

'Doesn't feel like it.' Fenchurch locked his own car. 'What have you been up to?'

'Under Mulholland's iron thumb, guv. She's getting worse.' Reed got up and rubbed her arms through her jacket. 'You got—'

Fenchurch's phone rang. Loftus. 'Sir, I'm outside.'

'Well, I'm upstairs with the Chancellor. We're waiting for you.'

'Five minutes, sir. Is Zachary with you?'

'He's on his way. And I'd take the lift if I was you, mm?'

'Sir.' Fenchurch got out. Bedlam. A woman shouting through a megaphone. 'What do we want? Zachary out!' The crowd chanted along with her. 'Zachary out! Zachary out! Zachary out!'

'Shit, that doesn't sound good.' Fenchurch set off towards the quad, Jaines Tower looming above, the lights twinkling in the frost. Could just about work out which room was Uttley's. He squeezed past a woman halfway down the path. 'Excuse me.'

Someone grabbed his arm. 'Fenchurch?' Gordon McLaren, hands on hips. Black leggings and a lilac blouse. 'Thought you were going to come to the vigil last night?'

'I came but I couldn't stay. Got called away when we arrived. I'm sorry.'

McLaren folded his arms. 'Why don't I believe you?'

'It's the truth. My boss is in hospital. Cancer.'

'Oh.' McLaren's eyebrows shot up. 'I'm . . . I'm really sorry.'

Fenchurch nodded down the path. 'Another protest against Zachary?'

'I thought they'd cancel it, given what's . . . happened.' McLaren snorted. 'Someone grabbed me in the common room, said it was peaceful. We came out here and someone threw a bottle.' He looked Fenchurch up and down. 'Glad the police are here.'

'We're here for another matter, sir. I suggest you leave.'

'I'm going, don't you worry.' McLaren sidled off as the crowd noise swelled up.

'Hey ho! Fascists go!'

Fenchurch walked towards the end of the path. At the end, the quad was blocked with students. Placards reading ZACHARY = SHITLER, GET BACK TO TRUMPTON and RIGHTFACTS IS FAKE NEWS!!!.

Zachary was halfway up the ramp, arms folded, no sign of his security muscle.

The woman with the megaphone was in his face, shouting, 'Hey ho! Fascists go!'

Zachary pointed past her and said something.

'Hey ho! Fascists go!' She pulled the megaphone away from her mouth and waved her arms, conducting the chanting.

Shit.

Shit, shit, shit.

It was Chloe.

Fenchurch barged through the crowd. 'Police!'

'Hey ho! Fascists go!'

Zachary was screaming at her, gripping her shoulders tight.

Fenchurch pushed between a couple. Then another. Ten bodies away from her. He pushed and pushed. Sam Edwards stood next to Chloe, hands cupped round his mouth.

Then Fenchurch was through. Chloe clocked him and she froze.

Fenchurch snatched the megaphone from her and stuck it to his mouth, holding down the button. 'This is the police! This protest is over! Please disperse and return to your rooms! Thank you!'

Boos rang out. A bottle flew past Fenchurch's ear, thunking on the ground and skidding.

'I'm serious! Go home or you will be arrested!'

Zachary got close to Fenchurch. 'You need to—'

Zachary's muscle bundled into Fenchurch, pushing him back. Not Brad. Some other ex-forces type. He made a one-man human shield around Zachary.

The crowd was thinning out, the students clearly not fancying an arrest on their records.

Not Chloe, though. She stood next to Fenchurch, jabbing a finger in the air at Zachary. 'Hey ho! Fascists go!'

So much like her bloody mother . . .

Fenchurch grabbed Zachary's arm. 'Sir, I need you to come with me.'

The bodyguard tore his hand free. Felt like he'd snapped the tendons.

Fenchurch flashed his warrant card. 'You're coming with me. Now!'

Zachary pointed at Chloe. 'She's the one you should be arresting! She started this!'

Chloe grabbed the megaphone from Fenchurch and swung it at Zachary. His bodyguard lurched forward, head-butting it out of the way, taking the blow himself.

Chloe almost toppled over. She grabbed the rail and held herself in place.

The megaphone clattered to the ground and rolled off into the quad. Chloe watched it go. Then her eyes bulged. She jolted forward and pushed Fenchurch.

He tumbled into Sam Edwards, the pair of them collapsing into a group of men.

A loud bang, then an echo round the quad.

A girl near Fenchurch screamed.

Chapter Thirty-One

The sound was so close to Fenchurch that his ears burned. Everything sounded underwater. Muffled, thick.

Fenchurch tried to push up, but Sam Edwards lay on him, pressing him down to the flagstones. He wriggled about, trying to get Sam to budge.

Chloe!

No . . .

No, no, no . . .

Eventually, he shook Sam off.

Then another scream.

Fenchurch rolled over.

A female student lay on the ground, a few feet away, clutching her leg. Her back arched as she let out another roar.

Chloe stood above her, mouth hanging open.

Fenchurch pushed himself up to standing. Students scattered around them, screaming and panicking. 'Get inside! Now!'

Chloe reached down for the megaphone and pressed it to her mouth. 'Get inside the university buildings! Now!'

Fenchurch stood and watched her. Impressed, but he couldn't push an image of her getting shot out of his mind. He pawed at her arm. 'Did you see something?'

'A flash of light.' Chloe pointed up at Jaines Tower. 'Something was sticking out of a window. A gun.'

Fenchurch pointed across the quad, away from the tower. 'Get inside!'

Sam vaulted the banister to get to the girl who'd been shot.

Fenchurch shuffled over to the stricken woman. 'Sam, can you get her inside? The shooter's still here.'

Sam nodded as he helped the girl to her feet, then started carrying her towards a door opposite the tower.

Chloe stopped near Fenchurch, following three Chinese students. 'You okay?'

Fenchurch couldn't focus on her. He checked the surrounding buildings, tried to figure out the trajectory of the bullet. He caught a glint of light from a window above the tower's entrance. 'Get down!'

Chloe dived to the ground.

The shot rattled around, a second blast coming seconds later.

The flagstones behind Chloe puffed up, dust pluming. She frowned at Fenchurch. 'You saved me?'

'Come on.' Fenchurch pulled her to her feet, his gaze shooting back to the first-floor window, just above the entrance. No guns, but movement. Maybe. 'Get them all inside, now!'

'Okay.' Chloe started herding the students.

Fenchurch powered up the ramp as fast as his gammy knee would let him. Inside Jaines Tower, students cowered and hid all over the foyer. The quad was empty now, the discarded megaphone lying in the middle.

Loftus sprinted down the staircase, followed by Mulholland. Neither noticed Fenchurch as they headed towards the entrance.

Fenchurch climbed the staircase, trying to ignore the pain in his knee, and emerged into a wide concourse with only four doors. Lecture theatres, probably. He tried to superimpose the downstairs layout up here. A janitor's store was over the far side. *Pray that the shooter's still in there.*

He inched across the giant rubber tiles. Movement blurred the door's security glass.

Was it his reflection?

More movement, light deflecting around it.

Definitely someone in there.

Something clunked, metal on metal.

Shit, the shooter was reloading.

Fenchurch snapped out his baton with a crack, loud like thunder. He crept forward and put his ear to the door. The window rattled, as if something was pressed against the frame. A man was speaking to himself, muttering. Hissing.

Fenchurch reached up and eased down the door handle, then nudged it open. He snuck into the office, taking it slowly.

The room was small, filled with chemicals and buckets. A rifle was mounted by the open window, pointing to the quad. The shooter stood next to it, silhouetted, the blinds flapping around him. Talking to himself. Muttering. Swearing. He spun round to face Fenchurch.

Richard Thwaite.

The Firearms Officer who killed Oliver Keane.

Trying to kill Fenchurch. Or his daughter.

'Richard, step away from the gun.'

Thwaite took one look at it. 'No!'

Fenchurch raised his baton, hoisting it up. 'Step away from the gun, Richard!'

Thwaite was practically hyperventilating. His head twitched, eyes bulging like he was having a stroke. 'No . . .'

'It's over, Richard.' Fenchurch stepped forward. And again. 'I need you to get down on your knees and put your hands behind your head.'

'No!'

Fenchurch took another step forward. Not far now. Inches from being able to strike. 'Come on, Richard. It's over. You're not going to kill again.'

Thwaite stomped towards Fenchurch, fists clenched.

Fenchurch swiped with his baton, lashing at Thwaite's knees. A scream and Thwaite stumbled backwards towards the window. Fenchurch lurched forward, pain spearing his knee, swiping at Thwaite's legs until he hit the floor arse-first, screaming.

Fenchurch grabbed his arm and got on top of him, shifting his weight, pushing Thwaite's arm up his spine. He wasn't going anywhere.

Fenchurch's knee was ready to pop. 'Why did you do it?'

Thwaite shook his head. As much as he could, cheek on the ground.

Something grabbed his arm and Fenchurch flinched. 'Easy.' Loftus.

Two uniforms powered into the room and grabbed Thwaite.

Fenchurch let his grip go and got up slowly. 'He should've been in custody!'

'I know, Simon.' Loftus's nostrils flared. 'I know.'

Fenchurch stepped aside to let the uniforms take Thwaite. 'Make sure he gets to Leman Street in one piece.'

'Sir.' Cuffs clicked and they lifted Thwaite but he was a dead weight. Another took his legs and carried him out. Didn't even move.

Loftus wiped his forehead. 'You okay?'

'Someone almost shot me, sir.'

'This could've been a hell of a lot worse.'

Fenchurch hobbled over to the window, moving like his old man after a bottle of whisky. The cold breeze slapped him in the face. The quad's flagstones were dented in two places, only one of them surrounded by blood.

No fatalities thanks to Chloe pushing me. Pushing me away. Or pushing me out of the way?

Christ, she saved me.

Fenchurch checked the matching windows at this height. The blinds rattled or hung open, a cop inside each one. The place was locked down. His shoulders slumped. 'Are you assuming that Thwaite's the only shooter?'

'We're not. Come on.' Loftus led him back out into the foyer. 'Being shot at is a traumatic experience, Inspector. I know you caught him, and well done and everything, but—'

'How is the girl who got shot?'

Loftus rested against the stairwell and pointed down at the foyer. Two paramedics were working at the gunshot wound, another two arriving with a gurney. 'Because of you, Inspector, we're dealing with an injury. A wound that can heal.'

Chloe stood next to a uniform, giving her statement. She made eye contact with Fenchurch. She held it, for once. Even added a slight grin.

Fenchurch mouthed 'Thanks.'

She shrugged, the smile on her lips flickering, almost daring to burst into flame. Then she turned back to the uniform. Her mature-student boyfriend was lurking around, hands in pockets, forehead creased.

Fenchurch pointed at Chloe, couldn't help but grin. 'She saved that woman, sir.'

'She did well out there.' Loftus nodded at Chloe. 'Your girl, eh?'

'She shouldn't have had to.'

'Simon, this probably isn't the time . . .' Loftus bared his teeth. 'But she organised a protest where someone got shot. A bloody flash mob.'

'She couldn't have known that would happen.'

'If she'd gone through the appropriate channels, we would've had officers in place. This would've been managed.'

'Sir, I . . .' Fenchurch threw up his hands. 'You honestly think that this is her fault?'

'Inspector, I suggest you don't take that tone with me.'

Fenchurch still held his baton. So tempting to lash out and batter Loftus with it. Knock a few teeth out. Throw him over the side of the barrier, watch him tumble down the stairs.

Loftus gave him a withering look then focused on the foyer instead. 'Oh, here we go.'

Zenna Abercrombie marched in through the side entrance, rubbing her forehead as she passed out orders to her suited ducklings.

'Inspector, our line here is that this isn't our mess, okay?'

Fenchurch tightened his grip on the baton.

'Thwaite is under the IPCC's care.' Loftus was still glaring at the door. Talking politics when Fenchurch's daughter almost got shot. Full-on *Game of Thrones* paranoia. 'Why on God's green earth did Abercrombie let him out of her sight?'

And why the hell can't you give up the golf-club bullshit for one minute?

'Not sure, sir.' Fenchurch pushed his baton back into the starting position and stuffed it in his holder. 'You want me out of here, sir?'

Loftus frowned at him. 'Why are you here, anyway?'

Fenchurch's turn to frown. Why was he here? Felt like they'd turned up a million years ago. Then it hit him. 'Zachary. Remember?'

'Of course. It was somewhat embarrassing to be sitting up there with Uttley, waiting.'

'I got held up by that protest.' Fenchurch pointed over to the foyer window where Zachary was being interviewed by a female DC. 'Same with him. How come you were already here?'

Loftus held Fenchurch's gaze for a few seconds. 'I was speaking to Rupert on a related matter.'

'We still need to speak to Zachary, sir.'

Loftus stared out of the window, huffing and puffing.

Zenna Abercrombie walked over towards them. 'Gentlemen, I need you to clear the area for forensics.'

Loftus led over to the stairwell. 'Oh, we're fine, Zenna. Thanks for asking.'

She shot him a glare. 'This isn't my fault.'

'Oh, it very much is.' Loftus licked his lips slowly. 'This is your murder suspect.'

'That's bullshit, Julian.'

'Let's see how the Director of Public Prosecutions feels about this, shall we? You may—'

'Julian, this isn't—'

'Zenna, Zenna, Zenna.' Loftus smiled at her, his tongue running round his lips. 'How about you and I grab a cup of tea while DI Fenchurch here does his job, mm?' He trained his smile on Fenchurch. 'Inspector, how about you go and have that word with our friend?'

Chapter Thirty-Two

'Through here, Inspector.' Zachary led Fenchurch into his office.

Brad was standing by the window, fiddling with his phone. Snap, and he was in Fenchurch's face.

'Brad, it's cool.' Zachary raised his palms. 'We're having a friendly chat. Go get me a coffee, yeah?'

'Boss.' Brad stepped back and adjusted his shades. He brushed against Fenchurch as he barged past.

Zachary collapsed into his chair and shrugged off his suit jacket. He picked up his fountain pen and ran his finger down it. 'This country . . . I swear . . .'

'Someone shot at me.' Fenchurch leaned against the window. 'That's the kind of—'

'You?' Zachary dropped his pen on the desk. 'I was the target, Inspector. Don't get me wrong, the bullet was much nearer you, but . . .' He brushed at his black eye, hidden behind make-up, the yellow and purple still clear. 'I'm no stranger to hate. The price of standing up for your beliefs. Not being a coward.'

Fenchurch focused on the view down to the quad. Forensics officers milled around the two gunshot sites, tiny ants dusting and measuring. A real drop from here. Be a shame for Zachary to fall out.

'So, Inspector, what's this about?'

Fenchurch left the window and took the chair in front of the desk. 'Let's start with Richard Thwaite.'

'Who?'

'The name doesn't mean anything to you?'

'Should it?' Zachary licked his lips. 'This is the man who tried to shoot me, is it?' He picked up his fountain pen again and twirled it round like a majorette with a baton. 'That poor girl. The one who got shot. Is she okay?'

'She'll live, but I suspect she'll be in physio for a while. But going back to Richard Thwaite.'

Zachary raised his right leg up and tapped the knee. 'I got shot in the knee when I was a boy. Out on a hunting trip with my pappy. Didn't your daughter save you?'

Fenchurch glared at him.

'Could Jen have been the target?' Zachary tossed his pen in the air and caught it. 'Sorry, Chloe.'

Fenchurch felt a stab in his heart. He brushed away his tear before it formed. He gripped his baton tight, still stowed in his jacket. One snap and he could bash the prick's teeth out. Haul him out of that window.

'Though I can see why you're worried. All those stories in the summer about you and Jen. You must be on edge all the time.'

'Earlier, when we spoke to you about her, you knew she was my daughter?'

Zachary tossed the pen on the desk again. 'It's a heartbreaking story. You have my deepest, deepest sympathies.' Looked like he meant it too.

Still, Fenchurch wanted to jam the pen in one of Zachary's eyes. Then the other.

'Girl's got daddy issues, though.' Zachary gave Fenchurch the up and down. 'And I can see why. Given what's happened to her, the memories she's got. You're a lot to live up to, aren't you? Real alpha-male type. Bet you play rugby.'

'Can't stand egg-chasing.' Fenchurch clasped his knees. 'You think someone targeted her?'

'I honestly don't know, and that's the truth, my friend. She's a great kid, bit messed up, but she's got hope.'

'That's the bugger that kills you.' Fenchurch reached over but Zachary picked up the fountain pen before he could grab it. 'I need to ask you a few other questions.'

'Can't this wait?'

'Sharon Reynolds.' Fenchurch left a pause, but Zachary just scowled. 'You might know her as Elektra De'Ath.'

Zachary's tongue flicked over his lips. 'Right.'

'We know about you and her.' *Keep it vague.*

Zachary tapped the pen on the desk. 'You'll have to enlighten me, my friend.'

'I thought the whole thing with these camgirls was that you'd watch exotic girls from America or Thailand or Australia, not from down the road.'

'This place is exotic to me.' Zachary pointed at the window. 'Okay, I'll bite. I started watching her before I came over here. Became fascinated by her. She's got great style, way better than most of the skanks on there. I was a bit of a goth in college, though that phase passed quickly.' He scratched out a line on the paper in front of him, the ink bubbling in the nib's trail. 'But I genuinely didn't know Elektra lived in this part of the city. And I sure as shit can't believe her name is Sharon.'

'We found her body at lunchtime.'

Zachary dropped the pen. 'Seriously?'

'No, I'm just making it up to spook you.' Fenchurch snatched the pen away, and put it way out of reach. 'Yes, we found her body. You sent her a message. Said you liked her style.'

Zachary bellowed out laughter. 'Christ, you're desperate.' He reached into his desk drawer for a Filofax. Fenchurch hadn't seen one in years. 'Before we go too far down this rabbit hole . . .' He flicked through and stopped at a page. 'When do you want my alibi for?'

'Let's start with between twelve and two yesterday.'

Zachary splayed the calendar across his desk and tapped at it with a finger. 'I was in a session with Chancellor Uttley. Eleven until three.' He waved at the door. 'Brad was with me all the time, before you start.' He snapped his Filofax shut. 'Listen, my friend. You might not sympathise with my politics, but I'm not a killer.'

'Why don't I believe you?'

'If you think I killed someone, based on me passing her a compliment, you should be arresting me. I'd love to see your pathetic prosecution getting taken apart by my defence team.'

Fenchurch stared at him. 'Okay. What about Zoe, then?'

Zachary's eyes narrowed to fine points. 'Who?'

'You sent her messages on Manor House.' Fenchurch spotted it, a little twitch on Zachary's forehead. Recognition. 'She's a client of Sam Edwards. Sam's girlfriend's been murdered. You connect to both of them. That's interesting.'

'This Zoe girl' — Zachary stuffed his Filofax back in his drawer — 'I know from camgirl message boards. She's . . . confused. Bisexual is probably the best way to put it. She watches the boys *and* the girls on Manor House. We were discussing them.'

'You were discussing boys?'

'I wasn't.'

'What about Sam Edwards?'

Zachary barked out a laugh. 'Zoe never mentioned him to me.'

'Here's an interesting thing.' Fenchurch leaned forward on his chair, like he was telling Zachary a deep, dark secret. 'Someone sent me a video of Sam and this Zoe having sex.' He shot a wink. 'And you've got a connection to both of them, haven't you?'

'How am I connected to Sam Edwards? I've never even met the kid.'

'His girlfriend was organising protests against you.'

Zachary groaned. 'The only time I spoke to Hannah was when I persuaded her not to throw her future away over this stupid protest.'

'You didn't show her this video file? Took it off her computer after you'd killed her? Think it'd be fun to send it to me?'

'Why would I?' Zachary held his gaze for a few seconds. 'Listen, you probably don't know this, but Jen— Chloe. She told me that she auditioned for that site.'

'I know.' Fenchurch leaned back in the chair. 'Someone sent me a video of her audition. Wasn't you, was it?'

'As far as I knew, that whole thing sickened her.'

'And yet you throw money at the girls on there?'

'I'm not breaking the law, Inspector.'

Fenchurch tossed the fountain pen for Zachary to catch. 'Look, whatever. This Zoe woman is a person of interest in this case. Any idea how I can get hold of her?'

'I don't even know if that's her real name. Like I said, I just chatted to her online.'

'You mind if I see these messages?'

Zachary smiled at him. 'They're encrypted. If you really want to see the content of those messages, then I'm going to need a warrant.'

'So you're hiding something?'

'I never share anything with law enforcement.'

'I'll be back with a warrant. You won't like it.'

Zachary whistled, and his bodyguard shot into the room, clutching a coffee. 'Brad, show the Inspector out.'

Fenchurch got up and leaned across the desk to Zachary. 'This isn't over.'

Fenchurch found Loftus in the Starbucks downstairs, overlooking the empty quad. Zenna Abercrombie clocked Fenchurch's approach to their table. The place was on lockdown after the shooting.

'Well, I've a few things to think about, Julian.' Zenna got to her feet and adjusted her trousers. 'I'll be in touch.'

'Preferably after you've got your house in order, mm?'

'I'm not the one who needs to cover their arse.' She walked off, giving Fenchurch a nod as she passed him.

Loftus took a sip from his coffee and grimaced. 'Charming woman.' His smile darkened. 'Simon, we need a chat.'

'A *chat*, great.'

'I've just read this message Zachary sent to the murder victim.' Loftus waited till Fenchurch sat then set his Airwave Pronto on the table. 'He liked her style. Really? That's enough to make him a suspect?'

'It's not just that, sir. He was in contact with a woman who . . .' Fenchurch realised he hadn't told Loftus about the video. About either video. 'There are connections between Zachary and the Hannah Nunn case.'

'Inspector!' Loftus thumped the table. 'We've got a suspect for both murders now. The Reynolds and Nunn families can grieve. Why on God's green earth are you trying to discredit everything we do?'

Fenchurch spotted Mulholland at the café door, lips pursed and smiling. 'When you asked me to work with DI Winter, sir, you said you don't want to be wrong and—'

'We've got another shooting here! By the same bloody guy as last time! Another bent cop. They seem to hover round you—'

'That's not—'

'Enough!' Another thump of the table and Zenna's abandoned coffee tipped over, sluicing to the floor. Loftus wasn't going to clean it up. 'I've got deaths piling up and you're not playing a team game. You need to stop. Now.'

Mulholland sat between them. 'Sir, I've seen what happens when—'

'Dawn, butt out.' Loftus didn't even look at her. 'DI Fenchurch, I need you to stop with this. Okay?'

'Sir, I—' Fenchurch pushed his chair back. Coffee was still dripping on the floor. 'Okay.'

Loftus looked over at Mulholland. 'Dawn, what do you want to tell us?'

'The IPCC have interviewed Thwaite, sir. I sat in and, well, he didn't speak. Not a word.'

'Well, then.' Loftus got to his feet and did up his buttons. 'Okay, Dawn. Let's you and me have a word with him. Now, Simon, I need you to head back to Leman Street and start on your statement, okay?'

Where the hell did this leave him?

Zachary was a slight suspect, connected to people by mysterious messages that they couldn't access. There was a motive, as clear as the fragments they had for Keane.

But . . .

His phone rang. Perfect. 'Sir, we need to keep Zachary as a suspect. This was based on solid intel.'

'That Zachary dated your daughter.' Mulholland's eyes were pleading with Loftus. 'You're letting your feelings make a mess of—'

'I'll tell you what's a mess. You, Dawn. When Chloe went missing, you made a blunder, and the more I think about it, the more it seems deliberate.'

'What are you talking about?' Her eyes kept darting over to Loftus. 'Sir, this is gibberish.'

'Gibberish?' Fenchurch folded his arms. 'You let the man who kidnapped my daughter go!'

Mulholland's glare could've sliced through him. 'Simon, you need—'

'Are you going to answer that?' Loftus was pointing at Fenchurch's trouser pocket.

'Right.' Fenchurch checked his phone.

Unknown number.

Bloody hell.

He answered it. 'Hello?'

'Simon, it's Jim.'

Fenchurch frowned. 'Jim?'

'Ormonde? Your father-in-law!'

Fenchurch gasped. 'Is Abi okay?'

'She's going into labour!'

Chapter Thirty-Three

Chloe was in an office on the first floor, sitting on a bench in front of a long table covered in laptops, giving her statement to DC Bridge. Chloe looked up at Fenchurch. 'Is she okay?'

'She'll live.' Fenchurch flashed a look at Bridge. 'Constable?' He waited for her to join him in the doorway. 'How's she doing?'

'She's . . .' Bridge frowned at Chloe. 'She's in shock, sir. Someone shot at her.'

'Have you finished?'

'Well, I've taken her statement, but DI Mulholland ordered me not to let her leave.'

'Give me a minute, okay?' Fenchurch didn't wait for a reply, just entered the room. 'Chloe.' He grimaced. 'Jennifer. Abi's gone into labour.'

'So?'

Chloe's boyfriend appeared in the hallway, frowning at Fenchurch. 'What's going on?'

'I need to speak to . . .' Fenchurch glanced at Chloe. 'Her.'

'Mate, can you butt out?'

Fenchurch shot him a furious glare. 'Sir, I need you to back off.'

'You're the one who—'

'Come on, sir.' Bridge led him away, Chloe's boyfriend grunting and glowering as he let her.

Chloe didn't look at him. 'He told you to butt out.'

'I heard.' Fenchurch sat next to Chloe. 'I want you to listen to me. Okay? I don't care who you think you are, who those animals led you to believe you are, but the woman who brought you into this world is giving birth to your brother. Right now. She needs you.'

A frown twitched on her forehead. 'Is she okay?'

'I need to find out.' Fenchurch swallowed down a lump in his throat and reached over, offering his hand. 'I'm going to the hospital now. I would like you to come with me.'

Chloe grabbed his hand and stood up, holding tight, like when she was little and he'd taken her last sweetie. 'Okay.'

Fenchurch led her out into the foyer, his heart thudding in his chest.

Her boyfriend blocked their progress. 'Jen, what the hell are you doing?'

'Pete, I . . . Sorry. I need to do this. Sorry.'

'Be strong, Jen.'

'Pete . . .'

'No, Jen. You *told* me to—'

'*Sir.*' Fenchurch ushered him to the side, still holding his daughter's hand. 'I need you to back off.'

Chloe let go of Fenchurch's hand. She tried to smile at Pete, anger knotting her forehead. Then she walked off, hugging herself tight.

'Jen?' Pete watched her go, his mouth hanging open. 'You need to be strong.'

'She's being very strong.' Fenchurch gave him what he thought was a reassuring smile. 'I won't let her leave my side. I swear.'

Chloe was much faster than her old man sprinting down the hospital corridors, but she kept pace as each automatic door slid open. Still wasn't speaking, but her presence—

Fenchurch slipped and stumbled on the floor, sliding across the lino. His knee felt like it had twisted inside out again.

'You okay?' Chloe stood over him, holding out a hand.

Fenchurch got up to a crouch and let her help him to his feet. 'Cracked my knee arresting someone the other day.'

'Your life is mental . . . You okay to keep going?'

'Should be.' Fenchurch started off at walking pace. No chance he was getting any more speed out of it. 'Thanks for coming with me.'

She sunk her head and walked ahead of him. He'd lost her again.

Round the corner, Jim stood in the doorway of the maternity ward, concern etched into his frown. He looked at Chloe, seemed to think nothing of it, then focused on Fenchurch. Then did a double take.

Fenchurch followed Chloe in, trying to make it feel natural, like nothing weird was going on.

Through the door, Abi lay in the bed, groaning and huffing. Evelyn sat next to her, clasping her daughter's hand. 'Oh my God.'

Abi frowned at Chloe. 'Sweet Jesus.' Her face knitted tight. 'Simon, what are you doing here?'

'Your dad phoned, told me you'd gone into labour?'

'It's going be hours yet.' Abi glared at her father. 'Dad, you could've waited!'

'He did the right thing.' Fenchurch got on the other side of the bed. 'I would've killed him if he'd kept it to himself.' He swallowed. 'The baby's definitely coming?'

'Two months early.' Abi looked over at her daughter. 'Just like you. Must be something wrong with me.'

A smile flashed across Chloe's lips. 'It's more likely to be him, isn't it?' Then the smile slipped away. 'I didn't know I was . . . That there was something wrong with me.'

Fenchurch locked eyes with her. 'There's nothing wrong with you.' Then Abi. 'With either of you.'

'Thanks for coming.' Abi smiled at Chloe. 'I know we've had our—' She choked. And again. 'Differences. But.' She started shaking. Rocking. Her stomach twitched, then her throat twisted, like a cat sicking up a fur ball. She moaned low and deep.

'Abi!' Fenchurch grabbed her arms. Couldn't keep her still. 'Abi?'

Evelyn shot up from her chair. 'What the hell is happening? Jim!'

Abi's chest rocked forward. Her arms tore at Fenchurch's grip. Hyperventilating. Shaking. Kicking. Her head twisted to the side and she groaned again.

'Stand clear!' A doctor nudged Fenchurch out of the way.

A nurse followed him in, then lowered Abi's head and pulled up the side rails. Then they grabbed the oxygen mask and stood over her.

Abi still shook, jerking wildly, clamping her teeth like a zombie biting at flesh.

'Out!' The doctor waved at the door, clutching a syringe in his free hand. 'I need the room!'

Chapter Thirty-Four

Fenchurch couldn't stand still. He paced around the hospital corridor, as much to keep his leg from locking as . . .

Through the metal door, Abi was still moaning low, that deep bass roar you got in the cinema. Groaning like something out of a horror film. But it was real. Acid stung at his guts.

He collapsed into the chair next to Chloe. She was fiddling on her phone. Googling, by the looks of it. She held it out to him. 'Could be epilepsy.'

Fenchurch squinted at the screen. 'Can't read that.'

'Don't you get eye tests in the police?'

'My sight's fine for most things. Up close, it's shocking.' Fenchurch took the phone and slipped on his glasses. 'She's never had epilepsy. I'd know. Your grand— Jim and Evelyn would, too.'

'Maybe.' Chloe took her phone back and fiddled with it. 'Heard of pre-eclampsia?'

'She was tested for it in the summer. Came back negative.'

Jim appeared at the end of the corridor. Evelyn stood next to him, tears streaming down her face. Jim stopped and shielded his wife. 'Any news?'

Fenchurch got to his feet. 'We're asking Dr Google.'

Jim blew air up his face. Couldn't take his eyes off Chloe. 'I feel sick.'

'You're not alone.'

'Does anyone want anything? Tea, coffee?' Evelyn's gaze settled on Chloe, her smile taking years of creases off her face. 'Have you eaten?'

'Not since lunchtime.' She bit her lip. 'I'd kill for a burrito.'

Jim frowned at Fenchurch. 'A burrito?'

The door clattered open and the doctor appeared. Mr Stephenson, the one who did the antenatal screenings. Another due next week. Grey skin, grey hair, grey shirt, lugging a dark-silver tablet PC. Heavyset, the kind of guy who knew his way round a scrum.

Fenchurch got up. 'How is she?'

'Well.' Stephenson consulted his tablet. 'As I'm sure you're aware, Mrs Fenchurch is going to be in labour for hours. At present, she's being sedated for her health.'

'What's wrong with her?'

'I'm running some tests.'

'The same ones you were supposed to run months ago?' Fenchurch wanted to grab him by the shoulders and scream at him. 'Did you miss something?'

'There's nothing to worry about.' Stephenson raised a finger to stop a question from Fenchurch. 'This is perfectly common in older mothers. In the vast majority of cases, it's something we can medicate.'

'And in the others?'

'We'll cross that bridge when we come to it. Medicine is all about diagnosis. You need evidence to figure out what is wrong.'

Fenchurch swallowed hard. 'How . . . how is the baby?'

'I'm afraid that's in the lap of the gods.' Stephenson clutched his tablet tight to his chest. 'We have a strong, healthy heartbeat, which a great sign. We'll get a better idea in the next four hours about whether baby will survive.'

Chloe's small hand wrapped around Fenchurch's sausage fingers. 'Can we see her?'

'She's under sedation. Nurse will be giving her full-time supervision.' Stephenson tried a warm smile, but it bounced off Fenchurch. 'We're doing everything we can, I assure you.'

Fenchurch could only nod. He got another squeeze from his daughter.

Stephenson scanned around the others. 'I'd recommend that you all go home. Grab some sleep, get something to eat. I won't be able to let anyone in until Mrs Fenchurch is awake in the morning.'

'Okay.' Evelyn smiled at him. 'Thank you, doctor.'

Jim wrapped his arm round his wife. 'You've got our number, haven't you?'

'Indeed.' Stephenson smiled at Fenchurch. 'I'll see you tomorrow.' He set off, swinging his arms like a sergeant major on the drill ground.

Jim pecked his wife on the top of her head. 'We need to book another night's stay, love.'

'Let's get it out of the way, then.' Evelyn frowned at her granddaughter. 'Do you want to come with us? Have some food?'

Chloe ignored them, staring into her father's eyes. 'We'll stay.' She pumped his hand. 'We'll stay.'

'Okay.' Jim grabbed his wife's shoulders and led her away.

'Thanks.' Fenchurch couldn't even think, he was so stressed. Nothing to do but wait. Impatience was his worst trait. He knew it, everyone knew it. If Loftus didn't, Mulholland would be telling him right about now.

Another pump of his hand. 'I want to stay, you know?'

Fenchurch clutched his daughter's hand tight, hoping against hope that she'd never let go again, that he'd be able to keep her close forever. 'When you were born, your mother was the same age as you are now. I wasn't much older. She dropped out of uni.' He pinched his nose. 'She got an Ordinary degree. Went back and did a teaching course when you were at nursery.'

'I never knew.' Chloe waved at Abi's room. 'Was it as bad as this?'

'None of that . . .' Fenchurch sighed. '. . . hyperventilating. That rocking back and forth. Like she's got a demon inside her. When you were born, I spent the night in the room with her, going through all the breathing exercises, holding her hand. I felt useless, but I kept her sane, I suppose. I was there.' The familiar prickle inside his nostrils. 'Jesus. I couldn't cope if I lost her.'

Chloe reached over and brushed a tear off his cheek. 'You cry a lot?'

'After you— After what happened, years after, I saw a counsellor. She told me I'd spent too long keeping it inside, turning myself into this empty husk. I couldn't feel anything. When I started to let it out, I couldn't stop. But I *felt* something again. All the pain. All this horror. Losing a child. And . . . I'm supposed to stop that shit from happening to other people but . . . But it happened to me.'

Chloe tightened her grip.

'Even with all that, I wouldn't change bringing you into the world. You were lucky, in a way. Could've had a much worse fate. You ended up with bad people, but they didn't bring you up badly.'

'How? How did that happen?'

'Someone I can never forgive, he saved your life. He—'

'Simon?' Fenchurch's dad was by the corner, frowning at them. 'What—'

Chloe bounced over to him, wrapping him in a hug. 'Grandpa!'

Fenchurch frowned. 'What the hell?'

Dad tried to prise himself out of the hug, but she kept hold of him. 'Simon, I've— Oh, shit.'

Jim appeared in the hallway, clutching a coffee. 'Evelyn phoned up and booked another couple of nights.' He took a sip. 'Ian.' Then his eyes bulged. 'What the hell? What's— Have you been meeting her behind our backs?'

'Jim, Chloe asked me to—'

'You're a selfish prick, Ian Fenchurch,' Jim snarled. 'What the hell's going on?'

'We've . . .' Dad grimaced. 'We've been meeting up. Every other week. For a coffee and a chat, you know?'

Fenchurch got between Dad and Chloe, nudging her. 'You didn't think to tell me?'

'Son, we—'

'I asked him not to.' Chloe dipped her head. 'I couldn't . . . couldn't.'

'Why him?' Jim held out his hands, coffee spraying through the lid of the cup, spattering the walls. 'Chloe, you remember us, don't you? I'm Grumpy. She's Mumpy. Don't you remember?' He reached over and grabbed his granddaughter. 'Chloe, it's Grumpy! You remember—'

'Shut up!' Chloe slapped his hands away. 'Shut up!' She pushed him back, sending his coffee flying through the air, and ran off down the corridor.

'Shit.' Fenchurch navigated the spreading coffee puddle and followed, hobbling through the hospital, trying to push through the burn in his knee. He lost her in the hospital entrance. He stopped by the WH Smith, spinning around, trying to find her.

Her disappearance eleven years earlier flashed in front of his eyes. Standing outside their flat, searching for her. Screaming.

He set off for the front door, almost skipping. She was at the cab rank, getting in the back of the first taxi. 'Chloe!'

He cut into a run and grabbed her arm. 'Chloe, stop!'

She pulled the door. 'Get away from me!'

'Chloe!' Fenchurch hauled the door out of her reach. 'Chloe!'

'Oi!' The cab driver tugged at Fenchurch's jacket. 'What the hell's going on here?'

'I'm police.' Fenchurch let go of the door and showed him his warrant card. 'This is my daughter. She's . . . It's complicated.'

'She doesn't want to speak to you. Now, cop or no cop, you clear off or I'll smash you into next week, mate.'

'Don't . . .' Fenchurch stared him down. 'Don't even begin to think that . . . My wife . . . Her mother . . . She's upstairs. My son might die!'

'Mate, I hear a lot of bullshit stories and that's reeking.'

Fenchurch ignored him, focusing his attention on his daughter. 'Hear me out!'

'Mate, you need to—'

'It's okay.' Chloe got out of the cab and nodded at the driver. 'We're cool.'

'Listen, sweetheart, if he's beating you or raping you or—'

Her head dipped. 'It's nothing like that.'

The driver glowered at her for a few seconds. 'Then piss off. Pair of you. Freaks.' He grabbed the door and smiled at a man in a tracksuit. 'Where to, sir?'

Fenchurch led Chloe over to the hospital wall, downwind of the smokers. 'You can leave if you want, but at least explain it to me. I want to understand. I want to know how you feel. I want to help.'

'Grandpa . . .' She let out a sigh. 'You and . . . Abi. You were too much. I couldn't deal with it.' She grabbed her hair, bunching it tight round her ears, like the pigtails she'd had when she'd been taken. 'The DNA evidence. I know who I am, what happened to me, who my parents . . . who *they* were, what they did to me.' She chanced a glance at him. 'Who my parents really are. But I can't deal with it.' She glared at him. 'You can't understand how hard it is to deal with something like this.'

'Really?' Fenchurch took his time. 'Someone took my daughter from me. I know how it is. But I want to understand what you're going through. Chloe, I want to help.'

'I can't even remember . . . that little girl who got abducted. I can't remember being her. And finding out that my parents did this to her?' She grabbed the hair at the side of her head and tugged it up to show the deep scar in her skull, surrounded by a bald patch. The sight of it stabbed Fenchurch in the heart like a spear. 'They took her from me, as well as you. All those memories . . . They're gone.' She let her hair down again. 'The only thing I remember, the only memory those bastards left me with was . . . Grandpa.'

'Dad . . .'

'I remember him, but I don't remember you. He's the only thing I can connect to. Wasn't too hard to find him. I met up with him, on the condition that he didn't tell anyone.' Her finger dug under her hair and rubbed at her scar. 'I found it easy to talk to him.'

Joy and hate burnt in his gut. 'That old bastard.'

'He's not so bad.'

'No, he's not.'

'Don't know about you, but I'm starving.' She let her hair flop down. 'Grandpa said you like Mexican?'

Chapter Thirty-Five

The server put the hot plate of sizzling chicken down near Fenchurch. Could almost taste it in the air. A flamenco version of a Tom Waits song blasted over the stereo.

Fenchurch tapped out a text to his dad. The server pointed at the card machine, so many tattoos on his hands that there was scarcely any skin visible. 'Fifteen eighty, mate.'

Fenchurch tapped his card on the machine and picked up the basket. Two silver tubes and two lemonades, straws poking out of the top.

Chloe was in a booth by the door.

Fenchurch set the tray down and shrugged off his jacket. 'Dig in.' He sat and grabbed his tube, started unwinding the tie. 'I'm starving.'

'Me too.' Chloe bit into the top of her burrito and chewed hungrily. She swallowed it down with a sip of lemonade. 'Thanks for this.'

'Don't mention it.'

Fenchurch watched her devouring the burrito, happiness tingling in his chest. 'So you like burritos?'

She frowned at him. 'Love them.'

'You know, I can list the London Chilangoes in order of quality. Even tempted to visit the Manchester one and see how it compares.'

'That's . . .' A laugh burst out of her mouth, along with half a pinto bean. She brushed it away with her napkin. 'Jesus. I thought I was bad.'

'I got hooked when I was based in the States, working with the FBI, catching serial killers.' He took another big bite. 'Can't live without them now.'

'Last summer I worked at a camp near Chicago.' Chloe chewed slowly. 'We'd go to this little Mexican canteen every day. Looked horrible from the outside, but the food was *so* good.'

'Never judge a book by its cover.'

'Never.' She brushed her hair behind her ears. Fenchurch caught a glimpse of her scar. 'When were you based over there?'

'2008 and 2009. Your mo—' Fenchurch grimaced through the acid gnawing away, drums beating in his ears. He chewed, couldn't taste a thing.

And it hit him like the hot sauce. Abi. Convulsing. Shaking. Sedated. No idea if his son was going to pull through, if . . .

'Abi and I had separated. I'd moved out. More like been kicked out for being a selfish prick. Bought a flat but kept searching for you. Obsessively.' He swallowed again, like the whole burrito was stuck in his throat. 'I asked to be given something I could really get stuck into, that'd make me forget. So my boss sent me over there to work with the serial killer task force. Supposed to become a subject-matter expert. Spent most of the time in Miami, which is a hellhole. Hunting down this guy who . . .' He exhaled slowly. 'You don't want to know. Anyway, I got homesick. Worried that you were . . . My boss sent me to Glasgow, spent six months there. Similar MO to . . . to the guy in the States. Caught the guy. But I wasn't getting any closer to finding you. Further away, in fact. Much further. So I applied for the job I've got now. Same grade, same pay, but I could handle the work in my sleep. Freed up a lot of my time to hunt for you.'

'I didn't know . . .' Chloe took a sip of lemonade. 'Think she'll be okay? Abi?'

'I hope so.' Fenchurch shrugged. Caught himself. 'That's what kept me going, you know. Hope. It'll kill you if you let it.'

'It paid off, didn't it?'

'This time.' Fenchurch held his burrito in front of his mouth. 'I used to have these dreams about you. Still do.' He tried to bat away the dream of her coming on to him. 'A lot of them were you and me in a park, sitting and talking. Sometimes they were about how I'd stolen your sweets. Then they'd turn weird, but . . . it kept me going. Through all that. It kept me going. We were watching basketball.'

She frowned. 'Basketball?'

'You remember?'

She picked up her burrito and stared into the mush. 'Maybe.'

'I can take you there.' Fenchurch reached into his pocket for a packet of wine gums and tossed them on the table. 'It's in Shoreditch. I used to take you there. You loved it. Used to eat these.'

She stared at the bag, chewing slowly. 'What did I say about being too forceful?' But she was smiling. The ice was melting.

'How's your degree?'

'I'm enjoying it, even though it's much harder than I expected.' She sucked in a blast of lemonade. 'But I love London. I hated growing up in Dorchester. So boring. Nothing ever happened there.'

'Too much happens here.' Fenchurch put his burrito down. 'I meant it when I said I could give you some money when I sell my flat. I want you to have it. I want to help.'

'Where is it?'

'Isle of Dogs. It's decent. Bought it off plan when . . . your mother and I split up. I was a wreck, staying with your grandparents.' Fenchurch got an image of his mother in her deathbed, worrying about her missing granddaughter as much as the cancer eating her flesh. 'It's worth a decent amount now.'

'Thanks, but I don't want anyone's charity.'

Just like her bloody mother . . .

'Chloe, if . . . all of this shit hadn't happened, I wouldn't have had to buy the bloody thing.' Fenchurch reached across the table and grabbed her wrists. 'That money would've been your college fund. I don't want you to have a shit life. You would've been fine. I just want the best for you. We both do.'

Chloe stroked his hands for a few seconds, rubbing slowly. 'Let me think about it, okay? I'll talk to Pete about it.'

'He's your boyfriend, right?'

She nodded, a warm grin all over her face. 'He's great, you know? He totally gets me.'

'Is he on your course?'

'We were in the same tutorial for a side course last year. Can't even remember what it was. Some piece-of-piss half-course. Conversational French, I think. Yeah, it was. Really basic and I've got an A-level in it.'

'And they still let you do it?'

'Didn't say I couldn't.' She gave a shrug. 'So that's where I met Pete.'

Fenchurch didn't want to mention the age gap. His phone blared out. Not Jim — Loftus. 'Shit, I need to take this.' He felt trapped, unable to decide between staying and going.

'It's okay.' Chloe smiled at him. 'I'm not going anywhere.' She picked up her burrito. 'Scoot.'

Fenchurch walked over to the wall and rested against it, just inside the front door. Close enough so he could still watch Chloe, close enough to smell the fresh tray of steak. 'Sir.'

'You okay?' Loftus was out of breath.

'I'm fine, sir. Just . . .' Pain jarred in his knee. 'Had some bad news.'

'Oh.' Loftus cleared his throat. 'Anyway, well. I need your assistance.'

Fenchurch left him hanging for a few seconds. 'What with?'

'Dawn and I are in with PC Thwaite. While we don't yet have your statement, with, ah, what's happened, well, there's something in your daughter's that we need to verify. Could prove crucial.'

Fenchurch frowned over at Chloe. Got a smile. 'What is it?'

'It's about the actual target of the shooting. We'd been operating on the basis that it was Zachary, but . . . Well, there's no connection we can find between him and Thwaite. Now Chloe, Jennifer, whatever she's called. She . . . In her statement, she said that she thought Zachary wasn't the target.' Loftus paused. 'You were.'

Fenchurch focused on Chloe, got a warm smile in return. Couldn't cope with losing her again. With someone shooting her.

How cruel it'd be, to spend all that time looking for her, only for him to be the one who went, leaving a hole in her life. One that she would remember.

'It's possible, sir. She did push me over. But I don't see why I would be a target. Nobody knew I'd be there.'

'That's what I thought. Do you know where she is?'

'With me, sir. It's . . . complicated.'

'I understand. Would you mind speaking to her about it?'

'Will do, sir.'

'Good stuff. Okay, well, I'm off to tear into the IPCC. Keep me apprised, okay?' Click.

Fenchurch pocketed his phone. Loftus . . . Some of the time he seemed fine, but every so often it felt like he could just destroy Fenchurch. And he seemed close to Mulholland. Too close.

Fenchurch walked over and sat opposite Chloe. He picked up his burrito. Wanted to eat it, but he had a bad taste in his mouth. He rested it on the carton and sucked down some lemonade.

'You seem tense.' Chloe was still chewing. Took as long as her mother did, grinding each morsel fifty times, unlike the one chew Fenchurch did. At most. 'Who was that?'

'My boss.'

'He used to work with Grandpa, didn't he?'

Docherty . . .

Another bite at Fenchurch's gut. 'No. That's someone else, and a whole other story.' He finished his lemonade. 'Back at the university, that shot. You saved me, pushed me out of the way. I can't thank you enough, but . . .'

Her turn to drop her burrito. 'I'll take that.' She grinned at him. 'It'll do.'

'No . . . You said they were aiming at me. Not Zachary?'

'I wish they'd shot that prick.'

'You hate him that much?'

'Worse.' She gasped. 'Can't believe I . . .'

'It's okay.'

'It's not. I was dating a Nazi. Based on how he looks. Found him on Tinder. I mean, Jesus.' She rolled her eyes at him. 'It's how it works now. Everything's online. I hate it.'

'I thought the idea was you get to know the real them, then you meet up?'

'Trouble is, Zachary doesn't know who he is. There's just a great big hole at the centre of his soul.' She picked at the last inch of burrito. 'I didn't know who he was at the time.' She pushed her tray across to the middle of the table. 'Go on, say it.'

'Say what?'

'That I like older guys?'

'There's nothing wrong with that. It's the Nazis I have a problem with.'

She smiled again. 'I've done some philosophy. Been reading Karl Popper. You heard of him?'

'Doesn't ring a bell.'

'There's this thing he calls the paradox of tolerance. If you extend tolerance to the intolerant, they'll destroy the tolerant ones and tolerance with it. They live outside society, so you shouldn't tolerate them. Defending tolerance doesn't mean you have to tolerate the intolerant.'

'I like that.'

'And Zachary is intolerant. Christ, I should've spotted him a mile off.'

'It's called growing up.' Fenchurch dared a grin. 'Your mother hates him. She was angry when he was voted in at your university. When I met him, I didn't trust him an inch.'

She snatched off a length of foil and started balling it up. 'Should I trust you?'

'I'd rather I earned your trust. But it's a different situation, anyway.'

She nodded. 'About that money . . . You don't know how difficult things have been for me since . . . they were arrested. Not that they were rich.'

'I meant what I said about the money. It's yours. Even if you never speak to me again, I want to make sure you're okay.' A shiver ran up Fenchurch's spine. 'But that video. Jesus, please take the money so that you don't have to do that.'

Tears soaked her cheeks. 'Jesus . . .'

'Do you want me to leave?'

'No, it just . . .' Her head dipped. 'I can't . . . Jesus.'

Fenchurch got up and sat on her side, hugging her tight.

'I thought that video was deleted.' She grabbed hold of him, her shoulders relaxing. 'But it wasn't. Nothing ever is. I can't believe you saw it . . . How?'

'Someone emailed me it. I want to find out who and throw them off a building. Now, who recorded it?'

A shiver ran through her. 'Sam.'

'Edwards?'

She nodded. 'He ran the audition. Said he'd deleted it straight away.'

'Okay.' Fenchurch let her go then got out of the booth. 'I'll be back.'

'What do you think you're doing?'

Fenchurch leaned forward to rest on the edge of the table. 'I'm going to knock his block off.'

'Why? What do you think that'll achieve?' She glared at him exactly like Abi would, those eyes tearing him apart. 'You think you can just waltz in and sort him out?'

Fenchurch wanted to go round there and batter the shit out of him.

Maybe drive him up to the Scottish Highlands, lose him in some remote bog nobody would ever find him in.

'I need to.'

'No. It's done, okay? I want nothing more to do with it. If I find out you've spoken to him . . . this is the last time you'll ever see me.'

But she was right. The violence — for so much of his life, acting as a channel for his anger — that needed to stop. It wouldn't solve anything. The video was out there and he didn't know if Sam had sent it or not.

But if that file came back? If someone else got sent it? Then he could do him under revenge porn laws.

But what good would any of it do? Abi was right, this was his daughter growing up. His little girl becoming a woman. Learning life the hard way.

He slumped back in the seat. 'Okay. Fine.'

'You're not going to beat him up?'

'I'm not.'

She grabbed his hands again. 'Thank you.'

Fenchurch soaked in her warmth through her hands. 'I'll help in whatever way you want. Just . . . Ask, okay? Anything, I want to help.'

'Okay.' Another squeeze then she frowned at him. 'You know your phone's ringing, don't you?'

'Kashmir' was blasting out. Fenchurch hadn't even noticed. The other punters in there had, a big man in a navy suit scowling at him as he messed about on his iPad.

Fenchurch checked the display. Reed. 'Kay, what's up?'

'I'm at the hospital. I thought you'd be here? They won't let me see Abi.'

Chapter Thirty-Six

The hospital canteen was buzzing with white noise. Fenchurch passed a couple who looked like they were dealing with bad news, then celebrating grandparents.

Reminded him of when they had it in their life, Abi's and his parents cracking open champagne after Chloe's birth, even though she was in an incubator for what felt like decades.

'There he is.' Dad's sausage fingers were wrapped round a steaming coffee mug. 'We were just talking about you, son.'

'All good, I hope.' Fenchurch took the chair between Dad and Reed. Couldn't sit still. He frowned. Chloe wasn't behind him. 'Shit. Where is—'

'I'm here.' Chloe sat next to Dad. 'You okay?'

Fenchurch shrugged. Too much in his head. Same as it ever was. But he was missing stuff. Obvious stuff. Phones ringing.

Or was it something to do with his wife being sedated while she was in labour?

He couldn't think about it.

'Dad, any more news about the baby?' Tried to sound casual, but his voice was a squeak.

'Spoke to the doctor about ten minutes ago, son.' Dad gripped Chloe's fingers tight. 'We won't get the blood tests back till midnight. Said everything else is okay, though. Midnight's the next update.'

Fenchurch glanced at his watch. Almost two sodding hours.

Dad hauled himself to his feet. 'Can I get you something, son?'

'Tea would go down a treat.'

'Coming up.' Dad walked over to the servery, his limp almost identical to the one Fenchurch had recently acquired. Chloe followed him over.

Reed stared into her tea. Chamomile, judging by the smell. 'Didn't think to tell me that one of my oldest friends was giving birth?'

'Kay, I'm sorry.' Fenchurch waved over at Dad. 'Been really busy. All this shit with Chloe.'

'Chloe?' Reed scowled at the servery. Dad had his arm wrapped around Chloe, even though she was about three inches taller than him. 'That's *her*?'

'Didn't think Dad had a new girlfriend, did you?'

'Jesus.'

'It's a long story, but . . . I think we might finally have her back.' Fenchurch clasped his hands together. 'For good, this time. Our daughter, accepting us. Talking to us. We went for a burrito and . . .'

'A burrito?'

'She loves them too.'

'What's wrong with her?' Reed was smiling. She patted him on the arm. 'I'm happy for you, guv. But . . . Next time, you tell me, okay?'

'There's not going to be a next time.' Fenchurch waited until she stopped laughing. His gut fell through the floor, leaving an empty vacuum. 'I'm scared, Kay. What if Abi . . .? What if our son . . . ?' The lump in his throat threatened to tear at his skin. 'I don't think I could cope if . . .'

'Hey, guv.' She rubbed his arm. 'It'll be fine.'

'You know that?'

'No, but . . . There's nothing you can do, is there?'

'What do you mean?'

'I mean, you can't change anything. All you can do is wait and see what happens. I know you hate that, but that's how it is. Abi might be fine. Your son might be fine. You just don't know. But your daughter's over there.'

Chloe was helping Dad make himself a coffee on the state-of-the-art machine.

He grimaced at Reed. 'She told me it was Sam Edwards who recorded her audition. I want to kill him.'

'Guv . . . You need to watch yourself. Mulholland's gunning for you.'

Fenchurch squeezed his thighs together. 'You getting anywhere with the case?'

'Stuck in the same situation as you, guv.' Reed waved around the canteen. 'Sitting around while other people do their work. Mulholland thinks you and I are too close, so she's sidelined me. Jon's the golden child now, practically running the investigation. I'm updating the bloody whiteboard.'

'What did you do?'

She slid her teacup across the table, some of the liquid sloshing over the side. 'Nothing.'

'Come on, Kay. Mulholland's a vindictive witch, but she's dealing with Loftus now. You said something to her, didn't you?'

'I suggested that we—' Reed sat up, all businesslike. 'Here's my thinking, guv. Keane had Hannah's and Sharon's computers. Those MacBooks. He was definitely up to something on them, but he was shot halfway through whatever it was. Which means he didn't get a chance to wipe his tracks. And those computers log everything. So I asked Lisa to unpick what he was doing.'

'And?'

'Mulholland found out. I'll let you guess the rest.' She took another sip of tea. 'But she'd done some of it. Keane had been running lots of searches, trying to find a particular file. Searching on all three machines.'

'Any idea what was in it?'

'The name didn't mean anything, just some numbers.' Reed sighed. 'Problem is, Mulholland's told Lisa to focus on Thwaite's background instead.'

***

Fenchurch stayed out in the corridor while Bridge snuck into the Incident Room. Mulholland was by the whiteboard, the pen squeaking as she scribbled. Five members of her team around her, acting like they'd won the Premier League, or at least secured a conviction.

Fenchurch set off to find a room.

Nelson and DI Winter walked towards him, sipping from coffees. Winter tilted his head to the side. 'Si, you still around?'

'Going to ask you the same thing.'

'The deal for getting credit for the case is that I've got to help Jon get this prosecution over the line.' Winter grinned at Nelson. 'Anyway, thought you'd left for the evening, Si?'

'Had to pick something up. For Abi.' Fenchurch scratched his ear. 'She's . . . gone into labour.'

Winter's mouth fell open. 'She okay?'

'Ish.'

'You should be with her.'

'Better go.'

'Hang on a sec, guv.' Nelson waited for Winter to enter the Incident Room, sucking coffee through the lid, the plastic rattling. 'The heating in your flat is broken.'

'So get it fixed, Jon.'

'Guv, I'm seriously busy.'

'And I'm not? Did you miss the bit where I said that Abi had gone into labour?'

'Thought you'd have a contract with someone?'

'I'll take a contract out on you.' Fenchurch grinned, but Nelson wasn't seeing the funny side of it. 'I'm doing you a favour, Jon. In case you've forgotten, you got caught shagging around and I'm letting you stay in my flat for free. Get a plumber in and we'll call that rent.'

'Right.' And with a nod, Nelson walked over to the Incident Room door. Cheeky bastard was going to grass to teacher, wasn't he?

Fenchurch led towards the meeting rooms, finding an empty one halfway down. He flicked on the lights and shut the door behind them. 'You think Keane was searching for a file?'

Bridge rested a laptop on the table. 'Well. It's more than that. Keane was doing a deep system audit on the laptop. By that I mean he was recreating everything that Hannah had done on the machine. All the files she opened, everything she searched for. There was a file he was interested in. IMG7329.mov.'

'A video, right? Any idea what was on it?'

'That's all I've got. Maybe you're better than me at guessing.'

'Does that match either file I got?'

'They were both renamed from the default. Something like JS underscore audition dot mov, and naughty boy dot mov.' Bridge swivelled the laptop around, showing a file system Fenchurch couldn't even process. 'But the thing is, that file was saved to the MacBook, but then Keane deleted it and wiped where it'd been. Locally and the server. It's gone forever.'

Fenchurch sighed. 'So you don't think you'll find it?'

'That's the other thing, sir.' Bridge glanced at Reed. She twisted her laptop back round and started typing. 'Jon's put me on the Thwaite investigation. I was searching through his emails and I found a load of photos someone had sent him.'

Fenchurch rubbed his forehead. 'I take it these weren't nice photos?'

'Thwaite having sex with a woman. Call this number if you don't want your wife to find out.'

'What did DI Mulholland say?'

'Very good. Have an apple, teacher's pet. That kind of thing.' Bridge turned the laptop around. The screen was filled with images of the same woman who Sam Edwards had been having sex with.

Zoe.

———

The Custody Suite was quiet. Far too quiet, given how late it was. Usually expect a few idiots from a fight in a curry house in by now. Big Martin sat behind the desk, watching some TV on his phone, propped up on the case. He collapsed it when he saw them, hauling out his earbuds in one fluid motion.

Fenchurch rested his arms on the high desk. 'Spotted you a mile off. Better than sleeping, I suppose.'

'Funny.'

'What are you watching?'

Martin folded his phone up in its wallet case. 'That *Shooter* show on Netflix. Very good. Much better than the film they made.' He stuffed it in his pocket. 'Anyway, you're after something, aren't you?'

Fenchurch scanned around the area. No smell of brimstone. 'Has DI Mulholland been down?'

'Yeah, brought Richard Thwaite down for processing.' Martin waited for Fenchurch's nod. 'Isn't shooting someone kind of his job?'

'Not when the suspect's unarmed.'

'Heard he was going for a knife?'

'True enough, I suppose.' Fenchurch drummed his thumbs on the desk. 'Any chance we can have a word with him on the QT?'

'I need to speak to Mulholland about it. Standing order.'

'Martin, mate. You owe me one.'

'Feels like I owe you five billion.' Martin opened his phone and propped it up on his table. 'Ten minutes, at the very most. And it never happened.'

———⌣———

Fenchurch tried to get Thwaite to look anywhere near him. 'Richard, who's blackmailing you?'

Thwaite frowned, fiddling with his neck. The St Christopher was missing. 'What are you talking about?'

'Your depression. I know the reason you were off for so long. You've got a secret and someone's blackmailing you. Am I right?'

Fenchurch didn't get a reply

Reed was sitting next to him. She pushed the emails across the table. 'I take it you called that number?'

'Why would I?' Thwaite nudged them back. 'This is spam. You open every email offering to make your cock bigger?'

Fenchurch smiled as he fanned out the pages on the table. 'Those emails don't attach photos of me at it with someone.'

Thwaite's face fell. 'What?'

'You're pretending you've never seen them before?'

'This is the first time.'

Fenchurch tapped at the images. The last one had Thwaite going down on his lover. 'But this is you, isn't it?'

'It does look like me; I'll give you that.'

'Are you saying it's been Photoshopped?'

'What's the point?' Thwaite let out a deep sigh. Guy seemed strangely serene, like he'd been living with the worst possible news for a long time and, now it was out, he could relax and let the shit swallow him up. No sense in fighting any more. 'It's me. Okay? Happy? I picked her up a while ago and . . . I can't get enough of her.' His fist clattered the table. 'I hate myself for it.'

'You, a cop, let yourself be blackmailed.' Fenchurch thumped the desk, cracking his wedding ring off the wood. 'Over something like this? In this day and age?'

'You don't understand.' Thwaite played with his imaginary St Christopher. 'My family. My religion. That's my whole life.'

Fenchurch stared at him long and hard. 'Whatever you want to do, so long as it's within the law, nobody else is allowed to give a shit. It's 2016. There's no reason for you to be ashamed of what you want to be.'

'My wife. She'd despise me for this.'

'Can't do the time, don't do the crime.'

'I know.' Thwaite nodded slowly. 'It's just . . . I spoke to the pastor at church. He tried to cleanse me. Wash away my sins. But the thoughts kept coming back.'

'I thought that'd be a couple of Hail Mary's for some common or garden adultery?'

'What?' Thwaite scowled at Fenchurch. 'You think that's it?'

Fenchurch frowned at Reed. Saw his reflection mirrored in hers. 'What am I missing?'

Thwaite nibbled at his lips. 'I've . . . I've got . . .' He held up the sheet, his hands shaking. 'She is a . . . a pre-op trans woman . . .'

Chapter Thirty-Seven

What?' Fenchurch's mouth hung open. He grabbed the sheets of paper back and started flicking through the pages, through Thwaite's self-hatred. Hard to pin it down, but Zoe didn't look like a man. She wore a black bra, possibly padded out. Skinny body, but looked curvy enough. 'This is a man?'

'She was born a man.' Thwaite's head hung low. 'Identifies as a woman.'

'But she's got a penis?'

'For now.' Thwaite huffed out a sigh. 'I'm pathetic, I know.'

'You're whatever you are, Richard. I'm disappointed that you felt so much shame about it that you let whoever this is make you do things.'

Things started to click into place, though. Zoe was a woman born a man.

'I need to speak to her.'

'Don't know her birth name.' Thwaite looked at the photos with a misty-eyed nostalgia, maybe seeing that there wasn't anything that bad in what he did. 'We met—' He sniffed. 'We met in a bar in Vauxhall. A lot of . . . these girls go there.'

'Was this just the once?'

'A few times.'

'How did you contact her?'

'She texts me.' Thwaite stared at the floor. 'I've got a burner at home, hidden away. For these sorts of things.'

'Can we—?'

'Too late. I threw it in the Thames when I went to the university. It's long gone.'

'When were you seeing her?'

'Last year. I went off with stress just after I went to the pastor. Like I said, he did his best but the thoughts returned after I came back to work.'

'Does Zoe know who you are? That you're a cop?'

'Every last detail.'

'Did you ever meet the blackmailers?'

'Whoever it is . . .' Thwaite tapped the page. 'I got these messages, telling me that they'd tell my wife if I didn't . . .'

'Didn't what?'

'They told me to shoot him, make it look like an accident.'

'So you planned to be on the team?'

'Pure luck. And I thought it was over. I'd wait out the IPCC investigation, they'd probably clear me. But it's never over. They sent me another message. Threatened to send a video file to my wife. Said they'd project it on my house.' Thwaite sounded close to hyperventilating. 'They told me to meet at the university. In a specific room. So I ran off. It's not like I was under surveillance. I checked. And turned up to meet, ready to kill, whoever was doing it. But I got to the room and I got caught. By you.'

'So you took the blame?'

'I didn't speak, which is the same thing. Kept quiet, all through the interview. Made me seem guilty.'

'But you are guilty. You murdered Oliver Keane.'

'But I didn't . . . shoot at you.'

Fenchurch waited until Thwaite looked up again. 'Because of this shit, you've . . .' He trailed off. Just didn't have the words any more.

Someone knocked on the door.

Mulholland. She'd found them. That was it, his career over.

Fenchurch walked over to the door and opened it, heart in his mouth.

Big Martin, frowning, twitching. 'Si, Mulholland's on her way down.'

——— ‿ ———

Fenchurch kept checking the corridor, in case Mulholland or any of her team found out he was even in the building. Expecting Nelson to have grassed. Reed seemed to read his mind and walked out of the room, giving them a barrier.

'Sir, I keep telling you.' Bridge slumped back in her chair and tucked her arms tight around her torso. 'I can't find Zoe, not in real life. People like her need to want to be found.'

Fenchurch was leaning against the desk, rubbing the cartilage in his knee until it clicked. 'I'm fed up of ghosts.' He sighed. 'So, all we know about Zoe is that she's had sex with Richard Thwaite on multiple occasions, paid for it with Sam Edwards, again on multiple occasions, and that she's spoken to Thomas Zachary on the Manor House website.'

'Pretty much.'

Fenchurch stared at her screen, the image of Thwaite and Zoe. 'Why was Zachary messaging her?'

Bridge lifted a shoulder. 'Maybe he's into trannies?'

'Have you read his stuff? He's much more likely . . .' Fenchurch swallowed, his thoughts catching in his throat. 'He's much more likely to be identifying her as a target.'

'True enough.' Bridge stifled a yawn. 'Do you mind if I get home, sir?'

'In a minute.' Fenchurch jabbed at her screen, pointing at the window into the MacBook's clone. 'Where did you get to with the Keane search?'

Bridge leaned forward, her fingers dancing across the keyboard. 'I was continuing the search, trying to figure out what Keane would've looked at next.'

'But didn't.'

'Right.'

'And?'

'And what?'

'Did you do it?'

'DI Mulholland stopped me, sir.'

'Can you do it now?'

Bridge glanced at the FitBit on her wrist and nodded. 'I'll see what I can do.' As she typed, the magic started happening in the window, searches running and folders opening. She clicked her tongue. 'Bingo.'

Reed came into the room and leaned against the back of her chair. 'What?'

'I've just found an email Hannah received with that attachment.'

'Can we see it?'

'That's the thing. The email's long deleted, and the file's missing. But I can see who she got it from.'

———

Fenchurch knocked on the door again. The flat seemed empty. No sounds or smells. No movement. 'Kid could be anywhere.'

'Studying in the library, out on the piss, having sex with someone's wife while they record it.' Reed was trying to peer in through the window. 'Anyway. What do you think is in this file?'

'A video. All we know is he sent it to Hannah and . . .'

And what?

Sending a file to your girlfriend isn't a crime. But if someone potentially kills her to get it. If they spent hours on that file on her laptop, tracing where it went afterwards, then . . . Then there's something to at least investigate. To delve into. If it's worth killing for, then it's of interest.

He thumped the door again. 'We can't burst in here. I've already done that. I'm off this case so I can't authorise a warrant.'

'So, we just give up?'

'Might have to, Kay.' Fenchurch pushed his hands deep into his pockets. 'I should be at the hospital with Abi. With Chloe.' His hands tightened to fists. 'Can't believe she's been seeing my old man behind my back. That lying bastard.'

Reed walked back towards her car. 'He's doing what he feels is right, though, isn't he?'

Fenchurch tried to trace it through. Any melting in Chloe had to be due to Dad's blowtorch. 'Maybe.'

'Guv.' Reed got out her phone. 'I'll call this in, see if I can get a location on Sam, okay?'

Keys jangled at the end of the path behind them. A skinny student stood there, hunched over and frowning. A record bag hung from a long strap. 'Can I help you?' West coast Scottish accent.

'Looking for Sam Edwards.' Fenchurch walked over and flashed his warrant card. 'He in?'

'How the hell am I supposed to know? I've just got back.' He squeezed between them and stuck his key in the lock.

'We need to speak to him as a matter of urgency.' Fenchurch stuffed his warrant card in his pocket and swapped it for a business card. 'If you could get him to give me a bell?'

'Aye, aye.' The student took the card and opened the door.

Fenchurch left him to it, though he walked away slowly, just in case Sam was lurking in there, hiding out from the cops.

'Here, pal?' The student was thumbing behind him. 'He's in his room.'

Fenchurch raced up the path, his knee wobbling underneath him, and stomped in the front door. 'Police!' He thumped on Sam Edwards's door. 'Open up!'

The door opened a crack and Sam peeked out.

Fenchurch pushed the door. It bounced off Sam's forehead, sending him backwards into the room. 'You!' He grabbed Sam's T-shirt. 'You were hiding, weren't you?'

'What? No!'

Fenchurch pulled him close. Stale aftershave wafted off the kid, mixed with sweat. 'You filmed Chloe's audition, didn't you?' He pushed his face into Sam's, their noses almost touching. 'Filmed her taking her clothes off, didn't you? Told her you'd deleted it, but you hadn't, had you? Eh?'

'I swear I deleted it.' Sam looked like he believed it, too. Then again, that's how the best liars work. He stopped struggling, resigned himself to whatever was coming. 'Jen's a mate. I was only trying to help.'

'By encouraging her to debase herself?' Fenchurch pushed down with his foot. 'You filthy pervert.'

'She needed money. A girl like Jen can earn—'

'Her. Name. Is. Chloe.' Fenchurch crouched over him, gripping his T-shirt, hissed at him. 'I'll kill you, you pervert.'

'I get that you're angry but—'

'No.' Fenchurch grabbed Sam's T-shirt, the fabric twisting round his fingers, and hauled him to his feet. 'Sam, I'll kill you and nobody will find your body.'

'Go ahead.' Sam hung there, a dead weight tearing the tendons in Fenchurch's fingers. 'I don't care.'

Reed stood in the doorway. 'Guv, what the hell?'

'Hannah's gone.' Sam sat on the edge of the bed, head in his hands. 'What else have I got to live for?'

Fenchurch stood over him, scanning his face, trying to spot the truth. 'You sent her a file, didn't you?'

Sam stared up at him. 'What the hell are you talking about?'

'It was a video. You and Zoe. We know she's a transgender woman.'

'So?' Sam scowled at him. 'You transphobic prick.'

'I heard what Zoe shouted at you. "Fuck me like I'm your girl-friend." Did you? Did you fuck her like you fucked Hannah? She knew Hannah, didn't she?'

'Shut up. If you'd listened, I told you that Hannah knew about it. All of it.'

'That's why you killed Hannah, isn't it?' Fenchurch nodded slowly. 'She saw the video of you with Zoe. Made her jealous, didn't it? That's what you argued about on Sunday.'

'We argued about what we were doing after university. It started as that, then . . .'

'Hannah wanted to leave you, but you didn't want her to go. So you killed her.'

Sam lashed out with his foot, stamping on Fenchurch's toes. Fenchurch swung round and caught a fist. Then wrapped his hand round Sam's, pulling his arm above Sam's head, arching his back.

'Guv! Stop it!'

Fenchurch let go of his arm, then grabbed hold of Sam's T-shirt, pulling him close. 'What was the video?'

Sam twisted to the side, gasping for breath. 'I don't know. It's probably me and Zoe, but I never shared it with Hannah. I swear.'

Fenchurch slackened off his grip. He let go, then stormed out of the room, out of the flat, into the cold night. Rain hit his head, small droplets.

Dirty little bastard. Surely it's easier to pull pints in a bar, or stack shelves in a Tesco. Like Chloe. All the shit she'd gone through and she was doing that. A fighter, never giving up. And Sam was debasing himself to anyone with a fiver in their hands.

'Guv?' Reed was following him, arms wide. 'Just because you're going through hell doesn't mean you can do that.'

'Kay, I'm sorry, but . . . He's lying to us.'

'Maybe, but he's also grieving.' She pushed him in the chest, looked dangerously close to going the full Essex. 'We need to give him space. Sound familiar?'

Fenchurch set off towards the car, fists clenched so tight his nails bit into his flesh.

Perfect time for his phone to ring. Least he heard it this time. It snapped him out of his stupidity. Abi, shit. He checked the display. Just Jon Nelson. He bounced the call and tapped out a text. 'Jon, just get a plumber in yourself.'

He looked over at Reed, looking like she'd gone way past Colchester, right out to Southend. Ready to batter the living shit out of any DIs who crossed her path.

His phone thrummed again. Nelson, calling back. He answered with a sigh. 'Jon, I told you, get—'

'Guv, I'm not calling about that. My mates in the drugs squad are pulling an all-nighter. Mulholland's trying to grab hold of their collar.'

'For Troy Danton?'

'No, Graham Pickersgill. Turns out Hannah's stalker was using that Go Fix Yourself shop as a front for dealing. Turns out he got his gear from Danton. Busted a drug ring. Maybe.'

'So why are you calling me?'

'We need your statement from Danton's arrest. His lawyer's trying to get it thrown out.'

'That's bollocks, Jon.'

'Yeah, well, nothing I can do about that, guv, other than to suggest you write it down.'

'I'll try and get some time this century, Jon.'

'Guv, look, I get it that you're pissed off. Sorry. If it's any help, Loftus got some clowns over from Cyber Crime to help us interview Pickersgill. They're going to convict him of stalking Hannah. We've got emails and text messages. Got his GPS from his phone. He was using his old university card so often that the guards just assumed he was a student.'

'Jon, if it's any use, he said he was in Hannah's corridor on Sunday night. See if you can press him for anything useful.'

'I'll try.'

'Save up enough of those brownie points and you can buy yourself a promotion.' Fenchurch killed the call.

Reed was behind the wheel of the pool car, scowling at him. 'You done?'

'Feels like it.'

'Not quite. Get in, you weasel.' Reed opened her door with a sigh. 'While you were being a prick to Jon, Lisa phoned. Turns out Hannah sent the file to someone we know.'

———

Fenchurch hammered on the door. Nice place in the arse end of Shoreditch, almost Hackney.

'How do you want to play this, guv?' Reed folded her arms and leaned against the wall. 'Go in gangbusters and tear him apart? Or just see what he says?'

Fenchurch hit the door again and checked the downstairs window.

A light pinged on.

The door rattled open and Younis stood there, arms crossed, dressing gown open to the waist, scrawny white flesh speckled with the occasional hair. He looked Fenchurch up and down, then repeated it with Reed. 'Well, well, well.' He opened his door wide. 'Two for the price of one.' The deep throb of that Lana Del Rey song boomed out from inside. 'What a pleasant surprise.'

'This isn't a social call.' Fenchurch stepped inside the flat onto engineered wood flooring, almost perfect. Black-and-white nudes lined the walls, a tasteful grey. 'Need to ask you about a video file.'

'What are you talking about?'

'Hannah Nunn sent you it.'

'She what, now?' Younis tugged his gown tight. 'Sam Edwards tell you? Oh, Fenchurch, you're such a bitter disappointment. You've got to take what that punk says with a whole salt mine, lover. He does so much off the books, I tell you, it's hard to get him on screen sometimes. Don't see what all the fuss is about.' He leered at Reed. 'He's not that big, either. Girthy, yes, but I've seen much longer.'

Reed laughed. 'You're a breath of fresh air, I swear.'

'Sure you pair don't want a little cuddle?'

'Quite sure.' Fenchurch stepped closer to Younis. 'I want to see that video file. Okay?'

'As much as I love you turning up at my doorstop, I'd rather it was after you'd popped a Viagra or two.'

Fenchurch wanted to grab him and throw him around the room. 'You think you're clever, don't you? That you'll get away with this forever. It catches up with you. Your type don't get to retire.'

'You're wrong, mate. I'm going to buy a Greek island. Piss off out of this by the time I'm forty. I won't be working the streets at your age.'

'And nobody will come to your island and hunt you down, eh?' Fenchurch looked Younis up and down. 'Besides, the second I prove it was you who sent those videos, I'll charge you with all these lovely new revenge porn crimes.' He pointed at the tasteful grey walls, the engineered flooring. 'You can kiss all this goodbye.'

'Why do you think it was me, eh?'

'Because you had access to those laptops, didn't you?'

'I did, did I?' Younis chuckled. 'Some crafty backdoor, yeah?'

'Something like that.'

'Much as I hate to admit it, you sexy beast, I'm not that good. Or clever. The kids I give these things to wipe them clean. Computer malware isn't like HIV, it doesn't hide around in your bones waiting for you to stop taking your meds.' Younis licked his lips. 'But, seeing as it's you,

I'll do some digging for you. That video of your daughter has clearly got to you.' He held up a finger. 'I'm a man of my word. I'll root out whoever sent you it. Give you a name. Or a body. Your choice.'

'Just a name and evidence.' Fenchurch folded his arms. He was blushing. Caught Reed noticing it. 'Hannah sent you an email, didn't she?'

'Back to this, eh? We've been over this, Fenchurch. She sent me lots of emails. Girl was needy.'

'This was on Sunday night at 11.05.'

'I don't remember.'

'That's bullshit. I want the truth. I want to see the email.'

'I can't show you.'

'So you do have it, then?' Fenchurch walked up to him. 'This is withholding evidence. I can do you—'

'Mate, there was nothing in it.'

'Then you won't mind me seeing a blank email, then, will you?'

'You're not leaving, are you?'

Fenchurch nodded. 'You're catching on.'

'Fine.' Younis led them through his flat into the living room. On a giant TV screen, Victoria Summerton was dancing, grinding her hips, her red corset barely containing her. Younis hit a key on his laptop. Lana Del Rey stopped and Victoria disappeared. Younis sat on his sofa, biting his lips, forehead creased. 'Okay.' He tapped at the laptop.

The screen filled with a video of a bedroom, Sam Edwards thrusting at Zoe, bent over on a bed. 'Fuck me like I'm your little bitch! Harder!' A different chunk of the video to the one Fenchurch had been sent. The lighting and bedding were from the same recording by the looks of things.

'This is what she sent you? I've seen this.'

'This is the original. I suspect you've seen a little edit of it.' Younis grinned. 'Keep watching.' He skipped the video on fifteen minutes.

Zoe lay on the bed, alone, wearing a gown, panting. Sam was nowhere to be seen. Zoe got up and sat in front of a dressing table, wiping at her make-up, her face visible in the mirror. She kissed the lipstick into a tissue. Then she adjusted the wig, long blonde locks, before yanking it off, silver hair tied down with a net.

Younis hit pause.

'Shit.' Fenchurch walked over to the screen and squinted. Look close enough at the features and you could see Thomas Zachary's face.

Chapter Thirty-Eight

Fenchurch glowered at Younis. 'I don't believe this.'

'Really?' Younis held his gaze for a few seconds, his forehead scored with deep frown lines, then shrugged. 'You've just watched that and you don't believe it?'

'But Zachary's alt right.' Fenchurch checked the face on the screen again. 'He said transsexuals should be drowned at birth.'

'There's that phrase "Methinks the lady doth protest too much"?' Younis leaned back on his sofa and crossed his legs. 'And you know about Ray Cohn?'

'Who?'

Younis rolled his eyes at Fenchurch. 'The next American President's first-ever lawyer. Heavily involved in McCarthyism, outing communists, real homophobe. Nasty, nasty bastard. Died of AIDS, telling everyone it was liver cancer. Turns out he was gay as a window.'

'Gay as a what?'

'Never mind.' Younis shut his laptop and put it down on the sofa next to him. 'I'm saying that if you think none of the alt right are lying about who they really are, then . . . They backed Milo Yiannopoulos until he slipped up.'

'He was out of the closet, though.'

'Good for their image. Fulfilling a quota, like one of those second-generation Indian guys who join UKIP.' Younis went back to his laptop and tapped at the keyboard. 'I've followed Zachary for a long time. Watched his videos, read his columns. You're right to say that Zachary wanted "gays and trannies"' — he added air quotes — 'to be shot at birth. Ironic, given that he's both.'

The screen filled with an image of Zachary as Zoe, bent over in front of Sam Edwards, screaming out and loving it.

'Why did Hannah send it to you?'

'I'm the one person she could trust, the one who had protection. I'm bulletproof, mate. Nobody would come after me.'

'I appreciate you showing us this.'

'Don't mention it, Fenchurch.' Younis puckered up and blew him a kiss. 'You owe me one, yeah?'

'No, I bloody don't.' Fenchurch held out his hand. 'Now, I need that as evidence, Dimitri.'

'Good one.' Younis slammed the lid of his laptop. 'Now, you can piss—'

The front door thumped. 'Police!'

Younis swung round, clutching his laptop tight to his chest. Uniformed officers bounded into the room, grabbing him and forcing him down on the sofa. Probably got a kick out of it.

Fenchurch had his warrant card out. 'I'm police!'

'I know you are.' Nelson stepped in the living room, shaking his head. 'Now what the bloody hell are you doing here?'

Fenchurch had to think fast. He stepped away from the couch, where Younis was being manhandled, shouting, 'I want a lawyer!'

Fenchurch took Nelson and Reed to the side. 'Jon, what the hell's going on?'

Nelson took their warrant cards and checked them out like he didn't know them. 'What are you doing here?'

'Investigating a lead.'

'On what case?'

'Kay is.' Fenchurch pointed at Reed. 'I was driving her to the hospital to see Abi.'

'Right.' Reed snatched her card back off Nelson. 'You want to be a dick about this, Jon?'

Nelson motioned them outside into the cold air. Stale smoke hung on the gentle breeze. Sounded like a rave nearby. 'The drugs squad had Younis on their radar. What you told me about Pickersgill, that opened the door. He started spilling. Talking about everything and everyone.'

'What did I say?'

'Him being in Hannah's corridor on Sunday.' Nelson got out his vape stick and took a deep suck, let it mist out through his nostrils. 'Kid was so scared we were going to stick the murder on him that he blabbed about drug deals. My mates in Middle Market Drugs have been after Younis for a while. Before he took over this patch, he was small fry on the street, but big in supplying. Pickersgill had been with him for a while now, that shop was a lot more than just giving some kids some dope.'

'Bloody hell, Jon.'

'Tell me about it.' Nelson put his vape stick away. 'So, what are you doing here? Really?'

'Asking him about an email he received from Hannah. It's on that laptop. Get that into evidence, Jon, and you'll be knighted.' Fenchurch started walking away. 'Catch you later.'

'Right.' Nelson headed back towards the flat then spun round. 'Pickersgill said the weirdest thing. Said he saw Thomas Zachary near Hannah's room, lurking around with Oliver Keane.'

'You sure about that? He must've been there very late?'

'Guy was obsessed. Said he wanted to watch Hannah sleeping.'

'Jesus.'

'Mulholland's trying to find Zachary now. He's not at his apartment. She was heading over to the paper.'

'Then let's see if he's at the university.'

———⌣———

Fenchurch got out of the lift in Jaines Tower and stormed across the carpet. 'Kay, is Lisa getting anywhere?'

Reed clutched her phone to her ear, staring into space as they walked. 'She's confirmed that the IP address for Zachary's account matches Zoe's.'

'So he was talking to himself? Why the hell would you do that?'

'Beats me, guv.' She was jogging to keep up. 'You think he killed Hannah because of this video?'

'A secret like that. It's big enough to kill over, wouldn't you think?' Fenchurch held open a fire door. 'I want to ask him that.'

'And not Mulholland.' Reed walked through the door. 'We better be careful here, guv. This might—' She stopped dead. 'Shit!'

A figure lay on the floor outside Zachary's office, groaning. Brad. Zachary's security guard.

Fenchurch raced over and crouched, his knee groaning.

Brad was muttering something about shooting. Then he stared right at Fenchurch. 'My gun!'

Fenchurch patted him down. A holster, empty. Jesus, nick him for that alone. The pistol was missing.

Shit. Shit. Shit.

Reed had her Airwave out already. 'Need medical assistance to—'

Fenchurch leaned in close, trying to hear what else he was muttering about. Gibberish. 'Who did this?'

Something crashed behind the door.

Reed locked eyes with Fenchurch. 'We need armed backup as well.'

Fenchurch grabbed Brad's collar. 'Who attacked you?'

'S-S-S-Sam.'

Shit.

Fenchurch crept over to office door and tried peering inside.

Sounded like glass smashing.

'Guv, they're five minutes out.' Reed killed the call. 'Told us to stay here.'

More glass, louder.

'We've not got a choice.' Fenchurch snapped out his baton. 'Mulholland will be here eventually. We need to get Zachary now. Stay with him.' He nudged the door open and peered inside, his heart pounding.

Sam Edwards was by the window, pointing a gun at Zachary. Brad's gun. Tears streamed down his cheeks. 'You motherfucker.'

Fenchurch sneaked in and crawled over to the armchair.

'Sam! Stop! You don't have to do this!'

'You motherfucker! You murdered her, didn't you?'

'Sam, let me go. This can be another of our secrets.'

'I'm sick of having secrets with you! What did she do, eh? Send the video to you? Start blackmailing you?'

'You sent it to her, you dumb homo. What did you expect her to do?'

Fenchurch stuck his head up. Sam was still pointing the gun at Zachary, his hands shaking.

'You filthy fag! This is your fault!'

Sam cocked the hammer. 'You filthy pervert.' Tears streamed down his face.

Fenchurch didn't have a choice. He stood up tall, baton raised. 'Stop!'

'Get back!' Sam grabbed Zachary and dug the pistol into his neck. He pushed him towards the window, his arm wrapped around Zachary's throat. 'I will push him out!'

'Sam, let him go, okay?' Fenchurch tossed his baton on the armchair in the middle of the room. 'I'm unarmed, Sam. Let him go. I know you're angry, but you need to let him go!'

'No way.' Sam nudged Zachary towards the open window, keeping the gun needling his throat. 'No. Way.'

'There's backup on the way here, Sam. You won't get out of here alive.'

'You think I *want* to do this?' Sam hit Zachary with the pistol butt, pushing him onto his knees. 'You think I want this animal to have killed Hannah?' He put a beefy arm around Zachary's throat and pointed the gun at his chin. 'Tell him.'

'No!'

'Tell. Him!'

Zachary choked. 'Let me go, Sam. This is all in your head.' He smiled at Sam. 'You ever fired one of those? It's harder than it looks on TV.'

'I'll take my chances that it does enough damage at this range.'

'Sam!' Fenchurch grabbed his baton, hid it behind his leg, and took a step forward. 'You're throwing away your future.' He took another step, careful that Sam didn't notice him.

'I don't care. This piece of filth dying is a price worth paying.'

'No. It's not.' Another step forward. 'If you let him go, you can walk away from this. It's not too late.'

'It's way too late.' Sam rested his finger on the trigger. 'I'll see you in hell, you—'

Fenchurch lashed out with his baton, smashing the metal into Sam's fist.

Sam screamed and the pistol thudded to the floor. Fenchurch kicked it away. Zachary fell forward. Sam slouched, rubbing his fingers.

Fenchurch held the baton above his head. 'Sam, I need you to back off, okay?'

Sam glowered at him, then complied, inching away and resting against the desk.

Fenchurch picked up the gun with his baton, then put it in an evidence bag.

Reed stood in the doorway, glowering at them. 'Guv, you okay?'

'Stay with Brad for me.' Fenchurch watched her go then helped Zachary up. 'You okay?'

Zachary didn't respond. He staggered over to the armchair and collapsed into it. 'You're prosecuting him, right?'

Fenchurch glanced out of the window. Blue lights flashed in the middle distance, still that precious five minutes away. He walked over to Zachary and crouched in front of him. 'You're going to tell me exactly what happened on Sunday night. How you murdered Hannah Nunn. Now.'

'You want the truth?' Zachary sucked in air, then barked out laughter. 'Someone sent me the video file, said we needed to talk about the content. I knew it was her. I didn't have a choice.'

Fenchurch frowned. 'Choice about what?'

'What do you think?' Zachary laughed again. 'I had to stop her sharing what she had.' He nodded over at Sam. 'This cheap slut hid a camera in a hotel room. He filmed himself making love to *her*!'

'You mean Zoe. You.'

'It's not as simple as that.'

'You were messaging her on that platform. Why? Were you working out who was the real you?'

'It's a game I play with myself. Sometimes it was on forums where other people could see it, but mostly it was just me. I was exploring how Zoe might interact with men, how to strike the right tone.' Zachary pointed his finger at Sam. 'But then that stupid fag worked out the truth. Didn't even know he was fucking me until last week.'

Sam stood to attention, looking like he was going to launch himself across the room. 'I got a film of me buggering you and you loving it. That makes you the *fag*.'

'You're a cheap piece of trash, Sam,' Zachary gasped. 'He filmed me taking off my make-up. My wig. He violated my privacy.'

'Growing up transgender where you did must've been difficult. But it's who you are, you shouldn't fight it.'

313

Zachary stared at the floor for long seconds. 'I've been this way most of my life. I hate myself for it. Wanting to be a woman. Acting like one. In so many ways Zoe is the real me and Thomas K. Zachary is the fiction. What I've built for myself, such a beautiful lie. Most days, dressing as Zachary felt like cross-dressing. Creating him, he was all I could do to stop feeling weak and pathetic. I *need* Thomas K. Zachary!' He shot to his feet, fists clenched. 'People respect me!' He slumped back in the chair. 'If they knew . . .'

'Why do you care about what people think?'

'Because I've created this! And it's worked for me! I have power, I have respect. It's a choice. It's all a choice, I don't need to listen to my body. I can ignore it and be who I want to be.' A smile flashed over Zachary's perfect teeth. 'Donald Trump shook my hand on election night, right after Clinton conceded. I was in the room. He put it on speaker, let us all hear. I've got his son on speed dial.'

Fenchurch grabbed his baton tighter. 'So you thought all that gave you the right to kill Hannah, did it?'

'Don't I? Don't I have the right?' Zachary crossed his legs and folded his arms. 'She was nothing. And I almost got away with it. Nobody saw or heard anything.' He huffed out a sigh. 'I went to her room to grab her laptop and she . . . she woke up . . . I tried to reason with her. Stop this video getting out. But the stupid bitch said she'd already sent it to someone. Then she attacked me. Punched me.' He pointed at his shiner. 'So I hit her, and she fell over. Called me Sam's bitch. I hit her again. And again. Then I strangled her. Couldn't stop. Didn't stop, until . . . she was gone.'

'And you raped her.'

'What?' Zachary bared his teeth. 'No.'

'Why did you go back?'

'What?'

'You returned to her room.'

'I didn't. Oliver Keane did. I forgot her laptop. In all that happened, I forgot to clear my tracks. I was in a bit of a state. Oliver said he'd help. He went back, took her laptop. Oliver must've raped her. Jesus. He had . . . certain predilections.'

'What do you mean by that?'

'Rape fantasies. Abductions. Back in Palo Alto, he used to find homeless women, abduct them, rape them, then leave their bodies. He did it here with some frat boy, picked up some skank from the street.'

'Sharon Reynolds? Elektra De'Ath.'

'Oh, Inspector. You know all their names.' Zachary's shoulders deflated. 'Oliver promised me it'd be fine, said he's covered it over so many times. Jesus. He promised he'd get it all off there. Make it as if she'd never sent that email.'

'But?'

'He watched the video, didn't he? Goaded me, taunted me. I couldn't forgive that.'

'So you got Thwaite to kill him.'

'That's the trouble with people, isn't it? You've all got dirty little secrets. Richard had his little fetish and he happened to be in a convenient position for me. But Oliver was just unreasonable. I thought we had an understanding, but no. He let me down . . .'

'You're a sick, sick bastard.' Sam was shaking his head, tears slicking his cheeks. 'Playing on people's fears, scaring them, while you live a lie yourself. You fucking hypocrite. But you're right. You are weak and pathetic.'

'Sam, you're the weak one. The pathetic wretch. You rent out your body to pay your way through college. Doesn't that sicken you?' Zachary got to his feet. 'It hurts me to see you emasculating yourself while all these privileged, entitled bitches preen and dance on video. A man shouldn't have to do what you do. It's against the natural order. It's not right.'

'I pity you, Thomas.'

'I don't want your *pity*, you freak.' Zachary looked Sam up and down. 'You took my secret to that witch, trying to impress her. She tried to blackmail me to leave. When she found that video, I killed her. I had no choice. Her blood is—'

'What?!'

'She found it on your laptop. A video of you making sweet, sweet love to me. Must've thought she'd struck gold when she recognised my face.'

Sam lurched forward, reaching for Zachary. 'I'm going to kill you!'

'Sam!' Fenchurch grabbed his T-shirt and pushed him away from Zachary. 'We need to let the system run through the process.'

'You're not going to get me that easily.' Zachary laughed at Fenchurch. 'You're pathetic. All that time hunting for your daughter. Jennifer. Chloe. Whatever her name is. She's a slut. I fucked her and fucked her and fucked her. Then she dumped me. Well, I found out who she really is. Sam here showed me the video.'

Fenchurch frowned at Sam. 'What?'

Sam hung his head. 'I didn't know what I was doing.'

'Zoe was interested in new girls. Sam wanted to impress her. Stupid cocksucker left his PC unlocked one time I was with him. So I sent the video to you, Fenchurch. Thought you might want to see what your darling daughter was up to.'

Fenchurch tightened his grip on his baton. 'Thomas Zachary, I'm arresting you for the murder of Hannah Nunn and of—'

An elbow cracked off Fenchurch's jaw. Something snapped his bad knee back and made it scream. A fist caught his jaw. He windmilled back and tumbled over the armchair. Someone screamed and something thudded to floor. Something crashed.

Fenchurch groaned. His head felt like someone had cut into it with a machete. He tried to sit up but fists pinned him down. He couldn't see who it was. Fingers groped his pockets. Then let go.

Fenchurch tried to push himself up to all fours. Couldn't put any weight on his knee. He blinked hard. He pushed himself up to standing . . .

Just in time to see Zachary fall out of the window, his scream fading as he tumbled towards the quad.

Chapter Thirty-Nine

Down below, the blue lights were nearby, uniforms spreading out across the quad. Floodlights shone on Zachary's corpse, splattered all over the concourse.

Sam stood next to him, staring hard, goading him.

Fenchurch grabbed Sam in a choke hold, pulling the baton round his throat. He stamped on Sam's ankle and pushed him over, jerking his arm up. Sam didn't resist. Fenchurch snapped handcuffs round Sam's wrists and got to his feet. He shut the window and locked it.

Sam sat up, the cuffs digging into his back. 'Good riddance.'

Reed stood in the doorway. 'Guv?'

'Kay . . .' Fenchurch tasted blood in his throat. 'Have you got—'

'What happened?'

'I—' Fenchurch shot a glare at Sam. 'I don't know.'

Fire burnt in Sam's eyes. 'You heard what Zachary said. He killed Hannah.'

'I was going to prosecute him. Now he'll be a martyr. Why did you kill him?'

Sam scowled at the door. 'If you're so interested in glory, you can lock up that shooter. Brad. Zachary's bodyguard. He shot at you outside.'

'Not Thwaite?'

'Who? No. It was him. He told me. Twist his arm enough and he'll tell you. He was going to kill Jen.'

Fenchurch's heart pounded. He left Sam and hobbled back through. Brad was groaning, propped up against the wall.

Reed talked into her Airwave. 'I think it's the sixteenth floor. Yes.'

Fenchurch held out his hand to Reed. 'Cuffs.'

'Guv?' She passed him her set.

Fenchurch snapped the second pair of cuffs on Brad.

Brad was fully conscious now, frowning at him. 'What the hell, dude?'

'I've heard a story about your extracurricular activities.'

Brad looked up. Then away.

'You were told to shoot my daughter.'

'Your daughter?'

'Chloe Fenchurch.' Fenchurch shrugged. 'Jennifer Simon.' The name didn't bite so hard now.

'Where's Thomas?'

'He's . . . dead.'

Brad seemed to deflate. 'She was the target. Zachary wanted her dead because she treated him badly, or something.'

Fenchurch couldn't speak. Couldn't move.

'But then you showed up, so I changed targets. Thomas said that if I killed you, it'd make things easier. But she saved you, didn't she?' Brad shook his head. 'We should've stuck with the plan.'

The lift door pinged open and three armed uniforms burst out. Fenchurch pointed at Brad. 'Take him to Leman Street. Now!'

'Sir.'

Fenchurch locked eyes with Reed. 'Kay, don't leave his side, okay?'

'Why?'

'He shot at Chloe. Shot at me.'

The other lift pinged and Bridge got out, lugging her laptop case. 'Sir?'

Fenchurch pointed back at the office. 'Through there, Lisa.'

'Sir.'

Reed's gaze followed Bridge into the office. 'Guv, what the hell happened through there?'

'Honestly?' Fenchurch pointed at the lump on his head. 'One of them attacked me. Next thing I know, Zachary's out of the window.'

'Sam pushed him?'

'Or he jumped. Couldn't accept what was going to happen to him. The truth was going to come out.'

'Guv . . .' Reed folded her arms. 'Loftus is on the way up. You better get your story straight.'

Fenchurch marched through to Zachary's office as quickly as his knee would let him.

Sam was staring out of the window, his whole body shaking.

Stupid bastard. He didn't need to kill him. If he did?

'Why now, Sam? Why didn't you kill him on Monday morning?'

Sam slumped against the wall. 'I thought Keane killed her. He'd been paying Hannah for cam shows. I thought he'd met up and gone over the score.' He laughed. Then his expression twisted into a scowl. 'That video got me thinking. You were very interested in it, weren't you?' He rubbed at his shaved head. 'Came into my flat, all that threatening about Jen, about how you're her dad, when what you were after was that video. Me and Zoe. I found it in my email, Hannah had emailed it to herself.'

'Was Hannah going to blackmail him?'

'I have no idea. She must've done.'

'She sent it to Younis. The only person who could protect her.'

Sam's fists curled tight, clanking the cuffs. 'She couldn't even rely on me to protect her.'

If Fenchurch was in the same situation . . .

Christ, *when* he was. When some craven animals had Abi . . . Three months pregnant, tied up in a basement. If it wasn't for Docherty, he'd have been out of the force. At best. At worst, he'd be in the adjacent cells to the idiots that . . . Abi had made him spare their lives.

Sam didn't have that angel on his shoulder, stopping him joining the side of the devils. He'd lost his other half and the kid wasn't handling it well.

Though pushing someone out of a window wasn't the best move anyone had ever made.

But it was Thomas Zachary. The man who'd tried to kill his daughter. Tried to kill him. Would've killed him were it not for Chloe.

Fenchurch stood over Sam, waiting until he looked up at him. 'Did you push him?'

Sam frowned at him. 'Are you saying I can get off?'

'Did you push him?'

Sam tugged at his ear. 'You were out of it. Didn't see what actually happened, did you? He attacked you, then he jumped out.'

'That the truth?'

'Does it matter?'

———

Fenchurch sat at Zachary's desk, trying to keep his breath steady. Could still hear Zachary's scream in his head, swelling and roaring as he neared the ground.

Stupid, stupid bastard.

Put Fenchurch in a difficult situation. Zachary had murdered. Hannah lay in the morgue. He was covered in Keane's blood, even if Thwaite pulled the trigger.

And he'd tried to kill Chloe.

Was it just Fenchurch's innate protection instinct?

Or did he want to give Sam Edwards the sort of second chance most people didn't get? The sort of second chance that people like Zachary insisted was only available to white, middle-class men. Men like Zachary and Christian Greenwood, the rapist of Sharon Reynolds. Men who thought the world was theirs, that it should bend to their whims. Crime and punishment was for other people, not them.

Sam Edwards, Zachary's ultimate sex fantasy. He'd played with fire, paying Sam to treat him like the girlfriend he'd pissed off, the girlfriend who was trying to kick him out of the university.

Lisa Bridge tapped his arm. 'Sir?' She was next to him, working at Zachary's machine. 'Are you okay?'

'I'm fine, Lisa. What's up?'

'Well, I've finished going through Zachary's computer.' She held up a finger. 'This is by no means a comprehensive analysis, but I've found the login for the email account that sent those videos to you.' She swivelled the monitor around and tapped a painted nail off the glass. 'I've also got videos and photos of Zoe with Sam Edwards and with Richard Thwaite.'

'What about the account he used to send Thwaite—'

'On here too.'

'Okay.' Fenchurch nodded slowly. 'That's good work.'

'Thanks, sir.'

The office door slid open and Loftus marched through, in full uniform, hands behind his back. He flashed a smile at Bridge. 'Lisa, give us a minute, would you?'

She rested a stapler on the keyboard to keep the machine from locking then left them to it.

Loftus perched on the arm of the easy chair and took off his cap. 'What are you doing here, Inspector?'

'Saving Sam Edwards, sir.'

'I meant, why here? Why now? Your wife's in labour, man.'

The memory stung Fenchurch. He shouldn't be here. He should be with Abi. 'I was following a lead, sir. DI Mulholland ordered DC Bridge and DS Reed to ignore—'

'Fenchurch, you need to let this go, okay? This petty feud between you and DI Mulholland. I don't get it.'

'I understand, sir, but it's not petty.'

'So what's it about?'

'It's . . . personal. She made a mess of something relating to my daughter's disappearance.'

'Fenchurch . . .' Loftus sighed like he was dealing with a child. 'I need you to grow up. Okay? Now that DCI Docherty isn't protecting you, you're going to be on a tightrope.'

'I'm treading the line carefully, sir.'

'Mm.' Loftus stared at him for a few seconds. 'You didn't try and save Zachary, did you? You let Sam Edwards throw him out.'

'Sir, I honestly don't know what happened. Zachary overpowered me.' Fenchurch pointed at the cut on his temple. 'When I came to, Zachary was already out of the window.'

'Sodding hell.' Loftus pinched his nose. 'This is *not* what I expected to happen. I wanted him in custody. It'll all come out, I suppose.' Loftus seemed to deflate as he sank into the chair. 'Well.'

'Sir, I need to get off.'

'Just a minute.' Loftus steepled his fingers. 'You've been playing games, haven't you? DS Nelson retrieved some evidence from the raid on Dimitri Younis's home. A video file. Next thing I know, you're off on some wild trip to arrest Zachary. Hunting for glory, were you?'

'I didn't want Mulholland to cover up another—'

'Fenchurch. Get out of my sight. As of Monday morning, you'll be reporting to Acting DCI Dawn Mulholland. I'll let you decide whether you want to hand in your resignation or maybe act like a grown-up for once?'

Chapter Forty

Fenchurch lucked out and found a parking space outside the hospital. He left the engine running and let the Beta Band track fade out. For once, he didn't sing along with the refrain.

Working for Mulholland.

No chance. Suddenly, Abi's move out to Kent or Essex seemed a hell of a lot better.

Mulholland was going to dig into what happened. Did Sam Edwards really deserve a second chance? Losing his girlfriend. Did he deserve to lose his future too?

Of course he did. If he did what they thought he'd done, Sam deserved life in prison. But it was never as simple as that.

Someone rapped on the window.

Fenchurch squinted at it. Couldn't see them through the frozen glass.

He killed the engine and got out.

Docherty, leaning on a walking stick, taking a deep drag on a cigarette. He'd lost even more weight, almost literally skin and bone, his muscle devoured by the disease. He took another long drag. 'Si.'

'Jesus, boss, should you be smoking?'

Docherty exhaled slowly, smoke snaking out of his nostrils. 'Nothing's going to save me, Si.' He took another suck. 'Doctor told me to get on with the bits of my bucket list I can actually still do.'

'And smoking in a car park is on it?'

Docherty managed a laugh, but it turned into a racking cough. 'Might get to see the Grand Canyon, if I'm lucky.' He took another drag, then went back to coughing his lungs up. 'But sod it, Si. I'm going to do everything I want to do.' Tears glistened on his cheeks. 'Not long left now.'

'Boss . . . I just . . .'

'I know, Si. I know.' Docherty exhaled. 'One of those things. That's all it is.'

'It's not right. You should have more time.'

'I've had a good innings, as they say.' Docherty put the cigarette to his lips and sucked in the burning air. 'I heard the news. Mulholland. Loftus asked me what I thought. Told him it was a mistake, but there you go.' He pressed his cigarette into the wall and tossed the butt into the bin. 'You need to watch your step from now on, Si. I really mean it.'

Fenchurch heard Zachary's dying scream again, swelling as he fell. He nodded at Docherty. 'Working for her. I don't . . . Can't.'

'I never got the problem between you.'

Fenchurch stared deep into his eyes. 'No, you don't.' He sucked in second-hand smoke. 'When Chloe—'

The hospital door burst open and Fenchurch's dad flew out, scowling in his direction. 'Simon! Abi's awake!'

⌣

Fenchurch powered along the corridor as fast as his knee would let him. 'What's wrong with her?'

'Doctor wouldn't tell me or Chloe, son.' Dad was panting. 'He's waiting for you.'

Fenchurch turned the corner, could see Abi's room from here.

Dad nudged his son's arm. 'Heard about Acting DCI Mulholland.'

'Jesus, Dad, how do you still hear stuff before me?'

'I've got the whole police station bugged.'

Fenchurch almost laughed. 'No, really?'

'Doc told me. Poor bugger.'

Fenchurch grabbed him. 'You need to stop hacking into police investigations, Dad.'

'What? I was just looking out for Chloe, son. That Sam geezer. He'd . . . Well, she asked me to check about that video. He swore he deleted it.'

Chloe peered out of the room. 'Dad.' Her frown deepened. 'Mum's . . .'

Dad . . . And she'd called Abi Mum . . .

Fenchurch grabbed her hand and squeezed. Wanted to stay holding it forever, to never let her go again.

She grimaced at him. 'Dad, Mum's—'

A scream tore out from behind her. Even drowned out Zachary's in his head. Not Abi . . . a baby.

'Come on.' Chloe led him into the room.

Abi was sweating, her face puffed up from painkillers. 'There you bloody are.' She reached out a hand for his. 'I need you here!'

Fenchurch got up close and kissed her forehead. 'Sorry, love. I'm—'

Felt like her grip was going to snap the bones in his hand. 'Where the hell have you been?'

'I had to help Kay. Something to do with the case.' Fenchurch grabbed her and pulled her tight. 'I thought we were losing you.'

'So you went to work when I'm giving birth?'

'I . . . I needed to focus on something other than worrying about you dying.'

'I'm never leaving you, Simon. Okay? I'm fine.' Abi held up the tiny ball of blankets, a shrivelled pink face peering out. 'Alan's fine.'

'Alan?'

'After Docherty.' Abi smiled. 'I hate the name, but it'll do.'

Fenchurch took the package from Abi and held baby Alan up to his face, getting that new-baby smell. 'He's perfect.'

The midwife was loitering around, her frown increasing the longer she looked at Alan.

Chloe sat on the bed next to her mother. 'My brother . . . Jesus.'

The midwife raced over, much faster than she looked like she could move. 'Oh no.' She grabbed the baby out of Fenchurch's grasp and started walking away.

Fenchurch followed. 'What's going on?'

'I need to put him in a ventilator.'

Fenchurch could only stand there while history repeated itself, as a midwife swept away his newborn baby from his arms.

About the Author

Photo © Kitty Harrison 2014

Ed James writes crime-fiction novels. *In For the Kill* is the fourth novel in his latest series, set on the gritty streets of East London and featuring DI Simon Fenchurch. His Scott Cullen series features a young Edinburgh detective constable investigating crimes from the bottom rung of the career ladder he's desperate to climb. Set four hundred miles south on the streets of East London, his DI Simon Fenchurch series features a detective with little to lose. Formerly an IT manager, Ed began writing on planes, trains and automobiles to fill his weekly commute to London. He now writes full-time and lives in the Scottish Borders, with his girlfriend and a menagerie of rescued animals.